On the Job
By Jack Nolan
ISBN: 978-1-9997156-5-6

Published by

PUBLISHING

i2i Publishing. Manchester.
www.i2ipublishing.co.uk

Authors Note

I would like to thank all my family, especially my Mum and Dad and all my friends who have joined me on my journey of writing this novel. As I have found, writing can be an isolating experience but one that brings me so much joy as this is one mountain I can say I have finally climbed. After five years of working relentlessly, experiencing mental highs and lows and hitting rejection after rejection, I can now look back with pride. Never give up on your dreams and keep climbing those mountains. I wouldn't have got this far without the support of my family who have believed in me. So, this is for them and everyone who has followed my personal journey and a special thank you to i2i Publishing for taking a chance on me. Without them taking a second thought or two with my work, then there's a chance I would have had to find another way around landing on this shelf! All the best and enjoy what's ahead of you.

Jack Nolan

"They say in life, where you start doesn't necessary mean that's where you're going to end, my Dad for example born in Ireland and lived a hard life. But look at him now, after immigrating over here in 1996 he's never looked back! What do I know anyway, like Dad says, I'm still a wee boy. The moral of this story is bad things happen to good people. I learnt that the hard way."

Chapter 1

2009 Saint Brooks High – Manchester

Vince was the first one to arrive in the classroom; he sat himself in the middle of the room. Vince gazed into the glossy window thinking of the last time his father took him to Ireland. Thinking how huge the mountains were, how extraordinary the views were from the hilltops overlooking the sea. At peace, Vince closed his eyes sinking into a daydream.

Vince was in Year 10 at school, at 15 years of age he was the youngest in his Year. He had a small build, he wasn't scrawny and he wasn't fat, he was somewhere in between. His hair was mousy brown. When he went to the barbers he always asked for short back and sides with a trim on top. He would rarely style his hair, so most of the time it was greasy and thrown to the side. Vince's father owned a pub at the end of Mary Lee Road called the 'Smoking Barrel,' it was a medium sized building and had a small beer garden at the back. Vince was considered a loner at school since his friends neglected him, but he wasn't fussed. There were two lads in the same year as Vince who spelt out bad news, Kane Crossling and Kevin Kingsland. These two partners in crime made Vince's life in school darker than the school toilets. Since Vince's friends abandoned him he kept himself to himself, he never bothered to try and socialise with people. Vince hated school even before Kane and Kevin came across him, it was the fact that the teachers didn't do their jobs and teach; Vince hated wasting his days at school knowing each day was going to be the same. Many times, he thought to himself it's pointless being there but there was nothing he could do, his Dad would often say just do your best and get a good job. Vince knew that his Dad just wanted him to work for him and wasn't arsed about what Vince wanted himself.

The noise at the back of the classroom rose with the muffled sounds of Kane Crossling and his gang creating mischief. Kane was the school's number one chocolate dealer and rumour has it that it's not just chocolate he sells. Everyone knew Kane's Dad didn't earn his mass of money by playing by the book. As the noise of the rowdy classroom increases Kane mumbles quietly to his friend Kevin, "Did you hear about what happened to big Dean from the estate?"

Kevin replied excitedly, "Yeah, I heard they cut his eyes out for looking at his bird."

A voice overhearing shouts from a distance, "I heard he was drowned in his own blood."

Kane's eyes open wide with cockiness, "No you're all wrong dickheads, Dean got into trouble with the wrong people and deserved to be shot in the head."

Kevin laughed, "BULL SHIT!"

Kane gripped Kevin by the collar and put his spare hand to his head in the shape of a gun. "Yeah he did, do you understand? He got popped in the head and splattered on the floor, question me again and you'll be the next mess that needs cleaning up around here."

Kevin looked at Kane confused, "Nah, nah I won't. I was only having a laugh bro; we're cool yeah just a joke init."

Kane looked Kevin in the eye holding a straight face, a smile slowly appears. "Did you see your face then, you fucking shit yourself. I can smell that runny fart dribbling down your leg."

Kevin's face lit up, "Fucking hell mate, that coke you've been on is fucking with your head, swear down its changing you. Hey, there's that Vince the Prince. The little gay boy. Look at him staring into space, he looks more twisted then you on a giro."

Kane looked over at Vince, "You know what, let's make his day more shitter than it already is."

Sean was quietly sitting there laughing with the boys, but he muttered a few words, "Come on boys, leave it for now. Can't we just chill for once without making a scene?"

Kevin responded, "Hey! You shouldn't be in our lesson big man anyway, Mr Wagger, we do as we want."

Kane snatched the Lucozade from Sean's hand as he was about to take a swig. "Speak up again and I'll be the one kicking your head in." Kane wacked the bottle over his brother's head and gave him a wink sharply turning to Kevin. "Hey big bollocks! Go and wind him up, it's about time we had some entertainment. It's boring as hell in here."

Kane's younger brother Sean Crossling was well-known as a tearaway. With his Dad's influence and Kane's motives, Sean wasn't too wise about his decisions. He was always trying to impress Kane but mostly ended up with a bad outcome on himself. The two brothers knew a lot of things they shouldn't at their age and this was reflected in their attitudes. Kane would hang around in a big group of lads. It was called 'Kane's gang.' Everyone was aware of them and the trouble they caused; even teachers feared having them in their class. Their names were black in the staff room and they were often gossiped about from the headmaster to the cover teacher, "Filthy skin headed rats" they were described as.

Kane's best friend Kevin believed he was the right-hand man, doing well in school didn't matter to him, he had already chosen his path. The only bind that kept him in the school yard was that there was money to be made. Kane's Dad was admired amongst the gang and Kevin, in particular, knew the in's and out's of their family business; he wanted in.

"There he is, the little pikey." Kane sniggered with a grey attitude.

Kevin and Sean laughed and chipped in. "My names Vince the leprechaun..."

"Where's mi pot of gold..."

Vince rose from the day dream and looked behind him. He knew that it was more than playful banter, Vince bit his tongue as the lads laughed him down. He knew they wanted a reaction from him. Vince was always on his own, ever since the people in his school found out his Dad was Irish. They soon did the maths that his Dad emigrated over here which made him a dirty immigrant in the eyes of the school lads. Vince's group of friends abandoned him through fear that Kane and his gang would make their lives hard through being associated to Vince.

All accept one, Chris, Vince's closest friend that he knew his entire life. Chris worked in Vince's Dads pub at weekend's, pot-collecting and occasionally sweet talking the odd customer. So, he was always around outside of school. Chris was a few years older than Vince as he left school 2 years before him. So, in school, young Vince had no one other than his books to carry.

Miss Maggie, who was teaching Maths to the class, lost a lot of patience with everyone in the room. Her eyes picked up on Kevin trying to be the class clown, but she sunk back into her black leather chair and played the next YouTube video, "How to get a 'C' in Maths." Whilst she left the computer on a loop she stared into her pocket mirror, her greasy hair was scraped back and full of knots. She wore the same black pencil skirt every day with her Oxford blazer from the 1970s. Maggie's eyes were black and covered in charcoal eye shadow, she was still intoxicated from the past weekend's bender. It wasn't hard to see as well, as she became known in the school for being Mrs Snooze, she had major bags under her eyes to show for it.

Kevin rose violently from his seat. "I SAID, HEY PIKEY WHY DONT YOU FUCK OFF OUT OF HERE!" The classroom froze from the laughter. There was no way anyone would ever speak over Kevin as they would be sailing a very bad boat. Kevin had broken many chairs in his time at school; smashing faces of those who tried to stand up to him was Kevin's norm. Now, you're probably thinking how on earth did Kevin get away with all his violent acts, well he was very wise about how he attacked. He played chess like a boxer; he waited for the teacher to leave the classroom on an errand. If she didn't leave he would text one of the lads from the school council to come in the classroom and say she or he was needed. Kevin was always thinking of new ways he could get teachers out of their lessons, so they wouldn't clock onto him. With the teacher being out of lesson he could cause whatever chaos he wanted; through fear, he controlled his classmates so no one would dare grass on him. A poor fucker at the back of the room got a chair rocketed at him; Kevin approached him and whispered down his ear what would happen if the word got out to the teachers. He said to him in quite a sinister tone, that they tripped and fell into the wall or any other excuse that had no part to play by him. Whether they were bleeding on the ground or unconscious slouched over a table, he had no remorse.

Vince grew furious inside but played himself calm on the outside. He wiped some dirt from his shoes, the black leather lace ups were old and tacky, they were hand me downs from Chris. Vince didn't mind this as it gave Vince a sense that Chris was always there with him. Vince combed his hair to the side with his fingers. Gathering his thoughts after one stroke, he gripped the work from his table and strolled up to Miss Maggie, who happened to be in a deep sleep.

"Miss Maggie, I've done your equations, go on have a look at them you washed out witch," Vince spoke with frustration. The room was still shaken by Kevin's roar. Kane had been following Vince with his eyes, glaring at him from the second he sat down at his table. Kane gave a nod to Kevin; Kevin knew that Kane was up for seeing some entertainment.

Vince walked slowly back to his desk, knowing he was in quite some trouble. The class started to make noises and sounds of "oooo." Someone from the corner of the classroom shouted out. "Rocket the bastard Kevin". Kevin smiled; his yellow teeth were revealed from his lips that covered them like red curtains. He clenched his fists and tensed his arms. The class started to chant like football hooligans. Soon the classroom became a gladiator's arena, with Kane sat at the top of it.

The room began to darken through Vince's eyes, looking down at Kevin, Vince violently pushed everything in his path out of the way and shouted, "Come on then you big ugly cunt." Vincent bravely stood his ground gesturing with his hands.

"Oh isn't this a change, little Vincent growing a pair." Kevin started to laugh then raged with anger moving towards Vincent. Kevin over shadowed Vince. He was broad and built like a brick shit house. His muscles raged with veins, the blood raced around his body. Tension was wearing thin between the two.

The violence was broken by Mr Gardiner as he was patrolling the corridors looking for a missing student, Sean Crossling. The door scraped open.

"Ay, YOU TWO! what's going on in here then? EVERYBODY BACK TO WORK!" Vince returned to his seat. "Miss Maggie, are you aware you have an extra student in your class?" Mr Gardiner gritted his teeth and looked across the room to witness Miss Maggie sound asleep. "MISS MAGGIE!" Mr Gardiner shouted. Miss Maggie jumped out of her skin to the over view of Mr Gardiner.

"Yes Mr Gardiner, I didn't mean to be rude, I was just daydreaming at this register, you're right I've got 24 students." Miss Maggie did a quick head count of the class. "And there are 25 students in here, so yes someone has snuck in here." Miss Maggie sniggered.

Mr Gardiner raised his voice so that the whole class could hear him clearly as he replied to Miss Maggie. "Well, if Kane Crossling is in here then there will be no doubt that Sean Crossling is in here two." Mr Gardiner skimmed the classroom tables with his eyes, "There he is, Mr Crossling you're coming with me."

Kane laughed and shouted, "Which one Sir, me or this little shit?" The whole class started to laugh as Kane stared down Mr Gardiner.

"Don't test me boy, SEAN get out now!" Mr Gardiner shouted.

Sean pulled away from his seat, picked up his bag and snatched at his Lucozade and followed Mr Gardiner out of the classroom, but before he went he whispered to Vince, "Dead Man Walking."

Vince knew he had a long day ahead of him. Kane and Kevin still had it in their heads to knock Vince out. Vince thought to himself as the clock ticked down that there was only 5 minutes left before the bell rang out for break.

At the back of the classroom, Kane and Kevin started talking about what they should do about the situation with Vince.

"Kevin, are you going to rocket him or what then?" Kane curiously spoke.

"Well, there's 5 mins to the end of lesson so fuck it. These minutes must be making Vince shit himself." Kevin answered.

Kane smirked looking at Kevin in a violent state, "Kevin mate, Vince deffo thinks that you're going to bomb him when the bell rings, it will be like fight night. Ding Ding!"

Kevin replied, "Nah Kane, the clock ticking down all day will be enough to torture him for one day. I'd rather leave him with the build-up of paranoia and anxiety."

Kane replied, "You nasty bastard, I wonder how much pressure he can take, got to admire your style though, mentally fucking with the guy's head. Can't believe him though. He called you an UGLY CUNT! He's got some balls that Vince."

Kevin started to look furiously at Vince then he looked back at Kane and spoke quietly to him. "I'll tell you what I'm going to do. I'll cut his balls off and then we'll see how big they are, and he's going to be the one who's the fucking ugly cunt after I've finished with him."

Vince sat in his chair shaking as the adrenaline rushed through his veins, "Shit what have I done," he said. Vince started to collect his thoughts and the anxiety of why the classroom had turned quiet dawned on him. The paranoia of why Kevin and Kane were silent. The room felt grey and all Vince could hear is the ticking of the clock and the scratching of pencils. "Tick tick tick". Vince watched the hands of the clock make a full turn of 60 seconds. Vince felt his neck get stiffer and stiffer, he was in shock with what just happened. "Scratch scratch". The sound of pencils went through him like chalk piercing through a blackboard. Vince felt the muscles in his neck lock, he was unable to look behind him to see what Kane and Kevin were doing. Vince's heart started to pound as his body started to shut itself down, second by second.

Vince put his head in his hands counting down the minutes for the lesson to be over, he tried to relax his body by breathing slow and steady, but his body couldn't keep up with the pace of his heart pumping the blood around his body. Though Vince felt fear inside, he was making himself mentally prepare for what may happen when the lesson ends. The bell to the end of the lesson rang out loud and echoed throughout the corridors, bouncing from classroom to classroom. Kane and Kevin rose from their seats.

"You know what, we'll ruff Vince up a little bit and see how long it takes for him to pop. I've got something in mind for him."

"What?" Kevin replied.

"Just you wait and see pal, you'll see." Kevin and Kane strolled past Vince, Kevin was staring Vince out.

"Just you wait boy, just you wait." Vince looked straight through the boys in a trance. Kevin was unpredictable. One second he could snap the next he was laughing and joking, this was one of the things Kevin loved to play on. "Yeah, that's right, keep fucking staring because that's all you can do big man. Remember that." The sound of paper scattered across the floor; just before Kane and Kevin left, Kevin threw his book at Vince.

"Get your arse picking that shit up you smelly pikey".

Kane put on his black Adidas hoodie; it had the famous white tram lines on the arms of it. "Kevin come on, it stinks of B.O. in here." The boys left the classroom, leaving Vince still stuck to his chair.

"You coming for a cig Kevin, can't be arsed with next lesson," moaned Kane.

"Yeah go on then I'll sling some of these Lucozade's out while we're there, get the boys to get rid of them," laughed Kane.

"Where did you get all them from anyway, you jammy basted" Kevin smirked, "Tesco, Morrison's?"

"Nah," Kane shrugged. "My Dad's mate Smiffy jacked them from the delivery vans; you know the one's that park outside Bargain Booze."

Kevin started laughing; his face lit up like Blackpool tower. "Smiffy... Fatso Smiffy haha, swear down he's funny him."

Kane pushed Kevin as they continued to laugh about Kane's Dads runner. "He's daft that Smiffy, he looks like an angry kid, that's what your brother Sean's going to be like with all the daft things he does". Kevin winked at Kane and smiled.

Kane replied. "Ay, you cheeky basted, Sean isn't ginger, true he is a little shit though. We'll have to get him to do some jobs for us, he's good like that."

Kane and Kevin would always go to the Astro for a cig. Reasons being that's where they operated. Wagging their second lesson gave them the first opportunity to sell to the other years who would come on the Astro at dinner. Plus, it gave them a quiet place to hang out with other members of their unit. At dinner, the Astro would be packed, flooded with hundreds of school kids. It had money to be made written all over it in the eyes of Kane. The other reason why the place was so popular was that it was a common place for fights to take place.

Kevin raised his eyebrow. "Have you give Aiden a text? He told me he was going to be on the Astro on second period. He belled me this morning moaning that he had Mr Smith for History and that he couldn't be arsed."

Kane zipped up his hoodie. "Err I ain't spoken to him pal, if he said he's going to be there he will be there. Plus, he's got my money so, he best be there!" Kevin pulled out his phone. "Fucking hell it's quarter to 11. Going to text big A then to make sure he's there." Kane scratched his head. "Ay, you know that Maxine from year 10?"

Kane unconsciously replied "Yeah."

"You know the small one, with purple highlights?"

Kane wasn't paying too much attention to Kevin as he was more interested in what he was planning to do tonight. "Na."

"You know, the one who was gettin onto Aiden, the dick tease?"

"Oh shit yeah, was she the one from that party we went to that time at Kyle Reef's gaff?"

The sun was shining in Kevin's face which made him squint "Yeah, fucking hell it's boiling. That sun is pissing me off."

"Yeah, what about her anyway?"

"Well her mate told me yesterday in that shit Maths lesson that she and Maxine have got fake ID, and they're going to the Dutch Birds."

Kane laughed ecstatically, "Bullshit. That Roxanne looks about 12."

Kevin sniggered, "These days, all girls need is a rack of boobs to get served anywhere. Haha, I was thinking we could take Aiden out with us and he will shit himself when he sees that Maxine".

The lads started pushing and shoving each other.

"It will be funny. Might get onto a piece of that Maxine myself," Kane replied.

Kevin looked confused and muddled. "Aiden's onto her though!"

"Do you think I'm arsed about Aiden, he works for me. If I say jump, he will fucking jump or else I'll cut off his legs. He best get my money, the scroat is testing my patience, It's either today or tomorrow he pays me or he won't be known as big A for much longer." Kane stood overlooking Kevin's height glaring at him.

"Kane, it's Aiden, our Aiden." There was a short pause between Kane and Kevin as they locked eye to eye.

"Aiden is a liberty taker Kevin, his shit doesn't add up."

Kevin shook his head looking down to the floor. "Liberties, it's 20 fucking pounds he owes you, that's only two 10 bags."

"Well that's a 20 bud. he should have had the money, it's principles."

"So you're just going to what?"

"There's doing him and teaching that fucker a lesson. We'll take him out with us, let him think I'm sweet with him, and when we bump into his love interest I'll pull her straight in front of his eyes."

Kevin frowned and Kane's evil smile was revealed. Kevin was broken in thoughts, he was quite upset, he liked Aiden a lot and couldn't change his fate. He knew that Kane would give him the go ahead to do Aiden in after the firework show.

"You got that Kevin?" Kane patronised.

"Yeah, but..."

"No fucking buts, Kevin."

Kane hit Kevin in the arm. "What the fuck dick head."

"Shut up and stop going on before they overhear." The boys were approaching smoker's corner. A muffled sound of plastic JD bags came from the corner. It was Aiden selling some Lucozade to the year 9 kids who were also out of lesson. Aiden stood tall around 5ft 11. He was medium built, and always seen with a cig in his hand; his hair was short, close to a skinhead like the rest of the clan. He had slits in his eyebrows, followed by a tramline on the right side of his head. He would wear a black hoody underneath his blazer with his hood up. His shoes were simple leather converse. He saw himself as a trendsetter and Mr Smooth with the school girls.

Whilst holding a cig in his mouth, Aiden greeted Kane and Kevin enthusiastically, "Yo boys! what's going down in the hood."

"The hoods going good!" Kane and Kevin shouted out.

Aiden frowned in curiosity. "What's going on boys? Ay, that little shit over there," Aiden pointed to the year 9 boy, "He tried to short change me when buying Aiden's happy meal of the day, 2 dairy milk and a Lucozade for a quid. I was like you mad bro?"

Kane smiled and spoke in an angry tone, "You're not the only one whose been short changed."

"What's with you Kane?"

Kevin piped up, "Leave it Kane; he's just pissed off that's all Aiden. That math lesson took it out of us."

Kane clenched his fists at the side of his legs. "Yeah, maths!"

"Thought things was good boys, Kane you snappy fucker. I'm just chilling init. Init."

Aiden grew nervous inside and began to take deeper drags on his cigarette, realising that he hadn't paid Kane back for the weed he bought.

"Shit Kane mate, ay when we go out tonight I'll pay you back for that bud, just forgot that's all mate. Had it in my hand, the money, this morning but I left it on the side by accident, rushing around the house."

Kane nodded his head and looked up to Aiden. "Yeah..."

Kevin broke the silence between the two. "So boys, Dutch Birds tonight or my gaff? Fuck that actually, my Mam's being a proper knob."

"Shame your Mam's hot," Aiden laughed.

Kane replied, "We'll meet up at 7 tonight then ay?"

Aiden buttoned up his blazer and smiled with relief, "I'm cool with that boys..."

Kane interrupted Aiden. "Listen, I've got to do something actually, so we'll be there at half 7, won't we Kevin?" The time was coming towards 12 o'clock and lunchtime wasn't far away. "Ay lads we better get selling these luco's, there's going to be bare people on here soon."

Though it was sunny, the wind was blowing strong, throwing the bed of sand on the ground in circles. The rain of students started to flood through the Astroturf's gate. The sound of footballs whistling through the air were a common thing to hear.

"There's the rest of the muppets," Aiden laughed. "Look there's Lucas haha, top guy him."

Kane's clan of misfits barged their way through all the people in their way, "Move before I shank ya," Lucas pushed his way through the crowd of people leading the way for other members. Lucas was black, he was the only member who was accepted in the clan who was allowed to grow his hair into an afro just so Kane and others could wind him up. Lucas chose to have short curly hair and was commonly seen with an afro comb wedged in it. His teeth were bright white which got him noticed by the girls. A lot of girls would do anything to get his attention. He wore black jeans to school with a white patterned piece of fabric on the back of his pants pocket.

"Luco Luco," a brown-haired girl muttered.

"It's actually Lucas, but yah." Lucas made a tutting sound with his lips as he made the exchange "Quid now yeah?" The girl passed over a pound coin.

"What about a kiss Lucas?"

"You can't see I'm busy?" Lucas and his pal Brad followed by other members of Kane's clan made it through the herd of people; Brad was very quiet and rarely spoke. You wouldn't know he was there half the time because he just nods and occasionally says a few words but when he was with Lucas he was more comfortable to talk. He was skinny and had the usual gang's haircut. People thought he was slow because he was always there hovering like a bee shrugging his shoulders and smiling.

"Brad, you there mate... Hello?" Lucas tapped on Brad's shoulder. "You there mate?"

"Yeah," Brad nodded.

"Are you going out tonight? "There will be girls man, bare little sticks of dynamite!" Lucas suggested.

"I don't know," Brad shrugged.

Lucas clocked Kane, Aiden and Kevin in the smoker's corner and headed over to them.

"Yo! Afro man," Aiden laughed. "Put that song on", Aiden grew excited like a little child on Christmas Eve.

Kevin burst out with the giggles, "When the Afro man walked through, the town houses went up for sale," and Kevin continued to giggle. "Yo Lucas, colt 45 and two zig zags baby, that's all we need, haha."

Aiden reached his arm out and shook Lucas's hand. "Safe man"

"Wargwan!" Lucas replied.

Brad smiled. "Alright mate," Kevin gestured to Brad. As the song played from Kevin's phone, Lucas started to sway his head.

"This is how you skank bro," Aiden replied. "You skanking tonight bro, Dutch Birds?"

"Deffo mandem, I'll be there skanking away, banging all the birds day by day."

"Fuck off," Kane laughed. "Are you pulling birds?"

Lucas's face wrinkled up, "Yeah blud."

The rest of the boys chipped in, "laughing my arse off mate, Kane's jell. Jealous, jealous guy." The atmosphere of banter came to an end when Kane spat his dummy out.

"I CAN HAVE ANY BIRD ME!" Kane rose in anger. "Just you's all fucking watch, yeah, you'll all be seeing me tonight causin' some fireworks with them ladies."

"Yeah yeah!" Aiden and Lucas commented. And even Brad nodded his head.

"Talk over me again and it will be the last time you do so."

"We're only joking," Aiden quietly spoke. Kane gripped Aiden though he was bigger built compared to Kane.

"Disrespect me again and I will cut out your tongue... Do you hear me?"

"Yeah." Kane released Aiden and took a swig of a lucozade.

Lucas broke the awkward silence. "So, what time are we out tonight? Six, seven?"

Kevin replied, "Half seven, outside Dutch Birds".

The bell rang out signalling the end of breaktime. The boys decided to go to their lessons as Kane, Kevin and Lucas were in the same class for Science. They were excited to see what Miss Mackie was wearing, the little dirty perverts.

Vince walked into the science block. He hadn't eaten at break as he was still shook up from lesson. Hunger pains started to dawn on him making him feel very sick. He wasn't fit for the lesson and unstable in state of mind. The situation he got himself into kept playing in his head.

"I should have done something," Vince whispered to himself. "I should have been braver. I'm too much of a coward. I'm an ant compared to Kane. What was I thinking?" Vince opened the science block doors; they squeaked open scraping along the floor. Vince walked down the science block, it was a narrow corridor with paint peeling off it; filled with old school posters and slogans. "Ofsted approves of Saint Brooks High" "Awarded Excellence". On the school posters there were words stated underneath the pictures of students in white text: "Strength" "Team work" and "Punctuality". Vince read these every time he walked down the corridor. Vince thought to himself, "They're so full of shit, this school, excellence yeah right." Vince plodded along the corridor, there were all types of people on their way to Science, the corridor was packed with students coming in and out. It was hectic. Vince past the popular kids and all the different types of groups on his way to class.

"Ay, its Vince", a voice shouted out.

"Vince the gay boy," another voice shouted in a dramatic voice. The comments were shouted across the corridor bouncing back and forth like a shuttle cock in a game of badminton. S11 was in Vince's reach, he saw his class going into lesson. Vince rushed his way past people, ignoring everyone. Vince saw the door closing before his very eyes. Bang! The door closed shut. Vince knocked on the door. He was growing anxious, he hated being late even for the most boring lessons. Mrs Mayer opened the door violently. Mrs Mayer's class had 3 rows of desks joined together, the walls were covered in work and diagrams of the solar system.

"You're late!" Mrs Mayer shouted as Vince walked through the door. Bang! Mrs Mayer closed the door with an attitude.

Vince sat at the back of the class, got out his texts books and buried his face in his arms and attempted to go to sleep.

"Right, now everyone get out your text books and turn to page 145. Today we will be learning about atoms."

The girls sat in front of Vince and started having a rant to Mrs Mayer. "Miss Miss, we did atoms the other day with Miss Clark when you were ill. She even did all the questions." Roxanne moaned.

"Oh really?" Mrs Mayer laughed.

"Yeah we did, didn't we girls."

"Well, where is it then hey?" Mrs Mayer walked over to Roxanne and Maxine and opened the girl's books. "Where is it then mmm?"

Maxine bickered. "Miss Clark gave us paper to do it on. She even collected it in," Roxanne pouted. "And marked it." Maxine kicked Roxanne under the table. "She might have marked it miss, she's next door. Want me to get her for you miss?" Maxine smiled. "Please."

"No, I'll pop around now. Everyone turn to the next page and do the extension activity."

Maxine pulled out her makeup bag and mirror and started to apply some rosy red lipstick. This was a common routine for Maxine, her hair was brown with purple highlights, and she wore fake eyelashes and often wore fake tan and often showed off her legs to all the school boys and that's not the only thing she would put on show. She wore black shoes that had a distinctive head of a rose on them. She wore a black school skirt that had pleats in it and the official Saint Brooks High jumper; she wore her sleeves up to her elbows.

Her headband matched her shoes as it had a black rose glued onto it.

"Roxanne, you got any of that eyeliner?"

Roxanne had frown marks across her head from posing in too many stupid positions. She wore a white shirt which you could see her bra through. This made her quite popular with the boys as she would dress like the stereotypical school hussy. Leather jacket with studs, baked in too much fake tan that made her look like little miss gingerbread woman.

"I wonder when Miss Mayer's is going to be back, swear she's a lesbian. What do you think Roxy?"

"Haha probably, you know." The two girls giggled between each other. "My names Mrs Mayer, license to kill rabbits...buzzzz."

"Haha imagine Miss with knickers saying 'Pussy Patrol' haha." Roxanne laughed hysterically crying with laughter.

"Shut up Maxine haha".

"I bet she's being Miss Clark's superman". Amber joined into the conversation putting on a deep voice, "Miss Clark you're my kryptonite." All the girls couldn't stop laughing.

"Girls you're going to make me smudge my make up!"

Mrs Mayer returned to the class. The room went quiet and the distant sound of other students talking simmered to a holt. The girls sat twitching staring at Mrs Mayer.

"Right, now, class..." Mrs Mayer was interrupted by the girl's hysterical laughter. "What's with you girls, I've been gone two minutes and all of a sudden you've all been popping happy pills!"

"Sorry miss," the girls wept.

"Settle down now, you have disrupted enough of my lesson."

"Ay girls," Maxine whispered. "Fuck off, will get you kept behind."

"Fuck off Maxine," Amber patronised. "Yeah, you will get us kept back after class sweaty knickers."

Maxine bluntly ignored the comments and stared into her mirror. She realised that there was a boy behind her with his head asleep on his book's. "Girls! Girls! Girls!" Maxine's whisper slightly increased.

"What!" Roxanne replied.

"That boy behind us is asleep."

"No way let me see," Roxanne turned her head and kicked Amber under the table.

"Ouch! What now?"

Maxine and Roxanne set off again with giggles. "There's a boy behind us fast asleep drooling from the mouth."

Amber looked behind herself, "Oh my god, shit no way, he's lying in his own saliva."

Vince was lying on the table with his eyes closed, trying to pass the time. It was the only lesson he could hide away from the world. So, he thought...

"Ay saliva boy!" Roxanne belched out. Vince ignored the straining tone of Roxanne's voice. Maxine and Amber started laughing. Roxanne put on an American accent and started taking the piss out of sleeping Vince. "Wake up dude! You're going to miss out on learning"

"Who is he?" Maxine's voice chuckled.

"Some geek, I can't see his face."

The girls continued to slag Vince off.

"Ay girls, watch this." Maxine started spinning her text book with her fingers and threw it at Vince. "I ya KA-POW, what about that girls for some kung Fu shit?"

"Shit," the girls panicked and turned back scribbling nonsense in their books. All but one. Maxine stared Vince out waiting for his reaction.

"What the fuck!" Vince shot up like a meerkat swaying his head left and right. In a tired tone of voice, Vince stared at Maxine. "What was that for you crank?" Vince looked down at the book which struck his head. Maxine Williams. "What's the need Maxine?"

"Eeew, never say my name again you little weasel."

"No way it's that Vince Haze." Roxanne pointed out. The room rose with noise of students talking.

Mrs Mayer sat in her chair reading emails from her computer. "What's the point, I should have been a zookeeper and I'd get the job after working with these animals."

Back in the corner of the classroom Maxine started to light up like a rocket.

"Eewwww you're that scroat everyone talks about," Maxine shouted.

Roxanne turned her chair around facing Vince and joined in with Maxine. "For fuck sake girls, I'm not in the mood for all of this." Vince scraped his hair back with his fingers. "Aw is the little leprechaun getting upset?"

Maxine pulled a backwards smile. "It's because he can't find his pot of gold." Roxanne and Maxine broke out in tears of laughter. Vince was angry after being woken up by the girls; he wanted the day to end. What a shit day it's been he thought.

"Here's your fucking book back you slag." Vince slid the book off his table. The book landed on the floor in front of Maxine's chair.

"Who are you calling a slag, you fucking freak? I'll get you done in you dirty immigrant." Maxine slowly became more aggressive and violent. "You're a little tramp, look at your fucking clothes."

Vince replied. "Clothes, clothes they're the same as yours, you dumb bitch."

"Ew, well they stink, you raw kid."

Roxanne laughed, "Haha you got murked by Vince."

"Shut up Roxanne." Maxine started texting on her phone. She was texting Aiden, 'That little shit Vince started on me in S11, calling me a slag and all sorts of shit X" Maxine looked at Vince and smiled; in a dark tone of voice she threatened Vince. "Immigrant I'm talking to you. Just you wait I'm going to get you battered. Do you really think you can talk to me like shit on a shoe?"

Roxanne piped up, "Leave it Maxine, we're only winding him up." Roxanne winked at Vince. Vince sat there confused, he clocked Roxanne wink at him.

What the fuck he thought to himself, I'm trapped in a room with these two skets doing my head in. Vince sighed and ignored the girls, he started to question himself. 'When have I ever had a good day at this place? Why does everyone give me shit? How come the teachers aren't as arsed as they make themselves out to be? I've been sat here getting shit for no reason. All I wanted was to pass time, not a game of 'Do you know who I am.' Jesus! Vince's head flooded with thoughts. 'Shit I hope I don't bump into Kane and Kevin, fucking wankers.

"Yeah I thought you would shut up you gipsy," Maxine patronised and sniggered.

Buzz Buzz! Maxine's phone rang in her pocket. It was a text from Aiden.

'What? Vince, he was giving grief to Kevin b4, he told me not long ago. Will sort it, meet you soon XXXX'

Maxine read the message and felt a warmth sensation. "ooo, Roxanne, Aiden gave me four kisses in his text. It's going to be such a great night tonight."

Maxine fluttered her eyelashes and grabbed her breasts "Tonight's going to get hot."

Vince turned away from the girls and stared out the window. He saw the lower years lining up outside the changing rooms, they had just come back from P.E. The teachers would give the students five minutes to get ready before their next lesson. This alerted Vince that it wasn't long until his lesson finished. The P.E kits were black shorts and polo shirts. There was a boy who caught Vince's attention outside. It was Sean Crossling, kicking a bottle around the floor with his younger pals. The P.E teachers shouted across to them, blowing their whistles to get their attention.

"Get inside and get changed!" Mr Russell shouted. Sean tackled one of his friends and kicked the bottle across the floor. The bottle flew up into the air and crashed onto the concrete facing the school benches. The outdoor parts of Saint Brooks High were linked to the school doors and the Astroturf. There were wooden benches and a small slope of grass where the school had built benches running across it. At dinner time, all the students would play a game of red arse whilst others would sit and watch for entertainment.

Vince sat nervously at the back of class. His hands began to shake and his teeth chattered. He felt a cold shiver down his spine. Paranoia kicked in, he kept putting his head in his arms and kept looking at the clock, then the door, then outside. Vince's danger radar was tingling. He sensed something happening and grew afraid inside.

There was nowhere for him to go. No one to run to, no one to put him at ease. The clock was ticking and ticking. Counting down the seconds seemed like an eternity. Vince heaved and brought up some sick. He swallowed it back down which made him feel worse. He felt his body cry out for food with hunger pains striking down on him. His body was in a spin, twirling like a washing machine. The school's Tannoy rang out and made an announcement. "Due to school regulations, we can't allow students to go outside at dinner today as electrical repairs are being made to the outside entrances." Typical, Vince thought to himself, the only day Kane and Kevin won't be able to go outside. It's like I'm destined to bump into the skinheads. How am I supposed to blend in now? Vince coughed and nearly heaved up some more sick. Tightly glued to his seat, Vince gripped his pencil and started to sweat. Vince looked up at the clock, watching the last-minute count down. 'Tik...Tik...Tik'. 'Ring ring ring.' The school's bell rang out. All the students jumped up from their seats and rushed to the door

"Great lesson guys!" Mrs Mayer muttered sarcastically. Maxine picked up her make-up bag and threw it inside her school bag. She swayed her hips left to right and turned around to Vince.

"Just you watch sweetheart, your day's going to go bad to worse Pikey." Maxine looked down at her phone. "Oops, looks like it's going to happen quicker than what I expected."

Roxanne stood near the door. "Come on Maxine, we're going to be late."

"Coming!" Maxine squeaked with excitement.

"Vince you have to leave, I've got another class coming in soon. There're students that want to learn, unlike you lot."

Vince pulled himself from the chair with his arms shaking. He picked up his books and emptied them into his bag. He slowly stepped across the classroom dragging his feet step by step.

"Can't you move any quicker? What's wrong with you?"

Vince replied, "You wouldn't care, you're just like all the teachers in the school. Fake." Vince pulled himself closer to the door.

"How dare you speak to me like that," Mrs Mayer's voice rose.

"You see Miss, this proves my point, you're unqualified to teach, yeah you've got a degree in teaching, yet you can't control a class of 20 kids and raise your voice to one."

Mrs Mayer frowned "Get out of my class room!"

Vince opened the door to the hell hole called school. The corridors were black. Someone had turned off all the lights, the corridor was empty. Vince felt shivers, he felt Kevin new where he was and was planning something. Halfway down the corridor was two toilets facing each other; girls and boys. The lights began to flicker creating a spooky atmosphere. All you could hear was the sound of Vince's footsteps. Walking through the corridor Vince started to slow down going towards the toilets. Vince felt intimidated by the walls coming outwards from the toilets. He sensed someone hiding behind them.

Maxine and Roxanne were hid behind the walls of the girl's toilet with their phones ready to record the action. Facing the girls was Kevin, Aiden and Kane. Maxine received a text from Aiden. 'He's coming I can hear his footsteps getting closer X.' The boys went into the toilets to have a quick piss.

"Is someone there? Hello." Vince shivered; no one responded.

The lights outside the toilet flickered on and off. Vince was petrified; paranoia was exploding inside him. Vince started to melt down. The dark corridor felt like a scene from a horror film. Vince took a deep breath and swelled some courage, continuing his journey down the corridor of darkness. He saw the fire exit signs glow at the end of the corridor.

What am I being a wreck for? Vince thought to himself, unconsciously aware of the danger lurking. Kane, Kevin and Aiden jumped out from the enclosed wall, their hoods strung from their heads.

"Ay, you little fuck, this just ain't going to be your day." Aiden gripped Vince up against the wall. Maxine and Roxanne watched what was going on from the side line, with Maxine's phone documenting what was going on, the girls held their breath, holding in their laughter. Vince froze in fear, a tear streamed down his face.

Kane and Kevin over shouted each other. "Welcome to hell short arse."

"This time there's nowhere for you to run." Kevin's face turned from white to red as he grew hungry with anger. "Like I said Vince you don't want to fuck with me, you dirty pikey."

Vince scanned his eyes across to her face, witnessing Roxanne stood in shock. Kevin grew aggressive like a raging bull.

"Twice in a day you've pissed me off, strike one you was lucky I didn't rip your head off, strike two giving shit to Maxine. One more strike and I'm going to fucking waste you." Kevin smashed Vince's head against the wall. "Do you fucking understand me?" Kevin spat in Vince's face. Aiden stared into the petrified face of Vince. "Let's fucking bog wash the cunt."

Kane whispered into Vince's ear. Collecting his dense thoughts, "Little Leprechaun, I'm going to steal your pot of gold and scatter it across this corridor."

Vince's eyes gushed like a waterfall, tears streaming down his face. "What the fuck are you on about? Please let me go!"

"Did you hear that boys," Aiden laughed. "Please let me go!" Aiden viciously punched Vince in the stomach. Vince's body shattered, being held up tight against the wall made him breathe hard for each breath. Seconds being there felt like a lifetime. "Let you go, do you think I'm finished with you?"

Vince screamed like a pig in a slaughterhouse. As Aiden punched him left, right and centre, each blow felt like a hammer hitting nails; Vince became a human punch bag. Sliding down the wall to his knees he shielded himself with his hands. Grabbing his bag for protection, Vince knew he wouldn't get out of this how he walked in.

Roxanne screamed, howling like a wolf. "Stop it! Stop it!" Maxine glared at her in disappointment.

Whilst she filmed everything on camera, Kane nodded to Kevin. Kevin gripped Aiden pulling him off Vince.

"What you fucking saying now Vince?" Aiden shouted in Vince's face. Leaving Vince with blood and spit dribbling down his face.

"We're done here Aiden," Kevin kicked Vince to the head, like a sly snake. It left a giant bruise on the side of his chin.

"Me and you Vince, we ain't done!" Aiden pulled Vince's bag from his hands and rifled through it looking for money or anything of use to him. He found nothing but rotten sandwiches at the bottom of his bag. Empty chocolate bar wrappers and school textbooks which hadn't been used. It was effortless taking Vince's bag as there was no fight inside him. Aiden opened the front pocket on the bag. Inside were pictures of Vince with his family. Photos of his mum who passed away, a variety of days out he had with his mum when he was a young child. Aiden sieved through the photos.

"Who's this slag? You're fucking Mam; she's not too bad; I'd smash her. I bet she was a prostitute with them legs." Aiden held the photograph in front of Vince's face. Vince covered his face and prayed inside hoping they would go. Aiden crouched down to the floor trying to get in line with the eyes of Vince. "Tell your Mam I'll be around tonight for a fuck". Aiden gently ripped the photograph in half "Oops," dropping the picture in front of Vince. Aiden stood up and emptied his bag all over the corridor throwing the photos like confetti.

"I told you we'd scatter your pot of gold," Kane winked at Vince. "It's time," Kane said to the boys. Maxine walked off with Aiden; they fluttered like birds down the corridor.

"You're so powerful babes, no one wants to be on your bad side." Maxine fluttered her eyelashes and wiggled her hips left to right.

"Too right babe, can't believe you let him give you shit, the little ferret," Aiden replied.

Roxanne felt disgusted after she witnessed a truly shocking act of cruelty. She thought the boys would have just shaken him up a bit and gave him a slap. Not a full-blown beating. She trailed behind Aiden and Maxine with her head bent down in shame.

Vince lay on the cold floor of the corridor, breathless with exhaustion. He lay there for what felt like only a couple of seconds, twenty minutes had flown past. Vince leant against the wall and looked at the mess that was left on the floor. All his childhood memories scattered like leaves in Autumn. Vince picked up the picture that was turned. He stared in disbelief, trying to condense what had just happened. He licked his dry lips, tasting his blood that slowly oozed from his mouth, sitting in shock and bruised like an apple. Vince started to shake like an old woman using a Zimmer frame. Scanning the pictures with his eyes Vince picked them up, gathering them together.

"I hate this school," he cried. His eyes filled up; bursting like balloons. His face turned red with all the blood rushing to his head. Vince held the photographs close to his chest and curled up in a ball. He sat under the flickering lights.

"School Of Excellence," Vince read a quote from the wall in front of him. "Lies, lies," Vince spoke angrily to himself. "Fucking lies!" he roared like a lion. The sound of Vince's voice echoed down the corridor. Vince bit his nails, staring at his shadow reflecting off the walls.

"Mum, why did you have to go? I need you. If you're with me in spirit, why can I not feel you?" Vince silently cried to himself, he forced himself to stand up. Even though he was short of breath he swung his bag around his shoulder and limped into the toilets. The smell of human waste hit Vince's nose. The sound of drains flushing and clanging through the room; the walls were covered in chewing gum. Vince walked slowly, limping up to the sink. Vince turned on the rusty tap washing his blood-stained face. He closed his eyes and re-opening them to the reflection in the mirror. Gritting his teeth, dark red blood concealed what was once white. The bruises were purple, lumping on Vince's skin. His face turned red like the devil. Vince grew hungry with anger. His breath changed pace, inhaling deeper and quicker. Vince looked deep into the reflection. He wiped away the tears that lay on his face. He watched the event play in his mind over and over like a video on loop. Vince whispered "What am I going to do? no one cares. Things would have been better if we didn't move here." Vince argued with himself, fighting his inner conflicts.

"Next time you will run Vince, you're smaller than they are. You're faster than they are." Vince rinsed some water in his mouth, spitting it into the sink. Brushing off the dirt from his clothes he marched out of the toilets. There was a spark in his walk. Vince felt a relief that his day was nearly over. He paced down the corridor and stood for a few minutes at the stairs.

"That's the one." Vince grinned, feeling his mousy brown hair he made his way down the spiral stairs. Holding onto the bannister with a tight grip, the bottom of the stairs led to an open space where students could go in free time. It was filled with benches, bins and flowers. Vince had never seen this place so quiet; he made his way to the student office. Vince knocked on the door.

"One minute," a voice shouted from behind the door. Vince stared through the window, hoping to lock eyes with someone. The door twisted open. A fat woman stood centre to the door.

"What's up love, oh what's happened to you? Come in." Vince walked through the door, the student office was a medium sized room with two computers and a noticeboard hung on the wall. It had a list of all the students that had bad attendance pinned on it. "Sit down, sit down", the fat women spoke gently. "What happened to you love? speak up." Vince stared into space. "It's alright love, my names Miss Thomson and I'm fully qualified in first aid." Miss Thomson sat facing Vince, her cheeks were chubby and she had a layer of fat around her neck that made her look like she had more than one chin. There was a brown wart just above her lip that had hairs growing around it. "Come on now love, speak up. What's the matter? How did you get all those bruises?"

Vince replied, "I tripped over my shoelace at the top of the Science stairs." Vince stared at the floor, tapping his feet on the grey carpet. Miss Thomson picked up some paperwork from her desk. "Well, that will explain those bruises... How did you do it again? Fell down the stairs?"

"Look I told Miss." Vince said feeling annoyed with himself. Miss Thomas started to fill in some paperwork, 'School Accidents.' Miss Thomas typed in Vince's name on her computer to add to his profile on the school system. She clicked under the attendance box onto accidents.

"From this information this isn't the first time you had a few cuts and bumps. Loss of balance walking up the stairs, bumping into walls, falling off your chair, slipping on ice. You're quite the stuntman aren't you Vince?"

"Or punching bag," Vince spoke quietly staring at his shoes. "Look, Miss, it's nearly the end of the day, can you sign me out. I don't want to get trampled by everyone when the bell goes." Vince thought to himself, I hope she lets me go. I don't want to bump into them again; Kevin still wants to do me in. Why didn't I just take the day off?

"Right then, follow me," Miss Thomas looked at her watch, stood up and walked through a door behind her leading towards the school's reception.

The reception had big glass doors that led to the outside. A small office set up and desk facing the doors. With a spiral staircase that planted itself in the middle of the room. It was a big room as it had staff toilets facing the stairs. Miss Thomas scanned her ID card across the door sensors and opened the doors for Vince.

"Have a safe journey home," Miss Thomas said as she walked through the door rummaging through her bag looking for a pack of cigs. Vince walked down the steps; each step he took made him feel amazed. He was so excited that each step he took, he was one step closer to home. The streets were dark as tarmac; the wind started to howl like a crying wolf.

"Fucking hell, hope it doesn't rain! That would be the icing on the cake." Vince's thoughts span around his head like a whirlwind. His hands were ice cold as he held his jacket. Vince stopped walking for a minute. He threw his jacket on, zipped it up and raised the hood. 'It's freezing.' Vince thought to himself how much he couldn't wait to get on the bus home. Vince smiled; a warm sensation shot through his body as he grew excited inside thinking about a nice hot shower. Vince imagined soaking in the water, breathing in the hot steam.

"Ahh," Vince made a gentle relaxing sound. Vince passed a street of houses dragging his feet. They still ached; he kept thinking whether to have a bath or a shower. The sky turned from blue to grey, big clouds started to join each other. The clouds hid the sun away so the streets went dark, the lamp-posts started to light up the street with an orange tint. 'Strange' Vince thought, 'it's only half three and it's getting really dark. Best get a move on.' Vince sauntered towards the bus stop hoping that no one would be there, it had just started to rain, Vince felt the drops hit his head. His jacket started to take a hit as the rain water came tumbling down him. Soaked from head to toe, Vince stepped up his pace forcing himself to move quicker. Making bigger steps, Vince was nearly there, only one street away from the bus stop. There was a group of lads at the bus stop. Vince couldn't make out who it was. Their hoods were up, with JD bags swinging.

"Shit". Vince panicked, "No way. It can't be." Vince slowed himself down and stared at the group. One was sat on a black moped wearing a matching helmet. Another one was sat under the shelter with a dog. The dog was a black staff wearing a choke neck chain. The other two lads stood in the middle. Vince tried to figure out who they were. The 101-bus turned onto the street. Vince could see it coming slowly travelling around the bend. It was an hourly wait for the 101 to pass. Vince started to put a step on.

"If I jump straight on the bus there won't be any time for that group to realise who I am." The bus was halfway down the street coming closer to its stop. Vince turned from a speed walk into a full-blown sprint for the bus, "Ahh" he yelped. Vince's leg was in a lot of pain as he put a lot of pressure on it. He felt like his leg was going to snap. With his feet springing from the concrete floor the bus started to slow itself down, turning its indicator on. Vince was just a few yards away from the shelter.

"Who the fuck's that," the lad on the moped shouted laughing like a chimp. The two unidentified figures turned around. Vince froze and stumbled back.

"K.. k.. Kane. K.. k.. Kevin." Vince stuttered under his breath. Kevin and Kane smiled

"I didn't think we'd bump into you so soon." The lad on the moped revved his engine repetitively a few times. Kane walked over to the lad on the moped and handed over an ounce of weed in exchange for £100.

"Nice one mate. Give me a bell later". The lad drove off down the street trying to pull wheelies. The bus drove closer to the stop.

Kevin approached Vince, "What a day it's been for you then, you little fucking scroat." Sounds of the Staff barking violently rose. Vince stumbled backwards. "Pikey, you fucking listening?"

Vince's face turned pale, his eyes watered through the wind blowing in his face. Vince ignored the comment making a leap of faith to get on the bus. "Crash," Vince fell to the floor, like a bag of falling bricks. Crumbling like dust, Kevin gave a vicious blow to Vince's head as he leapt forward to the bus. Sounds of the dog barking slowly dissolved from Vince's ears as he laid stone cold on the concrete floor, an orange glow covered his body coming from the street lights. His eyes shut tight. The sky turned darker than Vince's wounds. The clouds separated holding a dark purple tint. Lying there motionless as the bus drove past fading away into the gloom. Kevin and Kane evaporated into the darkness, with their JD bags trailing behind them. A shine of white light hit Vince's body again and again until one car stopped......

Chapter Two

"Stop going on with yourself Roxanne!" Maxine picked up a fuss.

"What happened was wrong Maxine, Aiden went too far." Roxanne stared at Maxine with a face of guilt.

"Why you arsed Roxanne? Go on?"

Roxanne looked down with her eyes, "I'm not."

"Why you being daft then? We're going out tonight with them. Did you see Aiden's arms so lean...? So, powerful?" Roxanne's face was straight. She pulled out her eyeliner looking into Maxine's mirror. "What is it with you?" Maxine replied looking back into the mirror at Roxanne's face.

"All your arsed about is Aiden, all we ever talk about is Aiden, Aiden this. Aiden that." Roxanne sulked and brushed her hair back.

The girls were getting ready for their night out in the Dutch birds. It was six o'clock.

"Am I not allowed to be excited Roxanne? He's the hottest guy in Saint Brooks High."

Roxanne laughed. "The hottest guy, aww you make me laugh Maxine."

Maxine walked over to her wardrobe and stripped off what was left of her uniform. White T shirt stained in fake tan and a tight pencil skirt rolled down her legs. Standing half naked Maxine shouted.

"Check these bad boys!" Roxanne looked deep into the mirror and sharply turned around.

"No way! What are them?"

Maxine giggled to herself, "Anne Summers Special."

Roxanne hissed to herself like a snake. "What the fuck. You wore them to school? No wonder you've been twitching for Aiden."

Maxine curled her hair around her fingers. With her free hand, she opened her underwear drawer. "You think these babies are hot. Wait till you see my ones for tonight." Maxine picked up a black laced thong with a matching laced bra. She held the thong in front of her hips. "Aiden's getting it tonight."

"Hey Miss Summers, you got a sexy fresh pair for me? I've only got Primarni one's for tonight." The girls laughed together; their excitement was building. But secretly guilt was building inside Roxanne.

"Haha, I'm going to get changed into these laces. I'll be back in a sec!" Roxanne silently laughed to herself.

"Best had, you porn star getting changed here would be a bit lez."

Maxine slapped her bum and gave a little wiggle. "You're just jealous."

Maxine skipped into the bathroom. Roxanne sat on the end of Maxine's bed. She started to brush her hair. Her clothes were laid out on the bed. Maxine's room was only big enough to fit a bed and wardrobe. The wall paper was white with black flower patterns. Her room was colour co-ordinated. But the floor was full of clothes; all mismatched and scattered.

Roxanne looked at her clothes, short black skirt and a skin tight black top; her face frowned as she looked in the mirror. Slowly rolling off her school uniform she sprawled out and stretched her arms on the bed. It was that time of the month so she felt sorry for herself with her hormones up and down. She picked up her plastic black high heels from the floor and sunk her feet into them. She held out her wafer-thin top, stretched it over her head and rolled the top down her body with her finely painted fingers. She threw on her fake leather jacket, looked in the mirror and kissed her glossed lips together. The bedroom door cracked open. Maxine walked in with her hair curled and a short red dress on. She pouted in the mirror, posing and looking at herself.

"What do you think Roxy?"

"You look sexy," Roxanne replied.

Maxine twirled her body and smiled into the mirror. "Hi Aiden," she winked.

"You're such a geek sometimes," Roxanne grunted.

"Shut up Roxanne, I've got to look my best." Maxine skipped over her scattered clothes and picked out a shoe box from her cupboard. She opened the box revealing leopard print high heels. They fit her feet as snug as her fluffy warm leopard print jacket. Roxanne started applying a top up of makeup to her face whilst Maxine fluttered around the room like a fairy.

"Are you ready yet?" Maxine ranted with energy.

"One minute," Roxanne belched.

"Come on, hurry up! We're going to be late. The lads are going to be there for half 7. It's quarter past now."

Roxanne brushed her face, adding her final touches. "Right come on then." Roxanne effortlessly said. Maxine marched through her door with Roxanne sulking behind her.

Aiden stood outside the Dutch Birds. A thin layer of frost lay across the streets making the streets slightly glitter. Every few minutes cars drove in and out of the pub's car park. Aiden's throat was dry. He could see his breath as he exhaled the smoke from his cigarette.

"Where the fuck are they?" Aiden whispered to himself. Aiden reached into his pocket as he felt his phone vibrating. It was Kevin ringing him. Aiden raised the phone to his ear. "Hello."

"Alright Aiden mate, we're nearly there. Are the girls there?"

"Nar I'm going to text them in a minute, it's fucking cheddar."

"Is Lucas with you?"

"Nar mate, he said he will come though, think a few other lads are coming out too."

"Okay mate safe."

"Safe." Aiden licked his lips. They were on the urge to becoming chapped. He tightened the strap on his leather gloves and put his phone back in his grey Nike bottoms. Aiden pulled up his matching hooded top, taking another drag on his cig, he pulled out his phone again and texted Maxine. 'How long you going to be? X.' Aiden stood on his own waiting for the first lot of people to arrive. The pub started to get busier and busier as more people arrived. The Dutch Birds was built with stone bricks, it's door was big and made of oak. It had two glass windows on either side of the door which had "Dutch Birds" engraved on the glass. Aiden finished off his cigarette; throwing the butt on the floor, he felt a tap on his back. Aiden jumped.

"Yo big A blood!" Shouted Lucas. "What's gwarning' and tings"

"Safe," Aiden replied. "Jesus I didn't see you there. You really are black as the night."

Lucas laughed. "Man! Did my eyes pop out at you? Or was it my teeth blinding ya". Aiden and Lucas laughed.

"What you doing here anyway pal?" Aiden smirked.

"Heard you's was all out tonight an' thought why not." Lucas was wearing his black jeans with white high top converse. He clipped a baseball cap around the fabric that supports his belt. He wore a fitted black jacket and a black T-shirt underneath with the words 'SWAG' written across it in white.

"Looking fresh r kid," Aiden bantered. "Looking swagger yourself haha."

The sky began to change; the clouds grew thicker and started to rain.

"You coming inside? It's madness this weather fam, I'm black I ain't used to this shit weather. Don't want my sneaks getting soaked. You coming inside?"

Aiden replied, "Yeah fuck it. I've been out her long enough."

Maxine and Roxanne were a few hundred yards away. They saw two figures walk into the pub. "

Roxanne, Roxanne it's starting to rain." The streets were empty; the orange street lights guided the way to the pub like the yellow brick road. Roxanne ignored Maxine as they walked up the street to the pub.

"Roxy my shoes, my bloody shoes are going to get ruined, get a fucking step on!" Maxine started to get stressed as she spent all night getting ready. "Shit shit. SHIT! My hair's going to get ruined." Roxanne chuckled to herself. "It can't get any worse than what it is."

"Shut up you we're nearly there now." Maxine panicked and tried to cover her hair with her hands. "Just use your bag."

Roxanne laughed at Maxine's expressions and tantrums. "Pathetic, it's only a little bit of rain not a tsunami flood or even a storm." Maxine walked side to side, she wasn't even drunk at this point but she didn't half kick up a fuss. "Ouch! I think I've got a blister on my foot." Roxanne looked at Maxine and smiled. "It's because you haven't broken them in. You're all over the place try and walk straight, come here and link me."

Maxine replied annoyed, "Move you lez you'd like that wouldn't you?" The girls squabbled all the way down the street until they reached the doors of the Dutch Birds.

"Go on then loud mouth!" Roxanne shouted.

Maxine strutted up to the doors of the Dutch Birds and peered through the window. "Oh my god he's in there. He's in there with Luco at the bar!" Maxine screamed with excitement. "Did you pick up my sister's ID off the side?" Maxine whispered and turned looking at Roxanne anxiously. Maxine's face turned pale under the mask of fake tan.

"Obviously," Roxanne groaned sarcastically.

Maxine checked herself out in the mirror, brushing off any powder from the makeup that may have landed on her. "It's show time Roxy!" Maxine pushed open the oak doors and fluttered inside with Roxanne trailing behind her.

The sound of loud cabaret music surrounded the room.

"Sweet Caroline." Kevin and Lucas were getting some drinks lined up. The smell of alcohol burrowed through every nook and cranny of the room. There was a row of tables with cushioned seats, the bar was made from matching oak wood. In the middle of the pub there was a dance floor which felt sticky when you walked across it. This was down to people spilling their beer. Maxine and Roxanne started dancing their way to their seats. "Sweet Caroline," Maxine fluttered singing.

"Good times never seemed so good," Roxanne joined in with the sing-song. The girls started swaying left to right.

Aiden scratched his stubble. "What you getting Lucas?"

"Man's getting the twisted eye, get me some Fosters," Lucas replied with a smile of excitement.

"Excuse me mate, al have 2 fosters and 2 Carlsberg." Aiden leant over the bar.

"Excuse me mate," Aiden shouted down the bar. A blond barmaid came to Aiden's attention.

"Girl you looking fine," Lucas locked eyes with her and started to flirt. The barmaid stood there and laughed feeling awkward.

"What can I get you?". The barmaid had blue eyes; she was slim dressed in black with a name tag saying "Jo." Her breasts were catching Lucas's attention. Lucas joined the queue of perverts who sat in the pub.

"Can I have two Fosters and Carlsberg?" Aiden scanned all the different types of beer on offer. Jo the barmaid rushed off to get the order as she didn't want to hang around much longer. She rushed to make the pints forgetting to ask them for ID. She pulled down on the pumps making the pints as quick as possible.

Rushing back to Aiden and Lucas she smiled, "Twelve pounds please." Aiden handed over a twenty-pound note. Jo opened the till and gave Aiden his change.

"Hot stuff, why don't you come and dance with me?" Lucas giddily shouted. The music volume increased, Jo had a straight face.

"I'm working."

Lucas smiled, "When do you finish?" Lucas tried his best to charm her but nothing seemed to work.

Jo winked at Lucas, "I finish way past your bed time." Jo ran to the next customer shouting to be served.

"She wants my dick," Lucas said beneath his breath.

As they carried their beer to the table Aiden laughed, "Shut up you dick."

"She's just playing hard to get, yeh get me." Lucas responded.

"Hi Aiden!" A voice screamed from over the left side of the pub.

"It's about time you got here Maxine; I've been waiting for you all night!" Aiden shouted back.

Lucas shouted across the room "Damn you girls are sexy, even you Roxanne ay!" Lucas bounced up to the girls and kissed them both on the cheek, putting his arm around Roxanne. "Sexy from head to toe." Lucas began to flirt with Roxanne.

"Did you not get us drinks?" Maxine spoke with an irritated tone.

"I didn't know you was here, I'll go and get you some. What you want?"

"Two blue WKD" Maxine shouted.

"Get me some shots," Roxanne replied energetically.

Aiden ran back to the bar. "Fucking women," Aiden said under his breath.

Kane and Kevin walked through the doors of the Dutch Birds, the pub atmosphere hit all their senses. The smell, the sounds and sight were overwhelming.

"There he is the prick, at the bar spending my money." Kane looked at Aiden like a target.

"Just get it off him now, save all the fuss," Kevin replied nervously.

"It won't teach him anything if I let this slip, people will think it's acceptable." Kane's blood boiled. "Go and get me a drink!" Kane's tone was furious, he walked over to the table where Lucas and the girls sat.

"Hi Kane," the girls giggled. Kane sat down, his face started to boil. His arms tensed. He sat back into the wooden couch chair. He smiled with disgust. "Alright, you girls are looking good, where's Aiden Lucas?"

Lucas pulled away from Roxanne's neck and stared at Kane. "What's happening G? He's at the bar." Lucas went back to caressing Roxanne.

"Stop it now, cheeky Monkey," Roxanne's eyes struck Lucas.

"Easy now girl, no one likes a racist."

"I'm not being racist. You're cute like a little monkey!" Kane sat there quietly like a kettle boiling water. He smelt of rich aftershave and cigarettes.

"Kane, how's you hun?" Maxine shouted above the music.

"I'm fine," Kane stood up in mid-conversation and walked through the small crowd of drunken people, making his way to the bar. "Boys you getting them drinks in or what? My throats like saw dust here."

"Two seconds Kane pal, just getting them in now," he replied sensing Kane's tension. Jo brought three bottles of WKD to Aiden and 2 bottles of Magners to Kevin. "Nice one love," Kevin kindly spoke.

"Yeah nice one Jo." Kane pulled daggers at Aiden, all his focus directed towards him. Aiden turned around with Kevin, all three of the boys made their way back to the table. The hairs on Aiden's arms stood on end, "When's the DJ coming on?"

Maxine buzzed with excitement when she saw Aiden with her WKDs.

"Yeah it's shit this old folk music." Roxanne chipped in.

"Ay what did Bob Marley ever do to you?" Lucas sat at the end of his seat. "It was a buffalo soldier!" Lucas started singing to the chorus. "Dreadlock Rasta", Lucas stood up, pulling Roxanne with him. "Skank it girl". Lucas started twirling next to Roxanne.

"Oh my god, what are you doing." Roxanne laughed.

Lucas and Maxine started dancing away; she ran to the table and picked up her WKD.

"Wait for me Luco!"

"Think that DJ comes on soon? Can't stand this auto play list." Kevin's voice pierced through the background music.

"Thank God for that," Maxine puffed out the remaining oxygen in her lungs.

"Kane mate I got you a WKD," Aiden frowned, sliding the drink across the table.

"What do you think I am? Some sort of bitch?" Kane replied in a dark tone. Aiden looked at Kevin in confusion and looked back at Kane.

"Ay, thought that was my WKD!" Maxine barked like a Jack Russell.

"I bought three; two for you and Maxine and one for Kane."

"WKDs are what bitches drink, are you making me out."

Aiden spoke over Kane. "No, I'm not!" Aiden burst out. Kane picked up his Mangers and started to down it. The DJ had just entered the pub; he set himself up at the back of the dance floor. Two people followed behind him, holding speakers. The DJ set up his desk and laptop, plugging his microphone in. "Yo, this is the track; I'm going to play a beat that will take you back." As the music faded up the DJ shouted "It's Day and Night!" the pub lights changed, the room went darker and lights above the dance floor started flashing the colours of the rainbow. Kane stared at Aiden like a preying lion.

"It's day and night, oh my God." Maxine drank the last bit of her bottle and jumped up pulling on Aiden. "Come on, come on Mr Hunk, let's get up." Aiden bounced his eyes at Kevin and Kane and got up.

"Yeah, I'm moving," Aiden quietly said. Maxine grabbed Aiden's hand.

"Ooo they're so soft and big." Maxine was dancing around Aiden like a stripper grinding her body against him full of lust. "Easy A. It's about time you joined in with me and Roxy!"

"Maxine have you seen these moves?" Lucas spun Roxanne with his hand and she coiled into his arms.

"It's about time you have a smile on your face," Maxine shouted over the music. The dance floor started to flood with more people.

The DJ made a song announcement, "Here's Gold digger, big it up for 2K9!"

Lyrics began to play, "She takes my money when I'm in need!" Lucas and the girls sang out loud. The room started to spin and Aiden froze.

"Shit," Aiden put his hand in his pocket and pulled out a five-pound note. The beer he was drinking went to his head. He slowly started to realise he had spent Kane's money on the girls' drinks. Aiden moved more into the crowd of dancers taking Maxine with him.

"Where we going, sexy boy?" Maxine grabbed Aiden's crotch.

"Some place more hectic." Aiden's pupils dissolved, everything became blurred. People bumped into him, spilling beer everywhere. Aiden let the drunken man pass.

"He just spilt beer on you!" Maxine shouted into Aiden's ear.

"What?" Aiden leaned onto Maxine. "It's alright", Aiden swayed back and forth like a boat on water. "He's my mate," Aiden slurred.

Maxine looked annoyed. "The Aiden I know wouldn't take that." Maxine grew annoyed inside.

Roxanne sensed Maxine's irritation, "Just chill out M... Maxine," Roxanne skipped back to Lucas.

"I ain't saying she's a GOLD digger," Lucas started to sing the same lyrics repetitively.

Aiden's senses started to crumble. Maxine was in Aiden's face. She grabbed his bare hands placing them on her hips.

"Kiss me," she provocatively whispered in his ears. Aiden looked down to Maxine. His neck leant forward, their noses touched. Maxine smiled.

"I'm yours," she fluttered her eyelashes and licked her lips. Maxine could taste the strawberry flavoured gloss on her lips. Aiden closed his eyes as Maxine put her tongue down Aiden's throat. The sounds of saliva washing against Aiden's lips could not be heard. You could not hear a pin drop because the room was so loud. Maxine bit Aiden's lip leaving a small bump. She wrapped her hands around his waist, digging her nails into his back beneath the top he wore. She scratched him like a cat, clawing him left right and centre. Aiden let his hands run free; he felt her fine red dress and made his way down to her hips and bum. Even though there was a crowd of people stood closely around them the pair did not care. Their tongues danced and grinded together with their jaws locked. Aiden squeezed Maxine's bum and attempted to crawl his hand up her leg.

"Slap my arse baby, you can." Aiden grew with excitement, his blood pressure dropped. He gently squeezed her bum first and dug his fingernails into her violently.

"I want you," Aiden spanked Maxine's bum.

"Not now, later!" Maxine smiled, her eyes lit up like a firework.

"I'm going for a piss."

"Okay," Maxine replied giving Aiden a kiss on his cheek, leaving a lipstick stain on his skin.

Aiden walked through the room that felt like it was spinning and made his way to the bog. Pushing his way through the people he leant left and swayed right, making his way to the wooden bathroom doors. The men's room stank of deposit waste that lingered onto your clothes. The smell of urine hit Aiden's nostrils. There was a metal pot for Aiden to let loose in, there were toilet cubes floating along the urinals soaked in yellow stains. Aiden pulled up his joggers and walked up to the condom machine that was mounted on the wall of damp wallpaper.

Kane scanned his eyes across the dance floor.

"Have you seen Lucas dancing with that Roxanne, he's gagging for it." Kevin broke the silence. Kane blanked Kevin staring onto the dance floor.

"I'll fucking kill him the twat, where is he?" Kane clenched his fist, finishing off his cider. He saw Lucas dancing around with the two girls. "Aiden best not of gone... The SHIT BAG!" Kane scratched his skinhead and put his hood up. Kevin saw the look on Kane's face, he knew he was about to lose his rag. Kane stood up placing his bottle on the table. He stretched his arms out taking a breath. He walked up to Lucas and the girls.

"Having a good time?" Kane asked.

"Yeah eye" Lucas replied.

The girls laughed and started to do some dirty dancing, "Yeah, it's great," the girls screamed. Maxine strutted up to Kane in a provocative manner. "Are YOU having a good time?" Maxine spoke in a sexual tone of voice. Kane looked at Maxine, staring at her breasts and swaying hips. "Want to dance with me?" Maxine looked into Kane's eyes and stroked his face. Kevin watched from the side line of the table.

"No way, what's he doing?" Kevin's heart began to beat heavier.

Maxine turned her body leaning into Kane; grinding her buttocks against Kane's crotch holding Kane's hand.

"Would you like to touch me?" Maxine grabbed Kane's hands rubbing them against her behind. Kane danced with Maxine but didn't talk too much. His hands caressed her body. She twirled around and pushed herself forward into Kane's body. She slipped her hands into Kane's joggers and kissed him. Kevin sat with his hands running through what was left of his hair, growing nervous inside. Lucas and Roxanne stared in shock.

Aiden made his way out of the toilets with a smile on his face. "I'm getting it tonight," he said to himself in a cocky manner. Aiden pushed through the crowds of people opening a window of Kane and Maxine snogging violently. "What the fuck!" Aiden shouted out. "You fucking slag... And you're my mate..."

Kane turned to Aiden with Maxine strapped to him like a belt.

"You fuck me over; I will fuck you over a hundred times more than you can imagine." Kevin shot up from his seat making his way into the crowd.

"You fucking slag Maxine," Aiden cried out as Maxine kissed Kane's neck. Kevin caught up to all the commotion. Aiden put one step forward and paced towards Kane furiously. Kevin gripped Aiden holding him back.

Kane shouted out, "Come on then big man, I'll show you whose fucking 'big.' Let him go Kevin, let's see what Aiden's all about!"

Aiden stood and stared for a minute. Tears ran from his eyes in anger, he swayed away turning his back and walked into the crowd aiming for the door.

Chapter Three

Vince opened his tired eyes, revealed was a warm room with a fireplace that burned logs and a wooden table that was placed at the back of the room. Vince felt the heat cover his face, he was lay on a brown fabric couch with a black bed cover over him. There were mounted wall lamps that were switched on to give the room a cosy feel. Not too dark but not too light. There was a fluffy brown rug that covered half the floor with a small coffee table sat on top of it. Vince lay effortlessly, he felt too comfortable and warm to move. He had no idea where he was, he believed he was in a dream lying in a log cabin in the heart of a forest. Vince heard people talking from a door behind him.

"Is he awake?" A young voice said.

"I don't know, I'll check on him now," an older woman's voice spoke up. The two people from behind the door walked into the room where Vince was lay.   Claire Harrison was a woman in her forties and mother to Daisy, she was a local drinker at the 'Smoking Barrel' and knew Vince's father very well. They lived at the top of Mary Lee Road at number twenty-four. Daisy Harrison was sixteen years old; she had black curly hair with a small sprinkle of freckle's on her face. She went to North Field High which was a very hard school to get in. She wore a long black silky gown. Daisy and her Mum Claire sat down at the table.

"What are we going to do if he doesn't come around Mum?" Daisy said with concern.

"Don't worry dear, he will come around, just go back into the kitchen and pour Vince some soup."

Daisy walked into the kitchen; the smell of tomato soup rose as she opened the door. The soup sat on the stove boiling away; it started to bubble like a Jacuzzi. Daisy turned the heat down giving it a quick stir; she poured it into a bowl.

Claire walked over to Vince putting her hand on his forehead, "Well you don't have a temperature thank God."

Vince re-opened his eyes and jumped out of his skin.

"Who are you...? What am I doing here? Where am I?" Claire tucked the covers around Vince and pulled a chair sitting in front of him.

"I'm Claire; I drove past you in my car. You were lay down on the street unconscious in the cold and rain next to the bus stop," Claire said calmly with care. "So I stopped my car and got out to see if you were okay, I then realised who you were so me and Daisy, my daughter, brought you back to my home. You must have fallen over Vince because you were unconscious and had bruises."

"How do you know my name? How do you even know me?" Vince looked confused. "You do look familiar."

"I'm a local at Mick's pub, your Dad's pub sorry. I know him well and I know he's going through a lot of stress at the minute so I didn't phone the emergency services to come to aid you because I didn't want your Dad getting startled, so I brought you here and cleaned you up. I'm only at the end of Mary Lee Road so when you're ready, in your own time, I'll drop you off home. Don't jump up too soon though, I've made some soup."

Vince replied with a smile, "Thank you... I really appreciate what you have done for me, but how did you know I was Mick's son?"

"I always see you pot collecting for your Dad with that boy Chris. Your Dad talks of you a lot, he pointed you out once or twice when he was telling me about you." Daisy walked over to where Vince was lay with a tray and a bowl of hot soup.

"Here have this, this should warm your body up" Daisy gave a subtle smile and passed Vince the soup.

"Thank you," Vince replied. "Tomato soup's my favourite."

"I'll just go and get some bread," Daisy walked back into the kitchen.

"Claire, I can't thank you enough for the kind hospitality." Vince started sipping away at his soup, Claire turned the telly on and sat at the table, Daisy came back into the room with a plate of buttered bread with a tray with two other bowls of soup on it.

"Here you go mum."

"Thanks love." Claire picked up a piece of bread and dipped it in her soup. "You can't beat crusty bread and soup."

Daisy and Claire felt a sense of good favour. They felt Vince's appreciation and started dipping their bread into the soup.

"It's nice and hot Claire," Vince said with his mind at peace.

Daisy brought a plate of crusty bread over to Vince, making a lot of eye contact. Vince stared at Daisy's body. She was wrapped up in a black silky night dress. Her eyes were blue with a small tint of green. Her eyebrows were black which matched her hair. She had naturally long eyelashes. Vince thought to himself her face is snow white like a beautiful swan but without an orange beak. "Thanks, Daisy." Daisy smiled at Vince gracefully making her way back to the table. Claire polished off her soup and picked up a washing basket.

"Right... I'm just going to sort some washing out?" Claire walked out the room leaving Vince and Daisy to themselves. Daisy sipped away and soaked her bread in the soup; she was the second one to polish off the soup. She walked into the kitchen and left the bowl on the side. She grabbed her chair and dragged it across the floor, placing it in front of Vince. She sat down.

"Are you finished?" Daisy asked with a cheeky manner.

"Not yet," Vince replied softly. Daisy's eyes twinkled as she frowned at Vince.

"What happened to you out there?" Daisy curiously asked.

"Nothing."

"I'm not buying that you just fell over, I'm not my Mum. What happened to you out there?" Daisy asked with a concerning voice. "You've got a bruise on your chin and cheek. You didn't just fall over, I'm not stupid," Daisy said with a hint of anguish. She then laughed and smiled. "Come on Vince, you can tell me." Daisy turned into a pestering puppy. Vince lay there shy and nervous, he had never spoken to a beautiful girl before. Vince didn't know what to say, he asked himself how can I even start, never mind what happened at the bus stop. Vince looked down at the bedding with a sad expression on his face, looking into the bowl of soup he saw a faint reflection.

"Well, how do I know I can trust you? I don't even know you."
Vince began to feel butterflies in his stomach. His hands started
to shake; it was not the cold running through his veins but
nervous energy.

"Fine then," Daisy looked at Vince; she started to get goose
bumps on her arms. Daisy was never loud and confident but
around Vince she felt intrigued.

"Don't say that... I'm just saying... Can't we talk about
something different? I've had such a hectic day." Vince looked at
Daisy with watery eyes.

"Well okay. How long you lived around here?" Daisy asked
sympathetically.

"I've lived here all my life"

Daisy shrugged. "How come I've never seen you around
then?"

"I don't really get out much, I tend to just help my Dad out
with the mess that's left in the pub."

Daisy giggled. "Haha, your housebound"

"Not really. I'm tired when I get in on most days so I either go
straight to bed or help out, depending how I feel." Vince kept
holding eye contact with Daisy. Vince had never felt so intimate
with a girl before, even though he had only just met Daisy.
He felt an instant connection to her. Daisy stroked off the
breadcrumbs that clung to her gown.

"This will keep the mice fed," Daisy's eyebrows slightly rose.

"What mice? You have rats in the house?" Vince laughed with
cheek.

"No! It's a saying; I best sweep them under the couch. My
Mum's a clean freak. She will go mad if there's a mess anywhere."
Daisy swept the crumbs under the couch, that Vince lay on, with
her feet. Daisy scratched her head, moving some hair behind her
ears. Vince sipped away at the remaining soup left in the bowl.
"Are you finished yet? You eat so slowly."

"Yeah," Vince said with a little rush of words. Daisy took the
bowl from Vince's hand and walked into the kitchen.

"I'm just going to wash these pots!" Daisy shouted through the door.

"Okay" Vince replied in a soft tone.

Vince started looking around the room; he felt a warm sense of home. Even though his feelings fluttered towards Daisy, he still didn't know these people. He felt at peace, a short escape from his harsh reality, Vince thought to himself. "These people are so kind, so thoughtful, they have good hearts. I should tell Daisy but I can't, I don't have courage." Daisy walked back into the room, the heat from the fire circulated the room.

"Daisy?" Vince burst from his lungs.

"Yeah?" Daisy sat down pulling her chair closer to Vince.

"Thanks." Vince replied.

Daisy's eyebrows moved central. "What for?"

"You know what for Daisy."

Daisy's eyes blinked. "No, don't be daft, I was scared myself, I thought you was dead. If it wasn't for my Mum recognising you, I don't know what I'd do. She's the one to thank, not me. I'm just glad you're here safe and sound, it would have been cruelty leaving you out in the rain." Daisy summarised what happened, it replayed in her mind. Vince felt a sensation of care. Daisy felt Vince's forehead. "Your fine, no fever." A thud of footsteps came from outside the door, Claire paced down the stairs with an empty washing basket and walked through the door.

"It's getting late now Daisy, come on, off to bed, it's 10:30." Vince looked at the Roman numeral clock that hung on the beige wall.

"I'll get off now." Vince pulled himself out of the cocoon of fabric.

"You can sleep down here for the night if you want. No rush." Claire smiled sincerely.

"Thanks Claire, but I must get moving, my Dad will start worrying if I don't get a move on...thanks though Claire." Vince smiled but felt like he had outstayed his welcome. He didn't want to leave but he tied his shoelaces and zipped up his jacket.

"I'll drop you off home; I can't send you back outside on your own into the wildness."

"I'll be alright. It's only a street or two away." Vince replied hovering his eyes at the clock.

"No, I'll take you home." Claire picked up her keys. "Are you coming Daisy?" Claire threw on her brown tweed jacket.

"Yeah, I'm coming Mum." Daisy looked at Vince and crossed her eyes back to Claire. All of them walked through the hallway and trailed across the carpet.

Claire opened the front door, cranking the key through it. The lock crunched open as Claire, Daisy and Vince walked through it. Claire drove a Volkswagen golf; the car looked knackered with scratches on it and a small bump.

"Are you sure you didn't run me over?" Vince laughed.

"What! No. What makes you say that?" Vince pointed to the bump on the bonnet. Daisy started to chuckle.

"That happened a few months ago," Claire began to giggle.

"Get in you two." Daisy and Vince jumped in the back of the car as Claire reversed out of the driveway. The rain bounced off the car windows, washing off the spray of mud that lay across the side of the car. "Vince, feel free to come around anytime. You're always welcome." Claire's eyes stared into the rear view mirror watching Vince.

"Thanks Claire, thanks for everything you've done for me tonight." Claire's eyes watered. The car arrived outside Vince's home, 'The Smoking Barrel.' "Well this is me."

Daisy put her hand on Vince's as he unstrapped his belt. "Stay out of trouble okay." Daisy said with concern. Vince got out the car leaving his pot of luck behind. He walked up the steps that led to the door. Squeak! the door opened, the sound of glass scraping together echoed through the room.

"We're closed!" Mick shouted. Mick was a medium sized man, aged 47. He originally had short black hair but as years went by life started to catch up on him. His hair began to turn silver and grew thinner leaving Mick looking grey in his appearance.

Mick lived most of his life in Ireland working on his Dad's farm. Hard work wasn't something new to him. His parents were very strict as they had to be because the crops wouldn't grow themselves. He had a plough horse called Spiorad, in English meaning Spirit. Mick gazed upon Vince, the room was dark, the light from the pool table was the only strong source of light. The bar was lit by logo's of a variety of brews. Carlsburg, Fosters, John Smith the full charade of alcoholic beverages.

"It's me, Dad!" Vince choked on his words feeling nervous.

"Oh right... Come here and give me a hand." Mick started to stack the empty pint glasses, the light from the pool table lit up Mick's face. "Where have you been?" Mick shouted at Vince as he walked closer with his head down.

"I've been at Chrissy's. I went there after school." Mick's forehead frowned.

"What's up with your face...? Look at me!" Mick grabbed Vince's face, his big chunky hands clinched onto Vince's skin. "What do you call this...Ay?" Mick stared at Vince seeing the victim in his eyes. "What happened to you?" Mick shouted aggressively ragging Vince by his collar.

The anxiety ricocheted like a bullet in broken pieces flying around Vince's body. His breathing locked and abdominal muscles tensed. Vince just wanted to breathe but his respiratory system was under attack by pressure and nerves. Vince felt the flood of embarrassment slice through him as he gazed upon Mick's eyes.

"What's this then?" Mick raged with anger.

Vince stumbled back. His arms started to shake. His face started to heat up and a flood of water broke out from his eyes.

"Get off me!" Vince cried out. "You don't care anyway."

Mick stared into Vince's eyes. He saw the little boy inside him and realised how much he had grown, how much he hadn't been there for his son, allowing Vince to come home with excuses every so often why he's bruised.

"Vince who did this to you?"

"Nobody!" Vince replied sobbing in tears.

"Nobody! How can I help you if you don't talk to me?" Mick released his hands from Vince. "Son, I'm here for you. Why can't you see that boy? Talk to me. Tell me!" Vince turned his back and headed for the stairs that lead up to his room. "Where are you going? Ay!" Vince ignored his Dad and paced forward. Mick followed behind him with the empty glasses in his hands. He placed them on the bar table. "Vince son, if you don't like school I've told you, you can come and work with me. But how dare you let people do this to you!" Mick felt himself getting irritated but tried not to get angry.

"I'm fine." Vince looked back at his Dad.

"Fine, fine... Are you right in the mind? Have you seen yourself in the mirror? Do you think it's fine that you come home looking like a walking corpse? Battered and bruised like rotten apple!" Vince paused as his head processed what Mick had just said.

"Why are you acting like you care? You never cared when you saw me bruised the first time. So why, all of a sudden, you care now?"

Mick stood tall and still, putting his hands on the bar table. "I know I haven't been the greatest Dad in the world. But I do care about you son. My life's been so hectic that I've shut myself away from everyone. Even you... my own son, my flesh and blood. And I've not made things easy for you. Coming over here calling a new country our home, well it's just how it is running this business, trying to keep shelter over our heads." Mick's eyes started to water. He started to think, looking down at the empty glasses, he pulled a bottle of brandy out from the side pouring himself a drink. He sat down on a stool staring into space.

"If Mum was here things would be different. I thought you stopped drinking, what happened to that, ay? Went down the pan like you've let everything else go." The sound of shattered glass echoed throughout the room. Mick threw his glass violently across the room.

"I loved your mother and I still do! I'd do anything for her to be back. Anything for her to walk on this earth with us again.

Don't you dare speak to me about your mother in vain!" Vince stood looking at Mick, his eyes puffed out red, swollen from an excessive amount of blood gathering around the muscles from his eyes. Cheek bones bruised, crumbling bone marrow ached Vince's jaws. Claire's pain killers had worn off. Vince started to feel physically and mentally exhausted. His head boiled like a kettle as Vince released his steam on Mick.

"Make your mind up. Do you want me to continue school and keep this up or stay here and work with you? What do you want me to do?" Vince screamed. "Go on then, go on then tell me, what am I supposed to do? I'm coming to a point where I just can't take it. Every day's a battle. A struggle to get through in one piece. They call me an IMMIGRANT Dad. They say I don't belong here and I don't." Vince banged his hand on the table bruising his fingers numb.

"You're angry enough to stand up to me hey? Brave enough to look me in the eye, strong enough to clench your fists. The answers right there, looking you straight in the face!" Vince's face reflected from the row of glasses facing the bar table. Mick bit his lip and rested his elbows on the bar, holding his face speaking softly. "Go to bed. Sleep, you need it. Take tomorrow off if you want." Mick rose from the stool and looked at Vince square. "But if you ever speak to me in this manner again, you won't wake up in the morning." Mick smiled and Vince subtly smiled back gritting his teeth. "So have a think about what you're going to do or you'll have me to deal with ay." Mick walked over to his son and hugged him. "It's not going to be easy. But try and get your head down. You're a clever boy, you take after your mother. But you have Irish blood so use it." Mick patted Vince on his head "Off to bed now son."

"What about the mess?" Vince replied wiping the tears from his face.

"Don't worry I'll sort it." Mick picked up a brush and shovel from behind the bar sweeping up the glass.

It was midnight. Vince dragged his feet up the battered old stairs. All Vince wanted was his bed so he could lie down and attempt to de-stress. An image of Daisy kept coming into his mind. Her dark curly hair and beautiful face kept reappearing. He had flashes of the day montage through his mind. He heard Kane and Kevin's voice scratch his ear's "Told you we would scatter your gold." "Fucking Pikey, immigrant." Vince collapsed on his bed. His bedroom lights were dead making the room dark. His mind shuffled thoughts with no ease. Left to right Vince tossed and turned. He yawned scratching his nose. "Irish Blood." "It's right it's in you." "Strong enough to clench your fists." Vince heard his father's voice override what Kane, Kevin and Aiden said to him that day. He heard his father's voice talk repetitively. "Strong" "Brave" "Irish blood."

Mick swept up the glass with a black shovel and wooden brush. He turned off all the remaining lights and locked the door. He sat back on the bar stool in darkness, leaving his thoughts to gather together. He went in and out of flashbacks to his past, repeating in his mind a variety of painful memories. Mick's hands shook as he went into a variety of painful trances.

Ireland

Mick carried the corpse of his father tucked away in a brown wooden coffin. His two brothers were next to him shoulder to shoulder crying hysterically, Morgan and Oden. Mick was the oldest brother out of the three and was full of pride. He did not shed a tear as he walked into the Catholic church; it was small with white paint on the outside. The church was known for being a place of happiness as it was a popular wedding reception and seen a lot of christened heads. Mick looked at all the people who gathered in respect to his father walking down on the wooden floor of Christ. Mick and his brothers walked slowly towards the alter.

"Sit down my children," the priest spoke in a calm voice holding warmth. "The light of God has shined above Vincent's head, leading the pathway of eternal life in the heavens." Mick daydreamed at the coffin in disbelief. It had not hit him that the creator of his life had left the world. Leaving Mick with the responsibility of looking over Oden and Morgan.

The brothers were close but this life changing experience tested the bond between them. They released the body of their father on the marble table of the altar; it was beautifully decorated with Jesus's cross and angels carved into the stone. The sun shined through the windows showing Saint George stained on the glass. All the windows had decorative illustrations of religious worshipers and rulers. Mick and his brothers sat at the front. Motionless Mick stared into space. The light shined across their heads.

"At least his poor heart can rest as he watches above with mother." Tears fell from Oden's face; his lips trembled shaking like his hands. Oden felt a soft touch on his hand as his eyes were sullen and blood shot red. Mick held his brother's hand's together tight and quietly sat there in a cold shiver.

2009 Saint Brooks High

Kevin walked through the school doors of Saint Brooks high with his head held high.

"My town." Kane said to himself as he looked across the atrium, all the students were walking past each other in their social groups. Kane spotted a few of his mob selling away,

Lucozade and chocolate. "That's what I like to see, the smell of money being made." As Kane made his way up the spiral staircase he looked across the balcony, overlooking his empire of grafters.

Lucas and Kevin walked towards the upstairs pathway to the entrance of the Science block.

"Yo, there's Kane I." Lucas tapped Kevin on the shoulder. "Look!"

"I can see him too! Come on, let's go and see him." Kevin replied feeling a sense of nerves.

"Did you see them last night, that Maxine's a right slag. One second she was on it with big A... The next minute on Kane like a smack head on heroin." Lucas chattered his lip's making sounds of chewing gum. He smacked his lips together slightly turning his snap back cap. It was white with black text on it spelling the words SWAG.

Kevin felt bad inside after last night, it wasn't the drink. Kevin wasn't having a hangover; he was drowning in a sorrow of sadness towards what happened between Kane and Aiden. One conflict after the other he thought. You don't do these things to mates. No matter how much you get angry. Kevin didn't want to talk but silently replied the words.

"I know."

Kane leant against the balcony, the steel frame felt cold as he rested his hands on it, he looked across the balcony to witness Kevin and Lucas heading in his direction. Kane scratched the side of his face. His eyes were puffed out, his breath smelt of cider. From the look of him, you could tell he didn't wash this morning as he still had sleep around his eyes, you could smell the tobacco on his blazer. Tired lines surfed under his eyes like waves. Tightness built around his face, he felt his jaw muscles stiffen on his neck. You could see red marks. Scratch marks!

Kevin approached Kane with Lucas closely at the side of him.

"Alright?" Kevin gestured to Kane.

"Yeah I'm good me, couldn't be better. You see this boys? Look down there!" Kane pointed his finger across the balcony,

"Year 7s, 8s, 9s, 10s and 11s all selling under one banner, my banner. That's some real shit right there. Anyone who tries to sell for themselves ends up a victim. The game works just the same. It's the same concept. Fear and retribution."

Kevin shook his head, "yeah I know. Everyone working like army ants for you."

"What's up with you?" Kane's nose flared.

"Nout." Kevin replied looking at the ground with his brown eyes.

Lucas shouted full of energy, "Yo boy's what lesson we got first?"

"Erm, don't know mate." Kane felt a little dazed. The aftermath of last night's drinks slowly started to affect him. Kevin pulled out his phone. He had the lesson's saved in notes on his D500 Samsung mobile phone.

"Its red week, we've got English first Maths, Science, P.E and business studies."

Kane laughed smiling at Lucas. "Ay, haha I didn't ask for a full running commentary did I Lucas!"

Kevin looked at Kane in disappointment. Nothing annoyed Kevin more than Kane being in an arsey mood. Kevin could handle his drinks; he rarely had bad after effects on alcohol, though he was still prone to getting leathered after a fair few pints. He looked at Lucas's cocky smile. Kevin was building up a small annoyance inside him towards the lads.

"Business Studies? You picked business studies for your option?" Lucas laughed and burped in Kevin's face tightening his leather strap bag.

"Yeah… And? You scruffy guy."

Sounds of students walking past the three started to increase as first period was well on its way.

"That's raw that! Smelly bastard you Lucas." Kane jumped over Kevin's words.

"Ay man's fresh, what you saying?" Lucas pulled up his jumper revealing his latest designer belt. "Easy man, man's got to be fresh to wear my SWAG fuckin LV mandem." Lucas began to feel himself get excited to the boy's reactions. Kevin and Kane locked eye to eye thinking the same thoughts.

"Harpuhey market ten pounds."

"Louis fake ton Cheetam Hill."

The school bell rang out setting off first lesson. "Ay dickheads, you can fuck off, this shit's genuine." Lucas's belt glowed as the sun light shone through the plastic roof cover of the science block.

"Yeah, yeah bull shit." Kane replied feeling full of energy. "Ay Kevin you coming English then G? Going to be the next Shakespeare, me."

"Yeah Kane," Lucas patronised throwing back his banter. "It's Mice of Men we're watching in English, fucking hell." The boys walked down the upper right wing corridor into the overriding mist of students flocking like sheep.

Chapter Four

Vince opened his eyes wide in a sudden shiver. It was ten in the morning.

"Shit I'm late, I'm late." Vince lay comfortably in his bed ranting to himself. The window in his bedroom was slightly open. The wind crawled its way inside sending a chilling breeze down Vince's spine. Vince tried to role his body left to right but the bed was too warm gluing him to the covers. The sound of Irish music was echoing up the stairs leaking through the gap in Vince's door. Mick would frequently listen to the Irish radio stations. It made him feel a sense of being back in Ireland.

"No nay never, No nay never no more!" the sound of Mick's voice singing along to the 'Wild Rover' pierced through Vince's ears.

"Right I best move then, I can't stand him singing." Vince made a dash attempt to drag himself from the comfort of his pillows. Vince picked up his pyjama bottoms that he kicked off in the night and threw them on, he felt the warmth of the fluffy cotton rub against his legs. "Dad!" Vince opened his bedroom door and shouted down the stairs. "Dad...Turn it down. It's ten o'clock, not ten at night. Mick shouted back up the stairs.

"I'm in good spirit my boy!" Vince looked around his room scanning through the piles of clothes on his floor.

He picked out two odd slippers. Both were Christmas gifts from last year and the year before that. Each year Vince would find himself getting new slippers underneath the pubs Christmas tree. The usual plastic tree that gets thrown up each year, it was only small and sat itself on a single rounded table. Each year Mick would go into the pub cellar and route through old bashed-in cardboard boxes of decorations. The cellar had two room's one for all the alcohol and beer barrels and a room for storage. It was dirty and needed a refurbish but it didn't bother Mick as it served its purpose.

The walls in Vince's room were damp, you could see the water damage spreading across the white painted walls. The dampness carried a black rash across the walls. Vince picked up some dirty underwear and started to wipe the thin layer of water that lay on top of his walls. He smudged the thick layer of dampness with an old pair of boxers. After a few minutes of wiping down the walls, Vince looked at the grey boxers. They had turned fully black and the fabric had absorbed the water. Vince walked out onto the landing and threw the boxers into the dirty washing.

"Dad! Dad! Turn the music down. I can hear it all the way up here!" Vince leaned over the balcony which led to the set of stairs and shouted down.

"Pack it in Vince," Mick slightly turned the radio down. "I'm going out to pick up some supplies for the pub. Do you want to come?"

Vince looked at his phone and read the time. "Its 20 past 10, I'm already running late for school." Vince gasped racing up and down the landing looking for his school uniform. "I told you... You can take the day off." Mick shouted up the stairs. Vince stood at the top of the stairs in his school pants then ran down the stairs without any top on.

"Oh right. I just thought that I should get myself in School." Vince walked through the bar door to witness his father sitting at the bar with fresh orange juice and porridge. Mick ate a spoon full of porridge, gulping it down his neck.

"Ah well, take the day off.... wait, do you have exams today?"

"No Dad." Vince gently replied.

"Oh righty then. You can wipe down these tables. And there's a black bag I need you to bring up from the cellar. It's heavy and in a thick tube shape. I need you to bring it up and put it in the back room where I used to store crates of bottles."

"Okay Dad. I'll phone in sick then." Vince shook his head with a smile.

"No need. I've already rang them." Mick gulped his glass of orange juice and burped. "Right then get your arse moving, I'm setting of now. And those tables better be bleeding shining when I'm back." Vince started laughing as Mick stood up from his seat and walked towards the door.

"Ey! Dad, move your arse." Mick smiled to himself and shouted back.

"I don't here you moving lazy arse. See you later."

Bang! Mick shut the door with some force and made his way to his white van.

Vince turned his head to the back door which lay behind the bar. He walked through it tiptoeing as the floor was freezing cold. There was a small kitchen set up in a box room on the right side. Vince walked into the kitchen.

"I should have kept them odd slippers on. It's freezing." Vince moaned to himself. He ploughed through the cupboard with his hands, searching for any box of cereal. Weetabix was Vince's favourite breakfast, there were only two Weetabix left in the packet, Vince pulled out the cereal box and got the milk from the fridge. He washed himself a fresh bowl in the sink and dried it off with a tea towel. He placed the Weetabix in the middle of the black bowl, pouring the milk then sprinkling sugar over the Weetabix like falling white snow. "That's what a real breakfast should look like, not a bowl of slimy porridge." Vince walked back into the bar and sat down on his Dad's bar stool. He started to eat away at his Weetabix whilst looking around the room. The pub was so silent in the mornings. The sun shined through the windows, the light bounced off the tables making the brown wood shine like varnish. After Vince demolished his cereal he pulled out a cloth which sat on the bar's sink. He threw his bowl in the sink, running some hot water over it. He walked up to the tables and started to wipe them down getting rid of beer stains that left a sticky sensation on the wood. "Wax on, wax off." Vince said to himself, quoting the Karate Kid.

It was his favourite film of all time. He fantasized being the kid that did the right thing. He saw the Karate Kid movies as a way of connecting with himself. "I wish I had someone like Miyagi, no one would fuck with me." Vince continued to clean the tables. "Well, I suppose being here today, doing these jobs beats getting beat up." Some tables had irritating stains that even bleach couldn't remove whilst others were an easy wipe over.

Vince went back upstairs into his room; he stripped of his school pants and rummaged through the mountain of clothes that piled on top of each other. Some grey Adidas joggers revealed themselves from the peak of the mountain. Vince threw them on and found a black vest which was unbranded. He pulled it over his head, stretching his arms through the vest. He picked up the odd pair of slippers and slid his feet inside them.

Vince made his way back downstairs. He turned off his Dad's radio then followed the path behind the back door which then lead onto the cellars stairway. There was mould on the walls with patches of dampness. The pub fell in silence, sounds of floorboards squeaking and the touch of a cold draft hit Vince in the face. At the top of the cellar stairway lay a small crate of beer that needed to be stored. Vince's legs stood firm as he bent over and picked up the crate. Vince looked down the steep slope of stairs, they were made of stone, let's put it this way, it would be a disaster to fall down these set of stairs as the cellar had concrete floors and brick walls. It was a death hazard waiting to happen. Vince swung one foot in front of the other. He had been down the stairs thousands of times; he knew each step well as his toes shivered as they felt the cold stone.

Vince's mind kept going on the blink, all the stress from yesterday had made him wake up feeling sick. The hair on his head stood up with grease and his face caked in gunk. Sleep fell beneath his eyes and tomato soup mixed with Weetabix reeked from Vince's breath. Reaching the bottom of the cellar stairs, there were two rooms, the storage room and a room full of beer barrels, draft pumps, the full gear that every pub cellar has; it had it all. In the storage room, there were wooden boxes, like the ones that were used for transporting objects in the old days. There was a cold draft which passed through the rooms which gave a spooky sense that someone was there, standing over the back of Vince, the rooms were frosty cold, there was a gloom which flattered the lights which shined from the ceilings of the roof. The coldness of the room clenched onto Vince's breath you could see the steam coming from the warmth of Vince's mouth.

Vince never smoked, so when it was cold, seeing his breath come out of his mouth like smoke was the closest experience of blowing smoke he had. Vince didn't bother about taking drugs as even though he was living a bad life he was ambitious that he had a lot to live for. School was just a passing point for Vince; learning how to stay mentally fit each day was like any other form of exercise like walking.

On the cellar floor was a big black bag, it looked like a body bag by the shape of it, like a sleeping person wrapped in layers of black plastic. Vince bent over, his knees cracked; he placed two hands around the bag. From one angle, it looked like Vince was bear hugging the bag. The object hidden beneath the plastic bag was heavy, maintaining grip was hard. Vince dug his fingernails into the bag and slowly placed it upwards leaning it against the wall.

"Fucking hell! What is it?" Vince groaned to himself, his back started to strike with pain as the weight he lifted was too heavy. Vince knew that his Dad would moan if he didn't move the object as he didn't ask a lot of Vince even though he always insisted on helping. Vince put his hands under the bottom of the bag lifting, bending his knees he held tight firmly around the waist of the bag. With all the strength in Vince's body, his muscles tired and bonded together as he lifted the bag. Each step he took up the stairs felt like a journey. Vince started breathing slower as he was chasing his breath, his abdominal muscles twinged and ached as the weight started to tear at his body. As Vince stepped up the stairs the bag felt heavier like clothes in water, dragging his body down. Fighting the stairs, Vince pushed his way through the opening of the cellar's door. He dragged the bag across the wooden floor behind the bar leading himself into the spare room which shared its space with the boiler and electric box. The room was dark and gloomy; the walls were bare, with no paper covering them. Vince threw the bag in the middle of the room and stared at it. At the back of the room were two windows which sat in a battered wooden bracket, the wood was rotting and the glass was covered in dark mould only allowing a little bit of natural light through them. There was a whistling sound which hissed through the gaps of the bricks. Next to the electric box were four switches. Vince slowly turned away from the bag and walked up to the switches. He pressed all four at the same time. Only one light came on but wasn't containing a consistent current as the light went on and off every few minutes. The floor was dirty; Vince could see the imprints of his shoes trodden along. Vince walked out of the room and left the door swinging open. He rifled for the wooden sweeping brush that hung next to the mop and bucket in the left corner of the bar. Vince walked back into the spare room and started sweeping the bed of dirt which slept on the floor. Half an hour flew past without Vince realising. There was a pile of dirt in the top right corner of the room which Vince built. The floor changed colour from black to light grey, you could see the plain concrete surface lie peacefully fresh. The sound of Mick's white van pulling onto the kerb outside the 'Smoking Barrel' echoed through the doors of the pub. Mick opened the door of his van, on the seat next to him was a blue plastic bag. Mick peered inside the bag and frowned with his eyebrows. He pulled down his sun visor and looked at his reflection in the mirror.

"Well you've done it now old boy I, fuckin hell." Mick rested his hands on the steering wheel; the keys were still in the car with the engine running. Mick twisted the key pulling it out of the ignition and put it in his trousers. The rear-view mirror revealed Mick's heated skin. On the dashboard sat a small paper medicine bag. In the glove compartment was a medium sized bottle of brandy. Mick opened the glove compartment and grabbed the bottle. Mick took a mouth full and swallowed; he felt a warm sensation lingering in his throat. He grabbed the paper medicine bag and put it inside his coat pocket, the plastic blue bag caught Mick's eye. Grabbing the bag with energy bouncing out of his seat, Mick slammed the door behind him. Walking through the swinging doors of his home Mick shouted.

"Vince! Where are you my lad?" Mick looked across the polished tables. "Good lad," Mick said to himself quietly.

"Yeah..." Vince's voice raised coming from the spare room.

"I'm in here." Mick walked towards the spare room, the floorboards creaked. Mick's eyes had to adjust to the darkness of the room. "What you doing in here?" Mick coughed and spat into a tissue.

"I didn't know where to put this bag? It's really heavy, it gave me a dead arm."

"Oh right... Open it." Vince turned to the bag and started to tear away at the plastic.

Mick revealed the objects which sat snug in his bag and held them in his hand. Vince ripped the plastic like wrapping paper. It was heavily layered in plastic, Vince clawed at the bag as his curiosity was running wild trying to get the plastic bin liners off. He felt a burst of excitement like a child on Christmas morning. Finally, underneath the mountain of plastic shreds revealed an old punch bag. It was as black as the night with a huge chunky rusty chain at the top of it. Vince's eyes lit up like Christmas lights as he turned to his Dad.

"There's a time that comes in a boy's life where he reaches the point of becoming a man. I know I've not been there to teach you how to become a man, as I've watched you grow from the shadows. But it's time for you to shine in the light. Before your Granddad settled down with your gran and bought the farm house he was a bare-knuckle fighter." Mick took a breath and released the air from his lungs, "Vincent the great he was known as." Mick gave Vince an old pair of laced up boxing gloves. "These were your Grandad's gloves he trained with." There was a slit in the gloves to put weights inside. Vincent would put the weights inside the gloves so when he trained his arms would become stronger, his blows would be harder and his knuckles would be tougher. "Here's a picture of your Grandad in his prime." Mick held the picture to Vince, his face was overwhelmed. He snatched the picture from Mick's fingertips.

Vince looked down at the picture; his Grandad wasn't a big man. He stood around the same height as Vince. He proudly showed off his muscles in the photograph with his fists clenched and his six-pack popping.

"How come you never told me this? I thought Grandad was a simple man?" Vince looked up to his Dad, staring at eye level.

"You never asked." Mick smiled running his fingers through what was left of his hair. "Right, go and get a shower, you stink!" Vince and Mick laughed together.

"It's because I've been doing job's for you old man" Vince replied back to Mick. Mick put his arm around his son.

"Thank's my boy, I know. Now go on, get a shower. I'll hang this up for you." Vince picked up the gloves and photograph and walked out of the room running upstairs to his bedroom. His footsteps going up the stairs was loud and fast as he paced to his bedroom. He stuck the picture on his wall with glue tack and threw his gloves on the bed. Vince looked at the picture for a couple of seconds.

"Irish blood," he whispered to himself. Vince ran across the landing, there was a spark in each step he took.

Vince jumped into his bath and turned on the shower head. The hot steam hit the sweat on his face. The grease glued inside his hair leaked down his neck,Vince picked up the Head & Shoulders, scrubbing his hair. Steam covered the small bathroom, water dripped down the windows and Vince took a humid breath as he rinsed his hair under the hot water.

Mick bent his knees and felt the rusty chain in his hands. He felt the texture of the rust and looked down at the bag. His eyes started to water and hands slightly shook.

Ireland 1994

"Come on Mick, stay for another round, you might get lucky." Oden collected the euros from the table leaving Mick a smug smile.

"I best be off; the wife will be going mad if I come home late. You know what she's like," Mick replied zipping up his brown tweed coat. "She hates being in the house on her own." Mick picked up a set of black leather gloves from the table.

"She's not on her own, she's minding baby Vince!" Oden shouted into his glass of brandy.

"Exactly, I should be back, Vince needs his Dad as well as his Mother." Mick necked the last bit of Vodka that stared at him from the table. His throat burned as he swallowed.

"Looking after children is a woman's job, drinking is a man's job," Oden sniggered, his drunken face was cherry red, his breath smelt of greed and selfishness with a stale scent of alcohol.

Mick looked at Oden in disbelief, "If Dad knew you was like this he'd twirl in his grave."

"Eye, he'd be doing back flips," Oden laughed and sang along to the country music which played in the background. Mick turned his legs towards the door and set off walking out the pub. "Ay, MICK! I fell into a burning ring of fire! I went down, down, down..." Mick turned his head back in disgrace as he pushed open the wooden doors of the Rusty Cage pub.

At the back of the bar sat two men dressed in dark clothes. They had been watching Mick and his brothers all night. One of the figures pulled out his phone and sent a text message. "He's just come out. The other two are still sat in the pub."

"Morgan, Morgan. Want a game of twenty-one then? Best of three, I bet you twenty euros." Oden pulled out some coins from his pocket and placed them on the table; twenty euros and five coins. "That's twenty-five euros. I bet you." Oden swayed his head and banged his hands on the table. "Come on play! Play! Play! I buy you a drink"

Morgan sat facing Oden; "I'm going back to the house soon." Morgan looked at his brown leather strap wrist watch. It was coming closer towards eleven pm.

"One game, don't be a sore loser. What... Why? Why so soon? You're going? ... One game? 25 euros?" Oden started to speak slowly and stutter on his words repeating himself. The effects of his drinking had started to tear away at him.

"I'm going to make a start on painting the barn tomorrow, the woods all rotten. It needs sorting so I'm going to head back and grab some sleep." Morgan held his patience with Oden. "Come on let's make our way back ay," Morgan threw on his grey trench coat.

"What are you doing? I'm going to get us both another round in." Oden held up his money "With my winnings... this could have been yours. You're a bad sportsman."

Morgan raised his voice louder over the music, "I'm going now! Are you coming?"

"I'm a grown man, you're not my mammy." Morgan buttoned up his jacket and followed the same path Mick had taken fifteen minutes earlier. "Wait!" Oden slurred loudly.

"What!" Morgan roared back at Oden. Morgan's patience was wearing.

"I need a piss."

Morgan waited at the door and laughed to himself. "The little bastard, he can't handle his beer. I should have been born before him the way I look after him"

The figures from the corner breathed heavily as they looked at Morgan. "You should have took the money you cunt."

Oden walked past the figures and planted his hands on their table.

"I'm sorry it didn't work out for you and your boss, you see it's been our home for generations. It would be disrespectful to move. Tell your man no hard feelings." The two figures looked up to Oden, one of them replied shaking Oden's hand.

"Eye no hard feelings." There was a short pause between Oden and the man who spoke as they looked at each other eye to eye.

2009 - Saint Brook High

"Where the fuck's Vince," Kane leant over to Kevin and whispered.

"How do I know Kane? I was with you all morning." Kevin started to doodle in his English book drawing a splif with his biro pen.

"You want to get on that later?" Kane scanned his eyes across the classroom trying to see where Vince was hiding.

"Nah, you're still rushed from last night!"

"I'm a real man me, no pain no game. I don't feel sick like you because I'm a man, not a bitch... You look like you're going to puke."

For the first time, all year, the English class fell in silence. Mrs Roberts had what seemed to be control over the class as she read Mice of Men out loud.

"You seen that glove on his left hand?"

"Yeah. I saw it."

"Well, that glove's full of Vaseline."

"Vaseline? What the hell for?"

"Well, I tell ya what Curley says, he's keepin' that hand soft for his wife." George studied the cards absorbedly.

"That's a dirty thing to tell around."

Kane actively listened in class for the first time. He was partially engaged to the story Miss Robert's was reading, his ears picked up at the line a glove of Vaseline. "Ay Kevin, that's what it must have felt like, Maxine's gash."

"What, you shagged her? Does Aiden know? Shit Kane," Kevin replied biting his finger nails.

"Wow, calm down. I told you I'd teach that fucker a lesson. She came on to me anyway. Made my job easier, she was gagging for it," Kane felt the scar on his neck and whispered in Kevin's ear. "Kinky bitch as well she was."

"Will the boys at the back be quiet please!" Miss Roberts choked on her tongue as she stared at Kane.

"Sorry Miss," Kevin spoke out loud.

Kane looked at Kevin confused and nudged him with his elbow. "What's up with you today. Apologizing. You right in the fuckin head."

"I want to hear the rest of the story." Kevin quietly spoke.

"Do you? Well, al buy you the fuckin book..." Kane stood up from his chair feeling a rush of anger. "Fuck you Miss, you fuckin slag. Al be as loud as I fucking please," Kane tucked in his chair and made his way towards Miss Roberts. All the other students put down their books and watched the violence unfold. "Ay Miss, you want me to be quiet? Who the fuck do you think I am?"

Miss Roberts cowered in the corner of her desk speechless and shaking. Trembling on her words Miss Roberts cried, "Sit back down" as tears fell from her eyes.

BANG...BANG! Kane smashed his hand across the wooden table. "Sit down ha ha, your weak like every little pawn in this school."

The room started to shake like a volcano erupting, "You're a fucking nobody Miss and your golden front row can't do fuck all." Kane turned his sight to the front row and walked slowly towards them with an intimidating smile glaring at every single one of them. He approached one end of the table and panned across staring at each student. "Specky four eyes...Spotty prick... Smelly bastard...Big fat cunt," Laughter started to rise from the rows behind. At the end of the row was a student staring at Kane with dirty looks. Kane made his way towards the star of the show "Alright GINGE... Are you the big man?" The student looked at Kane, his face built up with a frown. "What are you gonna do ay?... Fuck all, because you know who I am. You're a ginger cunt, that's all you'll ever be!" A smile revealed from Kane's face.

Sat behind Kane was Miss Roberts hiding behind her computer desk and she pulled a walkie-talkie from her draw.

"Student support needed for room E4... Requesting isolation team," Miss Roberts stumbled on her words.

Kane turned to Miss Roberts laughing like a child. "Ha ha who do you think you are? The POLICE? Detective Roberts calling back up. Ner Ner, Ner Ner!" Kane looked at the class and winked at Kevin.

"Dickhead." Kevin said under his breath.

"Looks like I'm a wanted man thanks to Miss, I'd love to stay but it looks like I'll be on my way." Kane laughed to himself picking up The Mice Of Men book on his way out.

Kane ran down the English block, he knew the isolation team would shortly be behind him. The sound of footsteps scurrying across the corridor echoed like a galloping horse.

"Stop!" A croaky voice shouted.

"Fuck off you slag!" Kane made his way out of the English block and ran past the library. He pulled out his phone and rang Sean. The phone rang but there was no answer. "Useless," Kane mumbled to himself. Looking through a list of numbers Kane typed in Lucas and pressed call.

Ring...Ring...Ring. The phone rang out for 15 seconds.

"Lucas it's Kane."

"Safe dog, what's barking?"

"You on astro? I'm getting a chase off the isolation twats, was seeing if you was there?"

"I'm not mate, I'm in lesson, fuck it I'll meet you there."

"Nice one Lucas." Kane ran down the stairs at the end of the English block which led to the atrium. The atrium was an open space filled with benches. The isolation team were only minutes behind Kane, he seen some on the balcony making their way down the middle stairway.

"Shit, I'm surrounded." Kane swiftly walked into the disabled toilets and closed the door. Sweat dripped down his face; he looked in the mirror laughing silently to himself. His phone buzzed as he received a text message from Lucas.

Where about's are you? There's bare isolation officers about, you convict. I used my fake toilet pass to get out of class!

Kane read the text and replied. *I'm in the disabled bog. Near stairway for English.* Kane walked up to the toilet and urinated all over the toilet seat.

"Them cleaners will have their work cut out in here" Kane thought to himself smiling away. Kane felt his phone vibrate in the palm of his hands.

There's loads of isolation officers walking towards the English stairway!

Kane heard the frustrated footsteps making their way down the stairs, the fuds of Miss Kay, the Isolation Warden, making her way down the stairs with a team of two echoed through the doors of the disabled toilet.

"Right, you make your way to the courtyard doors!" Miss Kay shouted to one of her colleagues. Kane silently laughed to himself. Sounds of footsteps grew louder as Miss Kay walked past the disabled toilet's, she stopped for a second to think. Kane heard the deep breaths of Miss Kay.

Miss Kay had blonde hair scraped into a ponytail, her skin had a grey tint. She wore long black pants and a white shirt; her ID card swung around her neck like a rifle on a sling. Skin tightly covered her face, the smell of cheap day perfume oozed from her clothes. Her eyes were brown which matched the roots of her hair. Stale coffee breath and cigarette stench often vapoured from Miss Kay's mouth, she was a chain smoker. Twenty a day simply wasn't enough for her. Her body was crying out for a nicotine rush but she had to hunt down Saint Brooks' number one Kane Crossley.

"He's got to be on the astro…... where else could he be?" Miss Kay spoke out loud to herself.

Sean looked at his phone sitting at the back of the class. "One missed call from Kane" his phone highlighted with an exclamation mark.

"What's he want?" Sean rang Kane to investigate the missed call.

Ring…Ring…Ring…Ring. Kane's phone started vibrating, a loud buzz came from his pocket.

"Shit! Fuck off Sean!" Kane declined the call whispering to himself. Miss Kay turned her head to the disabled toilets.

"What was that?" Miss Kay walked up to the disabled toilets door and put her ear to the door.

Kane slowly put down the lid of the toilet and sank into the toilet seat. Squeak! Kane's weight compressed against the plastic. Kane held his breath and turned his phone off. Miss Kay looked at the door handle. *Engaged,* ummmm!! looking at the red symbol on the door. Miss Kay's cheeks started to turn red, the reality hit her that she was listening to someone on the toilet. Unbeknown to her that Kane was right under her fingertips, she started to walk away from the disabled toilets feeling embarrassed.

Kane heard the steps of Miss Kay walking away from the door. Relief ran through Kane, but his adventure was not over yet as the fact remained he was trapped in a toilet. Kane stood up from the toilet seat, he walked towards the door and silently opened it peering through a small gap. The coast was clear. Kane turned on his phone sharply texting Lucas.

I'm going for it... Miss Kay's gone! See you there.

Kane burst into a sprint like an athlete, he legged it towards the doors of the courtyard; he jumped over a bench which blocked his path. The sound of his feet banging on the floor galloped like a horse at full speed. Kane's sight saw the glass windows which followed towards the doors. Faster and faster Kane ran like a maniac like a rat running into a trap. Four members of the isolation squad waited on the opposite side of the door with Miss Kay smiling in the middle. Kane's face dropped as his eyes met Miss Kay blocking his way.

Chapter Five

Daisy started daydreaming in her French class at The Academy of Arts. She couldn't get the image of Vince out of her head; the boy who lay in her front room. She kept thinking about his innocent stare and their eye contact. She felt obsessed and couldn't explain why her curiosity towards Vince kept growing.

"I wonder if he's okay?... I hope he doesn't get into trouble. What's wrong with you Daisy?... I wonder if I'll see him again... I hope I do. Wait. Maybe I should visit his Dad's pub and see if he's okay. " No, I can't... What if he's not there? He will think I'm weird or worse that I'm stalking him! My Mum goes in there all the time, maybe I could go with her. No... I can't just go in with my mum like a lapdog. Erm, wait, it's my Mum's birthday coming up. Maybe she could have a do in there! What daughter wouldn't go to her own mother's birthday! Perfect plan." Daisy thought to herself with excitement.

"Daisy, are you listening or are you away with the fairies?" Mr Davidson shouted as he marked the register. Daisy jumped out of her skin!

"No Sir."

"Why didn't you answer your name then?" Mr Davidson looked confused scratching his head. He picked up his glasses and looked back at the register marking Daisy in.

"Sorry Sir, I was reciting what I learned from last lesson." Daisy started writing in her book.

"And what is that?" Daisy panicked inside.

"Bonshure Sava bien Daisy" Daisy blurted out of her mouth.

"Yes, I taught you all more advanced words than that. Agreed, then you were away with the fairies."

Daisy felt stupid inside. "I hate French," She cursed under her breath. She planted her head on the table; sounds of other students answering the register rang out like an alarm in her head. "Get me out of here," she thought to herself sitting impatiently. Daisy plaited a strand of her hair and tied it with a black bobble. She wore flat black shoes which had little bows on them with knee-high socks. She wore a grey jumper with the Academy of Arts, Coat of Arms on it and a black blazer with the same logo. She looked out the window praying for the day to end like most school students, even though the lesson had just started. Daisy pulled her iPod out of her black skirt pocket and discretely coiled the head phones around her ears. She looked down at her iPod and clicked on shuffle. Her iPod played Katy Perry 'Thinking Of You'. Daisy heard the lyrics play through her mind.

'Thinking of you, what would you do if you were the one who was spending the night'. The song started to remind her of Vince lying on her couch, she started to see flashes of the event unfold like a flash back to that night. Images of his cold pale face and brown greasy hair scattered through Daisy's mind like a montage.

Daisy felt lost in the Academy. She didn't fit in, it was full of talented students who specialised in Dance or Music and other subjects known as the Arts. The only reason she got into the Academy was because her Aunty happened to be good friends with the Principal. Daisy had a gift for making dresses, she became very skilled with a sewing machine and asked for the finest fabrics every Christmas. Daisy kept her hobby quiet but her Aunty wore a dress made by Daisy for a party at the Principal's house. He asked where she got the dress from as her Aunty Jenny bragged that Daisy had made it. It was beautifully stitched with white fabric, knee length and decorated with patterns. The principal welcomed Daisy a place at the Academy of Arts doing GCSE Textiles as well as other default qualifications.

Vince grabbed the towel that was folded on the toilet seat as he stepped out of the bath. Steam covered the bathroom mirror. Vince wiped it with his hand and he looked at himself in the mirror for a few moments and started to dry his hair. He saw the markings on his skin; red stains and bruises fresh in the process of healing. Vince twitched. A shiver ran through him, drying himself off Vince wrapped the towel around his waist. As he stepped onto the landing the cold draft that circulated the air hit his naked body. Vince's bedroom door swung open holding onto its bracket with ease.

Vince looked across his floor scattered with clothes, a pair of old worn out jogging bottoms were hidden under boxers and socks. Vince buried his hand into the pile swirling his wrists dragging the pair into the light.

"There they are." Vince bit his lip throwing the bottoms swiftly on. He dived back into the pile like an Olympic swimmer going for gold; Vince's eyes caught onto a black vest top. Vince pulled the vest over his head stretching arms out wide; the vest felt tight and too small but that didn't faze Vince, he picked up the boxing gloves with excitement and shot down the stairs in a flash. Vince opened the door to the spare room and watched the punching bag swing gently from its chain. The chain made a subtle squeaking and you could hear the crunching of rust. The faulty light started to flicker matching the pace of Vince's movements towards the bag. Tying the laces on one of his gloves with the other glove he tied a knot holding the lace with his teeth. Vince pulled hard making a tight knot. The gloves felt damp but fitted snug as a gun in Vince's hands. Flashes of light continued to flicker from the faulty lights above. Vince released the pain he felt into each punch against the bag. The sounds of leather pounding echoed through the room. The bag swung left to right rattling the chains with a piercing squeaking sound, dust of the bag hovered in the air as Vince beat the bag viciously like a barking dog locking its jaw into each thrust. Vince howled like a wolf taking deep breaths trying to catch up with the pace of his heart tearing from Vince's chest. A burning sensation swirled around Vince's throat like a tornado, body fluids and acid flushed their way down his neck and continued to re-surface.

Vince hissed like a snake building up to full flow with his punches. Hiss…sss...sss…hss. Vince repetitively hit the stone-cold surface of the bag pounding each clenched fist into the leather. Bang...Bang…Bang! Sweat gathered on Vince's face and started to run like a tap all down his body soaking into the black vest. His light mousy brown hair went darker as the sweat pumped out of his pores. Vince stood side on repelling the swinging bag. Vince felt a rush of strength as he pelted combinations into the bag throwing a left and a right, stepping in, stepping out. Vince landed a right hook on the side of the bag, his knuckles cracked and rippled through his forearm. Despite the agonising pain of aching muscles Vince kept going at the bag fluently putting all his force into the thrusts. His eyebrows lowered and muscles raged pumping red blood cells around his body; the air felt thinner as Vince inhaled and exhaled the oxygen merging inside his body racing for the next breath.

Half an hour passed by, Mick sat at his bar listening to the slapping sounds of leather. His transparent glass of water started to move, you could see ripples in the glass from the sound waves of Vince releasing his fury. Mick looked down into the glass and saw his reflection.

"You're getting on a bit Mick." He said softly to himself staring across the bar towards the spare room. Finishing off the glass Mick walked towards the sink yawning, he turned on the tap and picked out a fresh glass filling it halfway. Bang... Bang...Bang. The noise of boxing gloves at full force echoed into the bar. Mick turned his head towards the spare room holding a glass in one hand and letting his other hang free.

Mick crept towards the spare room and opened the door watching Vince strike the bag. Mick leant against the dirty wall.

"Hit it boy!" Mick shouted tearing his voice box. The bag started to rock on the waves of power, Mick stood like an eagle overlooking Vince. "Right cross" Mick shouted. "Left hook...jab jab. 1 2 3 4 duck fast jabs." Mick walked behind Vince standing a foot away at the side of him. "In any fight, it's the man who's willing to die that's going to fucking win. The bags not going to hit you back Vince, someone real will."

"I know." Vince exhaled roaring like a lion cub.

"Then move," Mick whispered in Vince's ear with a caring tone. "In and out Vince, you're still standing static."

"I'm thinking..."

Mick spoke over Vince aggressively. "You don't have time to think, in the heat of the moment, just do and do it right the first time." Vince furiously staggered towards the bag punching repeatedly, his body was exhausted, Vince crumbled his arms around the bag. Sweat pumped from under Vince's armpits, his muscles were fully expanded.

"You can never afford to run out of gas Vince, outside of this room." Mick calmly spoke. Vince leant back from the bag. He felt his arms rip from the leather as the sweat set like glue, his hair stood up on end and goosebumps rushed across his body. Drowning in pain Vince looked at the bag, square on, visualising the faces of those who abuse him. A violent sound released into the room exiting from the mouth of Vince.

"ARGHHHH!" Vince pounded all his might into the bag for a further 30 seconds which felt like a life time. Hiss....hiss...hiss. Vince breathed quicker. His muscles released strength that he was unaware of, faster than a bullet, faster than a rocket. Vince left an explosion into the bag.

"Here, get some water, you'll dehydrate." Vince tore one hand free from the gloves, holding it between his armpit. They slid off with the sweat which whirled on the inside of the glove. Vince's hand was saturated and looked like he had spent a decade holding his hand in water. Red marks covered his knuckles with a drop of blood which had leaked from his split skin. Mick placed the glass in Vince's hand. Vince's hands started to shake whilst lifting the glass to his mouth. Gulp...gulp...gulp! Vince poured the water down his neck, when he got halfway he threw the water over himself. A combination of the two cooled down the body of Vince Haze.

Chapter Six

Maxine sat in her chair feeling smug, a vibrant smile opened up from her face. The sunlight shined through the Maths window glowing across Maxine's hair.

"That fuckin sun's doing my head in." Maxine stretched open her arms pushing her chest forward. "What did you make of last night then?"

Roxanne ripped a page from her book squeezing it with hands of guilt, .

"Well..." Maxine pursued, curling her hair around her fingers.

"Go on...Well what do you think?" Biting her lip Maxine looked at Roxanne with a grin.

"I don't know what I think... One second you was all over Aiden. Acting all loved up and then..." Maxine jumped over Roxanne's sentence laughing.

"And then what???"

"You was out of it, you sure fooled me as well as Aiden and Lucas." Roxanne frowned putting her head back down into the Maths book writing out equations.

"Anyway Sherlock, what happened with you and Lucas? You're keeping that quiet."

"Never you mind. You're my best mate, it doesn't mean I'm your twin." Roxanne continued to write out the questions from the board as Maxine's face started to change.

"And what's that supposed to mean hey?"

"Well you was going in to kiss Aiden then two minutes later you're with Kane."

"So?"

Roxanne replied in shock "So? It was Aiden's best mate. You played the field."

"Aiden fucked off and left me when we were dancing, Kane came and kept me company. Kane came on to me anyway."

"If you truly liked Aiden like you said why didn't you say no? Especially when you've been talking about him, all week."

Maxine's smile soon changed. "I was drunk and out for a good time"

"Yeah you sure was out for a good time, after it kicked off nearly you and Kane vanished." Roxanne looked at Maxine feeling concerned. She bit her lip and started to pick off the red nail varnish from last night.

"It was getting too warm inside so me and Kane went for a walk to the park, the cold air didn't seem to shake off the heat."

"Check you getting all poetic! Go on what happened then?" Roxanne felt her nerves rock inside, she wanted to hear the story but didn't know what to expect; like a guilty pleasure her temptation rapidly increased. "Go on dirty knickers what happened?" Roxanne slipped out.

"I'm getting to it, Jesus, one second your having a go at me the next your excited to hear like a kid listening out for Santa's bells at Christmas, you geek!"

"Shut up dirty bitch!" Roxanne laughed.

"He smacked my bum cheeks with his hand at first and started pinching me... He was drunk. He started getting raunchier the dirty fucker."

Roxanne's ears piped up, her eyes slightly widened. "What did he do next did he try and feel you down there?"

"What? No!" Maxine giggled to herself.

"You know, try and put his hands in areas." Roxanne courageously replied.

"Obviously he was gagging for me. And I kind of liked it. I felt wanted. I could feel his hard on against my hips when he kissed me." Maxine glanced at her phone. "It was pitch black and cold, when we were nearly at the park I put my hands in his pants... It was warm, I felt it, you know." Maxine's eyes lit up with excitement. "This is when things got more crazy. He dragged my hand deeper inside his joggers making me feel more than what I bargained for."

"Nar no way... He what???"

"He dragged me towards the benches. You know where the bushes are?"

"Yeah!" Roxanne gasped.

"He started kissing me and I felt his hand run up my back towards my neck. He grabbed the hair at the back of my head and forced me to get on my knees."

"Did he rape you? I knew he was a nutter!" Roxanne's face turned pale. She felt concerned and guilty that she had let her friend walk the streets with someone she didn't know.

Chapter Seven

Kane looked around him. "SHIT," he whispered under his breath.

"It's the end of the line for you." Miss Kay smiled to herself, "Did you really think that you could out run me?"

Kane fell in silence and looked desperately for a way out. "Fuck off you battered old goat," Kane replied feeling his anger building up inside.

Miss Kay turned to her colleague with a smile. "Did you hear that Mr Crossland? he seems to think he's the big 'I am' around here," Miss Kay laughed like a hissing snake.

"Do you not know who I am? It's Kane Crossling you slag... I'll get you kidnapped and buried."

"You're going straight to isolation Mr Big! And while we're at it empty your bag onto the floor," Miss Kay sniggered.

"Nar fuck off you can't search me...I've got nothing on me."

"If you have nothing to hide empty your bag then." Miss Kay started to raise her voice aggressively. A radio call came in on Miss Kay's walkie talkie.

"Have you found Kane Crossling?"

Miss Kay pressed a button on her walkie talkie, "Yes Mitchell he's here." Miss Kay spoke kindly but ascertive. "Get that bag emptied and hurry up! You're off to isolation sunshine!"

Kane saw Lucas in the corner of his eye, he was stood fifty yards behind Miss Kay and her round up gang. Lucas hadn't seen so much fuss about Kane in a long time. Lucas ran towards the group full of energy, Kane started to smile and glare.

"Show time," he mumbled under his breath. "Miss Kay..."

"What's happening? What am I missing eye?" Miss Kay turned her head into the sight of Lucas. "GET BACK TO LESSON!" She screamed across the courtyard. "you two get rid of him." Miss Kay shoved her colleagues towards Lucas. "Empty your bag! NOW!" Miss Kay made her move on Kane walking closer towards him, Kane turned himself moving his body towards the door. Stood behind the door was a team of five staff from the isolation office.

"Run Kane! RUN!" Lucas started to preach.

"Don't listen to your friend Kane, there's no more places to hide. You'll be seeing him shortly in isolation with the rest of your clan." Miss Kay patronised in the hope to humiliate him.

"What you doing Kane? Run! Move it or lose it! Mother Fucker!" Lucas ran around in circles around the two staff members of the Isolation team, "Way…way…You think I'm going left when I'm going right, haha… Easy now rude boy! Don't want to pull a muscle." Lucas chanted. "Come on Kane!" Lucas stared at one of the members of staff, he was a fat man with excess fat around his neck. He wore a grey cardigan with black pants and leather shoes. The glasses that sat on his nose looked flimsy and worn. His hair was brown and hung to one side of his head. "Come on fatty, come on… Razz, you deffo got bullied back in the day! Chase me shit flicker." Lucas belched across the courtyard, some students started to look through the side windows of their classrooms to see what was going on outside.

Kane opened his bag to Miss Kay, "See… Told you it was fuckin empty. Are we going then or what? Oh yeah and Miss?"

"Looks like you've made the right choice for once and yes?" Miss Kay replied with a smirk.

"Fuck you. YOU DIRTY goat! And that FAT cunt!" Miss Kay's cocky smirk soon faded.

"Get inside!" she said with anger.

Lucas chanted Kane's name telling him to run but he had already made his decision.

"Lucas get yourself off mate, I'm going in." Kane sparked up through his throat.

"In a bit yeah, text me!" Lucas ran to the opposite side of the courtyard where there were doors to get back inside the school, he galloped fast like a horse in a race. Out running the teachers, he vanished within the school premises. The isolation team gave up on Lucas as they weren't as interested in him as they were more engaged with Kane; the student who ran things.

All the members of the isolation team which stood behind Kane escorted him to the isolation room, number 12, a classroom hidden away from the normal classrooms for study. He felt like a convict being taken to court to be further investigated, whether he was to be charged with abuse or finer issues such as selling merchandise on school premises. Miss Kay opened a door which led to a long corridor of empty classrooms, isolated from the rest of the school Kane spoke out loud to himself.

"Fuck me, what's this prison? Miss what's the real reason your taking me here ay?"

"You'll soon be finding out, and have you forgot how you disrupted your previous lesson with violent intimidations towards your teacher?" Miss Kay opened the door to 12 feeling happy with herself that she caught Kane like a Police Officer on their first bust. "After you," Miss Kay patronised.

Kane walked into the room and looked around, it was literally an empty classroom with separated tables like an exam. There were no windows, partly so students couldn't escape or be distracted by students at break and lunch times. A white clock overlooked the seating arrangements; it was five past eleven.

"Sit down." Miss Kay gestured with her hands pointing at the chair in the middle. Kane glared at Miss Kay with an evil eye pulling a long dirty look.

"Where?"

"Just sit down on this chair." Miss Kay bickered pulling herself a chair out. Kane walked over to the chair that was pointed out and sat himself down. "So, Kane, I've got you here at last." Kane sat in silence listening to Miss Kay talking about the school's regulations.

"Look, its cost you and all your clan a lot of time to get me in here so what's the real reason? I could've just ran off and made you spend a full day running around after me, but I didn't because I'm intrigued to know why you sent an army out for me." Kane's eyebrows slightly raised and a cheeky grin started to reveal on his face.

"I'm the head of Isolation, I can call in more staff than I need at times and this conversation isn't about me. The reason we are here is because your English teacher called me on the radio." Miss Kay rolled up her sleeves.

"Miss please don't chat shit, I think we both know why you brought me here."

"How dare you swear at me, I am not some stand in Cover Teacher." Miss Kay stood up from the plastic chair; she turned herself to the desk in the corner picking up a black ring binder. "Right, let's see what we have here then." Kane sat looking up at Miss Kay, her shadow covered him in darkness.

"What's that?" Kane felt a small sense of anxiety of the unknown. "You've got no reason to keep me here. I'm walking out that door when I want but before I go, what's in that folder?"

Miss Kay sat back on the plastic chair; she felt the nervous energy which Kane tried to hide. Focusing on Miss Kay's face Kane stared deep into her eyes, his pupils widened and facial muscles started to tense. Miss Kay started to look through the ring binder, there was a thick amount of paper work shoved into plastic wallets with a variety of different student's names on them. James Scott, Bill Davis, Tom Andrews. Miss Kay sieved through her pages looking for the star of the show who sat in front of her.

"What's this then? Miss you're fucking weird you're a stalker. Why do you have a book full of students you freak!" Kane started to laugh to himself, "Miss you're not O... Kay, YOU!... Ay wait till I tell the boys this ha ha, they will never believe me!"

"I've been doing a report on your behaviour."

Kane interrupted Miss Kay laughing over her sentence. "No shit! You don't say. Miss, I know you fancy me. But you're not my type." Kane kicked his feet onto the table and rested his arms on his head.

"Kane I'm being serious! I'm cutting straight to the point. Have you been selling merchandise on the school premises? You do know we have a no selling policy in our school as it's illegal to do so? We have facilities for students to buy food and drinks here at Saint Brooks High."

"Miss you haven't got SHIT on me!" Kane shot up from his seat and pulled off his blazer shaking it onto the table.

"What are you doing?" Miss Kay screeched across the room.

"Look. I have nothing on me. No Lucozade's or chocolate. There's your proof, why don't you ring my Dad?" Miss Kay stared at Kane with a straight face, her mouth struggling to open

"Emptying your uniform doesn't prove anything. You're too smart to keep your profits on you and your merchandise and as far as I'm concerned, I will contact your Dad."

Kane smiled smugly scratching his eyebrow, his face relaxed and lips fell gently open. "Well, you haven't got any proof of your allegations, look you're wasting my time just give my Dad a bell, yeah? Do you fancy a cig? I'm gagging." Kane mimicked a smoking gesture with his fingers.

"Well Kane, what's this?" Miss Kay pulled out some pictures from her file of Kane selling Lucozade, took from the surveillance cameras in the school, she also pulled out six anonymous statements off students who came forward to say that they had been bullied to sell for Kane Crossling from a variety of different years.

Kane looked at the papers on the table in shock, "WHAT THE FUCK! You really are a freak. STALKER!" Kane grabbed the papers and tore them apart corner to corner. He snapped like a pit bull tearing the papers into pieces throwing them across the classroom, Kane smashed his hand across the table as he stood up from his chair, he pointed his fingers in a gun shape towards Miss Kay.

As she stared back at Kane she repeated the words, "You don't scare me. Kane... I'm taking this evidence straight to the head." Kane clenched his fist in fury.

"You should fear me for the same reason the Head does." Kane replied in an ominous voice and picked up his blazer staring at Miss Kay with a sinister smile. Miss Kay looked back bewildered and looked at the display of confetti across the classroom.

Saint Brooks High was coming towards an end; the clock was striking half three and hundreds of frustrated students were making their way out of the school. Most of the teachers sat back in their chairs with relief that the day was over. Sean made his way to the front entrance of the school trailing his JD bag behind him. The entrance flooded with students rushing to get outside, a wave started to build up blocking the entrance. Year 10 and 11 students pushed and shoved to get through the rows of other years.

Sean felt the roar of the crowd, it felt like the start of a football game, everyone clustering together like penguins fighting their way through hordes of people to the doors of escape. Lucas waited outside for Sean and Kane, he got out of lesson just before the bell rang out dodging the mad rush. Sean felt trapped within the crowd, drowning in a sea of claustrophobia.

"Fuckin' move out the way you cunts!" Sean shouted out amongst those who were in his way. Pushing his feet forward, swimming through the forest of people, Sean made his way closer towards the exits.

After a ten-minute battle for freedom of no school till the next morning, Sean saw Lucas standing against the bike poles, he approached him with amusement.

"What was going on before mate?" Lucas pulled a comedic face, his facial expressions were animated.

"Well my friend, it was madness. There was bare teacher's, Eye, bare staff, bare mans." Lucas replied in a playful deep voice.

"Just like Kane got a chase innit and that Miss Kay was onto him," Sean replied feeling laughter building its way through his throat. "He's a proper knob at times... People at dinner told me that he tried to hit that English teacher...Miss Roberts or something."

"Yeah that will be Kaneo," Lucas blurted.

Grey clouds started to gather above the school, the blue sky faded being digested by the rain clouds that were ready to burst at a moment's notice. Students started to flee from the school premises.

"Shit, it's going to rain." Sean noticed the clouds swirling in the sky, he pulled up his Adidas hoody hoping to keep himself dry. There was a figure walking towards the exit of the school with energy wearing a Nike hoody over his blazer and a shoulder strap bag around him.

"It's Kane!" Lucas shouted with enthusiasm. Kane walked through the school doors with a stone face.

"Who's been doing the rain dance? It's fucking pissing down out here!" Kane grunted.

"Definitely must be Lucas then."

"Sean...Shut up." Kane put his hands deep into the black school pants feeling for his phone; he pulled out his HTC Hero, the most advanced phone of the year.

"What is it?" Lucas urged, eagerly waiting for Sean and Kane to get a move on as the rain was starting to fall.

The boys started walking their usual root towards the bus stop; the wind started howling like a screaming bat. Hitting the backs of Sean, Kane and Lucas as they paced towards their destination.

"What did that Miss Kay say?" Sean asked Kane with a touch of concern.

"She was chatting bare shit about me, nothing to worry about though. I think she fancies me the pedo." An outbreak of laugher poured from the mouths of Sean and Lucas.

"WHAT? She fancies you?" Sean teased, with a tear rolling down his eye. "Yo! what makes you say that G?" Kane shrugged his shoulders putting his phone away.

"Well..."

"Well I heard there was a lot of noise coming from that Isolation room! Did you bang her?" Sean wept crying with laughter.

"SHUT IT!! or else al tell Dad you've been shagging men." Kane blasted Sean as he went past a stage of banter. "Yeah I thought you'd shut it...You little rent boy." Sean sank in silence looking at his reflection in the puddles on the pavement.

"What was it like though... what went on in their mate? She was ON TO YOU!" Lucas spoke with a concerned tone.

"Mate, she's been clocking me, like a detective and everything. Photos, statements even a folder dedicated to me." Sean listened in on the conversation keeping him quiet.

"WHAT THE FUCK? Pictures of what?" Lucas scrambled out of his mouth racing for his next sentence. "Pictures of you selling? SHIT! MATE." Lucas stared at Kane's iron face in disbelief. "You're fucked mate. Like proper fucked. They can kick you with this!" Lucas panicked feeling on edge. "Did they have any pictures of me? This is some next level shit!" Kane looked at Lucas his eyebrows lowered in a smooth motion.

"STOP WORRYING! They haven't got shit on you or any of the lads, It's bullshit anyway... She's just trying to scare me the stalker. That's all. And so fuckin what if she hands it all over to the Head. That cunt knows his place." Kane ranted like a convict fighting for freedom.

Chapter Eight

Daisy opened the white door to her home, walking inside she kicked her shoes off lying them on the floor of the hallway.

"Is anyone in? I'm home!" Daisy shouted through the house. She opened the door to her dining room and sat down on the brown couch. She looked at the clock that stared back at her with a glance. Twenty to four on the clock, she read the hands that sat snug hovering over roman numerals. "Ahhh!! Peace at last." Daisy sank back into the couch absorbing the soft materials the cushions had been stuffed with.

The house had a warm breeze which floated through the air. Daisy felt the warmth from the fire touch her soft beautiful face. She closed her eyes enjoying the heat drifting into a short dream. The smell of flowers fragranced through the air, tulips and blossoms and white roses lunged together making a site worth seeing. Their storks cuddled together inside a glass vase which was elegantly decorated with glass spirals leading to the top. On the wooden surface that the vase was sat upon was a card leaning in front of the glass.

Crank! Crank! The sound of keys opening the front door broke the silence. Daisy woke up from her catnap in a shake.

"Mum? Mum is that you?"

"Alright love, I'm just bringing this shopping through, could you give me a hand?" Claire spoke softly. Daisy stood up leaving a dent of where she had been sitting, she walked through the hallway and slid on her shiny leather shoes. Claire pulled out the plastic shopping bags from her car boot and brought them in the house piling them along the hallway. Daisy picked up the bags from the hallway and started to put away the fruit and veg. Claire walked into the kitchen and placed the shopping bags onto the floor.

"Can you go and get the final bag for us sweetheart? It's in the boot" Claire gently spoke.

"Yeah Mum." Daisy made her way outside and opened the boot of the car, picking up the shopping bag of milk. The three bottles of two litre milk started to ache at Daisy's arm as she carried it through the house. Her eyes caught onto the vase of flowers as she walked into the dining room. The smell of tulips ran through her nose like the scent of a perfume. She walked over to the flowers, releasing the milk onto the floor.

"Mum, who bought you these flowers? They're delightful. The roses are very pretty." Daisy looked down towards the card and picked it up. Reading the card in her head she grew curious.

"Thank you for a special evening once again, I hope you enjoyed the night. You've given my life hope that I can feel happiness and love once again. Thank you so much for taking care of Vince for me last week, I don't know what I'd have done if something happened to him. See you soon... Mick x"

Daisy looked at the card feeling shocked. She ran into the kitchen holding the card waving it in front of her mum.

"You didn't tell me you were dating!" Claire smiled at Daisy feeling like a loved-up teenager all over again.

"I'm not! We're just friends... Good friends."

"Mum, he bought you the most beautiful flowers I've ever seen, you can't be just friends." Claire started to blush and started to unload the shopping bags.

"We went out for dinner that's all. Just two friends eating. Go and get that milk you, anyway." Daisy started to smile as she walked into the dining room for the milk. "Put them in the fridge Daisy love." As Daisy opened the fridge and threw the milk inside she smiled to herself.

"Mum, I was thinking."

"About what?" Claire replied.

"Well you know like it's your birthday this Saturday. Could we all go in the Smoking Barrel to celebrate?" Daisy bit her lip and picked up the empty shopping bags.

"Of course we will. Hey, you're not trying to set me up with Mick are you, haha?" Daisy and Claire started laughing together.

"No Mum! You're just friends remember, haha so called good friends."

Chapter Nine

The school was silent and everyone had left except Miss Kay, she walked down the narrow corridor towards the Headmaster's office with the black ring binder in her hand. Her face was red and a stress rash started to break out on her neck, she felt heat build-up inside her. Knock knock. Miss Kay banged on the principal's door heavy like a hammer. Miss Kay heard footsteps walk towards the door, the door handle squeezed open.

"What is the meaning of this? Why did you repetitively knock on my door?" Mr Smith aggressively stared into the eyes of Miss Kay. "Do you ever stop pestering me?"

Miss Kay's face fell like a sand bag. "Mr Smith it's urgent! Very URGENT!" Miss Kay wept. Mr Smith opened his door wide allowing space for Miss Kay to walk inside.

"Well, you better come inside then."

Inside Mr Smith's office was a wall of school achievements and Ofsted reports. He had a computer table desk and a leather chair which was worn with patches of grey. Mr Smith sat himself down.

"Take a seat," Mr Smith said. Walking towards the chair Miss Kay felt depressed, her head looked towards the floor and slowly raised towards Mr Smith.

"Look, I've got a folder here with Kane Crossling's name on it and evidence in black and white that he's not just been bullying students and abusing teachers but... selling merchandise in our school. Not just the odd chocolate bar here and there, he's running an entire empire of student sellers." Mr Smith began to laugh.

"Is this some kind of joke? You're wasting my time." Miss Kay pulled out her folder and showed Mr Smith the photographs and the statements.

"Kane's clan is running this school a riot." Miss Kay's face turned purple and her eyes diluted. Mr Smith looked at the images placed in front of him and picked them up in his hands.

"Look Miss Kay, you're exaggerating but I admire your passion for right and wrong. But our school applies discipline to all and the students do co-operate as I heard Kane allowed you to take him in." Miss Kay looked at Mr Smith's face in anger, feeling furious inside Miss Kay raised her voice.

"You're not listening to me! He needs to be kicked out, he's controlling the students in this school." A loud bark came from Mr Smith as he looked at Miss Kay's deluded face.

Kane Crossling isn't no Alan Sugar, you're highly exaggerating. He's not a nice or kind student but he comes from a bad background and here at Saint Brooks High we offer an opportunity for every student to have a chance at leaving here with GCSEs. Every student has that right whether they misbehave or not." Mr Smith pulled out his side-draw and put on his glasses grabbing some paper work which sat underneath some newspapers. "Look, do you see these reports from Ofsted 'Outstanding!' 'Highest success rate' 'Saint Brooks High is one of the best schools in Manchester- Guardian' We can't let things like Kane Crossling blacken the school's good name. We have a reputation to keep, we have never kicked a student out of Saint Brooks High, I pride myself on that fact."

Miss Kay felt a bombshell crash inside her with shrapnel ricocheting through her body. "If you truly cared for what's best for the school, you'd kick Kane Crossling out!" Miss Kay picked up her ring binder and left the evidence on the table walking out of the office with a kick in her step.

"Close that door behind you!" Mr Smith ordered, biting his nails. Staring down at the photographs he picked them up with his hands and screwed them up inside his palm. "This is the last time she pesters me." He walked over to the bin striking each foot against the blue carpet throwing the picture into the bin violently like a basketball dunking through a hoop.

Chapter Ten

Vince sat on his bed mesmerised by the strength he never knew he had. His arms ached from all the motion he pursued. He looked at his wall and looked straight at his grandfather's photograph and stared in silence. Vince had never done any physical training to his body before, using energy on the bag. He had never thrown a punch but had taken many, he stood up from the bed and stretched his arms towards the air feeling a warm relief through his body.

"I am....I can...I will," he repeated to himself. Vince walked over to the mirror which watched him from the side of the room. He looked into the mirror feeling a sense of greatness, his bruises had started to fade and scars started to heal. Five minutes passed and Vince was still looking at his reflection in the mirror, he felt a cold breeze hover through the window that danced around his body. His hairs stood on chilled ends but inside he was heated and felt a sense of fire being set alight inside him, like a whirlwind sucking in all his weakness destroying his fears. Vince threw on a clean vest that slept with a pile of mismatched clothes. Walking past the landing and heading downstairs, Vince called out for his Dad.

"Dad? Dad you in here? Hello? Dad?" The smell of alcohol hit Vince's nostrils as he entered the bar. There was a note on the side of the bar, Vince investigated.

I've gone out to get some supplies. We're low on beer for a Do on Saturday so I'm going to get back later on. Chris phoned me and said that he'd come up at half 4 to help me bring in the supplies. See you soon. love Dad."

Vince's mind scrambled, "Shit what day is it today?" Vince bolted towards the pub's television and turned on GMTV. Vince read the date and time that the television gave out. "No way is it Friday! I've over slept." Vince ran around the room in a mad panic. "Shit! What should I do?" Vince thought to himself that it's too late to go to school, as his bus comes once an hour and he still wasn't ready or dressed. "Well I might as well have the day off and help my Dad out here," Vince said in realisation that missing today wouldn't make a difference to his GCSEs as the teachers he had today only played videos from YouTube.

Sitting at a table in the centre of the room, Vince started to brainstorm what he could do that would benefit his Dad today.

"Well the tables are clean, and everything seems to be in working order." Vince looked up at the lights. "There's not one bulb that's gone. Mmm..." Vince stood up and walked around the room picking at things he could do. He walked into the hallway, behind the bar and trod into the cellar and looked into the two rooms. The cellar had a distinctive musky smell that ignited with the stale air making a horrible tag team. Vince turned the switch on and a giant grey humidifier stood in the corner of the room on the left side. He looked around the room and saw rows of cardboard boxes un-neatly stacked taking up the whole room. "What a mess this is." Vince scanned his eyes across all the boxes, they were mostly cardboard boxes, a few plastic containers and two empty silver barrels.

"I might as well stack these boxes up and straighten the room." Vince ran back upstairs looking for any dirty old tops he could use for a cloth to wipe down the dust that imbedded itself to the cardboard boxes. He quickly dashed around the house running into every room looking for dirty clothes. He ran into his room at full speed, making a swan dive under his bed. Vince rumbled his hands under the bed pulling out an old pyjama top.

"That will do for now." Sprinting down the stairs, Vince felt an egg timer ticking down on his head, he wanted to clear at least one of the rooms in the cellar before his Dad came back as he wanted to help in any way he could.

"Right, where to start?" Vince approached the first box that stared him out. Bending on his knees Vince wiped over the box with his old pyjama top. The pyjama top had a picture of a worn out Dennis the Menace, a past favourite cartoon character from Vince's child hood. The dust absorbed the pyjama fabric like water. "Sorry Dennis," Vince quietly giggled to himself. "Every dog has his day but you're worn out now." Vince talked to the pyjama top as if it was a human being. Dust covered the full body of Dennis the Menace, his red and black top was no longer visible, caked in grey dust. Vince started to cough as dust floated into the air. "Come on Vince, there's not that many to do." Vince looked at the boxes on the floor, he was clearly lying to himself as there were plenty more to do. Vince curiously opened the box, inside were a variety of baby clothes and a silver rattle. Vince felt the soft fabric of the baby clothes and examined the rattle. *"Vince Haze"* was engraved onto it. Vince felt a deep sense of connection towards the rattle he held in his hands. Vince sniffed up a beautiful smell that rattled his nostrils as he breathed in. There was a smell of perfume which hadn't left the fabric of the baby clothes.

"No way! I remember this." Vince thought to himself. "I thought I lost this when we moved home." Clenching the rattle tightly Vince brought it to his ear and gently shook it. He placed the rattle back in the box and covered it with his old baby clothes. Picking the box up Vince walked back up the cellar stairs and placed it at the bottom of his stairway.

Vince felt a strange feeling of shock and disbelief. "No way!" Vince spoke out loud. Walking back into the cellar he paced up to the next box in his sight and bent his knees wiping away the filth. He peered his eyes inside the box. His heart rate increased as his curiosity took control over him, inside the box was old Christmas cards, hundreds of them, in fact, all stacked up inside; Vince didn't bother to root through as he knew he would make more of a mess. Vince tucked the pyjama top into his jogging bottoms as he picked up the box and moved it into a corner. Moving onto another box which caught Vince's sight he wiped it down and piled it on top of the previous box. Three hours past as he cleaned and straightened the room applying the same routine, wipe, wipe, lift and place.

Vince looked at the right and left corner of the room which you could see as soon as you walked in. The boxes which were piled up reminded Vince of school aid from when he was in primary school. Vince went into a trance, taking him back to

Mary Lee primary school when they donated shoe boxes filled with toys for the third world countries. Vince remembered sitting in the school hall looking out towards a pyramid of shoe boxes. Waking up from the day dream Vince smiled. "They sure won't know what's in these boxes."

Vince started to put the rest of the boxes on top of the pile, brushing down the dust he started to sneeze repeatedly. Achoo! Achoo! Snot started to run down Vince's nose, he felt the warm slime dribble on his skin. Vince wiped the pyjama top across his nose and took a huge sneeze into it.

"Fuck me!" Drying his nose Vince realised he didn't have a lot of time left before his Dad would be coming home. Searching through the last few boxes Vince came across a strange looking box. Vince walked closer to the box and bent down on his knees, in fact, Vince was not staring at a box but a large dark brown oak chest which had recently been attacked by mould and dust. Vince brushed over the chest wiping over the mould which was slowly developing. He felt the wood with his hands, on top of the chest was a cross carved into it. Feeling the grooves in the wood with his fingers, Vince slowly opened the lid of the chest, he felt the weight of the lid with his finger tips. Vince's eyebrows raised, his eyes zoomed into the deep depths of pictures, old newspaper articles from Ireland, objects such as plates with four leaf clovers painted on them and a small wooden crucifix. His heart started to pound and excitement blossomed. It took Vince a minute or two to take in what he had found beneath the clouds of dust. Sitting on the cold floor he pulled the chest closer to him looking over the newspaper articles. Vince read out the first headline he saw, 'Burning Barn.' Vince felt puzzled and shuffled through the other newspapers, 'The Irish Times, Ban Bridge Leader, The Ballymena Times.' All the articles were from the year 1996, Vince began skimming through the headlines. 'Arson Attacks…Farmers Flea…Random Farm Attack…Innocent woman dies in fire attack!' Looking in confusion and feeling deceived Vince further explored the chest, skim reading the articles.

"Farmer Mick Haze, Oden Haze and Morgan Haze lose their family home in a random arson attack. Unfortunately, Mick's wife Marie Kelly was trapped inside the farm house and lost her life trying to escape the fire. PC Daniels reports "The farmhouse on 38 Dromore Rd in Omagh had been attacked, set on fire at 11:30pm, fellow officers and myself got called to the sight at 9am the next morning. Our fire service arrived at 12pm thirty minutes after the fire had started. We are aware this was an intentional attack." Detective Moore leading the investigation stated that "This was no random attack, this was a murderous killing which was inhumane, the attack left no traces at the scene of the crime which is making the investigation hard but what we do know is that the farm house was burnt down with the use of petrol".

Vince started to fill up, tears fell like a rushing waterfall. "Arrghh" The room echoed the noises that came from Vince; they bounced from wall to wall howling up the stairs through the hallway. Shaking like a dying dog with Parkinson's, Vince hit his knuckles across the cold stone floor. "The fuckers! Bastards bastards...Arghh" A wild fire ran through the body of Vince, mixed emotions trampled his mind. In and out he breathed faster and faster, pushing himself away from the chest with feet arched, he lay back with his head touching the cold floor. Shivers struck his body sharp like lightning a flash of memories clashed through his brain. The cold started to climb through Vince's face turning his cheeks blue. Lying in silence staring into the darkness, Vince shook crazy as his heart was being attacked left right and centre. In a state of reality, he looked along the floor watching a spider run across his eyes. Rolling to the side Vince pulled himself up leaning back against the wall. He pulled out the dirty pyjama top turned it inside out and wiped his face. Eyes still blood shocked feeling shaken he stared into space for fifteen minutes and crawled forward.

"Mum!" Vince cried looking into the chest, picking up the photographs that were clung together with an elastic band. Amongst the pictures of the old farm house and family pictures of Mick, Oden and Morgan as young teenagers themselves and

Vincent Haze his grandad, there were pictures of his mother and himself as a baby. A photo taken at the hospital of Vince and his Mum lay in the hospital bed, only a few hours old.

Tears landed on the inside of the chest soaking into the new paper articles. Vince pulled away from the articles, underneath the papers was a green silky piece of fabric. Inside the fabric was a gold chain with a ring hooked around it. Vince felt the weight of the gold in his hand and held the ring in front of his eyes. An engraving inside the ring caught his eye. 'Love you always M & M' Vince coiled the chain around his four fingers clenching his hand into a fist. Tears ran down his cheeks, he could taste the salt touching his tongue. He felt abandoned as he sat to himself rocking in the darkness of the cold cellar, thoughts of being deceived by his father tornadoed through his mind.

"I can't believe you didn't fucking tell me." Vince shouted in pain towards the wall. "YOU CALL YOURSELF MY FATHER! And you hide this from me." Sobbing to himself Vince lowered his head into his shaking hands. Looking at the ring he kissed it squeezing it tightly with fingers of might. Vince peered into the chest silently crying, struggling to speak a mumbled noise sobbed from his lips. Feeling fragile Vince looked under the green silk, there was a white dress folded decorated with white beads and sequins. It was his mother's wedding dress untouched and not seen an ounce of sun light, which had only been worn once for fitting. The chest was like a time capsule preserving the past in a nutshell, a painful past indeed but a past which affected Vince to the bone as he was unaware of how his mother passed. He never talked about his mother's passing but the reality hit home that his father had been through it all. Sitting to himself in shock, Vince started to realise why his Dad hadn't told him the story and started to see his father in a different light, despite his anger he tried to calm himself.

Vince dragged himself to his feet, pushing himself up with his knees. Striding forward towards the chest he closed the lid. Bang! The chest locked shut; he pushed it forward towards the centre of the cardboard and plastic boxes. Snorting his nose Vince wiped the tear stained cheeks with the skin of his forearms. Unravelling the gold chain from his fingers he placed both the ring and the chain into his pocket and ran upstairs into the bathroom. It was ten past four and Vince knew Mick would be home soon with Chris so he turned on the tap splashing water onto his face. Once again he looked at himself in the mirror; still feeling shook up Vince grabbed the towel that rested on the bath side. Drying his face he looked at himself again.

"You'll be alright. It's okay." Vince lied to himself staring blankly ahead, his body turned towards the door following through with moving feet that trembled, Vince walked into his room. He sat on his bed with his head in his hands listening out for his Dad's van. Digging into his skin was the golden ring, he could feel its outline as the pressure of his body rested against the bed. Vince pulled the ring and chain from his pocket cupping it in his hand, rocking his hand from side to side all you could hear was the quiet whisper of chains crunching and grinding together in the palm.

The sound of a rusty old battered engine came rolling up the street. Vince's ears piped up from the daze as he heard the screaming of gravel being squashed by rubber tires, he put the gold under the pillow that lay on top of the bed and hurried out of the door running down the stairs.

"Fuck." Vince smashed his toe at the bottom of the stairs through rushing too fast. A striking pain of thunder splintered through his toe. Hopping on one leg Vince skipped towards the nearest table and chair.

Mick parked the van outside the 'Smoking Barrel' with Chris sat in the passenger seat.

"He's not been too well our Vince...You know, I think there's some kids at school who are giving Vince a beating. The fuckin bastards." One of Mick's eyebrows raised towards Chris.

"Whys that?" Chris replied scratching his freshly trimmed stubble.

"Eye. I don't know but they're fuckin brutal little fucks. Like hyenas. But Vince, you know, quiet lad he is, these last few days he's been like a fuckin raging bull." Chris's eyes squinted slightly as the sun glared through the window. "Like I hung a bag out for him in the spare room and… He's been at it like a red rag to a bull. He's good, he's good… Devil of a punch on him". Chris sat there thinking as he replied to Mick.

"When I was there at Saint Brooks High, I remember a lad in the same year as Vince. Cocky as shit because of his family's background. I think it was Kane… Kane Crossling. Think it might have a link to him." Mick replied feeling anxious his skin started to crawl and a sense of danger leached onto his skin.

"Crossling… Jimmy Crossling. Is that the kid's Dad? He's a right vicious bastard." Chris pulled down the sun visor tensing his arm.

"Yeah I think. Yeah it is. Jimmy Crossling's son."

"It wasn't too long ago was it that he got some man butchered, I heard…some lads who came in the other day mentioned it." Mick's mouth turned dry as he started to put the pieces together in his head.

"No doubt that his son is just as ruthless" Chris's face turned pale as he looked at Mick's eyebrows raise.

"Right we best get these barrels moved then, we've got about eighty people relying on us tomorrow and we shan't let them down."

Mick and Chris jumped out of the van closing the doors behind them. Mick opened the side boot on the van sliding it open. Inside the back of the van were twelve barrels of beer, ranging from all different brands contained inside the metal cylinders. On the bottom of the van at the side was a pull-out ramp where they rolled the barrels down on one by one.

Vince heard his Dad get out of the car with Chris, he stretched out his foot and jumped up sprinting towards the bar, behind the bar was a set of trainers Vince forgot to take upstairs last night. He slung them on his feet being cautious of the one foot that had the busted toe.

Mick banged on the door of the 'Smoking Barrel.' Knock Knock! Vince heard the bangs of the battering hammer of Mick's fists hit the thick wooden doors.

"I'm coming!" Vince shouted, a burst of energy sprung from his lungs. Vince ran to the door and unlocked it letting Mick through with the silver barrel rolling flat.

"Why did it take you so long to open the doors?" Mick asked.

"I banged my toe on the last step of the stairs an' I was looking for my shoes," Vince replied with a straight face that turned into a smile.

"Where do you want these Mick," Chris shouted across from behind Mick.

"In the spare room on the right." Mick yelled back rolling his barrel towards the door of the spare room.

"Alright Vince! Roll this in there for us whilst I get another." Chris smiled passing across the rolling barrel.

"Yeah course mate, you alright?" Chris walked back outside towards the van.

"I'm good mate, thanks." Replied Chris in a loud tone, reaching for the next lined up barrel. Mick opened the door to the spare room and rolled the barrel inside.

"How was school Vince?" Vince paused for a few seconds and scratched his head.

"I... I didn't go in Dad." Vince pushed the barrel through the door following Mick's trail.

"Why's that?" Mick asked with a concerned manner; bending his knees, tossing the barrel upright to a static stand still. Feeling anxious Vince looked up from the floor, looking at Mick's unshaven face.

"I overslept and didn't feel up for it... today we normally watch videos on YouTube so I've not missed much." Vince pulled excuse after excuse from his mouth, slowly rising in tone.

"It's alright." Mick replied, his eyes squinted and eyebrows raised. "What did you do with your time then?" An archway of frowns covered Mick's forehead. Vince spoke confidently, feeling a sense of purpose.

"I tidied up the left room in the cellar, I cleaned the boxes and stacked them against the wall. There's more storage space down there now."

A warm smile shined across Mick's face, "That's great Vince, it's good of you…. we could do with some more space." A bear sized arm gently hooked the shoulders of Vince. "Thank's my boy," Mick softly spoke looking into Vince's timid eyes.

Vince's mind started to spin, he kept thinking about the ring he had recently found, the headlines from the newspapers hit hard on his brain gasping for oxygen, he kept quiet pushing all thoughts to the back of his mind.

"I'll find the right moment, now's not the right time." Vince thought to himself, "Not now!" an unsettled whisper found its way from Vince's mouth.

"What's that?" Mick answered Vince as they walked back into the bar area.

"Nothing Dad, nothing." Chris past them both rolling the other barrels into the spare room.

"How many's left Chris?"

"There's two left at the back of the Van, be careful though because a bolt's come out of the ramp."

"So it still works?" Mick shouted as Chris rolled the barrels into the back.

"Yeah." Chris pulled the edge of the barrel flipping it upwards. He looked across the room, four silver barrels lined up one by one on the right side of the room. Looking forward he saw the black swaying punch bag hanging from a large hook. The light in the corner flickered on and off. "Al have to get that fixed." The hands of Chris leant against his hips as he planned in his head what he needed to do.

Squeaking sounds rumbled through the floor boards of the function room as Mick and Vince rolled the barrels across the wooden planks.

"Have you been on your bag?" Mick pushed the weight of the barrel forward, his veins grew thick as the blood pumped back and forth through his body.

"Nar…"

"O'right…Hey I'll see if Chris will have a spar with you," Mick laughed.

"Shut up Dad!... Sack that," Vince squirmed.

"Only a playful fight. It will be a good experience for you!"

"Dad, Chris is eighteen, I'm only fifteen. Nar. Definitely not."

Mick spat from his mouth. "Never mind then, as long as you don't fear the fight, because to me you sound like your scared."

Vince's face looked dazed, "Dad shut up," laughed Vince.

Mick smiled and winked, "I need you to work tomorrow night for me, pot collecting, me and Chris will be on the bar."

"Will do," Vince replied wondering to himself. "Dad what's the occasion?"

"It's one of the local's birthday tomorrow, you know that Claire from the bottom of Mary Lee Road. The one who gave you a lift last week." Vince felt a small feeling of excitement.

"No way?"

"I think her daughter Daisy's coming too!" Mick nodded and smiled.

"So that's why you won't have Chris a spar then hey haha, you don't want to get all bruised up… for Daisy. Ha ha ha," Mick laughed to himself.

"Dad shut it, I didn't even know about this before you just told me. I don't even like her anyway. I don't even KNOW her!" Vince felt nervous, Daisy had been in his subconscious over the past few days, last night he had a dream which she appeared in.

She stood in front of Vince holding a flower. The dream did not make any sense leaving Vince staring into space when he woke earlier that morning.

"Stop winding me up Dad, it's all you've done since you came in. Peck my head with this and that!" laughed Vince, his hand started to shake on and off, he started to feel butterflies flutter around his body.

Vince and Mick rolled the barrels into the spare room, catching up with Chris.

"How long does it take to move two barrels ay? What you two laughing at?" Chris muttered.

"Nothing," Vince responded hoping his Dad would shut up, Micks lips started to stretch open.

"Our Vince has a crush."

"Dad, seriously shut up." Vince spoke over his Dad before he could cause any more embarrassment. "I do not. Chris, he doesn't have a clue. I don't even know her... swear down!"

Chris burst out with tears of laughter, his cheeks turned purple. "oh is that why you took so long! Ay up, was you both having the father and son talk?"

"SHUT UP!" Mick and Vince both reacted at the same time. "It's all banter!" Chris replied trying to cool himself down.

All three, Mick, Vince and Chris started to hysterically laugh pointing at each other's faces.

"You should have seen your face!"

"You should have seen yourself then"

"Hahaha BANTER... The father and son moment!"

"Both of your faces just dropped!" All three contributed to the laughs, Mick had a distinctive laugh that sounded deep and croaky like grinding screws being blended. Vince's throat had a slight squeaky hiss when he laughed, Vince's face turned purple like beetroot. It had been a long time since the three musketeers had laughed like school children. Vince felt his stomach burn as he laughed heavily finding it hard to catch a breath, Vince's body bent forward.

"I can't breathe," Vince hissed like a snake as his abdominal muscles coiled.

Chapter Eleven

It was a cold and dark night, Kane waited by the corner of the street leaning against the lamp-post, he pulled out his HTC Hero and started to text Kevin.

Hurry up. Get here soon as mate.

Kane wore black track suit bottoms with a matching hoody it had white tram lines which stood out from the black, glowing when car lights shined across him. His hair was freshly cut, he could feel the cold wind strike his face turning the pale white cheeks into ice. Kane put his hands into his pocket feeling a metal object that slotted around his fingers like a glove. He tensed his fingers through the hollow holes of the object. He gently released his fingers from the pocket and pulled out his phone as it vibrated in his hand.

"Hello? Where are you?"

"I'm nearly there, one street away." Kevin replied running down the street catching up to Kane.

"Get them legs moving!" Kane shouted down the phone watching Kevin enter the street running towards him like a racehorse.

The pavement hit Kevin's feet, his Nike Air Max shoes started to wear, he looked barely visible as he was dressed fully in black from head to toe. The streetlights created silhouettes of Kevin's shadow as he manoeuvred through the night like a fully robed ninja, silent and deadly. Kevin approached Kane with nerves and a splash of adrenaline.

"About time." Kane made a sniggering comment towards Kevin as he was meant to meet Kane at seven thirty pm. It had now turned eight pm. "It's took you half an hour to get here! Are you taking the piss?" Kane aggressively spoke feeling pissed off.

"No mate... Honest. I was running as fast as I could, I had to get my Mam some bread and milk. So I had to go back on myself."

Kane's face fell straight and narrow cheek bones stiff. "You should know better." Kane stared into darkness flickering his eye towards the opposite street light.

"I'm sorry mate. I should've rang you but I thought I was going to make it." A short pause of silence fell between the two. "Look at me, would I ever let you down? Hey, have I ever in our friendship?" Kevin put his hand on Kane's back gently.

"No..." Kane replied grinding his teeth.

"I'm just late this once, right." Kevin said to Kane with a smug attitude.

"Okay." Kane bluntly replied. Kane's pocket started to vibrate he pulled out his phone and looked down at his screen.

"Aiden calling" the phone displayed. Kane let the phone ring a few times staring at Aiden's name on the screen. Each ring felt like a heartbeat, pressing answer on the phone Aiden's voice spoke out loud.

"I've got your money. Where are you?"

Kane replied in a resentful tone. "Park Field Avenue." Kane ended the call instantly.

"Is he coming?" Kevin asked as his nerves polluted his body.

A quiet sinister sound floated from Kane's mouth, "Yeah."

"I think I see him." Kevin looked towards the bottom of the street, an outline of a tall person came walking towards where Kane and Kevin were perched against the lamppost. Kevin's arm raised with goose bumps. His heart started to pound getting heavier and heavier, blood gushed through Kevin's veins. Shoulders tensed and hands numb. The cold air dehydrated Kane's throat, he coughed erupting thick green phlegm from his dry sandy tongue. Spitting on the floor Kane exhaled leaving hot steam into the atmosphere.

The thick black clouds covered the sky, hiding the stars which shone down. The light from the lamp-post revealed the boys like a spotlight. Kane's tram line bottoms reflected into Aiden's view catching the corner of his eyes.

"What you thinking Kane?" Kevin bit the skin from his lips tasting the dribbling blood, staining his plaque ridden teeth.

Closer and closer Aiden began to close in on the two, time seemed to feel slow. Kane turned his neck to the right side of the street, staring down Aiden like a missile locked onto its target waiting to explode with a lion's roar of might, Aiden stood meters away from Kevin and Kane's presence.

"I've got your fucking money." Aiden pulled out twenty pounds in five pound notes from his dark Nike hoody.

Holding the notes within his fingertips Aiden felt the smooth friction of paper slide. A blast of wind rattled the rage of Kane looking at the money Aiden held in his hand. A chill riddled through Kane's spine as he paused staring at Aiden's grey face. Aiden walked closer into Kane's personal space, his shoulders tensed and arms locked beside him. He looked up to Kane eye to eye. His eyes started to water with the wind blowing in his face, the short hair that grew from Aiden's head stood on end. Sweat trickled down the sides of Aiden's face, pushing his hand forward towards Kane with the money gripped with stiff fingers. Kane snatched the money leaving a silence between the two. Reaching into his pockets, Kane pulled out a pack of cigs and a lighter.

"Are we straight then?" closing in with tension Aiden asked.

Kane's eyes squinted and did not blink. "Straight, It will be fucking straight." Kane lit up his Richmond cigarette, taking a deep breath of tar he blew smoke from his mouth. He then pulled out the money in front of Aiden and rolled the wheel of his lighter. The yellow flame floated underneath Kane's hand holding the money. Kane felt the heat of the lighter increasing on his hand. The notes started to catch fire, ash fell from the money as it went up in smoke. Within seconds all the money had flaked away into ash landing on the concrete like snow.

"What the fuck are you doing?" Aiden felt puzzled as he gazed at the money burning. He could smell the fiery scent of burning paper. Kevin watched sharing the same reactions as Aiden. "You're fucked in the head you! You're fucking gone!" Aiden screeched into Kane's face. Kane stamped onto the ashes on the floor twisting one foot, looking at Aiden, Kane smiled.

Fury could not describe the feelings Aiden felt, he had struggled to gather the money and as he watched the money disintegrate he boomed with anger, his jaw hung loose and fingers twitched. "You're a fucking wanker, I'll fucking show you." Aiden sprung into Kane's direction with fists swaying left to right. Aiden windmilled his arms swirling towards Kane. Kevin pushed forward deflecting the waves of punches. "You were my best mate. You both were." Aiden gritted his teeth trying to jump forward past Kevin. "You're fucking crazy. Both of you."

"Go Aiden, just fucking go!" Kevin shouted advising Aiden to leave.

Kane slid his hand back into his pocket and fitted the metal object within his fingers. Kane launched a deadly blow to Aiden's face. Kevin looked in disbelief, a skinny silver knuckle duster coiled around Kane's knuckles.

"What the fuck?" Kevin panted as Kane viciously pounded his punches into Aiden's head, blood shattered everywhere like a fountain.

Swaying backwards, Aiden's cheek bones felt numb. Grooves outlined his face with cuts, holding his hands up blinded by blood Aiden fell over to his knees.

"Leave it now Kane… Leave it." Like a shark with a taste of blood, Kane pounced into a feeding frenzy.

"I'll fucking kill you Aiden, you're not so big now are you. You're nothing more than an untrustworthy sly bastard… You've fucked with the wrong man, this fuckin man!" Kane gripped the back of Aiden's head pulling it backwards as his body lay on the concrete pavement. Looking into Aiden's blood dripping face, Kane shouted violently, "I will fucking kill you! Do you understand? I will fucking kill you…You sly little rat." Kevin grabbed the back of Kane's shoulders and dragged him off Aiden with all his might. "Get off me!" Kane screeched, clenching his teeth, pushing Kevin back with one hand.

"COME ON! LET'S GO!... Kane come on!" Kevin gripped the back of Kane's jacket feeling tense and panicked. "Kane let's get out of here, leave it now!" Kane's grip on Aiden was locked like a pit bull with locked jaw. Kevin continued to pull Kane shouting to him "Let go! Let's go!" Kevin released his hands from Kane's back shouting into his ear. "Kane, I'm going mate, come on, come with me. Let's go! Let's go! He's unconscious come on! He's gone mate. Leave him for dead man."

The two lads scampered off into the darkness leaving Aiden's battered body lying on the cold concrete floor. Rain clouds started to hover over the streets and eventually burst pouring rain onto Aiden's body. The two silhouettes of Kane and Kevin sprinted towards an ally leaving shadows from every streetlight they passed. Adrenaline hit Kane hard as his hands started to shake. He slid the knuckle duster, stained with blood into his pocket. Blood thrust itself through his veins like a rollercoaster racing at full speed. His heart paced and eyes ran bloodshot.

Chapter Twelve

People started to gather outside the Smoking Barrel doors that opened at half seven. Claire had booked the entire function room for her private party.

Daisy sat behind the brown wooden table, there was a sticky sensation left on the wood from spilt beer. Across the crowd of people, family and friends, she noticed Vince clearing away bottles from tables. Stroking her curly black hair, she coiled a strand around her finger. Vince was working away and didn't notice Daisy was watching him. Moving back and forth from bar to table Chris shouted him over pulling away at the Fosters draught.

"Vince come give me a hand with this, the tills stopped working." Vince's ears pricked up over the loud speakers playing Take That.

"Never forget where you're coming from." The crowd gathered in the pub as they started to sing away; Vince approached Chris from behind the bar.

"Look, the button has jammed that's all." Vince replied pointing to the enter switch.

"Oh right, not used it in a while." Chris put pressure onto his thumb and popped the button back into place.

"You alright now mate?"

"Yeah fine now, get them bottles shifted," Chris grunted with a smile.

"Shut it you." Vince laughed picking up the empty bottles he left on the side earlier. He walked over to the big black bin and chucked the bottles into there. Walking out from behind the bar, Vince quickly scanned his eyes across the room picking out tables with lots of left bottles and empty glasses. He approached the closest table which had two empty glasses on it. He left the glasses sitting on the table and gathered other glasses from some of the other tables piling them all onto one table. After the table became half full he walked back behind the bar and pulled out a black bin liner and approached the table. He opened the bin liner wide and started to pick out the bottles placing them into the bag.

Mick walked into the room where everyone was singing and dancing to classic eighties' songs. He noticed Vince working away and walked towards him.

"Alright son." Mick spoke in a very mellow voice.

"Yeah. Just clearing this table." Mick patted Vince on the back pulling a warm smile.

"That's very good of you. See you've got some brains in you using that bin liner."

Vince threw the bottle he had in his hand into the bag. "Well, it saves me going back and forth from the bar." Mick winked and picked up a handful of the empty glasses.

"Well it won't hurt me getting any exercise." Vince laughed to himself and whispered under his breath.

"He's so bloody daft."

"Dancing queen only seventeen!" Claire bursted out from her breath screaming into the atmosphere. "Come on Daisy! Get up and dance with your Mum!" Claire ran to Daisy's seat and stretched out her hands. "Come on take my hand!" Daisy laughed at her drunken mother as she swayed side to side standing in front of her.

"Mum I know it's your birthday but you're embarrassing me."

"Come on, it's our tune. Hey, I'll buy you a drink come on, come on!" Claire dragged out her words in a slurring voice full of energy. Daisy stood up and held her mother's hand. "Dancing queen... Dancing queen!" Claire continued to pelt out the lyrics from her mouth as they walked onto the dance floor. "Come on Daisy give me a twirl." Daisy's face turned bright red changing to purple like a beetroot. She felt nervous energy crawl through her body as her mum forced her to dance.

A fat woman with blonde hair and a pan face came strolling up to Claire and Daisy. She wore a black dress and caked blocks of makeup on her face, carrying a bottle of blue WKD she swallowed a mouth full and screamed at the top of her lungs.

"CLAIRE! It's me Patty." Daisy and Claire turned their heads to the sight of Patty pointing her finger and moving her legs in sync with the Abba track. Claire threw her head side to side throwing her dark hair over her shoulder shimmering. "Shake it girl! I'm so glad you could make it. Where have you been all night?" Claire kissed Patty on the cheek. Daisy stood feeling awkward staring at the woman she had never seen before. Analysing her greasy fringe and wrinkled face Daisy shouted over the music to her mum interrupting her conversation with Patty.

"Mum get me a drink!"

"I'll be back in a minute Patty; come on Daisy I'll get you a drink."

"You better get your arse back here soon girl!" Patty replied with a cannon ball of energy.

Making their way to the bar, Daisy made awkward eye contact with Vince as he was working away. She took a deep breath and exhaled thinking to herself.

"OH GOD!"

Chris stood at the bar serving customers, he wore a black smart shirt and had a freshly trimmed stubble.

"Can I have two Vodka and Cokes please?" Claire asked Chris feeling excited but slightly annoyed how Daisy shouted over her conversation. Chris mixed together the drinks and passed them over the bar and looked at Daisy cautiously.

"That's six pounds please." Chris replied to Claire. Claire passed one of the drinks to Daisy and danced back up to Patty. Daisy made her way back to her seat and started to drink deeply from the glass. She hadn't eaten all day and the alcohol started to strike her brain.

Vince cleared all the tables with bottles except from one, one table which Daisy sat upon; he threw the black bin liner in the bin and Chris pulled him to one side as the bar became quieter.

"Vince, is that the girl your Dad was talking about earlier?" Vince let the sound of Chris's voice evaporate.

"No." Vince replied in a quiet tone. Sounds of glass breaking shattered through the plastic bin as Vince threw the bin liner,

"Yeah it is." Chris excitedly responded like a mithering dog. "I've seen you watching her discretely all night. Get in there lad."

Vince replied feeling a sense of nervousness, "Shut up!"

"Go on sunshine, make the move, she might like you too. I just served her... She's on Vodka and Coke."

"Shut up Chris, I'm working," Vince replied feeling all flustered. Walking back to the tables Vince felt nervous as he looked across at Daisy. He paced into the toilets in a hurry holding his breath.

The door squeaked behind him as it closed, he walked into the toilet and pulled up the seat. Unzipping his black pants, he flushed himself away from the noise of the party. Vince flushed the chain and walked up to the sink. Washing his hands with hot water Vince looked at himself in the mirror.

"I didn't see you there! Hi, you still using that? No way, what are you doing here?" Vince tried to prep himself before clearing Daisy's table, goose bumps started to appear on his forearms as he started talking to himself. "Right, now Vince, you're just going to pick up the empty glasses and walk away. Yeah easy. Keep it nice and simple. A brief hello never did any harm to anyone. Right come on... get yourself together." Drying his hands on his pants Vince looked towards the door and paced taking deep breaths, breathing in breathing out. His body bounced up and down like a Yoyo.

Vince walked out from the men's toilets, he felt his hands shake with nerves as he walked towards the table where Daisy sat with three empty glasses of Vodka and Coke. Vince's senses started to rumble, the song 'Rock DJ' started to rifle through his ears. Time turned slow as Vince felt each breath he took vanish from his lungs, his heart started beating rapidly like a firing machine gun. His eyes caught onto another table which was only meters away from Daisy's seat. Vince sharply turned to the table like a ricocheting piece of shrapnel. Daisy took a gulp from her drink noticing Vince's quick escape.

"Hiya Vince, you not saying hello?" Vince lay his eyes upon Daisy. She wore a silky black short dress that had small little white poker dots on it. In the centre of the dress was a ribbon that wrapped around her waist with a bow finish on the front. With matching shoes and a bow in her hair Daisy raised her glass to the opening of her mouth.

"Hi... I'm just working." Vince replied, a lightning bolt of nerves gushed through him. The effects of alcohol started to take its course on Daisy's head.

"Yeah, yeah. Working!" Daisy replied feeling a rush of courage and excitement. Giggling away to herself she spoke loudly. "You look different without bruises on your face!" Daisy smiled.

Vince stared back stuttering on his words. "Hey, you... I... I guess I...I do." Vince felt his veins pulse, his back started to sweat.

"Well are you going to sit down or go back to work?" Daisy gestured quotation marks with her fingers. Vince slowly walked towards the facing chair of Daisy. His heart rate started to simmer but under the table his leg quietly twitched. Feeling flirty and brave Daisy stared into Vince's face relaxing her shoulders. "You're not as ugly as I thought you were," Daisy's eyes fluttered. She picked up her glass taking another sip.

"Hey cheeky, shut it you." smiled Vince laughing. "Think I best water that glass down." Laughing back full of energy Daisy replied in shock!

"Hey, I'm not a lightweight! Do you drink?"

"No... well a little." Vince muttered feeling embarrassed.

"Haha, you've never drank have you?" Vince felt his cheeks slightly blush.

"Well, yeah, I have at Christmas."

Daisy replied in disbelief. "No way! Aww your so CUTE...You little featherweight." Daisy laughed to herself.

"Shut up!" A teardrop of sweat dribbled down the side of Vince's cheek. Vince wiped the sweat from his face with a tissue from his pocket. "You're cute."

"What? You must be mad," Vince replied feeling a sense of adventure.

Fluttering her eyelashes Daisy's eyes slightly widened, energetically she beckoned, "Do you want to dance?" Vince's face cooled down with a pale cast.

"I'm not the dancing type. I can't dance."

"Please." Replied Daisy in a soft tone.

"I'm working anyway. I best get back to work" Vince looked at Daisy's black hair with his blue eyes. "Or else my Dad will be on my case." Daisy stared into Vince's eyes, her heart started to skip.

"I'll help, I'm a good worker." A tingling sensation exploded through Vince's body, he felt butterflies dance inside him filling his heart with excitement. Not wanting to leave but feeling a paranoid presence of being watched.

"Well I'm just going to bin all the bottles outside, we'll see." Vince jumped up from his seat, passing the crowds of people that danced around the room like fairies. He walked back behind the bar, picking up the bin bag full of glass bottles.

"I'm just taking these out Chris."

"Ay, what happened with you and that girl. I seen you both laughing away. You smooth operator." Vince reacted feeling awkward.

"We was just talking. Talking never killed anyone. Besides I was shifting the bottles from her table."

"Yeah yeah, you can't fool me, Mr Romeo." Chris replied winding Vince up. Ignoring Chris, Vince picked up the bag with a tight grip as he walked outside, the sound of bottles scraped together.

Daisy watched Vince make his exit. A storm of butterflies whirl winded inside her body, she saw her mum ordering shots at the bar with Patty. Following Vince's exit, she jumped out of her seat rushing over to join in.

"Get me one Mum!" Three shots lined up on the wooden bar, as three hands picked them up. Throwing the alcohol to the back of her throat she felt a burning sensation ignite. Sparked full of energy and widened eyes, Daisy ran off to the front door of the pub to get some air outside.

Vince followed a pathway at the side of the pub which led to two waste containers, one was glass only and the other was general waste. The containers stank of cat urine, flipping the glass containers lid open with one hand he threw the bag from over his shoulder into the bin. A crashing sound of shattering glass reacted inside the container like an I.E.D explosion. The lid slammed back onto its plastic frame making a small bang. Vince heard footsteps walking down the side of the pub's pathway, it was dark and only the security sensor lights were shining.

Vince sensed the presence of another person watching him. He followed his footsteps back the way he came. Smash! Shatter! A glass fell to the concrete floor.

"DAISY! What you doing out here!" Vince questioned, feeling startled.

"I'm sorry about the glass. You made me jump...I got curious to where you disappeared to." Daisy spoke in an apologetic voice. The stars shone down on Daisy's face lighting up her beautiful features. Curly black hair and a button nose, Vince stared into her face.

"It's okay. It's cold we'll go back inside," Vince pointed the way with his hand.

"I told you I'm a good worker." Daisy seductively spoke pulling a smile, locking eyes with Vince for a moment that seemed endless. Gently tying her hands around the waist of Vince she squeezed him softly moving closer to his body. Closer and closer Vince's hips attached to Daisy's as their lips collided, the security lights went off like an eclipse creating darkness with only the moonlight shining on them both.

Standing stiff as a poker, Vince's feet stood solid to the ground, his heart pounded like a hammering nail. Goose bumps attacked Vince's body like a rash spreading all over the skin, adrenaline rushed through his heart. Vince's hands hung freely, in a trance he started to move his hands towards Daisy's hips.

Inside the pub everyone was cheerful and happy, touching near midnight the clock was well on its way to strike twelve. Claire danced around her group of friends fluttering like a bird, she shook her tail feathers staring into the distance looking at Mick. She hovered like a bee on a hunt for nectar pacing her way towards Mick.

"Hello gorgeous, thank you for this magnificent party!" Mick replied knowing too well he did nothing.

"Well, all these people are your friends, I just provided a space for you all...You could've picked any other pub." Claire smiled shaking her head to the music in the background.

"You've done more than that. You decorated the entire room for me... you played all my favourite songs. Er erm..." Claire looked back across the room like a meerkat. "See, look... You made a buffet for all my guests and made me that chocolate cake!"

Mick smiled and touched her hand. "You've been a very good friend to me Claire, you've helped me in more ways than one. It's the least I could do."

"Micky you're so sweet and thoughtful. I'm so lucky that I know you." Claire's heart warmed with boiling love inside her.

"It's getting late, so I'm going to close the doors soon. Do you want me to give you a lift home?"

Claire replied feeling flattered by kindness.

"Oh no! I can't make you drive me home. I'm not too far away. I'll walk it." Mick responded with energy and caring eyes.

"No, I'll run you, I insist."

"You've done far enough for me Mick. Thank you! You could call me a taxi." Mick pulled out his Nokia from his pocket and dialled a taxi firm.

"Hahaha MICK! I need to get you a new phone! That's what these kids call a brick!" Claire laughed like a school girl full of energy crying hysterically.

"Ay, it does the job, doesn't it?"

Back outside, Vince felt Daisy's tongue dance around his mouth. The night was silent; you could only hear the sound of lips locking together. Daisy pulled back after what seemed only a couple of minutes that stretched to half an hour. Time passed so quickly that both Vince and Daisy hadn't noticed a second pass. Feeling a taste of excitement Daisy skipped down the sideway path of the pub.

"Are you coming or what?" chanted Daisy full of energy. Vince paused and took a breath, he could taste Vodka and Coke on his tongue.

"Yeah! I'm coming." Vince walked quickly catching up to Daisy. Looking into Daisy's eyes Vince felt obliterated as it was the first time he had kissed a girl. After a couple minutes more he started to see her face turn pale and witness her body lean.

"I think... I'm going to be..." Daisy heaved, throwing up brown sick onto the floor. Her head started to spin while giving a powerful headache.

"SHIT! Are you okay?" Vince held Daisy feeling panicked. "Are you okay...Daisy? Daisy!" Daisy slouched towards the floor continuing to puke, tears started to build up in the corners of her eyes.

"I don't feel good." She sulked holding onto Vince for balance.

Sounds of a swinging door squeaked open, Claire walked through the door with Mick witnessing Daisy perched over Vince's stretched out arm.

"What's up!" Claire screamed, feeling like a bad mother she ran across to Daisy. Mick followed swiftly behind.

"I feel sick. Err...Mum. What are you doing here?" Brown sick rippled across the concrete floor leaking across the pavement onto the road. After five minutes of worrying Mick said to Vince.

"Get inside boy and tell Chris to lock up after everyone's gone. It's alright I'll handle this."

"Dad is she going to be alright?" Vince spoke with concern. "Of course she is, now get inside." Vince walked towards the doors of the 'Smoking Barrel' looking behind him he watched a taxi pull up on the pavement.

Mick opened the door of the taxi and assisted Claire with getting Daisy inside safely. He then approached the driver who sat with his window fully down. Mick pulled a twenty pound note from his pocket and passed it over to the driver.

"Take them to the end of Mary Lee Road estate. She will direct you from there!" Claire winded her window down and shouted from her seat.

"Thanks MICKY! See you soon." As the taxi span off down the street Mick looked into the stars for a moment and took the same steps Vince did five minutes earlier.

The sun's rays shined through the blinds of Mick's bedroom window. Quite a medium sized room which was wallpapered with bland pastel colours. Turning his head onto the left side of the cushion his eyes slightly opened but fast asleep snoring away like father Christmas after the midnight rush, Mick rolled his overweight body to the right side of the bed. A small wooden table rested at the side of his double bed. Watching over his body the table befriended the digital alarm clock which sat on top. Beep! Beep! Beep! The clock alarmed repeating sound after sound. Half asleep. stretching out a long arm and hitting the snooze button, Mick slowly started to open his eyes staring at the time...... 5:30am!!

"Shitting hell." Mick yawned extending his last word. Lying in bed Mick stared into space looking at the wall in front of him, after a few moments he leant over for his phone that snuggled under the thick white pillows. Clicking on the enter key to the Nokia, two unread messages from Claire appeared. His thick bushy eyebrows subtly rose, as sleep stuck to the corner of his eyes he read squinting.

Thank you for a wonderful birthday and once again a beautiful night. Hope I didn't drink too much haha. Just got in safe and sound. Daisy threw up a few times but she's okay. Won't be letting her off my lead again! Can't thank you enough for making my birthday amazing, will be in touch soon. Lots of love Claire xxxx

Mick smiled to himself and opened the second text message. *I can't stop thinking about you. I think I'm crazy. I can't wait to see you xxxx.*

Replying to the message, he clicked return and started to type away.

Dear Claire, hope you really did enjoy yourself last night it was truly great. Hope Daisy's alright, poor thing, curiosity is starting to grow on me why Vince and Daisy was outside. Young love ay. Hope I've not texted you too early. See you soon xx

Mick felt like a school boy after his first date, still feeling excited from his night with Claire a sharp scent of loss attacked Mick's heart.

Still in love with his wife who passed all them years ago, Mick started to fill up with tears in his eyes as his conscience started to tear away at his heart. Silently whispering to himself he started to whimper crying like a meowing kitten. No sound of pain scratched at his throat, only tears fell from the cheeks. In a state of loss, he heard his wife's voice.

"What's wrong Mick? It's okay love. You deserve to feel happy once again." Mick battled with his demons re-watching the event unfold from his eyes. Screams of agony flared through Mick's ears. Flashes of flames cross fired through his mind. Images of a burnt down house reflected into Mick's brain like water. His head sank into the thick white pillow like sinking sand. Looking back at his clock striking six he pulled onto his quilt dragging the covers off him. Pushing all the weight with his hands on the bed he leant forward in a sit up position.

"Fucking hell," Mick projected quietly. He allowed his feet to dangle off the bed then stood up half naked wearing black boxer shorts. As his stomach leant, the smell of body odour reeked; sweat gathered from his armpits streaming down Mick's body. He walked through his door creating large footsteps on the way to the bathroom. Crossing the landing Mick crept trying to create minimum noise as Vince was still sleeping. Opening the bathroom door Mick walked inside, his reflection bounced off the mirrors. He pulled a skanky towel from the cupboard that sat on the right side of the room and threw it on the toilet seat. Turning on the rusty tap connected to the shower he twisted on the hot water. Sounds of water hit the bathroom floor, Mick threw off his boxers then stepped into the shower over the bath. Steam started to cover the room as he tried to clear his mind; the sound of his wife's voice continued to beat like a drum.

"Why are you ignoring me? GET THE BABY!" Screams started to echo through Mick's ears, he wiped the tears from his face washing them away with water. He wiped both hands across his body soaking into the heat, Mick picked up the Imperial Leather bar of soap scrubbing himself crazy. The soap nourished his dark short hair, the sides started to show a silver tint of grey. Breathing heavily and slower he turned the running water off and stepped over the bath wall. Picking up the towel from the toilet seat Mick wrapped the towel around his waist. Water started dribbling from his feet leaking onto the cold floor, he wiped the steamy mirror looking into the layers of frown marks across his face and thick tired lines. His face turned red through the heat, Mick ran his fingers through his hair feeling the density with chunky fingers.

Chapter Thirteen

Park Hill estate was one of the most deprived areas in Manchester, there were rows of terraced houses lined up one after the other. The rows of terraced houses created a maze of streets for the people who lived there to run wild. Most of the homes were council owned and gangs of hooded teenagers lurked around every corner. It was a dangerous place to live, especially if you were elderly, muggings happened regularly and if you weren't known in the area you would be particularly victimised. A haven of the destruction, Park Hill was known throughout Manchester as trouble, like the people who lived in it, police sirens echoed through the streets bouncing off the maze of walls. Young children would play in the streets in pyjamas looking up to the older teenagers, the next generation of crime committers. The screeching sound of speeding cars was a common sound to hear. A black coated Mercedes Benz, E class was parked outside one of the houses at the end of the terrace row, it happened to be the biggest home on the estate. The Mercedes had 2 streaks on the sides of the vehicle and the original Mercedes Benz metal symbol that pointed out from the nose of the bonnet. It's silver and black alloys matched the silver trim around the windows. The registration plate of the car spelt out 'D4V3 666.' This car belonged to Dave Crossling known as the devil throughout Manchester. Father to Kane and Sean Crossling, Dave sat inside his house counting stacks of money on the glass table. Beside him was Scott Mitchell, Dave's trusted right-hand man.

"Pass me that stack Scott," Dave spoke in a deep voice full of testosterone, he counted the stack of money.

Dave was a medium sized bloke with a muscular build; he was no stranger to exercise. His head was shaven bald and his face looked square. He had thin eyebrows and green eyes, a scar remained at the back of his head, it had healed but left an outline. Dave scratched his dark stubble, wearing a black Louis Vuitton shirt which was stained in one million aftershaves.

"How's the kids doing then?" Scott enquired.

"Well, they're little shits as all teenagers are. Kane thinks he knows it all but knows fuck all!"

Scott picked dry skin from his lip and replied, "How's your other lad doing? Sean, is it?"

"He's the quieter one and doesn't answer back. His actions speak louder than words, every so often he will do something crazy."

Scott counted a thousand pounds and stacked it together putting it with a collection of other lined up stacks. Dave and Scott would always count their money together, so both of their minds were at peace that no one had the urge to take more than they should. Dave ruled the roost making a lot of his money through drugs but covered a wide range of crimes from the occasional armed robbery to taxing smaller dealers. Nicknamed the devil, Dave spent most of his early career kidnapping underworld figures in Manchester. He would severely torture these types of people and demand payment from them. Building up trusted members into his organisation, Dave's presence became known with criminals in the Manchester region but no one other than his accomplices knew who he actually was.

"He must take after me then," Scott replied with a smug face.

"Ay, you cheeky bastard he's my blood." Dave shouted across the table. "Right let's hurry up with this, the kids will be coming back soon and I don't want that little shit snatching at this." Scott nodded his head. He wore a white Ralf Lauren polo shirt with Armani light jeans and brown leather shoes.

"No worries, let's split it first and then bag it." Dave and Scott split the cash throwing it into black bin liners. Floods of money poured into the bags like a waterfall of paper. Tying a knot into the bag Scott smiled. "I best get myself a decent car like yours. I'm sick of getting taxi's everywhere." Dave folded his hands together staring at the clock on the wall.

"How much did you pay for it?"

"About fifty grand with another kid's insurance details on it. If I can remember rightly."

Scott pulled out a hundred pound from his share and slid it into his jean's pocket.

"Fuck me, that's not bad."

"It cost eight grand for the plate."

"Jesus Dave, I've got a little flat full of money, I need to start spending."

The dining room where Dave and Scott sat at the glass table was decorated with white wallpaper with black stripes, a white leather couch with black cushions and a television stood a few meters away from the table. A leg stretch away from the table was an open kitchen so all the rooms collided together. The kitchen was un-used and looked like a show home with wooden floor slats perfectly fitted. A clock sat four meters away from Dave's sight on the wall which connected to the kitchen. It was 3.35pm, the usual time Dave expected his kids to come in. Sean was always the first to get home, due to Kane being kept behind or meeting up with his friends.

The door gently squeaked open and footsteps tapped across the floor, walking through the hallway Sean popped his head into the room.

"Alright Dad? Alright Scott?"

"Yeah son, where's your brother?"

"I don't know Dad, last I heard he was with Kevin," Sean replied.

"Give him a text for us, tell him to get his arse in."

Sean walked into the dining area making his way towards the kitchen, "Have we got any yoghurts in?" Sean spoke quietly.

"Yeah and don't be eating us out of house and home."

Sean opened the doors to the American sized fridge and pulled out a cornflake Muller yoghurt. "Scott, do you want a drink mate?" Sean's voice raised slightly.

"Nah you're alright pal. I'm getting off soon." Scott pulled out his phone and called up a local taxi rank. "Alright mate, can I order a taxi for Park Hill estate on Dredington Street. Number 24." Scott put the phone down on the glass table.

"Sean get us a beer from the fridge... why didn't you ask me for a lift mate?"

Scott's frown raised. "I wouldn't want you to go out of your way. Plus, I never ask you for lift, you've done more than enough for me. I best get my own car soon." Sean walked over to the table and passed over a can of Carlsberg to his Dad. "You've got a license, haven't you?" Dave responded.

"Yeah"

"Then rent a car from one of the showrooms in town instead of buying one. That way they can't get a trace on it because it's all rented."

Scott's face looked baffled. "Why did you buy yours then and get it customized?" Sean stood listening to the conversation. Dave turned to Sean with his head.

"GO ON, FUCK OFF UPSTAIRS!" Sean walked out the room and ran up the stairs, Dave turned his head back to Scott speaking with a lower voice. "Remember last year when I got shot at by the Gucci's."

"Yeah" Scott replied in a concerned voice.

"Well, I got paranoid to fuck, so I ended up phoning some car specialist and got them to E-Guard the Mercedes for forty grand in cash."

"Fuck me that's a lot of money. What's an E-Guard?" Scott muttered.

"Listen mate, I've got run flat tyres with a steel bridge, but where your money really goes is into the bulletproof windows. They can deflect forty-four calibre rounds." Dave's eyebrows lowered. "I'm not fuckin about Scott, don't tell anyone." Scott smirked breaking into a laugh.

"Course not mate, I better get myself one of them James Bond cars then hey." Calming down with laughter Scott stared into Dave's green eyes.

"Get out of my house piss-taker and take your fucking money with you, you stingy cunt." Scott stood up from his seat.

"I think my taxi's here anyway, wind your neck in mate, haha." Scott walked towards the door that led to the hallway.

"I'll see you out." Dave followed behind Scott giving him a little slap across the back of his head. "Right, I'll be in touch soon mate," Dave spoke giving Scott a sharp nod.

A few hours passed and Dave sat on the couch passively watching the Jeremy Kyle show. His mind was on overdrive thinking about the next day. He had to be up early to meet Scott and meet with associates of his organisation, there were big plans due to be made. This kept Dave feeling anxious as pressure was creeping around the corner for him. Trying to relax, Dave picked up a spliff from a dark wooden coffee table. Feeling the texture of the rizzler with slim fingers he pulled out a lighter from his pocket and sparked up. The smell of cannabis started to circulate the open complex rooms, Dave's vision started to blur as his eyes diluted and shut closed. After taking in the whole joint he fell into a deep sleep with his legs kicked up and body sprawled out.

Crank! BANG! The front door chipped its way open echoing through the hallway. Dave woke from his snooze in a jumping shudder.

"Hey who's that?" Dave raised his voice aggressively.

"Who do you think it is?" Kane snidely replied, heart pumped still fuelled with adrenaline. Kane paced up the stairs like an athlete.

"Get here now!" Dave burnt out his lungs shouting at full pelt, roaring like a bear. The sounds of footsteps leaping back down the stairs bounced off the walls. Walking into the open spaced room Kane repeated the words.

"WHAT? What you been tipping weed?" Dave pulled himself up from the couch and slowly walked towards his son. Dave's shoulders flexed back and veins bulged from his forearms, bluntly ignoring Kane's remark.

"Where's my cut then?" Kane's face dropped with lowering frown's.

"What you on about?" Kane walked into the kitchen turning away from Dave ignorantly.

"Are you listening to me?" Kane ignored his Dad and opened the fridge, sounds of scraping feet muffled in the background clashing with the wooden floor.

"Fucking hell Dad the fridge is more or less EMPTY! You've cleaned us out with the munches." Kane spoke out loud giggling to himself, he started to slowly grit his teeth. Walking up to Kane from behind was Dave, watching him like a preying lion. Closer and closer, Dave closed the gap between him and Kane. "Where's all the fucking yoghurts?" Kane clenched his fist on the fridge handle looking further inside. As he pulled his head out of the fridge Dave gripped Kane's black hooded jumper with power, a small tearing sound sang a tune.

"You know full well what I'm talking about!" Kane's face froze and slowly turned red, his eye slightly twitched.

"I've not made a lot this week only eighty pounds." Feeling sweat gathering, Kane rumbled through his hooded jacket flaunting the money. Dave released his grip and snatched the notes from Kane's hand, then watching his Dad fold away the money into his pocket.

"That's for your fucking cheek." Feeling angered Kane held his tongue staring at his Dad for a couple of seconds, breaking the silence by walking towards the stairs.

Slouching along the floor with slow steps, Kane walked up the stairs into his room. Sean sat on his bed playing Call of Duty on the Play Station. Kane reacted to Sean's presence confused.

"What are you doing in here you geek? Get out."

"Come on man. I'm on a six-kill streak!" Sean replied with excitement.

"You on my account?"

"Yeah," Sean replied engaged with the screen.

"Alright then. Haha you best not get killed you little gay boy." Kane responded as he sat on the opposite side of the bed leaning over.

"Shut up, anyway why did Dad have a go at you?" Sean curiously asked as Kane pulled out hundred and fifty pounds, which was tucked inside his socks and quickly counted it like a card shuffling dealer. The room had brown carpet fitted over the floor boards, a double bed in the centre of the room with a forty inch plasma television set connected to a chipped Sky box. A wardrobe on the left side of the room stood tall with black doors, underneath Kane's feet was a carefully cut piece of carpet which wasn't noticeable unless analysed.

Kane pulled back the flap of the carpet revealing a square piece of floor board. Kane took the piece of wood out gently like a lid. Coming across a cardboard shoebox he pulled off the lid and threw the money inside joining a hefty bed of notes. Kane swiftly put the compartment back to its original form stroking his hand across the carpet layer.

"Nothing to do with you." Kane bluntly spoke.

"You know if Dad finds out he will batter you," Sean muttered.

"He's not going to." Kane walked over to Sean snatching the controller off him. "Is he mate?" Kane turned his head.

"No. But if he did, he'd go mad, you no he's brought us up to be equal. Not greedy." Kane replied in a quite spiteful tone of voice.

"That's my fucking money Sean. I earned it not him. So why should I give him everything? I make sure you're alright don't I? I graft for it!" Sean paused for a few seconds, his hands started to shake a little as he spoke nervously.

"Principles… He's given us everything, a home and food on the table." Kane raged inside, he grew hungry wanting to kick Sean's head in.

"FUCK OFF SEAN! Go on, fuck off." Kane pushed him out the room. "When you get older you'll see. He's nothing more than a selfish prick." Sean straddled through Kane's bedroom door falling onto the landing. "And you ate the last fucking yoghurt you little shit! If you wasn't my blood I'd smash your fucking face in you little runt." Sean picked himself up off the floor bravely answering back stuttering on his first few words. "Y… Y… You're fuckin adopted." Sean bolted off like a gazelle, fleeing into the bathroom locking the door behind him.

Chapter Fourteen

Vince swept the floor gathering all the dirt into one corner, shovelling it up. He walked into the spare room and grabbed a mop and bucket which was filled with soapy water. Mopping away removing dirt stains from the floor, Vince turned his head looking at the empty room. Considering it wasn't long ago since the pub was filled with people, it seemed like a hollow shell. Emptiness carried through the bar spreading across the whole function room. Vince felt a vibration in his trouser pocket buzz buzz. Vince pulled out his phone, there was a text message from an unknown number. Clicking onto the message Vince read out the text.

Hi it's Daisy. I'm sorry about last night I didn't know what was going on in my head. I'm feeling a lot better, I was only sick because I hadn't drank in a while or maybe I just drank too much! So just wanted to apologise, hope you're okay x

Vince felt a blast of excitement and curiosity wondering to himself how she got his number.

Kane walked down the stairs feeling hungry with earphones plugged into his ears. 50 Cent blasted from his iPod.

"Many men... wish death on me" Kane ranted the lyrics with energy holding a sinister tone. He walked into the living room, passing the glass table, he looked for a takeaway leaflet amongst a pile of letters.

"Where was you last night?" Dave shouted across sat on the couch watching television.

"I slept at Kevin's. We had to sort some shit out." Kane picked up a curry house leaflet and skimmed his eyes through the menu. Dave stared at the TV screen and replied.

"O'right" Kane's eye caught onto the chicken tikka curry, his eyes lit up. He pulled out his phone and dialled the number.

"Alright me mate can I have a chicken tikka curry" An Asian man's voice replied.

"Do you want a bottle of coke with that?" Kane responded. "Yeah go on then! I'll come and pick it up in twenty mins or so." Dave's head turned towards Kane with lowered eyebrows.

"Get your brother summat." Kane looked back with a nod and walked into the hallway for his shoes.

"Do you want out?" Kane shouted through into the room.

"Erm...Pass us that menu."

Kane opened the front door and slammed it behind him, the noise ricocheted through the house.

"The little fucking wanker. I'll fucking murder him when he gets back!" Dave jumped up from his seat slightly angry, he picked up his phone from the side table, he looked down to see an unknown caller had rung him which he had missed and a voice message waiting to be opened.

A croaky voice pierced through the phone growing louder in tone.

"I'll fucking murder you! DO YOU HERE? You've fucked with the wrong tribe. My fucking tribe, I'll kill you and all your fucking posers." The sound of a gunshot was the last sound heard from the voice message. Dave felt a ball of anxiety starting to snowball, he paced up the stairs into his bedroom.

The room was medium sized with sliding wardrobes on the left side and a set of draws on the right. There was a double bed with black covers lay on top with matching black carpet. Dave ran up to his wardrobe and slid open the doors. All his clothes hung on hangers, designer shirts, jeans, suits and jackets hung from a metal pole. Hidden away at the back of all his clothes was a black bulletproof vest which could stop nine millimetre bullets piercing through. Dave had a shelf inside his wardrobe which had a medium sized safe secured to it. It was black steel with a spinning dial locking system. Dave span the dial left to right opening the safe, inside was a thin pair of leather gloves, cocaine blocks and passports. There were stacks of money on the first shelf inside the safe. In the middle were three magazines from a nine-millimetre Berretta 92f pistol that slept beside a card box of nine millimetre shells. The pistol was chromed stainless steel with brown wooded grips; it had the devil engraved on the side of it. Dave took the gun from the shelf and released the magazine checking all fifteen rounds were loaded tightly. Clicking the magazine back into the firearm, swiping his thumb across the safety switch he tucked the pistol into his pants. He pulled out a black bag from his jacket pocket, storing it on the bottom shelf. Dave looked further into his wardrobe and threw a black thick gilet jacket onto his bed. The jacket had a hood which had a grey fluffy trim around the edges and optional sleeves attached. It was straight out of the Louis Vuitton catalogue as it had the letters LV on the inside of the jacket and hood with the recurring design, there was a stitched LV logo on the right side of the chest. Dave's eyes stared towards the bullet proof vest, he stripped off his shirt and picked up the vest from its hanger. He slid the vest over his muscular body, the mirror at the back of him reflected his broad shoulders. The vest fitted tightly on his body, securely fastened around him like a seatbelt. He threw on a fresh black shirt and picked up his gilet jacket. He picked up the spare cartridges and stored them away in his jacket pocket. As he felt his hands inside the pocket he realised an object was missing, his metal knuckle duster had vanished from the pouch in the jacket. Putting on the coat Dave looked at himself in the mirror zipping up the jacket.

"That little shits been rifling through my shit!" Dave shouted in an aggressive tone. Walking out onto the landing Dave shouted to Sean.

"Sean… SEAN I'm going out for a few days. I left some money on the side for you."

"Alright!" Sean replied from his bedroom. Dave ran down the stairs into the hallway and exited through the front door. Sounds of his car engine roaring down the street echoed through the maze of streets, his wheels screeched around the corners. The car accelerated quicker than a pouncing tiger, speeding hysterically towards Bradshaw Road.

Vince sat at the bar chair looking at the mopped floor and clear tables. He spent all morning clearing away clutter wiping away stains off the tables. He was looking at the text message Daisy had sent him. Feeling flustered with excitement Vince made his first text back to Daisy.

Hi Daisy, don't be daft. I'm glad you're feeling better. Don't apologise! It was special. Vince nervously continued to write. *I was thinking maybe we could meet up sometime, and go for a walk. Xx* Vince felt a sense of awkwardness but bravely pressed send.

"Shit!" Vince panicked to himself. "What have I done?" He felt his nerves expand, the sensation of butterflies started to twirl inside him. Within a matter of minutes, Vince's phone struck with vibrations. Vince opened the text message with paranoia.

Hey! I'm not too busy today, you're so cute saying it was special. I'm sorry for being really drunk though. I bet you wanted to batter me haha xx :)

Vince's heart pumped quickly, he was bewildered. He stood up from the chair with a giant smile. He ran upstairs onto his landing and jumped into the bathroom singing to himself.

"WOOO! Get in there Vince!" Vince posed in the mirror. "Who's the man! I'm the man!" He stripped off a hundred miles per hour and climbed into the shower. Singing away to himself Vince turned on the tap. "You're the best......around! Nothing's gonna ever keep you down!" Vince sang out loud to himself, it had been a very long time since he had experienced this kind of happiness.

Daisy applied some makeup gently on her face, she walked to her dressing table skipping away, she sat down on the cushioned stool. She straightened her black curly hair with GHD irons. She picked up her phone and texted Vince.

What about 2 today? Xx

Daisy glanced around her room looking for something to wear, she opened her wardrobe and scanned through all her tops, jeans and outfits. Swiping with her hands her eye caught onto a white short dress which had a black belt linked to the fabric. She pulled the dress from the hanger lying it along her single bed. Her bed had cream covers and pillows. Daisy pulled up the dress and covered her body with it looking into the mirror on her dressing table. Slightly squinting at herself she threw the dress over her body. Her arms and head popped out of the dress, she walked towards the window overlooking the streets.

A few hours past from half eleven to quarter to two, Vince was all ready to leave. He wore black jeans with matching converse. A striped blue shirt and Chris's tweed jacket, Chris had left the jacket in the hallway when he started his shift. He would occasionally forget to take it home through tiredness after a long day's work, Mick would usually drop Chris off home. Rushing to the car after a long night wasn't odd. Vince buttoned up the grey jacket, he looked at himself in a mirror that hung from one of the function room's walls. It had a wooden frame and polished glass which enhanced the size of the room. Vince brushed the sides of his mousy brown hair down. His hair was thick on top and greased with gel then combed to the right side. He tightened his shoelaces and pulled his phone out from his pocket and text Daisy.

He felt a bolt of ecstatic excitement blast through his body. Nervousness silently crept up Vince's leg, making its way towards his stomach. The butterflies turned from a tickling sensation to swarming bees. Vince was about to break his cycle of depression, he hoped everything would run smooth. Typing away on his phone, his hands started to shake.

Hi Daisy, do you want me to meet you at the end of Mary Lee Road? xx

Vince nervously text feeling a rise of anxiety. Vince brushed himself down and walked towards the door, sounds of footsteps strolled down the stairs from the hallway. A tired voice shouted.

"Vince, where you going?" Mick grinded from his lungs.

"I'm just going out Dad, for a few hours." Vince nervously replied, with hands deeply dug inside his pockets.

"Alright, ring me if you need me," Mick responded.

Vince exited from the main entrance, Mick walked behind him to lock the front door. He made his way to the bar and sat on the tall stool resting his head in his hands. Yawning away Mick glanced his eyes towards the alcohol and slowly turned his head behind him. Reassuring himself that the bar was empty, he leant towards the draft of Carling and searched for a glass. Fumbling his hands behind the bar desperately searching like an urging addiction, craving for the taste. Mick finally pulled down on the pump and poured himself a pint. Taking his first sip he felt anxious, nobody was in the pub except him. All alone and no jobs to keep him occupied Mick gulped the pint. His skin turned purple and cheeks bright red, he looked at himself in the reflection of the glass.

"Fuck sake... ARRGHH!" Mick bellowed into the atmosphere, he pulled out his Nokia mobile phone and slammed it onto the table. "Why Lord? Why!" Mick slammed his bare hands onto the bar. "WHY?" Mick silently stressed. He picked up the pint glass and poured the alcohol down his throat spilling all over his dirty white pyjama top. The Carling ran like a waterfall from Mick's quivering lips and down his chin.

BUZZ! BUZZ! Mick's Nokia sent sounds bouncing across the wood. Eyes blood shot and wrinkled, big bags under his eyes, Mick looked down at his phone. Pressing enter the name Morgan appeared on the screen.

"1 new message from Morgan," Mick read from the phone screen. "You alright Mick? Hope you're in good health, its Dad's birthday at the end of the month and I was wondering if you were coming up to the grave. Your welcome to stay at mine for a few days. Speak to you soon."

Mick stared at the text message for a few minutes. He sat still and made no noise, not a sound. In a trance of disbelief, he struggled to speak, tears ran down his face but no sound of weeping was heard. His face screwed up, frown marks left rows of embedded scars on his face. Holding his head with his hands, looking towards the floor a giant roar of emotion furiously cut open from his lips. After sitting in silence Mick stood from the stool, black bottoms hung around his hips, a grey robe fell open from his body as he banged onto the wooden table.

"AARGH WHY LORD? WHAT HAVE I DONE TO DESERVE SO MUCH PAIN!!! If hell is what you wish for me, why not take MY LIFE?" SMASH! SHATTER! Mick threw his glass onto the floor, glass crystals scattered across the wooden floor. Leaning his back against the wooden bar he slid to the floor closing his eyes.

Vince walked down Mary Lee Road, it was windy but not too extreme. The sun shined onto the pavement making Vince stand out like a silhouette. He squinted to see where he was walking. Mary Lee Road had rows of semi-detached houses and some single houses were all blocked together like Lego, cars would drive along the road frequently so all you could hear was the muttering of engines and tyres colliding with gravel. The clouds surfaced metaphorically like dancing sheep, fluffy and soft being herded by sheep dogs. Once the clouds cleared, they blocked the sun creating a cool and dry environment. The overcast created by flocking sheep recovered the sight back into Vince's eyes. Vince pulled out his phone to a text message from Daisy.

Will be there soon xx.

Vince continued to walk down towards the end of Mary Lee Road looking towards the traffic lights at the end of the street, he saw a young girl with black hair appear walking past the traffic lights towards him. Vince walked further towards the figure as he got closer he started to recognise who it was. His heart started to beat rapidly. They became only a few meters apart. Daisy smiled.

"Hi."

"You alright?" Vince gulped, his palms began to sweat.

"Yeah. Do you fancy going to the park?" Daisy asked.

"Er… yeah" Vince replied. Daisy and Vince walked up Mary Lee Road towards Broadhurst Park.

Daisy's facial muscle's slightly tensed as the sun rays hit her face.

Chapter Fifteen

A black Mercedes parked half on the pavement of Beverley Avenue, a block of flats overlooked the cars parked on the street. The view from the top overlooked the city of Manchester. It was six pm and as winter was approaching dark nights started to visit earlier.

"Smiffy, are you fucking listening?" Scott shouted.

Smiffy was a fat fellow who wore clothes strictly from JD's shelves. He was an old-school buddy of Dave's, they had grown up together. He made his living through scraping off the back of some of Dave's ventures. He wore matching sports clothes, black jogging bottoms and top with a Nike tick sown under his nipple. He was fond of KFC and fast food which resulted in his figure.

"Ay, fat arse, Dave's going to be here soon so you best cough up some info." Scott walked into his small kitchen and grabbed a bar of chocolate.

"Course I will, I always do. Give me a bit of that." Scott moved the chocolate towards him with his hand and laughed as Smiffy tried to take a piece.

"Fuck off you cheeky bastard!"

"Come on, I'm starving." Scott started to laugh.

"You walked in with Colonel's Fried fuckin chicken stinking my gaf out. You can do one Smiffy."

A loud knock was heard at the door. BANG! BANG! Scott answered the door to Dave.

"Jesus 'r' kid, don't break it down." Dave walked into the flat slightly wheezing.

"Sorry mate, is Smiffy here?"

"Yeah. He's been trying to eat my house apart." Smiffy sat on a red leather couch licking his fingers.

"Right lads I text you both earlier that some cunts sent me a death threat. Scott mentioned to me earlier that you've got some info on this shit, SMIFFY?" Dave's face wrinkled together, "So come on, I haven't got all day Smiffy, me and Scott have got shit to do." Scott sat down on the couch facing Smiffy and Dave sat beside him.

"Right, I was having a drink at the Eight Bell's in Ardwick and these heavy's came in. There was about seven of them and some young lads were with them. Some proper fuckin tearaways. And I heard this one, well a few actually talking loudly about the Devil." Dave's eyes lit up like a lighter, Scott scratched his head.

"Go on..." Dave intriguingly spoke.

"And then this big lad and I mean BIG gripped this scrawny kid by the neck and said who the fucks took the stash. This man starts crying weeping like a bitch. And utters the word Devil."

"Stop story telling Smiffy, spit it out," Scott interrupted.

"Well, he screams and he doesn't stop. The landlord kicks off and tells him to take whatever outside. This big man shouts in the scrawny fellow's face. I'M GONNA KILL YOU AND THIS FUCKIN DEVIL. I walked outside to light up and he's their gripping this kid throwing him about like a ragdoll. Shouting shit out like I'm gonna kill him and all his fuckin posers. So, the kid shouts back pleading in a croaky voice. I'll do it. I'll do it."

"Fuckin hell!" Scott spoke out loud as his lungs deflated. Dave grew angry inside.

"If he's as bold enough to threaten my life, I'm just as bold to take his." Dave passionately spoke. "Good work Smiffy." Dave passed Smiffy a couple of notes. "Can you get me that CCTV footage?"

"I'll see to it within the week."

Dave replied, "I want it posted through that door by tomorrow morning." Dave spoke with a serious tone.

"On that voicemail he had a croaky voice, didn't he?"

"Yeah. I think I may know who it is. We kidnapped him a few week ago. He's that newly christened drug dealer." Scott replied. "We'll watch that footage to confirm it's him. An I want to see who this cunt's working for!"

Kane walked down Parkinson Street to meet to meet Kevin, it was 8:10am and the lads were on their way to school. They arrived early to distribute their merchandise for the day with members of their clan. Lucas and a group of lads waited outside a shop perched on the corner of Regent street.

Walking towards the group Kevin mentioned briefly, "You heard anything from Aiden?"

"No," Kane replied. "I'm not arsed Kevin. Fuck him. He can sling it, I don't want that kid involved with us." Kevin didn't respond they continued to walk towards the group of lads.

"Easy boys!" Lucas blurted in high spirits.

"Alright." Kane and Kevin both replied.

"You got the load then eye? Got these lads to get the shit in." Kane swung a JD bag from his shoulder and passed it over to Lucas. Inside were Lucozade's and chocolate bars, Kane pulled out a pack of Richmond cigarettes.

"I'll tell you what lads, I fuckin need this," he grunted. Lucas passed out the merchandise between the gang of lads. "I want the money in my pocket by the end of the day. We'll meet back here."

A voice spoke out from the group of lads, "How much are you paying us?" Kane walked over towards the sound and looked at a young school boy.

"What year you in?"

"Year eight," The voice replied. The boy had his blazer buttoned up, he wore black leather shoes and had black spikey hair. Kane pulled the cigarette from his lips and exhaled the smoke. A smirk protruded from Kane's face.

"Listen kid, I don't fucking know you. But you're aware of me. Give me that bag, NOW." The boy passed over his school bag freshly loaded. Kane snatched the bag from his hands. "You're not getting fuck all." He swung the bag onto his shoulder and stared at the boy.

"Don't be grim G," Lucas urged.

"Cool it bro, this kid's got to learn his lesson. He's lucky I don't twist him up." Kane spoke in front of the group. He squared up towards the small boy, "You see this bag, it's mine." The boy looked back speechless feeling threatened.

The group of lads walked through the school gates laughing with banter. They walked into the school and split off into different directions. "Right lads I'll meet you all at dinner in the courtyard," Kane ordered.

The 'Smoking Barrel' was silent, Vince pulled the covers off his head. He looked towards the alarm clock that sat on his bedside table. 8:30am he read with his eyes.

"Shit! I'm going to be late." Vince lay in his bed but didn't move, trying to find the energy inside his body. He stretched looking upwards towards the ceiling then kicked his legs to the side. His school clothes were on the bannister facing the stairs. Scampering across the floor Vince climbed the mountain of clothes looking for boxer shorts and socks.

"Dad!" Vince shouted. "DAD!" Vince's voice echoed through the room lingering onto the landing.

"Yeah?" Mick shouted back still half asleep. "WHAT?" Mick belched.

"Have you got any spare socks?" Vince stood up and looked across the floor. He walked out onto the landing passing his school uniform walking into Mick's room. "Have you got some?"

Mick lay on his bed eyes closed heavily breathing, "There's some in that drawer." Mick slightly lifted his hand. Vince walked over to the draw and borrowed a pair of socks. He walked back onto the landing and threw the rest of his clothes on in a hurry. He paced down the stairs skipping his breakfast.

"Thanks Dad. See you when I get home." Vince ran out of the pub heading towards the bus stop.

Vince checked his pockets feeling anxious, searching for change. He waited for the 24 to pass, it was the quickest bus towards Saint Brooks High. Looking at his phone for the time, it was 8:45am. Vince felt a shiver of Mr Ahil's aggression for his lateness. He was his Tutor, every morning he would go through power point slides on 'How to be a good student' and all the school regulations. He always checked the student's clothes to check they were the official school uniform and ask to see everyone's pen and diary. Through rushing, Vince forgot his school bag but didn't realise.

The bus started to make its way down Mary Lee Road, Vince held his hand out waving it side to side. He felt the cold draft of the wind hit his body, his arms started to shake through the blazer as he waited patiently but feeling the stress. The bus eventually came to a stop. Whoosh! The doors of the bus swiped open, Vince stepped on board and threw a five pound note at the driver.

"Day saver please." The sound of the ticket box crunched as it printed off the day saver. Vince made his way to the top of the bus climbing the stairs.

Sitting at the front he saw a reflection in the window of all the seats being unattended and empty, he looked upon the concrete jungle of houses and roads. The bus picked up its pace and weaved between cars turning left at the bottom of Mary Lee Road. The vibrations made by the bus's engine rippled through Vince's seat. After a twenty minute journey the bus started to pass Saint Brooks High. Vince saw the school building through the window, it was a rectangular shaped building with standard orange tinted bricks. It had a fence built around the school which had an opening in the centre to enter the premises. There were other entrances but the centre entrance was most popular as it led straight to the South doors. Late comers had to go to Main Reception

Vince walked along the school path towards the building, he checked to see if the South doors were open but they were locked.

"Oh god," Vince sighed and walked towards the Reception with his head sloped towards the floor. He knocked on the glass door of the Reception and a woman who sat behind the desk pressed a switch to let him in.

"Alright love, come and sign yourself in." The woman had a gentle voice, she was in her forties and wore a white shirt and designer glasses glued to her eyes as she dismissed Vince.

Vince walked up a spiral staircase which centred itself in the receptions area. He passed the English corridor and turned left at the bottom moving towards his form room. M3 was a Math's classroom and his Tutor was the head of Maths, Mr Ahil was an Asian man who had a black beard and wore long white gowns called Dishdashas, his hair was thick black and a mole sat upon his cheek. He was a kind man but strict was an understatement.

"Right everybody, please get out your pens and pencils, rulers and diaries," Mr Ahil spoke loudly to the class. Vince pushed open the classroom door with a squeak, breaking the silence everyone in the room stared across to Vince.

"Sorry I'm late Mr Ahil, I missed the bus!" Vince spoke flustered with his eyes scrolling across the floor.

"Vince, please come in and sit down, it's half past the hour. Get out your equipment also." Vince sat himself down at the closest table.

"Shit." Vince muffled under his breath.

"Get out your equipment Vince!" Mr Ahil's voice started to raise louder.

"I...I... I haven't got anything Sir." Vince stuttered. Mr Ahil rose from his seat and walked around each table checking each student.

"It's good to see everyone's in full uniform. What did you say Vince?"

"I haven't got anything Sir, not even a pen," Vince proclaimed. A bolt of thunder sparked from Mr Ahil's voice.

"How dare you come into my classroom with no equipment and pounce in here late. I've been mellow all morning but you've broken that now."

"Sir, I'm sorry, I'm sorry, I missed the bus by seconds." The clock on the wall started to creep its way towards the next period of the day. A huge bell rang out through the speakers in the classroom which crossed every classroom.

"Right, I'm going to let you move on with the day, and attend your second period BUT I WILL NOT have this BEHAVIOUR again!" Mr Ahil's voice raised then simmered like waves in the sea.

Vince left his seat and walked out of the door with students rushing past him from behind. He stared into the corridors of what looked like frantically swimming fish. Students raced past each, dodging in and out, rushing to their next lesson. The day started to fly by. Vince stared through the window of his second lesson of the day, English. It was coming closer towards the end of the lesson and he noticed Kane and Kevin approaching the courtyard outside. The clouds gathered together in the sky looking all grey. Everyone outside seemed to be huddling together in groups and the sounds of footballs spiralling through the air seemed to have died down. Vince exited the classroom as the teacher gave him daggers for not having his pen. He walked along the balcony and headed towards the stairs stationed in the centre of the school building. People barged past Vince like he didn't exist, like a walking ghost transparent to others as they knocked into him like bowling balls. Vince's triceps started to lock, growing in intensity.

"Fuckin move you dickhead!" Vince's voice nearly shattered the glass window of transparency bouncing towards the ears of a taller student who barged past him. The figure of the boy's head turned and continued to walk forward. Vince felt his heart slowly heat as he reached the staircase. "For God's sake!" Vince thought to himself. At stairwell was a cluster of students walking down and others moving up, it was like a dual carriage way with two lanes. The friction of people didn't slide but rumbled and ruffled together. Anxiety started to clot inside Vince, his patience started to wear. With his neck growing stiff with the rest of his limbs he clenched his hands and squeezed hard. The sound of screaming girls screeched through the open space of the building. Vince felt the pressure of the colliding sexes clash.

Pressure struck his spine as people from behind started to prod his back.

Vince got to the bottom of the stairs holding back all his anger; he paced towards the courtyard doors to get some fresh air, in hope it would help cool him down. Passing the social groups, he pulled open the doors. Kane and Kevin were with their clan hovering around like bees. Some of the clan would stalk around the courtyard like scouts reporting back to the queen bee.

"So yeah this fuckin bird Maxine was all over me giving me the eye," Kane started to boast to his group. "And then the next minute I was on it. She was filthy gagging for it like a dog with his bone."

"Nah! Nah G! No way!" Lucas giggled to himself, "Take no notice lads, he's full of it." Sounds of giggles started to spread amongst the few.

"I fuckin SWEAR DOWN lads. Kaneo doesn't chat shit!" Kane bantered with Lucas and the other lads.

"Haha remember when you burned that sweaty immigrant!" Sean spoke up. "That Vince the prince?"

"Oh that dicked fam!" Lucas laughed. "WASTEMAN!" Lucas gently held out his fist towards Sean and tapped his hand.

"He knocks me sick that cunt. Greasy bastard. Nothing pisses me off more than people who don't belong here, this place is my town. He's not one of us." Kane pointed out with a nod of his head. "Look there he is the prick." Kevin stood watching everything that was going on, he picked up on Kane's aggression and tried to ease his temper.

"Cool it boys. Chill yeah."

"Kevin! Shut up."

Vince stood in the corner of the courtyard; he felt the cold breeze hit his face. He checked whether Daisy had sent him any texts. Putting the phone back into his pocket and looking around the square yard, Vince took a breath making awkward eye contact with Kane. He felt a small dose of fear creep up his spine as the last time he bumped into him wasn't far from memory. Bruised and battered reminders hit the light in Vince's eyes.

"Best get back inside," Vince thought to himself feeling a gathering of sweat. Vince slowly walked backwards scraping the wall behind him. His legs stopped moving standing stiff losing control, courageous thoughts started to alarm Vince's mind. "Stand firm, Vince. You're fine. Strength is in your heart." The inner voice inside Vince's head started to repeat growing louder. Vince's biceps started to intake more blood as it raced around his body. Fingers started to shake and nerves spiralled around him.

Kane barged past his group and spotted Vince leaning against the wall.

"Who's up for a fucking laugh! Come on lads!" Kane shouted to his peers. "Come on boys." The group followed behind Kane feeling the excitement spreading among them.

"What you gonna do Kane?" Sean shouted.

"Twist him up the little gimp" A voice shouted from behind.

"Waste man. Man, he stinks bro." Kane walked straight towards Vince with his shoulders back and chest out. The group shouted things out from the back.

"Dickhead... Dirty bastard. He's a little wanker!" The voices shouted out. Vince felt intimidated as he watched the crowd gather towards him. He heard the insults thrown over towards him as he stared at Kane's entertained smile.

"Alright there, Pikey bastard?" Kane's eyes lit up like a lighter, with a glowing smile.

"What do you want?" Vince spoke loudly.

"Calm down. I just came to say hello," Kane grinned.

Lucas started to laugh with a high pitch, "Ay, has he still got them pictures of his mam on him, what you were telling me about?" Lucas looked towards Kane. Vince stood quietly listening, feeling intimidated he looked towards the exit of the courtyard, Kane picked up on his nervous behaviour and moved closer towards him entering his personal space.

"Why don't you get them pictures out ay? So me and the lads can knock one out tonight over her."

"I'd rinse her me! If she was here," Lucas shouted with arrogance.

Glaring back at the group of lads he felt his heart beat harder with more intensity. The inner voices started to break up inside him.

"Hold, hold, don't back down." The voices started to drown out the fear motivating Vince to stand up for himself, turning his anger into strength. Vince held himself together as he felt emotionally unstable. The comments about his mother tipped him closer and closer towards a peak of aggression. All the training he had been doing, all the hours he spent on the bag punching his heart out had all been building up to this moment. FACING HIS FEARS! Vince launched himself forward swinging his fists wild like a spinning helicopter blade. He grabbed Kane with two hands and pushed him backwards. Kane scampered back onto his feet and stood at the back of the group watching everyone kick off. Feeling bewildered he laughed.

"I've finally released the DEVIL."

Falling onto the floor, Vince was then thrown against the wall behind him by Lucas and Kevin. Vince's arm stretched out towards Lucas's tie, he pulled the tie downwards clenching towards his neck. Repeatedly throwing punches and kneeing Lucas to the head.

"Aaarghhh!" Vince groaned as he unleashed the warrior within. Lucas was crouched towards the floor taking a shocking beating. Kevin tried to pull Vince off Lucas but his arms locked like a violent dog on lock jaw. "COME ON THEN YOU FUCKING PRICKS!" Vince bellowed at the peak of his lungs in a husky tone. Vince started to take a bruising off three members of the group. A giant crowd of people started running towards the scene and started to chant.

"Fight! Fight! Fight!…SHIT ITS VINCE!" Voices of students in the courtyard started to echo. Unable to fight back with his hands full Vince squeezed Lucas's throat harder until he coughed for air throwing him onto the floor. One of the lads caught onto Vince's hair whilst he was still attached to Lucas, he immediately threw a head butt straight to the lad's nose busting it open. Like a blood thirsty lion defending its pride, Vince roared, slashing his claws landing combinations into the second hooded figure. Everyone in the courtyard was shocked and started to surround the action. With the crowd shouting out Vince went into a dark state. His eyes diluted watching blood spray onto the figures lips and cheeks as he stained the person's skin with his bare hands.

The teachers on duty looked through the glass doors leading to the courtyard. They witnessed masses of students chanting like it was a final game of the FA. The teachers ran outside but were over-powered by students.

"GET TO YOUR LESSONS!" The voices of teachers rang like a telephone.

Inside the pit of people, Vince stood square on staring down at a hooded figure. Flames of courage burnt his heart.

"Come on then you fucking prick!" With blood shot eyes and a slightly red face the figure jumped towards Vince trying to drag him to the floor. With punches just below his face, Vince pelted each thrusting punch into the skin headed face of Kane's crew member. The figure started to go into berserk mode like he was chopping down trees with his rotating fists. Vince tried to step back in time but it was too late. A wild thrust connected with his face. Bruise marks started to boil on his cheeks. Vince swallowed some of the blood from his busted lip igniting his furious reaction. Retaliating like a bull, Vince dived towards the figure with strong combinations. Left, left, right hook followed with a left upper cut. The figures face dispersed firing back wild punches. Storming through the returning blows Vince attacked viciously firing his punches accurately. Vince moved in tight taking the figures fire. Vince gritted his teeth and snapped his hand out towards the hooded student's jumper catching onto it like a hook. He tore his jumper but placed himself in a dominant position punching into his skull. The figure started to cry, blood merged upon his face. Vince released his grip and stared at him on the floor. A tear of anger rolled down the side of Vince's face.

"Is there anybody else?" He shouted with a husky voice. His heart rate was pulsing and body shook leaving his hands to rattle. The sound of the bell rang out ending the break. The teachers still struggled to move the crowd.

Kane looked towards Vince and stood quietly with Sean by his side.

"Fuckin hell," Sean hissed. Kevin helped Lucas to his feet and vanished into the crowd. Members of Kane's clan re-grouped behind Kane staring in disbelief. The voices of the crowds shouted into the air.

"Drop him"

"Vince the prince, Vince the prince"

"Go on you little leprechaun!" The voices continued like an audience at a Colosseum. Vince stood and stared into Kane's eyes. But all Kane responded with was a smile.

After ten minutes of lesson wasted outside, Miss Kay was called on the radio. Within a couple of minutes she was there with a team of ten.

"Everyone back to your lessons!" She screamed out loud with other colleagues. The crowd started to evaporate, Kane picked up on Miss Kay's presence and fled with his pack of wolves. Still standing bruised and torn, Vince watched the crowd disappear. His heart was still pumped and adrenaline still surfacing. A woman walked up behind Vince, as he watched the hooded figure scamper along the floor catching his feet he ran with a limp. A hand touched Vince. Vince turned sharply on edge.

"You're coming with me Vince." Miss Kay spoke in a shocked tone. Miss Kay and Vince walked through the hallway of the school towards the Isolation corridor. After all the noise and violence the silence felt unusual to Vince's ears.

"What am I doing about my lesson? What's going on?" Vince panicked.

"Calm down. Calm down. That lesson is the least of your worries." Miss Kay replied gently.

Vince placed his hands on the table and stared at them as they shook. Tear after tear ran down his face. Vince felt a snowballing of emotion crash through him. His face turned purple as he wept. "Arrgh!" Sounds mumbled under his breath. "Four years," he muttered. Miss Kay had never experienced sitting in front of an emotional wreck of a student, her Sherlock brain switched on as she attempted to investigate.

"What do you mean four years? Vince, it's okay. You can talk to me." Vince's face crinkled up and tear streaks lay on his skin like road lines. "I'm just going to get you some tissue Vince, would you like some water?" Vince looked at the table with weeping sounds but didn't reply. His breaths were quicker and a lump clung to his throat. He heard Miss Kay leaving the room with the twisting of a door knob.

All alone in the square room, Vince heard the voices in his head. All was silent giving Vince nothing but the sound of his thoughts. He kept seeing images in his head of the blood and Kane's smile.

"Why was he smiling?" Vince questioned himself. Vince heard the door handle twist as Miss Kay walked back into the room with a plastic white cup of water and tissues. She placed them on the table in front of Vince.

"Here you go, I got you some water just in case." Vince stared at the water but picked up the tissues and dried his face. His eyes were still watery just waiting to leak at any moment. "So, what did you mean by four years?" Miss Kay spoke with concern.

"I...I..." Vince stuttered. "What am I... I ... here for?" Mumbled Vince.

"I'm here to help you Vince. And to investigate what happened outside. I came across your record yesterday and you've had more accidents in the school than any other student has and it grabbed my attention." Miss Kay spoke eagerly trying to get a response. Vince tilted his head upwards towards Miss Kay.

Vince gathered his words together, "Kane and his mob have been making my life at school a living hell! And I don't understand why this school allows him to run it. I don't get why you care all of a sudden. You teachers are all the same." A few tears dropped from Vince's eyelids. Miss Kay looked back annoyed.

"I'm not like any of the teachers at this school. I'm not classed as one so don't refer to me as one. I'm the Head of Isolation."

"See, you don't listen, you're all the same to me." Vince spoke with attitude.

"Vince I need you to tell me what happened out there, I can help you. Kane Crossling and those associated to him have been bullying other students like yourself and causing chaos to the school's merchandise through their distribution of Lucozade and chocolate." Vince sat and took no notice of Miss Kay.

"Miss, when can I go?"

"Well you were involved in a fight and it's against the school's policy to let you leave this room till half three."

"What?" Vince spoke louder. "I'm the victim in all of this. I'm the victim." Vince's blood started to boil like a pan of water on a hob.

"Tell me what happened out there?" Miss Kay urged.

"All I did was defend myself and stood up to that pack of hyenas. And you want to cage me in here like an animal." Vince started to raise his voice.

"Look Vince, I want to help you." Miss Kay replied.

"Help me? You're locking me in here all day and that's classed as help."

Miss Kay shrugged. "Look Vince, we can go to the Headmaster and you can tell him about your experience at the school. You could be a great asset to show the Principal what a monster Kane is. He might take action." Vince listened carefully slightly shaking his head.

Chapter Sixteen

The road was quiet outside the 'Smoking Barrel, Mick threw on some plain clothes, a dark coloured shirt and black pants with leather shoes. Bang! Bang! A loud knock at the door beated like a drum waking Mick from his daydream. Mick ran down the stairs and shouted towards the door.

"We're closed!"

"Closed?" The voice shouted back. "It's me, your brother Oden." Mick cranked open the thick wooden door.

"Why didn't you let me know you were visiting?" The thick open wooden doors revealed Oden dressed in a black woven jacket with black suit pants and pointed leather shoes. His hair was coloured black but was trimmed on the sides blending into the outlined stubble.

"What's with the long face? I thought you'd be happy to see me." Oden snubbed.

"You could've rang to let me know." Oden walked through the doors of the 'Smoking Barrel' and looked around nodding his head.

"You've changed it since I was last here."

"Not much, just added a few mirrors to the walls."

"Was going to say the room felt bigger," Oden scratched his chin and spoke mildly "Can I have a drink then or what?" Mick walked over to the bar.

"We haven't got much in to be fair, it wasn't too long ago we had a do." Oden looked towards the bar and his eyes caught onto a bottle of Martel brandy.

"Can I have a drop of that?" Oden pointed towards the bottle with his finger.

"It will cost you." Mick laughed grabbing the bottle and two glasses. Mick and Oden sat down at the bar as Mick poured the brandy blurting out a few words.

"What brings you here then?" Oden picked up the glass raising it to his mouth before taking a swig.

"Well, it's Da's birthday at the end of the month, and I thought I'd come and see you before we go up to the cemetery." A small silence was left between them as Mick poured the brandy down his throat. "You are coming, aren't you?" Oden curiously asked. Mick banged the glass onto the table and replied softly.

"Yeah."

Mick sat on the stool and stared into Oden's face.

"Remember that time when we were only little and Dad made us stay up all night planting seeds." Oden shook his head with a smile.

"Yeah. Morgan always got out of it. Golden boy."

"He'd always say life's a seed." Mick's eyes slightly watered.

"You know I finally get what he meant all these years." The sound of glass tapped the wooden bar table, Oden's head tilted towards the glass.

"He was a good man. A great man. He would've done the right thing."

Mick's eyes widened. "Right thing? What...?" Oden pulled a smug face, his cheeks tensed and throat burned.

"Nothing."

Mick tensed his hands. "Go on."

Oden polished off his glass and turned his body towards Mick. "Well, Da would have done something if he was still here." Mick's face scrunched together with his eyebrows touching, in an aggressive tone he spoke loudly.

"He was an old man Oden. It would've killed him. Seeing his home burn to ashes."

"Killed him like it's been destroying you for how many years?" Oden replied boldly. "Do you think Da would've wanted us to do nothing about it? They didn't just take our home. They took away our life."

"SHUT UP! You selfish bastard. They took the mother of my child away from me. You fucking idiot. You come here to talk to me about revenge."

"You know it's right. Them fuckers are going to pay. Every single one of them!"

"I will not be a part of this! I have Vince to care for. And if he ever found out, what type of a father would I be ay?"

"One that cares." Oden responded. Mick listened with a pause, the comment floated around his head brewing anger. He pulled out from the bar table and stood on his feet.

"It's time you should be going." Oden looked inside his glass.

"I'm not finished," He commented.

"Yes you are." Mick snatched the brandy from the table and put it on the alcohol shelf.

The creaking of the wooden door pushed open, Vince walked into the 'Smoking Barrel' with a swollen face and a busted lip. His face was sweating and eyes squinting. Mick looked across the bar witnessing his son's injuries.

"Vince, are you okay? What happened to you?" Oden span around on his chair towards Vince.

"Alright, Oden?"

"Jesus Christ that's going to be a whopper." Oden clowned.

"Come here son, sit down. I'll get you some frozen peas." Oden stared deeply into Vince's eyes.

"What happened to you?"

"It's nothing." Mick walked back into the room with a bag of frozen peas.

"Take this Vince," Mick spoke with care, feeling concerned he sat beside Vince. "So what happened to you?"

"Really it's nothing." Vince leant the peas against his cheeks. "I'm gonna go and take a shower."

"You aren't leaving until you tell me what happened boy." Mick's voice raised.

"I... I got into a fight. Well this kid was intimidating me. I couldn't take it no more. I couldn't digest the fear any longer." Vince's hand slightly shook tapping the bar with his fingernails.

"Who was it?" Mick responded.

"A group of them."

"Fuckin hell, you took on a gang. How many was there?"

"Around eight but not all of them jumped in."

"He definitely takes after his uncle Oden." Oden smiled.

"Do you want me to go in and talk to the Head?"

"No. I'm alright."

"You best get the lad a drink. He's fuckin earned it!"

"He's too young for all that."

"He's got Irish blood in him. Of course he can drink. That's in our blood too!"

Vince laughed. "I'm alright Oden. I'll pass on that one."

"Shouldn't you get going now Oden? It's getting late." Oden smiled and started to laugh.

"I thought I'd stay for supper," Oden cracked up and laughed with hysterics. "I'm only joking. I go back tonight. My flights at eight so I best be on my way."

"It's good to see you Uncle Oden."

"I, It's good to see you too, keep out of trouble you." Mick walked towards the door with Oden.

"Next time let me know when you're coming up. And don't do anything STUPID!" Mick lowered his voice but spoke with intensity.

"See you soon laddie!" Oden shouted back towards Vince. A muffled bye was heard in response. "See you a few days before Dad's birthday then." Oden instructed as he walked through the wooden doors of the 'Smoking Barrel'.

A few days passed and Vince hadn't gone back to school. He stood in the spare room bending down towards the floor picking up an old pair of boxing gloves. He looked at the punch bag and started to shadow box, pushing out a variety of combinations into thin air. Hiss! Hiss! Vince exhaled. He stood on his side and moved in and out moving closer towards the bag.

"Arrghhh!" Vince shouted as he lay a punch into the leather. He punched right, he punched left repeating his thrusts. The bag swung wild as Vince turned his back. He got down on all fours and started to do push ups building his body stronger, Vince felt a craving of energy to enhance his training. The sound of footsteps was heard as Vince proceeded with crunches, the door opened and Mick walked inside.

"It's 8am, are you going in school today?"

Vince replied breathless. "No."

"O'right. When you going back in then?"

"I'll go back in a few days, I don't want anyone to see my face. It's still puffed out." Vince chewed on the skin inside his mouth.

"Why don't you go to the boxing gym?" Mick watched Vince force his body forward working his abdominal muscles.

"I've not really thought of it," Vince replied.

"Well you've locked yourself in here for a week and that's great. All I heard last night was you hitting that bag for hours on end. That takes some energy." Vince jumped to his feet and walked up to his Dad.

"I'm gonna get a shower. Let me know if there's anything you need doing."

"I'll hold you to that!" Vince laughed as he walked out of the room running up the stairs as he headed towards the bathroom.

Kane and Sean walked towards the bus stop, it was a dry day but the wind blew heavy making the streets cold. There was a short silence between the two boys as they approached the stop. The sound of cars drove past the streets and plastic bags blew along with the wind. Kane wore a black Nike jumper under his blazer, he pulled the hood over his head. The strong wind started to irritate him, his face turned slightly red due to the cold.

"Fuck sake. This weather's doing my head in" Outburst Kane.

"I know!" Sean replied. "You know what Kane? I can't believe how Vince went on a rampage. He took on nearly half of the lads we had with us."

Kane smiled and his eyebrows rose. "I know...I didn't think Lucas could get any blacker. But his face is fucked up royal!"

"And the other two lads who was selling for us, he wiped them out. He's was fucking well mad, I would've banged him out obviously, but why have soldiers if you don't use them."

Kane burst out with laughter, "Who do you think you are Mr Big? He wouldn't've touched you."

Sean shouted back quickly. "Yeah… because he knows."

"Shut up Sean. Come on get a step on we're gonna miss this bus. Time is money." Kane and Sean sprung into a light jog. "Come on you snail, I can see it stopping." Sean started to gasp for air.

"Fucking hell, it best stop." The number 182 bus slowed down as it reached the stop. Kane and Sean flashed their week passes like FBI badges and ran up the stairs of the double decker bus. Sitting at the front of the upstairs seats, Sean stared into space looking at the passing cars, he turned his head slightly in Kane's direction. "So what you going to do about him?" Kane sat with his feet kicked up against the glass window.

"Vince?"

"Yeah."

"I've been thinking." Sean stared back into the window watching the traffic lights change.

"Are you going to jump him? You've got to do something. What if other people start coming out of their place because of him. We've got to send a message. So everyone's reminded why you don't fuck with us." Kane scratched his head and pulled out his lighter and started to flick the flame on and off.

"I suppose you're right. But how do you suppose we do that?" Sean's face glowed with excitement.

"Well, I'd gather all the lads together and wait for him to come out of school and attack him. At that time, everyone would be coming out. So they would see how dangerous we are."

"And what message would that leave?" Kane sighed. "You see, this is why I run things. You're too predictable and don't see the bigger picture."

"Huh?" Sean muttered. The bus slowly arrived outside the school, Saint Brooks High stood tall looking over all of the flooding students. Kane stood up from his seat and pushed Sean towards the stairs.

"Come on, get a move on." Kane's voice raised. The two boys jumped off the bus and joined into the flood of students walking down the pathway to the school's entrance.

Vince sat in the function room at the table. There was a glass of pure orange filled to the top just waiting to be drunk. Vince picked up the glass and took a deep swig of the juice. The flavour of orange was sharp down his throat giving him a fresh sensation. He looked at his phone and read the recent texts from Daisy.

Mick shouted from the hallway, "I'm going to go out for a bit Vince. I'll be back in a few hours."

"Okay." Vince started to create a new message to Daisy.

Hi Daisy, I know you're in school today but I couldn't help but text you and tell you how beautiful you are. I was just thinking to myself that it's been a week or two since we last went out and I was wondering if you'd like to come up to mine when you finish school plus my Dad's going out for a few hours xxx

Vince pressed the send button on his mobile and picked up the glass finishing off the orange juice.

Mick walked into the room and headed straight towards the door. He wore black timberland boots and a black waterproof jacket.

"See you later Vince. Give me a ring if you need anything."

"Thanks Dad, will do." Vince replied with a small sense of excitement building up inside him. The sound of the door banged as Mick shut it behind him. Vince's phone vibrated, he looked down towards his screen and opened the text message from Daisy.

Hi Vince, I'm in lesson at the moment. I'll give you a ring on my break so keep your ears open for it. And yeah that sounds good. I'll give you a text when I get out and meet you. Xxx

Vince felt joy as he replied to the message.

Okay. Look forward to our phone call. And it's okay, I'll meet you at your school if you want xxx

Vince pushed the table forward by an inch and stood up from his chair. He walked over to the sink behind the bar and placed the glass in it. He turned on the tap and swilled the glass with soapy water scrubbing it with a bristle brush. Ring! Ring! Ring! Ring! The landline phone rang loudly making Vince jumped, he looked across the bar for a tea towel to dry his hands on. He then ran into the hallway where the telephone was based, mounted on the wall in a plastic frame. Vince answered the phone to a male voice with a strong Irish accent similar to his Dad's.

"Hello? Hello, is Mick there please."

Vince replied, "No, he's out at the moment. Who is it?"

"Is that Vince?"

Vince's face looked puzzled. "Yeah."

The voice replied. "It's me, your Uncle Morgan."

"I thought you sounded familiar Uncle Morgan."

"It's good to hear from you love. How's your Dad?"

Vince pushed the phone closer to his ear as he listened to the levels of his voice go up and down. "He's doing alright, I suppose. He's not moaned in a while so that's probably a good sign."

"Hahaha I, it is. Well can you tell him I rang?"

"Yeah," Vince agreed with a smile.

Chapter Seventeen

Kane Crossling walked into his English lesson and sat down next to Kevin. The teacher didn't make any eye contact with him as he walked through the door. The class was calm with a little chant of small talk from other students but the biggest news on the street was that Vince fought off Kane's clan and a lot of students were glamorising his victory. Two copies of the book 'Of Mice & Men' sat on the shared table between Kane and Kevin. Kevin pulled his chair in.

"Everyone's talking about it."

"I know." Aiden squeezed on his black biro pen.

"He's really made a mess of Lucas. I went to his last night and I couldn't get him out of the house. It's really affected him. I think he's embarrassed."

Kane revealed a blunt face. "Lucas isn't a fighter, he's a top lad but nothing more than a poser."

"Are you not even arsed about what happened? Vince made us look pathetic."

"Don't worry, I'm sorting it. Must admit though, he's a right little pit bull isn't he when he's all fired up. I've been waiting for him to snap for a long time."

"Right now class, all turn your books to Chapter Six." The English teacher shouted out loud. The class were coming towards the end of the book building up to the pages of when Lennie dies by the hand of George. The class was silent as the teacher read out the sentences in a Southern American accent.

"George took off his hat. He said shakily, "Take off your hat, Lennie. The air feels fine." Lennie removed his hat dutifully and laid it on the ground in front of him. The shadow in the valley was bluer, and the evening came fast. On the wind the sound of crashing in the brush came to them. Lennie said, "Tell me how it's gonna be." George had been listening to the distant sounds. For a moment he was business-like. "Look across the river Lennie an' I'll tell you so you can almost see it."

The whole class was engaged with the story, even Kane's ears had opened as he followed the sentences with his eyes. He heard the teacher's voice continue with a poor accent.

"And George raised the gun and steadied it, and he brought the mussel of it close to the back of Lennie's head. The hand shook violently, but his face set and his hand steadied. He pulled the trigger."

The class sat in silence shocked. A few voices of other students shouted out.

"That's bullshit!"

"George is a NOB MISS!"

Kane sat in silence, his mind reflected on a time from his past, a memory from his childhood re-sparked from the text he engaged with.

<u>Manchester 2002 Park Hill Estate</u>

The sound of cars screeching fell silent as the clock struck twelve. Inside the house of 224, the Victorian house at the end of the terrace block lay eight-year-old Kane Crossling in his bed. He was woken by a noise but couldn't identify with the sound he heard. Kane looked across his bedroom, facing his bed was Sean's bed. Sean lay fast asleep unconscious to the world.

Kane pulled the covers off him and crept out of the bedroom onto the landing. The wooden floor boards slightly squeaked as each tiptoe created pressure. Upstairs was dark and gloomy, Kane wore a Manchester United pair of pyjamas, the logo was faintly printed on the right hand side of the top. Kane slowly made his way down the stairs sliding his hand against the mounted bannister. He heard sounds of somebody crying, Kane knew he should have stayed in bed but he couldn't stop his curiosity.

There was a wooden door that led to the open space of the living room and kitchen. The door had a top glass window, Kane snuck behind the door and slightly moved his head up peeping through the glass. A man sat on a chair mounted to it with a rope.

"Where's my fucking money?" Dave roared violently. Crash! Crunch! The sound of the man's face being beaten by Dave drummed into Kane's ears.

"Are you listening?" Scott kicked the chair onto the floor and repeatedly kicked him. The screams from his gagged mouth poured with blood. Dave crouched down and looked at the man's face.

"Listen to me you thieving prick. I'm the fucking Devil. And you can tell God I send my regards." A pool of blood clotted onto the floor. Dave and Scott brutally beat the man, his lungs collapsed and ribs punctured vital organs causing him to drown in his own blood. The man muttered his last words in agony.

"See you in hell." The man coughed spewing blood.

"You're already in hell. Arrrghh!" Dave savagely responded tearing the man's body like a rag doll.

"What we going to do about the money?" Scott's heart rate increased.

"You've got to think about the bigger picture. One less problem to deal with." Dave made his last kick to the man's head. The body was battered, blood ran from the victim's mouth. His face wasn't recognisable. As the room fell in silence Kane ran up the stairs quickly…

2009 Manchester 'Smoking Barrel'

Vince looked at himself in the mirror upstairs, he wore a white polo shirt and denim jeans with some grey converse pumps. His hair was washed for the first time and a scent of coconut varnished his skin. His face was still swollen and black bruises sat under his eyes like leeches. Vince took no notice to his facial appearance, the fact he still looked in pain didn't faze him. He looked down at his phone receiving a text message from Daisy.

Hi Vince, my Mum said she would drop me off at yours. Will be there soon xx

Vince looked at the time, in the corner of the screen it was 3:45pm.

Vince pounded his way down stairs with a bottle of air freshener, he sprayed the bottle into the air trying to hide the musky smell of alcohol. Fifteen minutes had passed and a knock at the door banged away.

"Shit. This must be her." Vince walked to the entrance of the pub and opened the door revealing Daisy with a blue dress.

"Sorry I'm late, I stopped off at mine to get changed. WHAT ON EARTH HAPPENED TO YOUR FACE?" Daisy's eyes glared open wide. Vince felt intimidated and nervous.

"What? It's nothing. I... I just had some trouble that's all." Vince backed away slowly from Daisy.

"Oh my god, are you okay? I'm sorry for shouting. Why didn't you tell me?" Daisy's face showed concern with frown marks.

Vince replied feeling a little shaken. "I didn't want to worry you. Please sit down I'll get you a drink, what do you fancy?" Vince led Daisy towards a table and chair as he ran towards the bar grabbing two fresh glasses. He ran back to the table with two glasses of water.

"What happened to you?"

"I got into a fight at school. It's nothing to worry about." Vince tried to reassure Daisy but it wasn't stopping her digging for more information.

"Who did this to you? What are the school doing about it?" Daisy started to pant.

"Well, it was a few lads that's all and the school's shit, they don't have a clue." Vince's hands lay on the table, Daisy's hands moved closer towards him as she tucked in her chair. She put her hands lightly on top of his.

"Vince I care about you. I really do and you can talk to me about anything. Don't be afraid." Vince looked into Daisy's eyes and felt relief. Daisy leaned forward looking into Vince's poor face and kissed his swollen lips. Vince's eyes gazed into Daisy's face.

"You're so beautiful." Daisy started to blossom with red cheeks slightly appearing.

The two love birds whispered to each other, Vince pulled back from his chair and smiled. He held his hand out towards Daisy and stood up. She took his hand and stood up.

"What's wrong?"

"Nothing" Vince replied. He tugged onto Daisy's hand and led her to the bar. "Do you want anything tastier than water?" Daisy's face glowed and eyebrows gently raised.

"Your Dad will kill us if we drink all of his stock." Vince giggled quietly and grabbed a bottle of J20 fresh orange from the side fridge.

"Here, which one's your favourite?"

"I'm alright thanks Vince, honest." Vince grabbed two glasses and shrugged his face pulling a smile.

"We can share then." Daisy looked into Vince's blue eyes, she felt her heart race as Vince smiled back. "Mmm," muttered Vince. "Have you ever had a private tour around this pub?"

"No," Daisy gently replied, twisting strands of her hair with her fingertips.

"Well come on then." Vince excitedly whispered taking Daisy's hand.

Vince pointed with his free hand towards the pictures on the walls.

"I don't know too much about these pictures, but they've been there for as long as I can remember." The pictures that hung on the walls were paintings and illustrations of horse shoes and farm animals.

"Is that one a horse?" Daisy spoke with curiosity pointing her finger towards a painting of a black mare stood in a field.

"I think so. It's too big to be a donkey," Vince replied with a burst of laughter. Vince pulled gently on Daisy's hand leading her into the hallway.

"Where do them two doors lead to?" Daisy spoke intrigued. Reaching out with his hand towards the door handle Vince's voice chuckled.

"This is where I sleep, down there's my bedroom." Daisy looked puzzled and opened the door.

"Really? It can't be. It smells down here." Daisy peered her eyes into the room. Vince burst out laughing.

"I can't believe it haha. I got you!"

"Shut up," Daisy laughed. "I knew it wasn't your bedroom."

"Yeah, yeah," Vince chuckled. Vince tugged onto Daisy's hand gently, "Come on Daisy," Vince smiled. The pair quietly crept up the stairs and walked along the squeaking floorboards of the landing. Moving towards Vince's bedroom the pair fell quiet. "Sorry for the mess," Vince spoke feeling embarrassed at the mountain of clothes piled on the floor.

"It's okay," Daisy smiled. "My rooms ten times as messy, brushes everywhere, makeup, my old dolls I had as a child. At least your clothes are folded," Daisy laughed.

"I am sorry for the mess though Daisy, I've just got that many clothes that I can't fit them all in my wardrobe." Daisy sat on the bed, her hair fell beside her shoulders and her eyes widened.

"Does that TV work?" Daisy pointed addressing an old dusty box television that rested on a shelf.

"I think so. I've not used it in years." Vince pulled himself up from the bed and walked towards the TV caked in dust; he pressed the on button. The television screen lit up but the images were fuzzy, moving the metal aerial side to side trying to get the best connection, after a two minute struggle the picture became fairly clear.

"Check you Mr Handy Man," Daisy grinned. Vince walked back towards the bed with a rectangular remote in his hand.

"What do you want to watch?" Daisy playfully snatched the remote from Vince's palm.

"Erm..." Staring at the television screen flicking through the channels Daisy came across channel 4.

"Have you made your mind up?" Vince laughed.

"No. Haha. Shut up." Daisy bantered. "These adverts do my head in so much, we could watch Mr and Mrs Smith. It's just come on." Daisy smiled.

"Ay, they're good, channel 4, aren't they? I'm surprised this TV still works. And yeah course. So, you see yourself as a bit of an action-packed girl ay." Vince laughed as they both sat back on the bed.

"No! Haha. It's a good film, I've been told." Daisy pinched Vince's arm. "Shhh, I'm trying to watch the film." Vince slightly squeezed Daisy's hand. The pair snuggled together on the bed passing comments about the film, joking and laughing at each other.

Dave lay on Scott's red couch holding a spliff in one hand as the room fell gloomy with smoke. With closed eyes and music playing in the background, Dave tried to relax wearing a grey Ralf Lauren tracksuit.

"I don't fucking get it! I'm the biggest known fucking boss around here. And some little bastard wants to kill me and make a name for himself. He's already fucking dead. I knew it... I knew it. We should've got rid of him when we had him by the throat." Scott walked into the room from his kitchen with two McDonald bags.

"I was going to dish them out but fuck it."

"Scott, they give you the bag so you don't have to plate your food."

"Yeah yeah, I know, but I thought. You know what fuck it just get that down you." Dave laughed as he took a drag and reached into the paper bag with one hand pulling out a big mac.

"What time did Smiffy say that he'd drop that video off ?" Dave blurted into the atmosphere.

"Half five he said he'd be here, unless he's stopped off at KFC." Mumbled Scott as he chewed his big mac with a grin.

"He knows how important this shit is so he shouldn't be fucking about." The sound of a repetitive knock hit Scott's door with urgency. A smile unfolded from Dave's face as Scott leapt up from the couch. Crank! The door knob twisted open to the sight of Smiffy standing saturated in the rain. Breathing heavily with a slight wheeze, he rested his hand on the outside frame of the flat. Scott looked at him with concern.

"What happened to you? Come in but take them fucking shoes off."

"Some fucker drove past me in his car and splashed a fucking tsunami at me." Smiffy caught his breath and kicked off his shoes. "And then to top it all off your lift is broke... I had to run up them bastard stairs. Six floors." Smiffy exhaled the remaining oxygen and tasted the thick liquid at the back of his throat bubbling. Scott burst out into laughter walking back to his seat holding a cheesy smile.

"Have you heard this?" Scott belched addressing Dave.

"Yeah...Smiffy did you bring the tape." Smiffy passed a blue bag over to Dave and sat on the couch with his socks touching the carpet. Opening the plastic blue bag with aggression, Dave's fingernails clawed and tore the plastic. Smiffy's feet gasped for air whilst polluting it with a fungus smell waking Dave's sharp senses of sight and smell, black holey socks entered the corner of his eye.

"Where's your shoes you sweaty fucker?"

"I didn't want him fucking up my floor with his dirty muddy shoes." Scott swallowed a piece of his burger.

Smiffy sat there quietly with innocence, until his urge overtook him.

"Scott, can I have a bite mate?"

"Two words Smith, FUCK OFF," Scott stuck his fingers up towards Smiffy.

Dave stood up from the couch glaring towards the television. He walked towards Scott's dusty old tape player and inserted the video. Crunch! The old device streamed the CCTV footage onto the plasma TV set.

"This best be the right tape Smiffy."

"It is, it is." Smiffy replied staring at the fuzzy screen.

"Give it a bang, it will sort it out." Dave tried Scott's suggestion which made the tape player make a hissing sound, after a two minute wait the footage started to respond.

"See I told you it would work."

"Shut it Scott." Dave's eyes glued to the screen as he watched through the moving images.

"There he is. Stop it there!" Smiffy shouted energetically. Dave watched a tattooed neck stocky figure walk outside the pub, as the footage continued to play he watched the event unfold that Smiffy had recently spoke about. "See, look there he is. The twat head." Dave's hands clenched and his spine stiffened.

"Do you recognise him Scott?"

"Yeah, it's that scrawny bastard..."

The one who's gripped him, he's THE FUCKER WHOSE SPOOKED HIM."

Anger raged inside Dave's body, he stood tall and stormed into Scott's kitchen pulling out his pistol onto the kitchen table.

"Who the fuck is that tattooed necked fucking wanker?"

"It's a snake tattoo." Smiffy shouted into the kitchen. Dave gripped the gun tightly walking back into the living room.

"AND I'M THE FUCKING DEVIL!"

Kane stood alone outside Saint Brooks High, he gazed his eyes towards the school doors and looked at his phone checking the time. The flood of students had already evaporated and left a silence that sat across the school. Kane waited testing his own patience, fifteen minutes passed as he stood waiting. Kane's phone vibrated.

Where are you?

Kane glanced over the text messages from Kevin and Sean. He clicked reply and text back.

I've been held back, in detention. Kane looked through the glass doors looking deep into the open complex of the school.

A figure of a student walked towards the school doors, as he opened the glass door Kane stared.

"Vince."

"Move Kane I don't want no trouble." Kane stood in Vince's path blocking his exit. "I said fuckin move!" Vince's voice raised full of aggression.

"Calm down," Kane remarked. "I want to talk to you..."

Vince spoke over Kane.

"Talk to me? You want to talk to me. After all the times you made my life a nightmare. You're not right in the fucking head."

"I was testing you. Seeing how much you can take. And you passed with flying colours!" Kane spoke in a sinister tone.

"What the fuck?" Vince shouted projecting towards Kane. "Listen to me Vince. Me and you are the same breed."

"Same breed? You make people's lives a living hell, mine especially." Kane held his hands up.

"Don't be too hasty Vince, think about the bigger picture." Vince felt an explosion of confusion, his forehead frowned creating waves of caution.

Vince passed the wavering arms of Kane and continued his journey home towards the bus stop.

Mick pulled a battered old suitcase from under his bed. He piled clothes inside un-ironed. Boxers, socks, pants and shirts layered like pasta in a lasagne dish. Zip! Mick zipped the case shut and stood it upwards as his legs dangled from the bed, the case mirrored his emotions. Dull, dark and alone. A faint ticking noise was heard, Mick tilted his head down towards his wrists, a black leather strap watch snugly fit with a golden face. Mick undid the strap turning the watch onto its back, the casing which concealed the battery had markings scratched onto the circular metal plate.

Vincent Haze 01/08/1944. His eyes glazed with a layer of tears, Mick strapped the watch back to his wrist standing up reaching towards the suitcase. The sound of wheels spinning and grinding along the floor was pulled across the landing. As Mick engaged with his set of stairs he picked the case up and wobbled down the stairs with it, tucking it away under the bar.

A knock at the door banged loudly! Vince walked through the door saturated in rain water.

"What happened to you?" Mick enquired.

"It started chucking it down proper bad when I got off the bus."

"Take your shoes off, I can hear them squeaking from here, I've already mopped the floor so try not to make a mess." The sound of wet feet squelched across the floor into the hallway, he kicked off his shoes and ran upstairs into the bathroom stripping off and drying himself down.

Kane waited at the bus stop, glued to his head was a black hood with a Nike tick stitched on the chest. He heard the laughter of a group of teenaged girls walking towards the stop. Kane ignored the sounds of hissing placing his earphones snugly inside his ears. He discretely pulled out his phone and started to play his favourite songs. Miming the lyrics to Afro Mans 'Colt 45' rap. Kane squinted his eyes as he watched cars pass.

"Aaaahhh!" The sound of teenage girls screamed. "It's him, it's him. Go on Maxine!" An excited female voice was heard.

"Shut up girls!" Maxine's deeper voice overpowered. Kane sat down on the bus stop's bench and leant his head to the side of the shelters frame. Kane's eyes followed the passing cars repeating over and over until the pattern was broken by the herd of teenage girls all dressed in slutty clothes, short skirts, illuminous tut tut and skin tight tops, all revealing different coloured bra's.

"What the fuck do you call this? Peter pan and the lost boys?"

"yes, we're fairies!" A voice giggled.

"We seen what you did to Aiden's face" The same voice replied. Amongst the crowd of teenaged girls was Roxanne. She stood quietly only muttering a few words. "Let's go Maxine."

Kane started to grow agitated.

"Move!"

"Shut up." A voice from the back shouted. "Hey Maxine was he good or what?"

"Yeah, Maxine?" The voices started to pitch higher. Kane's eyebrow twitched, his eyes slowly dilated.

"Kane's got a little one!" The group started to wind Kane up as Maxine had filled them all in on their night out. Kane's throat boiled like a pan absorbing into his tongue. Maxine made her way towards the bench where he sat.

"Do you want to do it again?" Maxine giggled to herself resting her hand on Kane's leg.

Jumping from his seat Kane growled howling aggression.

"Fuck off the lot of you. Go on, I'll slap every fucking one of you sluts!" Kane violently pushed Maxine back into her crowd, a vein pulsed on the right side of his head.

"What the fuck are you doing you dickhead?" Maxine shrieked.

"Go on! FUCK OFF!" Kane yelled like a lunatic. The group of girls walked away wavering as Kane clenched his fists.

"Come on girls, let's go," Roxanne spoke feeling agitated. Kane stood on his toes shouting down the street, like a game of tennis, scattering insults back and forth.

The girls faded into the night the further they walked down the street. Rain clouds started to cover Kane's head. Kane heard the sound of an approaching vehicle, gasping hydraulics screamed as Kane perched his head towards the sight of the bus. Holding out his hand with a grey face the bus came to a gentle stop.

Mick sat downstairs in the function room on the comfy seats. He reached into his pocket pulling out a white pill that sat in a plastic container, swallowing hard Mick threw his head back as the pill scratched his tonsils. He picked up a freshly made glass of water and choked down each gulp of water.

Vince came thudding down the stairs dressed in grey jogging bottoms and a matching hooded top.

"What's this?" Vince stumbled across the old suitcase neatly tucked to one side under the bar. Wheeling it into the open space of the room Vince repeated himself. Mick sat in silence for a minute or two whilst Vince looked at him.

"It's your grandad's birthday next week. I'm going to Ireland for a few days. Well, until next week." Mick replied in a gentle tone. Mick's eyes were blood shot, his face was sullen. Grey hair started to sprout on his jaw bone, with eyes glued towards the suitcase Vince responded quietly.

"Oh, right," Vince gently put the case back under the bar.

"I've spoken to Chris and he said he'd come up to keep an eye on you when I'm gone," Mick's voice raised slightly.

"Okay," Vince replied.

The sound of the pub's landline phone started to ring in the hallway. Mick stood up feeling a burning sensation in his back and approached the phone in the hallway.

"Hello, Mick it's Morgan, which day are you coming over?" Mick continued with the conversation, Vince walked past, running up the stairs. The sounds of Mick's voice grew quieter as Vince entered his room.

Kane opened the door to his house, Dave's car was nowhere to be seen on the street.

"FUCK SAKE! I'm fucking soaked!" Kane shouted echoing through the house. Sean sat on the couch watching MTV. Taking no notice of Kane's entrance. Sean picked up the remote and increased the volume. "Have you had anything to eat?" Kane asked.

"Yeah, a frozen pizza," Sean replied with his eyes glued to the TV.

"Did you save us any?"

"I didn't think you wanted it." Water dripped onto the floor creating dampness. Kane squeaked across the floor into the kitchen.

"Nice one dickhead." Kane's snake like arms slivered towards the fridge.

"Why's there no food? Where's Dad?" Sean's head turned slightly.

"I don't know. What's with the all questions?" Sean asked lying back relaxed on the couch.

"God sake! I'm just gonna order a kebab instead. It's shit in here, you eat all the fuckin food. You little fat shit."

Sean responded feeling annoyed. "What do you expect me to do? Starve?"

"Shut up you little bitch!" Kane shouted as he rooted through the cupboards. Kane ran upstairs and ripped off his school uniform. He pulled out his phone and clicked on Kevin's number. Ring ring! Ring ring! Kane held down on the loud speaker icon so he could talk hands-free. Pulling off his white shirt he heard Kevin's voice respond.

"What's up?" Standing over the phone topless, Kane replied with enthusiasm.

"Alright mate, my Dad's fucked off for a few days, so will you round up the lads and we'll get fucked at mine. I've got a shit load of bud and beer."

"Will do. It's midweek though."

"Fuck it mate. I can't wait till Friday. I've got some news for you all too!"

Kevin spoke with monotone.

"What is it?"

"I'll tell you later, I'm getting ready so make the fuckin calls dickhead!" Kane heard the sound of the phone call ending with a beep. He walked towards his wardrobe and pulled out a fresh track suit.

Thirty minutes had passed and Kane's cravings had started to take over him as he waited for his friends to arrive. Unable to sit still he rushed towards his Dad's room and ploughed through his Dad's drawers with urgency, in search of any loose cannabis. His eyes glowed at a plastic bag which contained half an ounce of cannabis, he picked up the bag with his finger and thumb. A giggle ran down his throat with blood pumping wild.

"Yes! Get in there." Kane shouted bouncing off all four walls with excitement. Sean curiously investigated Kane's excitement,

"What's up with you?"

"Nothing…Keep an eye on that door, the lads are coming up soon."

"What for?"

"It's nowt to do with you pal." Sean sat back on the couch with a bowlof chicken noodles which steamed the words tasty across his lips.

Kane examined the bag with his eyes, "Just under half an ounce. It's going to be a long night." A huge grin perched on Kane's face, opening the bag Kane held it under his nose taking a deep breath inhaling the scent of cannabis. "Let's get fucking high!" Kane giggled to himself childishly. "Are they here yet?"

Kane shouted down the stairs as he danced around the landing full of energy.

"How am I supposed to know?"

"Shut up you little shit." Kane walked into his room and crashed on the bed. With two feet spread and glued to the floor Kane pulled out a rizla, pinched a handful of cannabis then sprinkled it onto the thin paper and roled a spliff. His phone vibrated in his pocket but occupied by the drugs he didn't feel it.

BANG! BANG! A loud knock at the door echoed. Sean jumped from his seat and peered through the side window.

"Kane!" Sean shouted promptly. "The lads are here."

"Alright!" Kane replied loudly. He finished off his freshly rolled spliff and put it in his pocket with the cannabis wrapped in his other. Running across the landing and down the stairs Kane muttered.

"Get the key Sean. Get the key."

"Two minutes lads." The sound of an impatient group of teenagers piped up.

"Fuckin hell, you knew we were coming you dick." Kane heard the moaning comments from behind the door.

"Hey, shut it you numpties."

The noise of crunching keys finally opened the door.

"Alright boys!" Kane smiled.

"It's about time G" Lucas reacted.

"Fucking hell you got wigged!"

"Don't be at it Kane" Lucas softly mumbled.

"Shit! I didn't think you could get any blacker!" A few of the lads laughed. "Come in boys," Kane walked into his open living room space. "Can I get you anything? Even some fucking frozen peas?" Lucas ignored Kane's remark and sat on the couch.

"You alright, Sean mate?"

"Not too bad. Just been putting up with Kane." Lucas laughed pulling a smile.

"Tell me about it haha."

"Shut up you little gay boys."

"So, what did you drag us all down here for then?"

"Boys, I got you all something!" Kane gasped.

"What's that?" Some of the lads replied.

"Here we go! One of Kane's bright ideas." Kevin commented looking at Kane's face full of excitement. There was more behind his enthusiasm then he was letting out. Kane revealed the bag of cannabis and flaunted it in the lad's faces.

"Let's get fucked boys! Let's get high bitches!" Kane screamed like a school girl at their first concert.

"What about your Dad?" A voice spoke up.

"Fuck him. He's gone away for a few days the twat."

"So this is the reason you dragged us all down here." Kevin spoke out loud.

"Calm down you stress head and sit down." Kane pulled out the spliff he made earlier and passed it across to Kevin. "I was saving this one for myself so light it up." Kane walked over to his breakfast table with the lads following behind. "Chill out, everyone will get some" Kane opened the plastic bag of cannabis and emptied it onto the table. The pile of cannabis gathered like a mountain. Spreading its scent like blowing leaves on a hill side, the smell glued to their clothes and the walls of the room.

"That reeks! Isn't that Dad's Black Widow! He'll go sick. It's his stash." Sean squealed picking his nails. Some of the lads felt a conscious outburst of paranoia and small rumbles of anxiety, Kane looked at the faces of worried sheep.

"Shut the fuck up Sean. He's not going to notice, he's got too much shit as it is." Kane addressed his friends with ease. "Look if he says ought... I'll tell him straight I smoked it all and ate everything in the cupboards. You pussies!" Kane welcomed his friends to dive into the stash as he walked over to his iPod that sat tight in its docking station.

Pressing hard with his finger onto the centre of the iPod the screen turned on with a black and white face. He scrolled through the play list and clicked onto a 50cent album. The lads crashed onto the couches waving spliffs in their hands.

"Say Domperella and Alice I don't need shit. I stay high all the time I'm on the good shit. I stay high all the time I'm on some hood shit!" Lucas sang out loud starting to feel the effects. The room started to gloom with smoke. Kane looked across the room staring at his tribe, he stretched out on the couch gathering his thoughts.

"It's a tune mate, proper tune!" Kevin giggled relaxing into the couch, waiting for the chorus Kevin sang loudly.

"I'm high all the time, I smoke the good shit! Every time I hold up then I tell them roll up roll up. Yes, boys. Get hyped get hyped!"

"Kevin"

"Yes mate?"

"Your singing it all wrong G. Man don't even know the words fam!" Lucas laughed putting on a deep voice.

Kane smiled at the sight of everyone enjoying themselves. He kept clock watching, waiting for the right moment to spill his thoughts. Sitting calmly and quieter than usual the lads started to notice.

"What's up with you?" Kevin shouted across to Kane. The sound of rap music in the background turned muffled. Lifting the spliff to his mouth and taking a deep inhale of cannabis Kane's eyes glowed red like a neon light.

"Well. I've been thinking."

"About what?" Kevin's voice choked on concern.

"Lads listen up. Listen." Everyone in the room turned towards Kane. "I've been thinking. Thinking about getting that what's his face, that Vince on our team." The room fell silent with everyone mythed.

"What the fuck? He fucked up my face. And you want him on our side. He embarrassed you Kane in front of the whole school. He wasted our best kids in the year below?" Kevin's face lay shocked.

"No fucking way," Sean spoke up.

"He's got a fuckin point, we should wipe that immigrant out." A voice blurted out from the side of the room. Kane turned his head to the side and looked at the unknown face.

"Who's he with?"

"He's one of us, he's my mate from the year below," Lucas spoke still boiled with anger.

"What's your name?"

"Tom," the lad replied nervously. Kane stood up from his couch and slowly approached Tom.

"Listen to me Tom," Kane gently spoke grabbing the boy by his shirt. "I need soldiers who have balls." Kane threw Tom into the centre of the room. "I need people who can take a hit. As well as give it out." Kane slapped Tom on the back of the head.

"Ay, chill out yeah. We're all friends here." Lucas muttered feeling intimidated. Kane's eyes boiled redder as he looked deeper into Tom's face.

"Are you fucking listening to me? Are you fucking listening? I need men not mice." Kane started to roar.

"I'm listening."

"Are you fuckin listening?"

"Yeah," Tom whimpered with a head smaller than Kane and shortly cut black hair. "Yeah."

The sound of tearing fabric was heard as Kane threw Tom to the floor. Leaning over Tom's body Kane's face moved closer towards his face as he screamed down Tom's ears.

"I need people with a pair of balls not cowards like you." Tom covered his face with fragile hands.

"That's enough!" Kevin shouted on the edge of his feet.

"Stop it Kane. Don't be at it." Lucas whined. Still engaged in a trance Kane heard the sounds of the boys shouting as he stared down the eyes of young Tom.

"Cowards crawl to the floor and whimper. Whilst those with demons can attack wildly AT ANY FUCKING MOMENT!" Kane shouted violently in Tom's face with a smile arousing.

Eyes closed in fear and hands tightly covering his face, Kane gripped Tom by the collar of his shirt and raised him forward.

"You see it doesn't matter how big the dog is, it's how loud the smallest one barks as well as it's bite," Kane whispered in a sinister tone with saliva dripping from his lips. Kane's posture crouched as he faced Tom, he saw coward written all over his face. Before standing he passed on the words. "You are still yet to prove yourself." Kane glared with dark eyes standing up sharply. "Calm down everybody. We're all friends here." Kane pulled Tom up with his hand as he sat in shock.

"Aren't we?" Kane's face squared towards Tom. "Tom?" Kane opened his arms wide towards the group. "Anyone want a can?" The lads all sat quietly staring at Kane who stood central in the middle of the room, an awkward vibe spread through the room as Tom scampered behind the couch where Lucas was sitting. Lucas signalled to Tom that he was leaving. The rest of the crowd disappeared all but one stayed sat in the room.

"Kevin, you know I'm right." Kane spoke up feeling annoyed, frown marks were left embedded on his forehead as he sat there with a smug expression.

Chapter Eighteen

Mick stood in the centre of the function room, it was 8am and the air felt thin. His suitcase stood beside his feet as he looked at his watch. The sounds of creaking floor boards squeaked as Mick moved closer towards the front door holding himself firm. Vince slid his hands down the banister attached to the stairs before walking into the bar area witnessing Mick standing still and quiet.

Mick heard Vince creeping and slowly turned his face towards him, gently looking down at Vince's eyes.

"What times Chris coming?"

"He should be here soon," Mick quietly spoke.

"Was you going to say bye, or what?" Vince's facial expressions showed his emotions.

"I didn't want to wake you son, I left a note and we spoke about this, you knew I was going today." Vince felt sad inside and walked closer to his Dad.

"Dad, I didn't mean to anger you before you go, just let me know when your there. Is there anything you want me to do here while you're gone." A smile revealed from Mick's face as he saw a reflection of himself in Vince. "Well... Have the tables been wiped?"

"Yeah."

"Then just make sure this place is how it looks now when I come back, I left Chris in charge of this place and it's still giving me the chills." Vince laughed at his father's humour and muttered.

"It will be fine ay."

The sound of Chris's van crunched on the pavement outside the 'Smoking Barrel' as the sound waves of a beep crashed into the air exiting the vehicle.

"That must be Chris then." Mick bent forward to pick up his case and reached for the plastic handle.

"It's alright, I've got it, I've got it." Vince snatched at the handle and wheeled it forward through the front door, Mick followed behind wearing a brown tweed jacket with matching pants with leather shoes. Chris's van sat on the pavement as he jumped out to assist Vince.

"Alright there, kiddo? I'll take that off you bud." Vince passed the suitcase towards Chris as he threw it into the back of the van. Mick looked at Vince and put his arm around his shoulder.

"I won't be gone long." Jumping into the passenger seat Mick winded the window down and said his final words before Chris and him set off. "Don't forget to lock up. And there's some money on the side for the week, have a good day at school son."

"See you when I get back matey," Chris shouted out the window with his thumbs held up as he revved on the engine. As the van drove off Mick leant over the horn and beeped at Vince. BEEP! BEEP!

Mick's face turned grey as they were getting closer to the airport, he held his thoughts inside his head but he knew it wasn't long until he was getting out, he started to leak emotions.

"You okay Mick? It won't be long now hey until you're on the plane. It goes fast in there once you check in." Mick nodded his head. "You're not nervous about flying are you?" Chris watched Mick's reaction through the mirror.

"No! It's just, you know, things on the other side."

Sounds of the suitcase slid back and forth in the back of the van as the other cars on the road drove past. A minor whistling noise was heard in the background from a hidden hole in the van creating a bumpy experience for the two. The radio played over the surrounding sounds.

"Fucking hell, did you see that Volkswagen then? Jesus, it nearly went right up the back of us." Mick clenched onto a handle above his head.

"Fuckers," Mick responded.

"You know Vince will be alright with me, don't you? I'll keep a good watch over him."

"I know," Mick replied. "It's just... I haven't been back here in a while. It makes me itch."

"You're meeting Morgan over there, ain't you. So you'll have a place to stay."

"It's not that. You ever get that feeling that you shouldn't be going back to a place."

"No."

"Maybe it's because you're young, but trust me you'll get it one day."

"Mick, you'll be fine, trust me." Mick stared out the window and slowly released his grip from the handle above his head, taking a deep breath he noticed the architecture of Manchester Airport. "It's terminal three, isn't it?"

"Yeah."

As the van parked outside the entrance bay Mick sat quietly in the passenger seat. "You know it's my father's birthday tomorrow and every year I visit him." Mick glared straight ahead of him. "It's not that I'm ashamed that I still grieve for him, it's the shit that got left after he went. That I didn't only lose my father, but everything I had over there. My life." Micks eyes glazed with un-hatched tears. "And every time I go back there it's not his ghost that haunts me, it's his spirit inside me." Chris stared at Mick listening to the stress in his voice, he felt Mick's pain. Mick twisted a handle which opened the van's door. He stepped outside and walked towards the back of the van. Chris jumped out at the same time and approached Mick swiftly.

"You know you don't have to go Mick?" Mick's face flattened firmly.

"I'm going." Mick opened the back of the van as Chris pulled his suitcase onto the ground. Mick held his hand out towards Chris and shook his hand tightly, "I'll be okay Chris. Thanks again for everything." Mick pulled out twenty pounds from his pocket and placed it in Chris's hand.

"No, no Mick. You don't have to do that."

"It's for the lift." Mick wheeled his suitcase towards the sliding doors of terminal three. Chris watched his father figure as he jumped back into the van, with his window down Chris beeped at Mick and ignited the engine.

Walking into the Terminal Mick turned back and watched Chris's van leave the grounds, he pulled out a medical bottle from his inside coat pocket and poured some pills into his hand. Throwing them to the back of his throat Mick walked towards the closest bin and dropped the plastic container.

The morning air was fresh, the sound of tweeting birds could be heard in the distance from Vince's window. Another school day was awaiting Vince. Tossing and turning in his bed, rolling left to right trying to catch the last couple of minutes before his alarm clock rang out. Then hearing the first wave of subtle ringing sounds until his phone raised in volume, ring…Ring….RING! Vince struggled to open his eyes, lacking in energy. He swooped his arm under the pillow and turned to the opposite side of the bed burying his head under the covers. The alarm rang for a good five minutes before Vince turned back over, eyes full of sleep unable to open them fully, he jumped out of his bed slamming the alarm on snooze.

"Yawn!" Vince's mouth opened wide as he walked across the mammoth of recently left clothes.

Creeping across the landing Vince walked into his father's room to pick up a fresh towel. He saw the outlined covers of where Mick had recently laid. The digital alarm clock that sat on Mick's side table showed the numbers 7:40am. Vince pulled a fresh towel from Mick's wardrobe and ran into the shower full of urgency. As Vince followed his usual morning routine his phone, which sat on the covers of his single bed, started to vibrate. Unable to hear with the sounds of crashing water, the phone continued to vibrate without a second of a break. It wasn't a thread of messages from Daisy but an unknown number calling.

Throwing on his clothes Vince put the same busted shoes on and creased blazer, with his hair still wet he picked up his phone and glanced at the six missed calls.

"What the fuck? Who's that?" Vince curiously thought to himself, he felt a small presence of paranoia slowly kick into his body. Half an hour had passed as he continued to pursue his morning duties, all ready for the day with half a bowl of cereal bedded to the back of his throat. Vince walked onto his street and continued his journey to the bus stop. As he followed his usual path he noticed that there wasn't a cloud in the sky, it seemed like an almost perfect morning if he didn't have to waste his day in school.

Vince became in view of the bus stop, he could see only one figure sat at the shelter. As he walked down the street his inner voice started to try and figure out who the suspicious unknown calls were from, but he just couldn't think who it could be, mumbling to himself Vince continued to try and work it out.

"Well it can't be my Dad, because he's just gone and if there was an emergency he'd ring on Morgan's phone. Fuck knows, prob's just prank callers." Vince got closer to the bus stop, he saw somebody wearing dark clothes with a hooded jacket. As Vince approached the shelter he felt a spiral of nervous energy. The hooded figure slowly raised his head from the floor and uncovered his face.

"WHY HAVENT YOU ANSWERED MY CALLS AY?" Kane Crossling's voice was intimidating, with a slight tone of aggression and a false smile. Vince's heart skipped a beat as he looked upon Kane.

"I didn't know it was you, I was in the shower. Any way what the fuck do you want?" Vince spoke nervously with a touch of confidence.

"Calm down. Calm down! Alright. I'm not FUCKING weird right." A shiver ran down Kane's spine. "Listen to me yeah. Chill." Kane pulled out a cigarette. "I know we haven't seen eye to eye but school's school init. I've got no shit with you yeah. To be honest I respect you man." Vince felt a snowballing of confusion, his shoulders became un-tensed as he relaxed into a moment of oddness. Still feeling slightly weird about the situation, Vince turned his back and started to walk away from the bus stop, everything seemed unreal. "Hey, listen to me," Kane shouted as he sprung from the bus shelter's seat. "Vince, where you going ay? Look mate, all along I've been testing you, from day one like one of them exams, to see if you'll either pass or fail. I've done some bad things to you." Kane stood in front of Vince blocking his path. "But through this you've become stronger hey? So, a little thank you would be nice." Kane smiled glaring into Vince's face. Vince looked around him and saw the school bus approaching the stop.

"What do you want Kane? Look I'm going to miss this bus now."

"Fuck school," Kane sniggered. "Look man let's just go town init. Me and you bro." Vince looked down at his beaten-up shoes and scanned his eyes at the moving bus.

"Why would I go town when I don't have a penny?" Vince shrugged.

"What you gonna do then hey, go school. First lesson, second lesson, break, third lesson - all that shit or just fuck it for the day. Besides fuck the Maths, the teachers don't give a fuck anyway! Go on... waste your day." Vince walked back to the seat of the bus shelter and questioned himself whether to stop the bus. He sat back falling into a deep stare watching the school bus pass his eyes. Kane's face lightened with excitement. "Fucking get in there son! So, town for the day, innit." Pulling a smile Kane sat down next to Vince. "Come on mate cheer up. It's gonna be a good day. The teachers won't even notice you're not in."

Vince sat quietly for a moment, everything didn't make sense.

"Fuck it. Alright, I'll come. You mad-head."

Kane laughed at Vince and looked at the bus timetable which was mounted to the wall of the shelter.

"Sweet! One should be here soon, twenty to nine. Role on the 182." Vince felt the cold metal from the bench shiver down his fingers, the wind blew his hair across his face. Kane's voice seemed to lose tone as Vince sat in a daydream listening to all sorts of uselessness coming from Kane's mouth.

Chapter Nineteen

Dave murdered his car down Oldham Road with full throttle force. The Mercedes engine tore apart the road roaring like a striking lion. Dave pulled out his mobile phone and struck the steering wheel with one hand as he reduced his speed for the speed cameras.

"Scott, I think we've got the bastard. Smiffy's just text me saying the geezers in the pub, I'm on my way to pick you up, be ready mate." Dave spoke with intensity as sweat dripped down his forehead.

"Alright mate. I'll be outside with cap and gown." Scott laughed.

"Scott don't fuck about now. Just be ready alright. I'm five minutes away."

Scott pulled out his work clothes from his closet and a leather bag. He threw in a black balaclava and some nasty surprises. He threw on a black shirt and black pants with a leather jacket on top and made his way out of the flat. The clock struck twelve, mid-day, but the environment Scott lived in felt quiet and eerie even though it was touching towards the afternoon. He would usually hear the screams of people arguing in the streets and witness teenage lads causing chaos on their BMX bikes, but the streets were empty. He leant against a street light as he waited for Dave to pick him up. He heard the sound of a whizzing car screaming through the estate, there was no doubt in Scott's mind that it was just some stupid kids joy riding. But no, Dave's Mercedes crunching the tarmac pulled up beside him. Dave's window dropped down smoothly as he popped his head outside.

"You gettin in then or what?"

"Open the boot then." Scott walked to the back of the car and threw in his leather bag. He entered the car sitting in the passenger seat to face Dave.

"What's the pub called again?" Scott asked.

"I don't know but it doesn't matter Smiffy's text me the address anyway, it's near Portland street."

"Nar it's not. I think it's called the Eight Bells in erm... Fucking Ardwick." Dave looked down at his phone and revved the engine.

"Shit yeah!" The Mercedes accelerated forward with a thrust of wind streaking across it, the sound of the engine bounced from the flats and spiralled through the maze of urban architecture. Dave could feel his blood pressure heighten as the colour of his face started to change, he felt his heart beat erratically.

"Did you get the stuff?" Dave spoke out loud.

"Yeah, it's all in the bag."

"Good." Dave drove up Lime Street and saw the Eight Bells on the corner, it was a small shabby building with the usual standard box shaped design with the name printed on the front of the building.

Dave stopped the car a couple of yards away from the entrance of the pub, feeling his body race with energy he kept his cool and stared at the building.

"What you thinking then, mate?" Scott opened the glove compartment and pulled out Dave's knuckle duster which was hidden underneath the cars paperwork. He tried it on then slid it off placing it inside his jacket pocket.

"Right we'll go in the pub and get a drink and watch what's going on. That other heavy might be in there, the fucking runt."

"Two birds, one stone, then hopefully." Dave pulled open his car door and shouted to Scott.

"Come on then." Scott jumped out of the car and followed behind catching up to Dave. Dave felt vibrations in his pocket, he reached inside and answered his phone.

"Where are you? You best get here quick. You never know when these types of people come and go!" Smiffy blurted down the phone.

"We're here now." Dave threw his phone back into his pocket.

"Fucking hell he never stops going on." Dave and Scott entered the Eight Bells fully fuelled, Smiffy greeted them with excitement at the entrance of the Public House.

"Welcome boys glad you're here, it's good to see you." Dave grabbed Smiffy to one side and pushed him towards the men's toilets whilst Scott scanned the room for the dealer.

"SMIFFY, you better shut the fuck up mate. I've given you a pat on the back, right. You're going to get me noticed the way you keep jumping about like a giddy dog." Dave spoke directly into Smiffy's ear, "SO SHUT THE FUCK UP and get us a round in."

Dave sat down on a stool at a small table.

Scott saw a young teenaged lad matching the description of the video he saw.

"Fucking hell," Scott mumbled quietly under his breath.

"He's only a kid." Scott joined Dave at the table with dark eyes.

"What's up with you? You found him?"

"Yeah, he looks quite young."

"Where is he?" Dave scanned his eyes towards the bar.

"Him? I remember now, we have definitely taxed him before and he's trying to take me out, fucking little shit! No respect." Dave spoke with anger and frustration in his voice. "Where's Smiffy gone?"

"Think he went for a shit. Then he's getting us a round in."

Time started to pass inside the Eight Bells, you could hear the smokers gathering outside the pub and hear the sound of people shouting at the television sets that were showing the sports channels. The smell of alcohol burrowed in every corner of the room. The dealer sat on the same stool texting away on his phone oblivious to his unfolding future. The second round of pints evaporated into their bodies, Dave's eyes were fixed on his target. The conversations in the pub started to raise as the pub became rowdier. Speaking over the background noises Scott whispered into Dave's ear, slowly rising in pitch.

"Why don't we wait for the big fish and take him. We've already kidnapped this little fish before." Feeling a sense of anger Dave resisted as his bulletproof vest made it slower for him to intake oxygen.

"Because this little fish escaped our nets last time and is threatening to kill a shark." The two spoke in proverbs metaphorically to each other which started to brew disagreements. "He's a loose cannon, he needs teaching a lesson, once and for all. You know that!" Dave placed his empty glass on the table firmly.

"In a few years that could be one of your kids." Scott empathized.

"Like it or not this little fucker's getting it. You can't be going tame on me Scotty. You know the code, it's us or them. Age!!! didn't stop him from doing what he's done, so he must face the consequence of his actions and threats, regardless." Dave's voice rose with conflict. "He's going boys, he's on the move."

Smiffy laughed, "He's bouncing."

Dave jumped up from his seat, "That's our queue." Scott stood up and thanked Smiffy for the pint. The two walked out of the pub shoving the drunken crowd to the side. Dave clicked on his keys to open the car, the two jumped inside. Dave's heart was beating fast and his energy started to spiral out of control, he was determined and dangerous. The adrenaline was pumping. Speeding up the street, his car swerved left crossing the junction erratically. A hysterical laughter emerged from his lungs as he caught up to the dealer.

"FUCK IT!"

"What the fuck are you doing?" Scott shouted as the car moved closer towards the totally unaware dealer. CRASH!

The sound of a thud was heard as Dave clipped the dealer's legs. Screams was heard from outside the car. Dave jumped out of the car and opened the boot, he pulled a balaclava out of the leather bag and a weighted object. He held the object behind his back as he approached the dealer lying on his back. The dealer saw the figure of a tall man walking towards him, he reached for a pistol that snugly fitted in-between his skin and the elastic on his Nike jogging bottoms.

"WHAT THE FUCK ARE YOU DOING WITH THAT!" Dave roared kicking the dealer in his groin. Dave pulled out the metal object from behind his back, Scott's sawn-off shotgun fully loaded and waiting to explode at a moment's notice.

Tears streamed from the dealer's gravelled cut face.

"I'll fucking kill you. You don't know who you're fucking with." Screamed the dealer. Scott walked over to the collapsed body.

"Fucking hell that looks nasty, don't think he'll be walking anytime soon." Scott felt the adrenaline rush through his body, in slight shock from the car colliding he leaned over to the body and picked up the dealer's pistol. The dealer screamed like a dying dog in immense pain, Dave shoved the two barrels from the shot gun firmly into the dealer's mouth.

"SHUT UP AND LISTEN TO ME! I'm the fucking devil." In broad daylight in the isolated streets Scott picked up the dealer and threw him into the boot of the car placing a sack on his head.

Dave felt his heart explode, with blood shooting left, right and centre, his hands were all shaky, hair on his arms stood upright. Scott felt his heart beat intensely as he didn't expect things to pan out like this.

"What the fucking hell Dave!"

"That twat wasn't going to out run me. No fucking chance mate."

"Fucking hell! Fucking hell! It's broad fucking daylight."

"Did you see anyone?" Dave laughed and smiled feeling his anxiety disappear, he felt more determined than ever to start taking out his enemies.

"No! But you never checked for any people. All it takes is someone to note down the Reg Plate and we're goners mate." Dave listened bluntly, but took no notice of Scott as he cruised out of the area. "Listen to me Dave, at least tell me next time you get a bright idea. SHIT! AHH." Tears of laughter streamed down Dave's face.

"Did you see his face? His fucking face! He even tried to shoot me the fucking idiot. Even after I clipped him."

"We've always been alright when it comes to Police right, because we're normally discreet. So beware of that shit. Turn left here it's a quicker way to the mill." The car drove off into the concrete jungle of roads and buildings of Manchester.

Chapter Twenty

Mick walked up to the terminal check in, he saw rows of queues lined up at a variety of different check ins. He looked across at each queue and saw a list of different airlines, Mick looked down at his boarding papers. He saw the British Airways logo on his paper work and joined the never-ending line of people.

"I'm getting too old for all this waiting around," Mick laughed to himself stroking the side of his head.

Inside Mick felt his emotions take over, he felt himself melting down. His eyes felt heavy and the suitcase he was pulling felt like a mammoth task. Not as young as he once was time had caught up with him, Mick raised his free hand and held his chest. He could feel the pulsing of his heart. Trying to block his emotions to create a clear mind, Mick continued to fall down the mountain. His demons inside boiled which changed the way he walked and moved, his posture leant and his bones felt weak. After an hour wait, Mick was next to check in his luggage, he had been watching the family in front of him stand for the same period of time. He heard their family squabbles which created a small touch of humour.

"If only my problems were as petty as that." Mick thought to himself still holding himself. The family he saw reminded him of what he could've also had in his life, but the stress inside him created bitter thoughts.

"Next please." The British Airways employee shouted towards Mick, he stumbled to the check in as he watched the other family walk into security.

"Sorry I was daydreaming," Mick apologised and placed his suitcase onto the scale, after the case was weighed the woman scanned it through, Mick waited impatiently to be told what procedures he had to tackle next before he could get into duty free. After all the security checks had taken place, Mick entered duty-free, he walked through all of the shops to pass the time but ended up sitting in a bar area drinking a pint of chilled Fosters.

Mick's legs started to ache through all the waiting around but the taste of alcohol started to make him loosen up.

Mick looked at the television in the bar area which showed all the flights, his gate was opening in thirty minutes. He felt his jaw bone start to lock stiffer as he yawned, he started to see images inside of past events which happened to him.

"Please, Mick don't go."

"Go on Micky get another round in. It's not going to kill ya? Hahaha."

"Do the right thing."

"Dad don't leave me."

"You know I love Mick."

The images flashed before Mick's eyes like a montage, his eyes stared into space as he saw the mental images on the inside taking a strain on his heart. A tear rolled down Mick's face, he could taste the salt on his tongue.

"Could all British Airways passengers please go to gate nineteen? thank you." Mick woke from the trance through the sound of a Tannoy. Mick pulled out his phone and texted Chris.

Alright mate, just had one for the road. Just to let you know I'm boarding and will see you when I get back. Make sure Vince is okay for me, keep a close eye you know what he's like. Thanks again. Mick.

Mick scrolled through his phone and sent Morgan a message to let him know he was flying out.

After all the stress Mick walked to his gateway and boarded the plane. The day was still clear without a cloud in the sky. Everything seemed almost perfect until the plane set off up the runway, Mick clenched the arm rest on his chair with eyes tightly closed. He could feel the whole plane shaking crazily, all the vibrations travelled through his spine onto the floor of the plane. His chest pounded like a drum, hard and loud, each breath felt like a chore.

Chris parked his van outside the 'Smoking Barrel' and unlocked the door to the pub. Chris shouted to see if Vince had returned home from school. He stumbled upon a bunch of brown envelopes and placed them on a wooden table in the middle of the function room. He walked behind the bar and grabbed an orange J20. Sitting back in the chair at the table, Chris opened the envelopes, he started to scan through them. One of the letters grabbed his attention it had HM Revenue Customs stamped on it.

"Fucking hell! I don't understand how this is even possible. Where on earth has it all come from? Shit. Shit. I don't fucking believe this." Chris stormed out of the 'Smoking Barrel' furious and confused.

Pacing towards his van he opened the back of it where crates of beer stared back at him.

"Fuck sake. Why didn't you tell me old man?" Chris spoke under his breath with upset and anger.

Walking down the street of Mary Lee Road was Vince on his way back from town.

"Alright Chris?" Vince shouted with a smile.

"Yeah." Chris pulled his head out from the back of the van with a crate of beer.

"Do you need a hand?"

"Nar, it's alright mate, oh actually, go on then you may as well make yourself useful." Vince walked towards the van and picked up a crate of beer.

"What's with the JD bag?" Chris kicked the door open making space for Vince to follow.

"I had PE today so I needed more space than normal in my bag."

"Oh right." Chris acknowledged. Vince glanced at the envelopes on the table on his way to the store room.

"What's all that about?"

"You know the usual junk mail you get. Will you support the labour party? It's bull shit innit."

"I suppose," Vince laughed.

"What's with the serious face Chris? Haha, girl trouble now hey?" Vince bantered.

"What you on about you little nugget head?" Chris pulled a cheesy smile and gave Vince a wink. "So how's you and your miss's then? Oooh Daisy!"

"Shut up, you muppet, I'm alright."

"Wasn't asking about you mate!"

"Its good ha ha everything's fine."

The two released the crates into the store room.

"Right, go on get another one in then, I'm right behind you." On the way out of the pub, Chris picked up the letters and shoved them snugly into his jean pockets.

"Which one do you want me to get?" Vince shouted from outside.

"Any, whatever's easiest."

Inside the 'Smoking Barrel' didn't feel the same without Mick's presence even though it had only been one day. The whole pub seemed lifeless, like there was something missing. Maybe it was the energy Mick created when he walked into the room, the sound of his voice not being heard for the first time, in a long time in his family home felt strange.

Chris sat down at the closest table after he finished manoeuvring the crates of beer, Vince sat down beside him placing two glasses of water on the table.

"I'm sweating now!"

Chris shrugged. "Weakling."

"Nah, it's not that they're too heavy, you know what I mean."

"What you doing tonight then? Fancy going out somewhere?" Vince replied feeling a burst of happiness. "I'm going to see Daisy."

"Oh right, selling me out hey." Chris laughed.

"I best go and get a shower, see you in a bit." Vince left the room in a hurry whilst the sweat dribbled down his neck. Chris waited until he could hear him slam the bathroom door shut and opened the letter from his pocket, glancing into misery.

Mick arrived at Ireland's Galway Airport feeling nervous, he hadn't caught much sleep on the plane and still felt uneasy. Morgan waited outside the airport in a beaten down car, as Mick walked through the exit he heard a beeping sound from Morgan's car and noticed him gesturing. Mick walked up to the car pulling his suitcase behind him.

"Alright there Mick? Throw your baggage in the back." Mick pulled open the stiff boot of the car and threw his case inside.

"Alright?"

"Alright Mick? It's good to see ya." Mick frowned and shook his head as the car left the airport onto a motorway.

"I've spoken to Oden, he said that he'll meet us at the cemetery."

"Oh." Mick replied quietly gazing into the road.

"You know he's been alright lately. I've been keeping an eye on him and he seems... well he seems okay."

"You remember when we were younger and he'd chase the cows on the field."

"Yeah."

"He was never okay," Mick grinned. A smile appeared on Morgan's face.

"Ay, we all chased them fucking cows but I know what you mean, haha. He wasn't okay, in fact, he started it."

The sound of laughter burst from the car, it had been a long time since Mick and Morgan had bonded as brothers. After a forty-minute car journey, they arrived at Bohermore Cemetery where the energy between the two simmered to a low.

"Doesn't seem that long ago since we were here last." Morgan's eyes lowered as he parked outside the stone gate entrance. Crunch! Morgan pushed open his car door followed by Mick. The clouds moved gently across the sky, dancing in front of the floating sea. The sound of stones crunched amongst their shoes as they walked towards their parent's grave. A silhouette of a man dressed darkly in the distance sat on a bench facing the gravestone of Vincent Haze and his wife Bridget Haze.

Mick looked across all of the gravestones, he felt the reminding feelings burrow inside him. The silhouette of the man sitting on the bench became recognisable as distance between them got smaller.

"I've been here all morning." The man spoke turning his face towards Mick and Morgan.

"Oden, how are you there?"

"Grand."

"This place always feels the same despite what the weather is." Morgan leaned forward to shake Oden's hand.

"It's good to see you brother." Oden looked at Mick and smiled shaking Morgan's hand.

"As I say, grand." Mick looked away and walked towards his father's grave.

"Happy birthday father." Mick cleared away the rotten decomposed flowers that lay in his father's bed, digging deep into his pocket Mick pulled out a small wooden cross painted white and pushed its base into the damp grass. He closed his eyes making a small prayer leaning down on one knee. The world fell silent in Mick's ears, the sound of Oden and Morgan talking muffled into a blur.

"It still gives me shivers this place, I don't know what it is. But every time I read our parents' names on them stones, it's surreal to believe that they're gone." Oden leaned towards the floor with his back arched from the bench. Slowly turning to Morgan's ear, Oden's voice turned slightly deeper. "You know what? I can still feel the heat from the fire on my face and it burns inside me." A tear ran down Morgan's face.

"I know." He whispered.

Vince ran down Mary Lee road full of energy, his hair was combed back and a spray of aftershave lingered around him. Full of excitement and feeling fresh Vince couldn't wait to arrive at

Daisy's house. After five minutes of dashing he saw a young girl with black curly hair making her way up the street.

"Daisy!"

"Hi Vince! I thought I'd surprise you and meet you halfway." Vince analysed Daisy's outfit admiring her beautiful features, feeling a shyness spring inside him.

"You look beautiful," Vince muttered.

"Awww, you're so sweet Vince." Daisy walked beside Vince holding his hand. "So, what you done today?"

"Nothing really," Smiled Vince squeezing Daisy's palm tightly.

"Are they new shoes?" Daisy looked down towards Vince's feet.

"No, I got them ages ago. It's just, well, I thought I'd wear them for a special occasion."

"You really are a cutie." Daisy leaned towards Vince kissing him on his cheek, they shared a stare for a couple of seconds.

"So, what should we do tonight?" Vince smirked playfully. "Well, My Mum's going out for the night so maybe we could cuddle up on the couch. Watch a film, get a bowl of popcorn and I don't know he he."

"Sounds good, sounds pretty good to me."

Daisy and Vince arrived at the end of Mary Lee Road and strolled towards Daisy's house. Daisy skipped towards her front door pulling Vince along with her. She pushed her key inside the door and twisted it left. The sound of the UK's top 40 music played on the radio from the kitchen. It was heard all through the house.

"Bulletproof, haha that's hilarious."

"My Mum must've forgot to turn it off when she went out!"

"Hey what's this one? Mah mahhh, mah mah, mahhh. Ha ha Lady Ga Ga! I wanna hold them like they do in Texas please!" Vince danced around Daisy's front room laughing and singing.

"Shut up you!" Daisy laughed walking into the kitchen. "Do you want a drink?"

"Yeah, go on then." Vince followed behind Daisy like a lost puppy. Vince stood behind Daisy as she poured him a drink of Coke, he placed his hands on her hips. She wore black leggings that sat along her skin with perfection, he gently felt the side of her body with his hands making his way to her shoulders. She wore a dark flowery top that felt smooth on Vince's skin. Daisy turned her head towards Vince looking backwards and kissed his lips.

"Stop it naughty bum. Behave!"

"What! I've not done anything," Vince laughed, running his fingers through his hair.

"Here's your drink." Vince took the drink from Daisy's hand and walked into her front room. He took a sip and placed it on the centre table. Daisy ran up to Vince and coiled her leg around him.

"I've missed you, munchkin." Vince rested his hands on her lower half and started to slowly kiss Daisy as he walked backwards falling onto the couch.

The sky glowed with stars twinkling and flashing lights from street lamp-posts, rows of fast food havens opened their doors letting the smell of greasy food express their flavours into the night air. Dave gently released his foot on the acceleration of the car as Scott daydreamed ahead.

"Do you fancy a Kebab? I'm starving." Scott stared blankly ahead as the car came to a steady stop outside an Indian takeaway. "Suit yourself then." Dave exited the car and walked into the scent of fast food.

Scott looked down towards the glove compartment and opened the collapsing lid. His eyes looked upon a black snub nosed revolver. He closed the compartment and re-opened it, slamming it closed he pulled down the sun visor and stared at himself in the reflecting mirror.

"FUCK!" Dave walked back towards his car with a white bag full of food.

"I got you a burger. Are you alright?"

"Yeah," Scott replied taking the bag from Dave's hands digging into the paper wrapped parcel of food.

"Watch the leather, that grease stains shit." Dave tore the paper away that held his kebab in place and took a huge bite, then threw it back in the bag. Dave turned his key in the ignition and reached for his steering wheel licking his lips. "Right, how long we been gone now?"

"About an hour."

"Right, we'll go back to the warehouse, and we'll sort out the kid." Scott bit into his burger swallowing hard.

"What we doing about that big fish then?"

"We'll fry this little fish first. Make him squeal some information up about the big fish. Then eat the bastard."

Dave revved his engine with might as he cruised down the busy road. His Mercedes growled like a panther hunting down its prey, closing in on the distance between his location and where they were holding the dealer.

The car shortly arrived outside an abandoned warehouse within one of Manchester's districts. A layer of graffiti had found itself a new home on the warehouse as it bathed in a cake full of dust with shattered windows and stale damp air circulating the building. The smell of vomit and urine streamed into the atmosphere where the drug dealer was left to drown in fear. With legs and arms tied together and glass scattered across the floor with no sight of any light, he heard Dave and Scott enter the warehouse. Struggling to breathe, he was suffocating with the sack tied around his head. He kicked and wiggled his body like a worm rolling himself into more stress. Broken glass entered bare feet biting like a rat as his body wiggled in a panicking state.

Wearing black balaclavas and dark clothes, Dave and Scott entered the flea ridden environment transporting some tools. They walked through a corridor invaded with cobwebs as they entered the room where they had left the dealer.

"Hello, hello, hello, you again?" Dave booted the dealer in the stomach repeatedly and pulled off the black sack revealing his blood coughing face. "What is your fucking name!" Dave aggressively shouted beating the unfortunate victim's body violently.

"KARL NELSON!" he cried spitting blood.

"So Karl, who gave you the job to try and do me in then huh?" Scott leant towards the floor where Karl was lying and spoke gently down his ear.

"Answer my questions and I'll let you go." Scott pulled out the snub-nosed revolver and held it in front of Karl's face. "Because I'm not in the fucking mood for games!" Scott put one shell into the cylinder of the gun and span the casing shut pointing it straight to Karl's knee cap. "If you want to fucking walk again I suggest you tell us who the fuck this guy is!" Scott pulled back the hammer on the pistol and shouted in Karl's face. "I was never great at maths but what's the chances that if I pull this trigger your leg's going to blow straight off!"

"One in six, pull the FUCKING TRIGGER!" Dave barked.

Karl screamed louder than a woman giving birth with tears streaming down his face.

With his last words, "I'll fucking kill you! You fucking wanker." CLICK! Scott pulled the trigger and a silence entered the room as no bullet exited the pistol. Karl released a deep breath as sweat poured down his face. Breaking the silence Dave continued to roar.

"One in five, you're still alive! Tell me who the fuck sent you to kill me." Dave's eyes turned red with blood shot matching his cheeks. Veins pumped adrenaline through his body pulsing out of his neck. "I'm the fucking devil! Who the fuck sent you, you little fucking rodent?" Dave kicked into Karl's injuries violently. "Scott! Pull back that hammer and blow this little fucker's leg off! You're in no fucking position to threaten me!" Dave ripped his balaclava off and stared deep into Karl's eyes. "I'm... The Fucking... Devil." Dave broke his words apart with energy in a sinister manner. "WHO THE FUCK SENT YOU?"

"FUCK YOU! I'm not afraid of you. I'm not afraid of anyone. You don't know who you're fucking with, DAVE!" A bolt of confusion crossed Dave's face. Scott's eyes lit up just as baffled as Dave himself. "WHERE DID YOU HEAR THAT NAME? PULL THE FUCKING TRIGGER!" Scott drew back the hammer and clenched his fist around the grip of the pistol. "Pull it, FUCKING pull it!" CLICK! The hammer of the pistol locked back into its original position with no bullet fired. "Again, again! No fucking games now! Shoot this prick!" Dave grew more violent, he kicked Karl from head to toe. Screams and blood poured from Karl's face. Like a lamb to the slaughter house, helpless with no hope, fate corrupted with violence, blood and no way out. Karl lay helplessly with a stubborn jaw.

"Haha! I know you're fucking name and I know who you are. You're going to die. I know who you fucking are, DEVIL haha!" Karl laughed and hissed hysterically whilst he coughed up blood and choked. Dave thrust his arms towards Karl's neck making him swallow his blood, ragging him left to right like a ragdoll.

"Who sent you? WHO IS HE?" Dave shouted repetitively as Scott digged the pistol deep into Karl's fleshy leg. Karl's head shook, his eyes started to lose their colour, his breathes grew erratic and body shook immensely with tears streaming down his face.

"C C Carmen" Karl retched with a grin. "BIG C. I'm going to kill you for the big man. You fucking pussy."

"Scott give me the fucking gun!" Dave shouted over Karl's hysterical screams.

"LOOK AT ME!!" Dave gripped Karl's hair. "Look at me, I'm going to kill you and your fucking clan." Pulling back the hammer the cylinder rotated, aliening the number of seconds Karl had to gaze into the barrel of his own gun before the next shot was fired.

"Our Father, who's art in heaven, hallowed be thy name. Thy Kingdom come, thy will be done on earth, as it is in heaven. Give us this day our daily bread. And forgive us our trespasses, as we forgive those who trespass against us. Lead us not into temptation, but deliver us from evil. For thine is the kingdom, the power and the glory, forever and ever. Amen." Mick sat still holding the Rosary beads gently around his hands as he sat beside his father's grave with a tilted head. Then looking upwards he noticed Morgan and Oden sitting on the facing bench. They sat quietly watching Mick until a sudden sound became apparent from Oden's mouth.

"You know what we need? A good old drink. There's one not too far from here!"

"I" Morgan agreed shaking his head.

"I suppose," Mick shrugged his shoulders raking chipped fingernails through what was left of his hair. Oden slapped his hands on ridged knees and stood up.

"Come on then. No time like the present." Morgan pulled his hands away from his face and stood up opening a hand to Mick.

"Come on Mick, first rounds on me hey." Mick grabbed Morgan's hand and pulled himself up from the ground, he looked back at their parent's stone.

"Happy Birthday Dad. Goodbye Mother. Until we meet again." Oden buttoned his jacket and Morgan gently squeezed Mick's shoulder. The three were once again joined together by one day that called on sadness. Fragile emotions blew in the wind, Mick walked slowly as Oden marched ahead. The blue sky didn't seem so fresh anymore as stale air became noticeable by Mick's nose.

Mick licked his top lip whilst looking back at all the different stones.

"It's crazy to believe one day all we become is a lifeless body rotting in the ground. Morgan make sure I burn and free my soul from this pain." Mick spoke with upset.

"Don't talk like that! Right! Get your head together!" Mick and Morgan arrived at the car shortly after Oden. Oden leant against the rusty old car.

"Hey, still driving that old banger. Haha, things never change."

"I can still call you a taxi."

"I, you can." Morgan turned his head slightly to Mick and mumbled, "Fucking prick." He walked up to the car and twisted his keys in the lock, Oden opened the left-hand side door and jumped into the front passenger seat. Mick jumped in the back and fastened his seat belt. Morgan started his engine and proceeded towards the nearest bar.

A bolt of energy rumbled inside Oden's chest as he burst into a ditty.

"I'm going to make a good sharp axe. Shining steel tempered in the fire. Will chop you down like an old dead tree! Dirty old town dirty old town. Dirty old TOWN".

Morgan turned on the radio to drown out Oden's noise. "Dirty old town. Dirty old town. Dirty old town." Oden mellowed, open mouthed. Mick rose with a smile and started to laugh.

The radio was poor as all it played was crackling connections, he pulled out a tape from a slot at the side of his door and injected his favourite track. The tape crackled and popped.

"It's not going to play, it's fucked!" Mick pointed out. A screeching sound echoed inside the car from the cassette player, after the high-pitched sound ended the song started to play.

"Here we go!" Morgan shouted

"D d der der d d der" Morgan tapped his fingers on the steering wheel and started to hum the start of the song. "The taste... of love is sweet!"

"Johnny fuckin Cash," Oden whinged whilst Morgan sang along with the chorus.

"I fell into a burning ring of fire, I went down, down, down but the flames went HIGHER!". The energy had spread contagiously throughout the car. All three started to contribute to the singing, even Mick's mouth started to move.

Eventually they arrived at a pub named the 'Horses Wagon.' It was painted white with black outlines and benches lined up outside.

"Finally, we're here! Just like old times." Morgan lowered the music and released his seat belt.

"If I remember rightly…" Oden stopped for a few seconds to think, "First rounds on you." Oden gestured to Morgan. Mick opened his door with a face resuming straight. Raising his eyes Morgan strolled towards the entrance.

"Come on then. I don't remember including you on the first round."

"Very funny," Oden pushed open the front door of the pub and walked straight in directing Morgan towards the bar whilst himself and Mick found a table.

The smell of pub grub spiralled into the air, greasy beef burgers and chunky chips.

"Mmm, the food does smell good here!" Oden slid a menu across the table towards Mick.

"I'm not hungry." Morgan returned to the table with three pints of Guinness clenched together.

"Who wants a burger? I'm fucking starving. Morgan you've got legs." Morgan put the glasses onto the table and snatched the twenty euro note from Oden's opened hand.

"So do you!" Morgan walked back towards the bar with his tail between his legs, Oden started to laugh as he watched Morgan pace.

"I'll have cheese, sauce and every damn thing."

"You have no fucking respect," Mick hissed into his glass.

"I'm joking. It's a joke. You're too serious Mick." Mick bit his lip and drank deep into the glass gulping away at the ale. Morgan eventually returned to the table.

"You can fuck off now. I'm staying put."

"Where's my change? Fucking thief."

"I got myself a burger and some chips for us all."

"Out of my fucking money! Now that's disrespectful, using another man's money." Oden said slightly more aggressively.

"SHUT UP Oden," Mick glared. After a twenty minute wait the food arrived at their table, two plates and a basket of chips.

"It's about fucking. Fuck me! Is that it?" Oden complained to the waiter shaking his head.

"Ignorant twat." Mick grabbed a handful of chips and started to swallow them whole.

"What happened to you not being hungry?" Oden spoke with a mouth full of food.

"I've told you Oden. Shut your mouth. Alright."

Morgan smiled pulling the burger towards his mouth, noticing Oden getting more agitated with him.

"Mmmm, it doesn't half smell good. In fact, it smells even better when it's not your pennies. Look at the size of it." Morgan winked at Oden's angered face.

"Morgan."

"Yeah?"

"SHUT YOUR FUCKING PIE WHOLE. Fucking gob shite." Morgan laughed loudly in Oden's face.

"It's only a joke. Mr FUCKIN langer." Mick coughed and started to laugh along with Morgan as slight tears left Mick's eye.

"LANGER!" Mick screeched. Oden stood up from the table and took the last swig from his glass pointing his fingers at both Mick and Morgan.

"Fuck you and fuck you. You pair of wiggling maggots!" Oden walked into the direction of the toilets as the table filled with laughter.

A couple of hours passed and row's of empty glasses had gathered on the table where all three sat.

"You know, I just fucking love ya, both of ya! Fuckers!!" Oden's face lifted with colour, bright red cheeks and wide eyes stared deep at them both. Mick sat quietly listening, only adding here and there to the conversation. "I'm going for a piss again. Fuck me and my liver."

"It's your bowels, well, bladder."

"Whatever it is, I don't care. I... I got to take one." Oden stumbled from his chair and followed the same path he made earlier, only this time was slightly different. He bumped into others walking, swaying from side to side around the room.

"I best go to the toilet as well." Mick walked towards the toilets feeling the effects of alcohol hit him all at once. "Oh, dearie me," Mick swallowed a ball of saliva that had over produced to the back of his throat, he could taste the mellow scent of Guinness.

Walking towards the toilet Mick stumbled gently but did not lose his step. He pushed open the wooden swinging doors to the smell of urine. Stood leaning on the wall Oden stared into space as his body fluids entered the urinal. Mick walked towards the closest urinal and unbuttoned the top of his pants.

"You alright Oden?"

"I'm grand," replied Oden oblivious. Mick walked towards the sink and started to wash his hands.

"Do you ever think, what on earth is going on?" Oden slurred

"What?" Oden zipped up his pants and strolled towards the sink with smell of alcohol lingering. He scratched his head and looked blankly into the mirror that stood above the sink.

"Do you?"

"What are you going on about? Oden."

"And it burns, burns burns. The ring of fire. La la la laaa." Mick looked up to the mirror and stared into Oden's eyes deeply. "It makes you think doesn't it. Makes you wonder."

"You're slurring. I don't know what you're on about." Oden tilted his head left to right and stood behind Mick placing his hand on his shoulder.

"There's not a fucking day I forget," whispered Oden. "Not a night I don't wake up shivering." Mick turned off the tap and grabbed a couple of paper towels. "I DON'T KNOW WHAT BURNS INSIDE ME MORE, THE FACT WE DIDN'T DO ANYTHING OR... THAT WE LOST EVERYTHING!" Oden shouted with tears. "I CAN'T STAND IT ANYMORE!"

"Your drunk Oden. There is nothing we could've done. NOTHING!" Mick raised his voice in pain and fury. "NOTHING! UNDERSTAND! NOTHING!"

"I don't fucking understand how you don't care!"

"How fucking dare you!" Mick spoke louder. "HOW FUCKING DARE YOU! I DID'NT ONLY LOSE OUR MA AND PA! I LOST MY WIFE!"

"That should give you more of a fucking reason you idiot. Them bastards took Vince's mother away from him!" Oden and Mick looked at each other in anger and disgust, Mick turned to Oden and gripped him by the collar of his shirt.

"This is exactly why I hate coming back here! YOU CAN'T LET GO!"

"I KNOW exactly WHO DID THIS!" Oden shouted over Mick's voice.

"What?"

"I KNOW WHO THEY ARE!" Mick pushed all his body weight onto Oden pressing him up against the wall.

"Do not do anything that will bring more danger to our family! YOU HAVE NEVER UNDERSTOOD"

"HELP ME DO THIS! MAKE THIS RIGHT MICK, for our parents, your wife and Vince."

"You fucking leave Vince out of this!" Mick pressed harder.

"At least for the life we once had. We have nothing."

"No Oden. You have nothing. I will not bring danger onto my family," Mick pushed Oden onto the floor.

"That's good! Get angry Mick. Get fucking mad!" Oden hissed to himself like a rattle snake.

"I'm fucking telling you Oden." Mick pointed his finger towards him with upset in his voice. Mick walked over Oden's drunken torso. Looking up towards Mick's moving body Oden screamed.

"IT'S THE ONLY WAY!"

Mick slammed the toilet door behind him and faded into the crowd of intoxicated people.

Lying on the couch snuggling together Vince kissed Daisy passionately locking lips. Daisy looked at Vince and smiled, he started to hum with his lips. Daisy held her hand out towards Vince.

"Stop singing that song!" She laughed with a glowing seductive smile.

"What is it? You don't like Lady Gaga hey?"

"Shut up, come on I want to show you something." Vince smiled taking Daisy by her hand as she walked upstairs towards her bedroom. "My mum won't get back till the early hours of the morning."

"Oh right," Vince shook his head. Daisy twisted the door handle and pushed her way into her room. The smell of perfume vapoured into the air, the bed had red poker dot duvet covers and pictures on the wall, photographs sat neatly on the shelves. Filled with past memories in print, Daisy pointed to them.

"This was me when I was five."

"No way is that you?"

"Yeah it is, look at my eyes, they haven't changed." Vince looked at Daisy's eyes closely.

"Oh yeah."

"And this one, it was my eleventh birthday." Daisy pointed to a picture that had her and a group of girls in the photo.

"Are they still your friends?"

"No!"

Oh! Why, what happened?"

"Well, you see her there, the one with the pink top?"

"Yeah."

"Well she was called Katie Parker," Daisy spoke raising in tone, "She turned all my friends against me."

"Why? Hardly friends then were they." Vince said with concern.

"It doesn't matter anyway, it was years ago." Daisy picked up the photo and threw it under the bed. "Come and lie down with me." Daisy raised her eyebrow gently and pulled a warm smile.

"Okay." Vince fell onto the bed laying next to Daisy. "You know you can tell me what happened."

"Well, let's just say she was a horrible person. Kiss me!" Vince crawled towards Daisy and kissed her lips snuggling up to her.

An hour passed and the two lay together talking about their pasts, after they shared stories about how horrible schools can be and people who have affected them the vibe in the room between them changed. Finally Vince had met somebody he really liked and was lucky that his relationship with Daisy had progressed into absolute trust. The energy inside Vince grew, his attraction towards Daisy became magnetic.

Vince reached for the lamp at the side of the bed and pressed the off switch.

"Vince, I'm scared," Daisy spoke quietly.

"Don't worry, I'm right here." Vince put his arm around her body and gently squeezed tighter. Daisy lightly kissed Vince's lips and pulled the T-shirt that glued to Vince's body. A shiver of excitement crawled down Vince's spine rushing like blood beating to the heart. Daisy held her hands on his body and pulled off his top, she inhaled oxygen through her nose whilst her lips were locked. Taking fast paced breaths, she whispered into his ear.

"I love you Vince." Running her fingers through his hair, Daisy gradually came to Vince's shoulders.

The heat from the bedroom cooled down into the early hours of the morning. The wind blew a cold draft into the air from Daisy's open window. All was quiet as the hours passed by revealing the morning sun from the closed venetian blinds. What once was a neatly tidied room had become a nest of lust with underwear scattered on the floor and clothing randomly thrown. Daisy and Vince lay together shaped like spoons in a trance of a dream world state of consciousness.

Chapter Twenty-One

The school week flew by as talk of Vince and Kane had spread throughout, diluting confusion amongst students. It was at the beginning of the weekend all over again, life had started to dramatically change for Vince as people looked at him differently. Slight behaviours started to become experimental, he still felt like himself but his eyes had become exposed to Kane's influence and manipulating personality. Walking out of the school yard with Kane, Vince stared blankly ahead.

"What you got planned for the weekend?" Kane spoke over the noise of the school yard.

"I don't really know. My Dad comes home this Sunday."

"Sounds good. You doing anything tonight."

"I don't know. Just going to go home. See what needs to be done."

"Me and Sean and some others are meeting up. You should come." Vince bit dry skin from his lip as they exited the school yard.

"I don't know, you know. The pub's a mess, it needs sorting out. My Dad will go mad if he sees it."

"Don't be a turd. Do it when you get in."

"KANO!" A voice shouted from behind.

Kane turned his head and looked behind him.

"Alright lads!" Lucas and Sean approached from behind.

"Safe Vince," Lucas muttered.

"Alright Vince. You out with us tonight?"

"He's too busy," Kane laughed. "Too busy to chill with us bro."

"Don't be a waste man. Come out fam! Eye" Lucas spoke as if they had always been friends.

"I'll see, yeah." Vince felt slight pressure feeling uncomfortable heading towards the bus stop. The small crowd followed as they shared the same stop. Nudging Vince, Sean addressed him.

"Come on! You know you want to pal. It will be a top laugh, it's a fucking weekend!"

Lucas spoke quietly to Kane, "Have you seen Kevin today?"

"Nah, he didn't come in."

"Bit weird innit?"

"I'll give him a text and tell him to meet us innit?" Sean became more boisterous with Vince, putting his arm around him and talking to him with excitement.

"Trust mate. Tonight's going to be wild!"

The group eventually arrived at the bus stop and Vince's eye caught onto a passing bus.

"Shit. That's my bus. Ill speak to you later boys."

"I'll drop you a text," Kane shouted as Vince entered the bus. "Tonight will be good," Kane pulled a gentle smile. Vince flashed his day saver to the driver and sat upstairs overlooking the street ahead of him from a different perspective. The sound of the bus's engine were heard throughout the bus, the vibrations swam through all the passenger seats. Vince pulled his phone from his pocket and glanced at the screen. Scrolling through his contacts he started to text Daisy.

Hi babes, hope you're okay. School's been a bit weird. Xxxx

Vince clicked send on his phone feeling slightly odd.

Buzz Buzz! Vince's phone vibrated with a response from Daisy.

I'm okay thanks. What's up? Xxxx

Vince bit his lip and started to text back.

I've sort of made some friends. And they want me to go out with them. Feels awkward xxxx

Daisy replied. *You should go out with them. It will do you good. :) xxxx.* Twenty minutes passed and Vince could see his stop at the top of Mary Lee Lane, he pressed the bell and paced down the stairs thanking the driver.

The clouds started to collaborate with each other creating a gloomy atmosphere along the street, blurring all the blue from the sky. The streetlights tinted orange as a cold breeze blew down Vince's back.

Vince entered the 'Smoking Barrel,' he heard Chris on the landline stood in the hallway behind the bar.

"Hello?" The phone crackled as Chris spoke loudly.

"Hello. Hello."

"Chris it's me Mick. Just to let you know I'll be back tomorrow, I should arrive at the airport at one. Can you pick me up around that time?"

"Yeah course I will. One on the dot; I can do that."

"How's things over there?"

"I'll see you tomorrow at one."

"Oh, Okay." Vince threw his school blazer onto the closest table followed by his bag.

"Who was that?"

"It was your Dad. He's coming home tomorrow." Chris hung the phone back on the wall. Vince walked past Chris into the hallway.

"Oh, I thought he was coming back on Sunday. I'm going to get changed out of these clothes." Vince ran upstairs and threw on an old track suit. He looked at himself in the mirror and pulled up the hood and glanced at the JD bag which was thrown into the corner of his room. Picking up the bag Vince dug his hands into the bottom of it pulling out the cardboard box containing the shoes Kane got him. Vince pulled open the lid of the box and stared at the Nike trainers. They were black with a bright white tick with matching white rims with air bubbles. Vince slid his feet into the shoes, he had never experienced wearing expensive trainers that fit perfectly. Standing upright, Vince felt the bounce in the shoe, he felt taller than usual glancing at his feet. He sat back on the bed and pulled out his phone.

Where's everyone meeting tonight? Vince texted Kane.

Vince didn't feel like his usual self, he felt an excitement inside him that sprung around his body.

"They can't be that bad." Vince spoke to his reflection. "Fuck it, I'll go out with them once and see what their big hype is. I'm not doing anything anyway, I'm just going to be sat here on my own aren't I" Vince felt his phone vibrate.

Alright mate. Yeah we're meeting outside Tommy's Chippy. The one near Broadhurst park."

Taking one last glance at himself in the mirror Vince zipped up his hooded jacket and smiled. Leaving his room Vince shouted to Chris.

"I'm going out mate."

"Alright pal. Give me a ring in a bit. I'll pick you up."

"Nice one Chris. Alright I'm off now." Vince walked through the function space and left by the front entrance.

Chris arrived back at the pub with Mick, the journey home covered the usual conversations with the usual chit chat about what happened over there and how everyone was. Mick started to stare at the floor.

"Have I had any post?" Chris gently paused and released a muttering response.

"Yeah." Mick turned his head towards Chris still holding a deep stare. "I best get off I'm exhausted," Chris turned towards the door holding a lump in his throat, he quickly pushed the wooden door forward.

"Wait up Chris." Chris paused cautiously with his hands feeling glued to the door.

"Where is the post?" Mick's feet thudded as he approached Chris's spooked body language.

"It's just here. I picked it up yesterday morning." Chris reached into the side pocket of his black North Face jacket and revealed the letters. One of which had been opened with torn edges.

"Are you okay Chris? You look sheepish?" Chris nodded with widened eyes and gulped.

"Yeah." His eyes started to build up with a glaze of water, his eyes dilated with an extending circumference. Chris held the letters folded in his hand and moved it forward towards Mick holding eye contact. Chris felt nervous and his hands shook gently, he could feel the anxiety boil inside him, the thoughts of the unknown reaction from Mick terrified him.

"Did you open my letter?" Mick's tone changed as he recognised the envelope. He pulled out the letter and glanced at the mess he was in. "You have no right to read into my personal stuff."

"I didn't intend to." Chris panicked. "It was just there."

"Why did you hide it?"

"Well, you was away, I wanted everything to be okay. I was scared Vince would find it, so I took it."

"Don't you DARE root through my SHIT again. I trusted you to take care of things back here. THAT LETTER IS NONE OF YOUR CONCERN. "

Chris whimpered building up a volcano of anger and aggression. "WHOSE NAME IS ON THAT LETTER?"

"Yours."

"EXACTLY, NOW GET OUT OF HERE!" Mick aggressively raised his voice assertively. Chris turned back towards the door with his head faced towards his feet. Mick followed him outside fuelled with emotion.

"You was never going to even tell me, was you?" Chris looked at Mick as he pulled open the door of his van. The sound of the vans engine choked on the fuel and slowly reversed out from the concrete path. Chris un-winded his window and popped his head out, "TWENTY-FIVE GRAND MICK. Fucking hell. Why didn't you tell me?" Chris hit the steering wheel of the car with his fist as Mick watched Chris's actions in disbelief.

The park turned quieter as the boys dispersed into the night, Sean walked beside Kane leading the group's direction.

"What did you think of that brick hahaha?"

"It was fucking stupid." Kane exhaled smoke from his cigarette and grew irritated. "You could've hit me you dick."

"I knew you was behind the counter, what's the chances?"

"Fuck off Sean."

"You're always a twat to me, even when we do something good." Kevin piped up with a stern tone, "Crazy shit man. Stop being mad, it's not like we got caught. Then there would be a reason to be pissed." Lucas laughed to himself, "True shit bro, you get me."

"That Vince shit himself!" Sean mocked.

"I suppose he is still yet to prove himself," Kevin smiled.

"I told you he's not one of us." Lucas mumbled loudly, "Mans a pussy innit."

Kane frowned and dismissed the immature comments. "The first time is always overwhelming, he could've ran or worse sabotage what we did."

"I suppose." Kevin acknowledged rolling a cigarette.

Sunday morning, birds singing, the sun fighting to get through the clouds. Picking up his phone Vince text Daisy

"I heard my Dad raise his voice at Chris yesterday when he left, like proper angry. I didn't say out when I seen him this morning but it's awkward. Chris hasn't spoken to me, not even text me, so I don't know what to say."

Daisy responded quickly tapping away on her phone reassuringly.

"Don't worry about it. It's probably over nothing they'll be friends again tomorrow."

Vince read the text and pushed his thoughts to the back of his mind. Vince started to walk down Mary Lee Road heading aimlessly, "What am I doing with myself?" Vince questioned himself talking softly under his breath.

The sun surprisingly broke through the cloud's hitting Vince's face, the day was warm and Vince hadn't experienced the sun's glow in a long time. He felt the warmth on his face and smiled to himself. He picked up his phone and dialled Daisy's number.

"Hi Daisy," Vince chirped.

"Hey."

"Do you fancy going for a walk? I know it's a bit random, but I just thought I haven't seen you the past few days and well you know..."

"Yeah." Daisy interrupted smiling to herself.

"That's great. I'm already on foot so I could come and meet you."

"Well, I'm not ready."

"Oh," Vince paused to himself thinking what he could do to pass the wait. "It will take me about twenty minutes to get to yours."

"I've not even done my makeup!" Vince stressed to himself and paused trying to think of a solution.

"My Mum's going out in an hour around 1pm. Come down to mine around then." Vince refrained from saying what he thought and agreed, he stared at his phone's screen and checked the time.

"11:23am God sake!!!" Vince mumbled to himself. "I might as well just go back home," Vince moaned.

Chapter Twenty-Two

Vince's phone started to ring out, 'Kane' appeared on the screen.
"Hello?"
"Alright Vince mate? It's Kane."
"Alright"
"You busy?"
Vince felt discomfort and blurted, "I've got to go." Feeling shaken Vince turned off his mobile phone and headed home jittery. Checking his pockets, he became alarmed. "Shit, I haven't got my keys." Vince banged on the wooden doors awaiting a response from Mick on the inside.
"Dad!" Vince shouted knocking harder on the door. Creek! Mick twisted the key on the door and pulled it open.
"Alright son. What you up to?"
"I've just been out with a few friends."
"Oh," Mick nodded. Vince stepped inside his home and headed to his bedroom. "Ah Son, will you do the locking up for us, the keys on the side?"
"Yeah." Vince grabbed the keys and locked the pub's doors tight and headed to his room.

Vince woke the following morning hearing the thick wooden door being banged on repetitively.
"I'm coming Dad, I'll be there in a second!" Vince shouted throwing on his grey jogging bottoms and a matching top. The wooden doors of the 'Smoking Barrel' rocked with heavy knocks. Still half asleep, Vince opened the lock to the doors and pulled them open.
A tall figure wearing a tweed jacket and tailored trousers, carrying a travel bag in his right hand, towered over Vince. He had short dark hair which had started to mature grey. His eyes had shallow tints of darkness which stood out from his unshaven face.
"Vince, where's your Dad?" Oden spoke friendly.
"Alright Uncle Oden? He went out before with Chris."

"Oh, right, can I come in for a drink then and wait for him to get back?" Oden licked his lips and walked inside the pub following behind.

"Yeah, course, come in." Vince walked to the bar as Oden found himself a seat. "What do you want?"

"Just get me an orange juice." Vince went behind the bar and opened the side fridge that sat neatly underneath the wooden interior. He grabbed at the half empty bottle of orange juice and poured the liquid into a brandy glass.

"How's your Dad?" Vince walked to Oden's table and placed the glass in front of him.

"He's alright, I suppose."

"Good," Oden replied softly. "When's he due back?"

"He shouldn't be too long, he set off a while ago."

"So, you've left school know ay?" Pulling out the facing chair Vince sat down and responded.

"Nar, I've still got this year, then I'm done." Oden scratched the hairs on his face and smiled.

"Have you got any plans then ay, you going to be working with your old man?"

"I don't know, probably. I don't really have any plans."

The room was empty and the sound of a van was heard parking outside. Chris jumped out the van followed by Mick.

"Fucking hell that woman never shut up. I thought we'd never leave."

Mick shrugged with a smirk, "She didn't mean any harm, if it wasn't for her taking a liking to you we wouldn't have got them barrels on the cheap."

Chris's face lit up with a light glow of red, "Shut up!" The two broke into laughter as they walked into the 'Smoking Barrel.'

"Alright there Mick?" A deeper voice than Vince's spoke out with a familiar Irish accent.

"Oden?" Mick's face changed dramatically as he looked across at Oden sat at the table with Vince.

"That's my name. It's nice to see you too."

"What are you doing down here Oden?" Mick's eyebrows raised with concern.

"I thought I'd stop by for a visit." Mick felt anxious, his hands started to shake slightly.

"Chris, take Vince with you to unload the lighter load from the van and take them into the storeroom around the back." Mick dug his hands deep into his pockets and clenched the van keys. He pulled them out and threw them to Chris.

"Come on Vince, come and give me a hand pal."

The sound of Vince's chair squeaked across the wooden floor as he left the room. Mick approached Oden and sat in the facing chair, he looked into his eyes nervously sensing a negative energy.

"Oden, what's wrong?" Mick softly spoke.

"There's nothing wrong. Look at me, I'm fine. Can't your brother come to visit?" Odens face frowned slowly. Taking a deep breath and exhaling, Mick stood and walked over to the bar. He picked up an empty glass that sat along the wooden surface and poured himself a drink. The brandy stained the glass as it hit the bottom and rose to the top.

"I see that you've helped yourself to a drink."

"Vince got me this. What's wrong with you Mick?" Oden took a sip of his orange juice and scanned his eyes across to Mick.

"What's wrong? You didn't ring me to tell me you was coming, you didn't let me know anything. And the last time we spoke we didn't... well, let's just say... get on and you just come here out of the blue." Mick grew angry inside with past affairs on his mind.

"I came to say I'm sorry! ALRIGHT! Jesus Christ! Can't a man apologise? Brother to brother." Mick bit his tongue feeling a rush of guilt.

"Look Oden I worry about you and when you come here out the blue, it plays on my mind because usually something's happened, Either with Morgan or other things." Mick picked up the bottle of brandy which sat behind the bar and walked over to Oden. "I'm sorry for over-reacting. It's just..." Mick's voice started to crumble as he continued his sentence. "It's been on my head, I kept thinking that you was going to do something crazy. I've not slept right in fucking weeks because of you." Oden listened feeling his brothers fear, he starred down at the empty glass on the table which was filled with orange juice. He poured himself a glass of brandy and replied gently.

"Morgan's fine. He's still a pain but he's alright."

"You're a fucker," Mick revealed a smile.

"You know what I'm fucking on about."

"I take it you're going to ask if you can stay for a few days then," Mick looked to the side of Oden's feet where a travelling bag leant against him.

"I'm staying at the travel lodge."

"Oh."

"I best be going anyway Mick, I'll see you around." Oden stood taking the last drop of his drink and exited by the wooden doors.

Chapter Twenty-Three

Six months past, school finally came to an end, Vince moved into full time work with his father. Turning seventeen, Mick became aware of the extra pair of hands he had, he made sure that Vince could drive the work van so he could assist Chris on daily routines. Chris still played a large role in keeping the pub existing as he battled and tore with his emotional connection to the pub.

Kane had grown into his tailor-made shoes and put forth some more steps in his future path.

Daisy was still Vince's partner in crime but little did she know what was going on in the flipside to his coin.

September 2009 'The Smoking Barrel.'

Vince pulled into the paved path outside his home with Chris sat beside him.

"I can't believe you're driving now," Chris grinned.

"I know." The two got out of the van slamming the doors behind them. "Should we get the barrels out?" Vince asked. Chris paused, his ears perked.

"Is that the sound of people chanting." Vince walked forward towards the door hearing the muffled sounds of people talking over each other. The door creaked open by Vince's hand, revealing a small crowd of people chanting at the pub's television set. It was United vs Arsenal and some of the locals used the pub as a haven.

"This is strange, we normally only have a handful of casual people. The only time this place gets more hectic is well, when we do private functions." Chris spoke bewildered to himself.

Mick stood behind the bar feeling smug.

"That will be two pound fifty."

"Thanks mate," a well-rounded figured bloke mumbled walking back to his seat.

"UNITED!" The older men shouted as their team came close to score.

"Alright Dad!" Vince glowed. "What's happening in here?"

"We're making money son, that's what we're doing!" Mick smiled.

"Vince come and make yourself useful boy, get behind here." Mick walked into the back corridor followed by Chris.

"Mick we've got them fresh barrels."

"Good, good." Mick leant forward falling deeper towards Chris. "You know what I heard."

"What?"

"That Eight Bells has been shut down."

"No way!"

"I know, strange isn't it. But I think it's going to get better for us now."

"What happened then?"

"I heard one of the blokes that came in here saying that it's been raided by the Police. Shut down! Every one chucked out! Something to do with drugs being held there and sold, all sorts of shit going on."

"Always knew it was dodgy."

"But now people have been coming in and out of here."

"Mick, we best be careful who we're going to attract in here."

"I know, then we will be screwed."

"I'll go and take over from Vince." Chris walked towards Vince, heading towards the interior of the bar Vince stood pouring drinks. "Keep an eye out for anything dodgy or suspicious." Chris spoke quietly, whispering into Vince's ear. Shaking his head with a slight nod Vince gave customers their change.

"I've got to run and check something."

"It's alright, I was gonna take over from you." The sound of the crowd shouting created a new energy in the pub, something was different other than all the noise. It was almost like the place had lost an element of what it was intended for.

Once the noise had died down and the crowd had disbursed no one sat casually. It felt like an illusion how such a place could hold so much sound for there then to be none. 10:30 pm struck the clock, which was still early in the eyes of what the business is. Thud! Bang! Bear like hands, similar to Mick's thudded on the wooden door entrance.

WE'RE OPEN!" Mick shouted from behind the bar.

Wearing a black thick woven fabric Crombie and matching top hat, saturated in water from the hailing rain that dribbled down the rim of his hat, a voice, still sore from a husky cold, Oden shouted out.

"I SOLD MY HOUSE!!"

"What? What are you doing here?" Mick held confusion and came out from behind the bar. "What's in the bag?"

"Sixty thousand Euros!!!!"

"You can't be here!"

"You're the only family I have Mick, I have nowhere to go, well and Morgan."

Keeping calm, Mick followed up smoothly, "There's a travel lodge just down the road. I'll phone you a taxi. Something you're familiar with, you'll be right at home."

Rushing footsteps from upstairs came crashing down.

"Shit, I've not sorted the van out and it's raining. God sake." Vince arrived in the function area where Mick and Oden stood locking eye to eye. "Alright?" Vince awkwardly spoke breaking the stare.

"How are you Vince?" Oden spoke addressing Vince as he slowly stepped backwards. Oden walked intrudingly towards a seat faced only meters away from Mick.

"How much is it for the night at the hotel?"

"forty-five to fifty pounds." Mick responded adamantly. "Oh, can you get me a glass of water kid?" Vince looked to his Dad, Mick nodded. Vince picked out a glass and filled it with water placing it on Oden's table.

"That's all you'll be getting." Picking up the glass firmly with grazed hands Oden gulped half the glass.

"No better way to clench the thirst." Holding his thoughts, he entered his hand into the coats deepest pocket and pulled out a handy amount of money. Oden shuffled it in his hands slightly licking his finger and began to count quickly to himself.

"Go and straighten your room Vince." Mick demanded with concern. Vince headed upstairs getting out of the way.

"Why give money to strangers. I'll pay you for the cost of one night in that hotel." Oden put sixty pounds on the bar and looked at Mick's stern face.

"Upstairs, there's a spare room. One night only!!"

The following morning Vince woke at six am to the sounds of someone stumbling along the landing creaking the floor boards. Throwing on a dressing gown from the floor, Vince explored popping his head from around his door. It was the figure of Oden heading downstairs.

"What the heck is he doing?" Vince thought to himself following Oden's path along the landing. The wooden planks creaked as Vince got to the top of the stairs. Snooping quietly he slid his hands along the bannister and entered the function space from behind the bar. "Where is he?" Vince scanned his eyes across the room with Oden nowhere to be seen. Vince pulled open the door to the fridge and grabbed an Orange J20, his ears opened awaiting the smallest sound.

Oden found his way into the cellar where all the stock and barrels were stored, dark and gloomy with a mild light twinkling, he searched for a small confined space, holding the leather bag in his right hand, stacks of musky wooden boxes and stainless steel barrels stared at Oden in the face. He shifted them left and right trying to find a concealed area within the room. He made his way past the obstacles towards one of the corners in the room where wooden boxes lay on top of each other. He dropped the bag beside him onto the floor and started to rearrange the placement of the boxes. Sliding his nails across hidden groves on the box in hand, he managed to find an opening. Odens eyes glanced inside.

"Empty wine bottles?" The empty bottles sat snugly together wrapped in soft cloth. He started to make a new section in the room for the boxes to stand. One by one he rooted sniffing out the dust that layered until he came across one that caught his eye. "Newspapers? Why would you store old papers Mick? Nevertheless." Oden placed the box in front of him, he brushed away the dust on the outside of the box and smiled. "This is the one." Oden unzipped his bag, Vince lurked in the shadows and discreetly looked across the opening of the cellar door, unnoticed he watched Oden dig his hands into his bag.

Oden gripped stacks of Euros and Pounds from his bag that valued more than what he had told and started to fill the wooden box like a safe deposit box. Freshly grouped stacks glued together on top of each other with elastic bands keeping them tight. The last object inside his bag was covered by a dirty rag of fabric, it had a weighted feel to it. Oden started to unravel the fabric but stopped after a couple of seconds with eyes squinted then placed it on top of the money finishing off with the lasagne layers of newspaper. Oden closed the box with concentrated force, patting his hand's on top of it.

"Alright Oden, what you doing down here?" Vince broke the silence. Slightly jumping, Oden placed the box in the corner and started to stack other boxes on top.

"I'm looking for your Dad's secret stash of beer, I know he's got one somewhere, I know he doesn't keep his best stuff on the bar." Vince didn't buy his lies but played along holding back his suspicions.

"I'm not sure, I think he has some good stuff upstairs you might not have found."

"All I can find down here is empty bottles of the stuff." Oden referred to the bottles left out along the floor.

"I'll find you something, don't let him know you've been rooting though, he'll go mad."

"I won't, promise. Lead the way Vince." Vince walked back up the stairs of the cellar to the bar and started to look for some high-volume alcohol drinks. "What about this Brandy here?"

"I don't know what make it is because it's in a single glass bottle. But you can try some." Oden took the bottle from his hands and swigged it down his neck. "Don't drink it all, it's my Dads."

"FUCKING HELL! That's a good one. O I." Vince laughed at Oden's reaction to the drink, they both started to giggle between one another. The sound of footsteps from Mick entered the bar area.

"What's all this fuss about?"

"Nothing Dad." Vince swiftly moved the bottle under the bar table.

"Vince go and get yourself ready. I need you to run some errands for me." Mick placed the van keys on the table. "Come on Vince, did you hear me boy?" Vince ran upstairs towards his bedroom, Oden watched as he left.

"You know you shouldn't be too hard on him, he's a good kid."

"He is a good lad."

"I'll best be getting out of your way soon. Don't want to out-stay my welcome."

Mick laughed. "We've been getting busier lately you know."

"That's grand."

"What you planning to do down here?"

"Well, I take each day as it comes, I guess. I'm going into town at some point."

Mick bit the skin from his lip and looked underneath the bar.

"You've sneaked some of my Brandy." Mick grabbed it placing it on the bar's table whilst picking up two glasses.

"It was all Vince."

"What's he like that lad?" Mick poured himself a glass and looked towards Oden. "Do you want one?"

"Oh I Mick, you know me."

"It's never a great start to the day without one." Mick slid Oden's glass forward towards him. "I've been thinking." Mick paused in thought. "I could do with an extra pair of hands."

"You have plenty, don't you? Vince and that other lad."

"I do have Vince and Chris but it's difficult putting too many hours on them. What I'm trying to say is....." Oden stood listening with care. "I've been thinking....and you can come and work for me, well with me."

"I don't want to be rude."

"Oden.... I can change my mind."

"Alright then. Yeah. Thanks Mick." Oden spoke quickly.

"I'll have to charge you rent though. I've still got a family to feed."

Oden smiled. "I am your family."

Vince returned dressed for work and entered the bar area.

"Thanks Mick." Oden opened his hand to Mick respectfully feeling a sense of belonging.

"What's going on?"

"Your Dad's letting me stay boy."

"Well he can be an extra pair of hands at least here I can keep him out of trouble." Oden laughed along with Mick's smirking smile.

"That's great to hear. Welcome aboard Uncle Oden. Your taking this first shift." Vince laughed on his way to the door.

"Less of the cheek. I'm still your Uncle." Oden bantered.

Vince picked out his mobile and called Daisy.

"Morning baby." was the first words that jumped out.

"Hello boo." Replied Daisy.

"What you doing?"

"You know, I'm on my way to college."

"I knew that. I just didn't think."

"What you doing today?"

"Well, Oden's here, so I don't know what my Dad will have me do."

"Why didn't you tell me."

"He came late last night."

"Did anything happen."

"Well he's still here, so something must've happened, Dad's letting him work with us."

"Oh right."

"Do you fancy coming down to mine tonight. I'll pick you up from college."

Erm. I don't know. I've got an assignment that's got to be in, in two days."

"I'll still pick you up."

"You sure. Don't want to mess up your plans."

"What plans you on about?"

"Your probably working today so I don't want to get in the way."

"What are you on about? I always pick you up. I'll be there at half two."

"No Vince, I've got to get my work done."

"I'll drop you off home, just save you getting the bus, that's all." Vince ended the call and shrugged. "Bloody Heckers." he muttered to himself.

A couple of hours passed, Vince straightened the bar space and grabbed himself a sandwich. Daydreaming into the ham that sat stuck to the butter Vince opened his mouth and took a bite. His curiosity had been growing, creeping up on him from the back of his mind. "What's in that box," Vince thought to himself looking at his clock. "Shit!! I better get moving."

Vince arrived outside the college where Daisy studied. Waves of students passed by the streets in their own social groups. Caught in the mist of the majority Daisy saw Vince's van parked on the side walk of Newton Street. Manchester College over looked everyone with an intimidating authentic 20th century old school feel. Traffic queued on the road facing, Vince scanned his eyes through the rows. Bang! Vince jumped and turned his head to the passenger window. He opened the door as he leaned across.

"Where was you?" Daisy entered with a snide smile.

"I'm, here, aren't I?"

"Yeah. But I didn't see you."

"So."

"So what?" Vince clicked his indicator right and waited for another car to let him drive off the pavement.

Manchester was busy with a flow of cars streaming along the roads along with bus drivers causing hazards.

"Aren't you glad you're not on that?" Vince referenced the bus in front. With an acknowledging smirk Daisy spoke.

"Yeah, still gonna take about an hour though in this traffic."

"At least you've got me."

"Oh, I'm flattered." Vince felt the negative energy and turned on the radio.

"You shouldn't have come."

"I wanted to help you out."

"Oh, only when you feel like it." Vince felt a panic inside he couldn't understand why Daisy was behaving unusual.

"If you didn't want a lift from me, why didn't you jump on that bus? Why did you get in with me then? Can't you be happy that I wanted to pick you up and be with you as much as I can?"

Daisy stared feeling angry. "So, when we was supposed to see each other the other day you were busy and you didn't even let me know."

"I forgot, I didn't mean to."

"Oh, so it's nice to get a text about, errm…..let me see." Daisy looked down at her phone. "Thirty minutes before we were going to spend time together."

"You've been going out every other night and leaving in the early hours of the morning when were together. With no reason or explanation."

Vince gulped gathering saliva. "I've had to do extra hours at the pub. Sorting out things."

"What things?"

"Pub shit."

"Go on."

"Do I need to give you a full commentary of my day, what's the matter with you?" Vince pushed down the acceleration with his foot and over took the bus.

"What you doing?"

"It's doing my head in going slug speed." Vince aggressively broke his tone.

"Let me out, I'm walking."

"Why you being stupid? You're not."

"See, you never listen to me."

Vince grew in frustration. "I'm not letting you get out here on Mosley Road with dickheads who we know live round here."

Vince came onto Mary Lee Road still boiled with anxiety and frustration. Daisy continued to create noise down his ear for answers he could not give. He knew that if he told her what he had become a part of, she would leave him. He could not take the outcome which came with the truth behind his mysterious actions.

"Your nearly home now look." Daisy leaned against her arm looking out of the passenger window.

"Finally." Vince pulled up outside her home. "Look, will you let it go?" Vince spoke gently.

"I just feel like there's something going on and you won't tell me."

"Nothing's going on, I've got a lot on with my Dad not being his old self."

"You said Oden's come back."

"Exactly."

"You said he's been helping out as well."

"Yeah and I've been having to show him how things work?"

"Oh." Daisy replied feeling more secure with herself.

Daisy placed her hand on Vince's and looked at him in the eye. "You need to start telling me things, that's what I'm here for, OK?" Daisy watched Vince's face turn neutral and kissed him on his cheek.

"Hey." Vince held out his lips.

"I'm still angry with you." Daisy smiled playfully. Daisy opened the car door and stepped out.

"You can come in if you want."

"Oh no, its fine. I'll end up distracting you and your work."

"True, well have a good night working. I'll ring you when I've got this essay out of the way."

"Okays." Vince smiled watching Daisy run towards the door of her house, he pushed his feet on the pedals and continued to drive forward down the road.

Kane pulled up outside his house in a Volkswagen Golf, he entered holding anger.

"SEAN! WHERE ARE YOU?" Kane shouted marching up the stairs. "SEAN!" Creek!

"What the FUCK is with all this shouting going on?" Dave entered the landing furious from being woken by Kane. "Stop your fucking going on you little shithead. He's in his room asleep, like a normal little fuck up." Dave reached his hand forward with a thrust and caught onto Kane's top.

"Get the fuck of me, I'll fucking smash your head in." Kane ruffled with Dave trying to get free.

"Don't fuck with me you little shit it's too fucking early. Fuck off back to bed you dickhead." Dave released Kane and forcefully pushed him along the landing. Kane disregarded his father and continued his journey along the landing.

"Sean!" Kane shouted pushing open his bedroom door. Lay with jittering eyes snuggled to his pillow Sean's eyes rolled open.

"What? What do you want?" A confused tired look glued to Sean's face.

"Are you taking the piss? I rang you six times. You was supposed to meet with me at five am to pick up."

"I'm still at school."

"What the flying fuck has that got to do with out?? You gotta do exactly what I tell ya." Sean sat up from the warmth of his pillow. "What the FUCK. How dare you. You work with ME don't you?"

"Yeah." Sean muttered.

"Not for me?"

"Yeah."

"Then you better start acting like it."

"Okay...Okay. Stop going on about it. Will you get out of my room now?" Sean spoke still feeling unconscious.

"DON'T YOU FUCKING CROSS THE MARK WITH ME, you cheeky little bastard." Kane jumped onto Sean's bed and gripped him by his head digging it into the pillow. "3pm today, I'll be there at the gates, don't fucking be late." Kane grinded his teeth one inch from Sean's ear raising in volume holding aggression. "Now get your arse up, we've got shit to do." Kane pulled the covers from his bed and dragged him by the ear. "Get moving." Sean lunged across the room hopping on his feet. Kane left the room defused and entered his bedroom whilst lurking hands entered his pockets.

He leaned towards the floor feeling the fabric of the carpet awaiting his fingers to come across the hidden slot in the floorboards. The wooden opening to the floor board revealed illegal substances coiled and sealed by plastic containers. A square clingfilmed package of squashed cannabis leaves and strands combined together exited Kane's hand, entering the space, in replacement of a set of prepacked disposable plastic bags in various sizes. Bags filled with supplements all ready to hit the streets clustered into Kane's palm, then slipping deep into his concealed inner pocket of his sports top.

Kane's ear pricked upwards, the sound of creeping footsteps alerted him. Slick with style he smoothly closed the wooden floorboard lid. A quiet tap hit his door.

"You ready?" Sean glanced watching Kane spring to his feet.

"Come on, let's get off." Kane bounced with confidence past Sean whipping a fresh set of car keys from his back pocket.

Closing the door to the house, Sean's eyes peered to a Grey Volkswagen Golf, with a private registration plate attached KC 666. Kane pressed the fob unlocking the car and entered the driver's seat. Crunch! Sean entered slamming the door.

"Ring the lads Sean." Sean picked up a phone that slotted into its holder.

"Fucking brick this." Sean referred to the Nokia, throw away mobile, Kane had been using for business. Scrolling down the contacts list Sean stopped at Kevin's number.

"Kevin?" Sean stared at Kane waiting for a response as he started the car. Kane twisted the keys into the receiving slot, twisting hard pushing down on the accelerator, placing the gear stick into first from neutral position. Kane accelerated pushing the car forward and shook his head briefly to Sean.

"No, Vince" Kane spoke softly. Sean dialled and looked for a speaker phone indicator.

Vince sat in his van that was parked at the bottom of Mary Lee road in a stationary position. He stared into the dark clouds as the day was turning towards night. He felt a sense of peace with his eyes shut momentarily, the sound of other cars passing awoke him back into reality. He turned the engine back on and scanned through the radio making a move back towards the 'Smoking Barrel.' Vibrations were felt within his pocket, he pulled it out and pressed the loud speaker indicator.

"Vince, it's Kane…. I've got work lined up for you. Where are you? It's a drop off I need."

"Oh." Vince replied unaffected by Kane's words. "Where are you?"

"Meet me on Mersey Road, be quick about it." Vince heard the call end and pushed down on the accelerator picking up speed down Mary Lee Road. Passing his home heading towards the end of the road he turned left and headed towards Mersey Road.

Dave sat in Scott's flat, the television was heard playing in the distance of the room. Dave waited patiently for Scott to enter whilst engaging with himself, on old, but not forgotten priorities.

"It's been ten months since we dealt with that little fish, Scott."

"I've told you." Scott replied from the kitchen. "I've been working on it, just wait alright."

"I guess only time will tell Scott, waiting seems like all I've been doing. We've searched every place in Manchester and not a word or mention. He's probably in a different city." Scott entered the room with a folder and scrunched up paperwork and notes. "What's all that shit you've got?"

"I've been telling you, I've been on it." Dave's eyes sparkled like a lighter crossing along the paper.

"What is it?" Scott dropped the paperwork on the centre of the table in front of them. A list of names and numbers appeared on the paper, along with brief notes of other criminals connected to their underworld branding. Documents of drug and money exchanges were collaborated with Scott's accounted information.

"Look, these are all our contacts right? Suppliers and links, people who work for us, people who want in."

"So? You're losing it Scott. This looks impressive but it's like Sherlock Homes shit."

"Just give me five minutes right." Scott scrolled his fingers down the list of names. "Martin Cahill, Irish connected, he said to me that he's been dealing with a man named Carmen, he operated in and out of Manchester but is always on the move."

"I don't know a Carmen?" Dave appeared confused.

"He told me what he looked like and he fits the same description of this Big C feller? Round, fat, well stocky big and bald."

"NO FUCKING WAY!"

"He said…"

"It's FUCKING him! I seen that tape, so did you. He's got to be the one." Scott pulled out his mobile and started to dial the number.

"07952188766" Scott spoke out loud pushing the numbers on his phone and dialled it clicking the speaker indicator on his phone.

"Scott." An husky Irish accent voice spoke.

"I've got Dave here."

"Greeting's Devil."

"No fucking games Martin, you know why I'm in touch?"

"yeh, a little birdie told me that you had some beef you need sorting."

"Yeah, if that's what you want to call it."

"Have you heard from your man?" Scott over spoke.

"I don't recall Carmen as one of mine." Martin laughed.

"Listen to me Cahill !! Is his pet name Big C, because that little cunt is going to get it ??"

"Hush hush! You do have a temper."

"I'm not wasting bullets on the wrong fucker."

"Wait." Martin paused on the opposite line of the phone. "I'll arrange something but in return you'll have to do something for me. A favour let's say."

"What's your price?" "No charge but one job I need doing."

"Big? Small?"

"Well considering you want one dead man, I want one myself." Dave bit his lip.

"Personal or business?"

"That's not required, I'll send over both details in a text Dave."

"Yeah ok?"

"Don't fuck it up."

"Why do they call me the devil." The phone line ended and Scott smiled.

"I smell a dead shark."

Vince drove down Mosley Road and witnessed Kane's parked inside a carpark of a closed supermarket. Vince pulled into the car park and continued the journey towards Kane's before coming to a gentle stop. Sean sat in the front passenger seat with Kevin and Lucas seated in the back. Kane pressed the electric remote to take down his window.

"Yes Vince I." Lucas shouted from the back.

"Fuckin rip that bro. Nice rims."

"Shut up man and pass me that package." Kane shouted into the back. Kevin took the package from Lucas and passed it forward to Kane. "Vince, this is an important job. There will be some good money in this for you. You know after this you could get your own place." Vince's mind grew excited.

"What's in the package?"

"This is one that you just do and don't ask. It's nothing out of the ordinary. You've just got to drop this off for me."

"Where do you want me to take it?" "I'll send you details in a text." Kane leaned through his car window and passed it to Vince, a brown cardboard box with tape covered around all seals. "Shit I almost forgot, this is for you." Kane pulled out a sealed envelope and passed it across.

"What is it?"

"For the work you've already done for me."

"Oh, thanks. I best get this sorted then, send us that text." Kane closed his window and drove off with some speed with music playing loud beating from the inside to the outside of his car.

Daisy sat on the bed in her bedroom, the radio played subtle in the background. 12:04am glared on the digital clock. She lay back on fluffy cushions coiling into the quilt. Her eyes shut but continued to open as she tossed and turned under the covers. The room was in darkness with the curtains closed shut. Her senses enhanced as she could hear the swaying of the trees in the garden becoming hit by howling wind. Something didn't feel right, her mind and body felt anxious as her breathing became shallow with short bursts. Daisy dug her head under the pillow in desperation to sleep. After thirty minutes had passed her mind could not fall to the ease of dream world. She moved her body, sitting upwards and turned to her lamp on the bedside table, switching it on.

"What's wrong with me?" Daisy held herself tight as restlessness attacked her body.

Looking through the draw attached to the bedside table, Daisy found a small cardboard rectangle package similar to a tube of Colgate. She opened it up revealing a pregnancy test. Creeping towards the bathroom she placed herself on the toilet with legs placed apart, desperate to know the result.

"I can't be, can I. This really can't be happening." After a five-minute wait for her body to settle, the test was done. Daisy flushed the toilet and sat on the toilet seat in her dressing gown.

"Fuck! Come on..... appear." Anxiously waiting she become more and more nervous hoping that she was over thinking things. She looked at her mobile and saw the photograph of Vince and her together. With panic rushing its way to her brain she clicked towards Vince's mobile number and started to create a text message.

Daisy's eyes slowly looked towards the pregnancy test, fingers jittering. Daisy pulled the test closer to her eyes.

"Nooo!! This can't be right." Tears began to fall from her face as her eyes recognised the positive symbol. A scream of shock exited her lungs with her neck muscles tensing as she whispered to herself. "I'm only seventeen, I'm still at college, No... this can't be happening." Daisy cried feeling alone. She continued to write out a text message to Vince, her world felt hopeless. All of her aspirations had become rattled, her life had come to its first major unexpected crisis.

The night gloomed with dissolving stars that once lit up the concrete roads along with lamp-post shine. Vince received the information from Kane and guided himself to the drop off point which was outside a beaten down garage in the neighbourhood of Collyhurst. One of Manchester's recognised areas with a high rate of poverty and crime. Vince placed the envelope inside his glove compartment for safe keeping and stepped outside his van with the package. 1am hit the clock on Vince's mobile screen, the streets were empty. With a tea spoon of hunger Vince banged his hands against the metal garage shutters.

"Hello. Is anyone in? I've been sent by Kane Crossling." Not a sound responded. Vince made one last attempt to gain some attention. "I've got the package for you, I work with Kane." Vince banged on the shutter with cold hands. "Hello, is anyone inside? I've got the package." Vince shouted brushing his hand across his fringe. Vince made his way back to the van before he heard the shutters opening. Vince turned back to the sight of a scrawny figured man standing in the middle of the garage shutters. He wore tattoos across his body stained with oil, wielding a distinctive scar across his face from ear to chin with a comfortable worn darkened vest top.

"I didn't expect you to be here. I fuckin only just got the text." The figure spoke revealing his blackened teeth stained by unkown care. Vince cautiously walked forward towards the man. "Let's have it here then." Vince couldn't take his eyes off his face. A face he would definitely not forget, he needed not ask questions to increase his presence for the visit.

"Kane said it's all there and that you've got what he needs."

"Are you sure about that?"

"I'll phone him if you like."

"No need, it's right here." The man picked up a plastic bag which had some weight to it. Vince had become familiar with the way the packaging had been made. The plastic bag was wrapped multiple times again following a similar pattern with tape. "Here, you can tell him it's what we agreed. And just to let him know, it's none refundable." The man spoke in a scally northern accent and stared into Vince's eyes as he passed him the bag. "You've got a clean face." Vince looked down catching a closer glimpse at the man's arms as he accepted the package. He quickly analysed the needle holes in his arms and made quick assumptions.

"I best be off then." Vince moved quickly feeling a slight intimidation as he heard the shutters closing.

"See you around pretty boy." The man assertively shouted.

A couple of hours passed and the morning sun started to wake with its light hitting the environment, all people of Manchester called home. After a long night on the job Vince phoned Kane to tell him the successful news of receiving his contents with no stress.

"Kane it's me. I've got your stuff and I'll pass yours on my way back home. Where do you want it?"

"Fuck me that's a welcome change. You're eager, come to the usual place then." Kane yawned feeling a rush of excitement.

Vince arrived outside house 121 on Ardwick Green, he noticed Kane standing outside the run down building, walking towards his car as he parked outside.

"Here it is mate. That's it yeah." Vince handed the parcel over to Kane.

"Good work mate, do you want to come in?"

"To be honest with you I'm fucked. I'll best be heading off."

"Listen Vince, the reason why I got you to do this job is because I trust you. I know your head's in the right place." Kane glanced back towards the house. "Unlike some of them in there."

"Don't worry about it."

"Thanks, I'll bell you some time soon." Kane connected his hand with Vince's and headed off back into the house. "Safe bro." Kane shouted as Vince left in his van.

Thirty minutes passed and Vince made his way back to his desired bed, with closed eyes fuel less. After seven hours passed Vince awoke to the sound of his phone vibrate. He cuddled his cushion and stretched out one arm towards it. He grabbed the phone irritated still stung by the tiredness.

We need to meet. Vince read the message without taking too much notice. Lying in his bed for another hour, waking up with eyes flashing on and off with a closed shutter. Feeling an unexpected emptiness inside, unable to figure out what was going on within himself he ignored it, making excuses.

"I need some food me. I feel weird. Must be deprived." Vince thought to himself. "I best make a move, but it's warm though under these covers. Come on Vince get up." Vince's mind spiralled with thoughts as he stared at the facing wall. "Shit, I wonder what Odens stashing? Go on Vince move. One big jump up it's all you need." Vince finally pushed himself to get out of his bed.

The sound of chatter came from the function room, Vince's ears perked up.

"That's good to hear love." A female voice spoke softly. Vince entered. Daisy's mum Claire was sat on a table with Mick talking about the latest news with the family.

"Alright there?" Vince spoke kindly.

"You alright love. Haven't had a chance to see you."

"I know. You know what it's like with Daisy's exams and college work."

"I know yeah. It's nice to see you, your Dad's been telling me how busy you've been."

"I know, I'm worn out."

"What you doing today Vince?" Mick spoke out.

"Well, I'm on top with the work so can I have the day off?"

"Go on Mick. Everyone needs a break, he's still only young." Claire smiled.

"I suppose then."

"I'll leave you two to it then. I best get ready."

"Alright son."

"See you around Vince. I'll probably see you later if you come around to ours." Claire said politely.

Vince stepped towards the cellar and heard their conversation continue in the distance.

"Oden came back a couple days ago."

"What happened" Claire asked intrigued.

"He came here, so I let him stay the night and strangely I felt like I somehow reconnected with him. I just got this warm feeling the next day and I couldn't see him go. I offered him a chance to earn his keep."

"That's great, I'm glad for you."

"I just hope he will stay out of trouble and feel connected with us. I can't deal with any more bad news."

"Things will start looking up for you. You've got to start thinking positive and look forward to things." Claire spoke with care and warmth leaning over the table giving Mick a discreet kiss on his cheek.

"You are right."

"I know I am."

Mick smiled.

Vince entered the dusty and musky cellar with an element of curious excitement whilst texting Daisy back.

"*Okays xxx.*" Vince explored the room and made his way to the area where Oden seedily rummaged. Vince analysed the boxes seeking any clues that might emerge in the direction to the box Oden was fondling. Vince moved the row of boxes and disassembled them on the ground getting hotter towards the altered box.

"It's got to be this box. It looks like the dust has been recently wiped of it." Vince noticed a slit on the wood top lid. He slid his nails into the seal and pushed it open like a detective. "Get in lad!" Vince shouted quietly to himself, as he placed it on the floor, he kneeled. "Old newspapers. Come on there's got to be something more interesting in here." Vince felt the delicate paper with his hands and rolled it along. "Mmm." Vince mumbled. He gathered the paper and carefully took it out of the box. He found a bulging amount of fabric coiled like a snake skin. "What's this?" Vince held the fabric coiled object in his hand. "It's heavy this." Vince's curiosity took full control over his body with his hands automatically de-coiling the object. Fine wraps held the object covered together tightly, Vince's fingers began to feel the shape of the object. Still unaware he untied knot's that kept the object concealed.

Vince's eyes dropped to what he had found within his hands, he could feel cold metal in his palms. "Fucking hell. Fuck me." Vince held an old pistol in his hands that had started to slightly rust. "A fucking gun. What the fuck is he doing with this?" It was an old Russian Makarov pistol with surely an unknown story behind it. He dug his hands deeper into the box instinctively revealing thousands of pounds, including euros all lined up on top of each other. "Shit! What's going on here?" Vince held back his urge to count it and covered it back up with the newspaper leaving the gun out. Vince held the pistol in his hand with an outstretched arm pointing it into a corner.

Feeling a sentiment of power, he momentarily practised aiming and mumbled to himself. "I'll fucking kill you. You fucking bastard. Get on the fucking floor!" Vince deluded himself feeling an adrenaline charge inside him. "Fuckin hell." Vince shivered. Looking at the pistol he ejected the magazine with the pressure of a pressed finger on a metal catch. A metal cartridge slid from the bottom of the handle. Vince's eyes popped, "I can't believe I've found this." Vince's once pure heart had become more contaminated the longer he explored the parts of the gun. He slid the cartridge back into the gun's grip handle, scanning his eyes at the nine millimetre rounds. Vince felt a shift inside him unlike no other feeling. He covered the gun back up with the fabric material lightly caressing it and dug it into his jogging bottoms. Before he left, he neatly packed away the boxes exactly how Oden had left them and moved quickly upstairs to his bedroom.

Energised power ran through Vince's body, he pulled up the mattress from his bed and lay the gun on the wooden panel bracket flattening it down with the mattress, everything seemed ordinary. Clothes scattered on the floor with mismatched socks and boxer shorts, un-noticeable differences made. Vince sat on his bed checking everything felt okay, he pulled out his phone and had received a text message from Daisy.

"Come mine tonight." Vince recognised, after scrolling through his text chat, that she had not been adding any kiss symbols to her texts and began to analyse with caution.

"Something must be up." Vince spoke cooling down from the pacing blood pumping around his body.

The shabby bricked house of 121 Ardwick Green lay as a nesting ground for Kane's business ventures. Inside was contaminated with dampness and mould bonding to everything within sight. It wasn't occupied by anyone other than Kane and his fellow gang members. The smell of dust was thick in the air but went unnoticed to Kane's explosive excitement as he placed his recently purchased package on a torn ironing board.

"Lads get over here." Shouted Kane with urgency.

"Are you getting it open or what or are you just going to stare at it?" Sean spoke in a cheeky manner hovering over Kane with the others alongside. Kane pulled out a knife and stabbed it into the package, a chalk like substance of white dust puffed from the torn slit in the bag.

"This is the one boys." Kane smiled as he started to tear away at the plastic bag wrapping.

"Yo! That's fucking sick that, I !! It's like fuckin Scar Face innit? Can I have a taste?" Kane nodded allowing Lucas to poke his finger lightly onto the snow coated cocaine block. Lucas sucked his finger glazing his tongue on the substance. "That's tasteful bro."

Kevin looked cautiously at the block.

"This is the first time we've got a block, don't you think we should check it's all sweet?"

"Our supplier Dean never lets us down." Kane replied.

"Yeah, but we've never got something as big as this before."

"Start bagging this up then and if anything looks odd let me know."

"Right get that knife off the side Lucas. Sean go and get the bags." Kevin ordered as Kane sat back on a skanky couch rolling a spliff.

After twenty-five minutes passed a collection of bags started to stack up.

"Watch it doesn't get everywhere. It's fuckin money this." Kane shouted from his seat.

Kevin spoke aghast.

"Stop for a minute! Wait a second! Kane get here... boys chill." Kane jumped from his seat and re-grouped around the ironing board. Kevin scooped a handful of the brick and smelt it lightly without inhaling.

"What the fuck are you doing?" Lucas shouted.

"Let me have some, that's bang on." Sean whined.

"Your idiots, man can you not smell that soapy scent?" Kevin put the cocaine back on the platform and spread it out crushing it with his fingers. "What you doing that for? I'll take this out of your cut if we keep losing shit." Kane spoke assertively.

"Look, smell it...it's deffo a mix." Kane felt his stomach turn. He bent his head ever so slightly and started to smell the product. He rolled his fingers through the substance crunching scoops in his hand. The group stared anxiously waiting for Kane to speak as he groomed with wondering fingers.

"BULLSHIT! IT'S FUCKING GRAINS OF WASHING POWDER AND FUCKING PRETTY BOY POWDER, I'LL FUCKING KILL THE CUNT!! Twenty grand for a bag of shite, who the fuck does he think he is the cheeky disrespectful CUNT!" Kane explicitly jarred wild.

"Don't worry man. WE'LL FUCKIN TEACH THAT DICKHEAD A LESSON!" Kevin hungered. "I knew it though, I don't trust that scrawny fuck up... Deans a fuckin dead man."

Kane snapped ferociously like an impatient caveman and pushed over the Ironing board. The powder raised into the air ballooning as the rest fell to the ground like sand.

"Get Vince on the line. Get him on the fuckin phone."

"Let me sort this Kane. I'm just as fuming as all of you. I'll send him a message." Sean spoke out.

"Do you think you're a fuckin big man Sean? You want to fucking play gangster, go on then fuckin do it." Sean became more affected by Kane's presence. The atmosphere in the room cooked, boiling with ego and testosterone. Kane felt his hands shake, anger like no other encircling inside him.

"I want this Dean! I want my fuckin money! I want compensation!" Kane's veins busted.

Arriving outside Daisy's house Vince walked towards her door and made a couple knocks. Daisy came towards the door and opened it, she wore a brown fluffy dressing gown with her hair tied back in a bobble.

"Come in." Daisy stared. Vince walked through the doorway into the hall. "I'm just sitting in my room, come up." Vince followed Daisy up her stairs and crept along her landing into her bedroom.

"You alight?"

"Erm. Yeah."

"I know your annoyed with me."

"I'm not."

"You know I've been busy and it's my first proper day off so I've come to see you."

"I've been busy too."

"Exactly, so we both have been here, there and everywhere." Vince attempted to give Daisy a hug as he wrapped his arms around her as she sat on the edge of her bed brushing him away. Vince sat next to her, he felt an unusual vibe coming from her. Placing his hand on her knee he smiled.

"So? What you been up to hey? I bet you've done great on them tests of yours."

"I don't think I have." Daisy's energy was unwilling.

"Don't say that, I know you, you always give everything so it will all work out."

"Yeah."

"Maybe you've just knocked yourself out so you might feel a bit lifeless but I'm here now so let's have some me and you time." Vince pushed verbally trying to create ease. He started to kiss her neck lightly and her cheek, "Daisy boo." Vince spoke softly.

"VINCE" Daisy spoke firmly.

"What? What's wrong?" Daisy crossed her legs and stared into space. A silence was left between them for a couple of minutes, Vince felt shook up by Daisy's tone. The room represented Daisy's thoughts, messy, untidy and in need of a good clean, she could not persist. Tears started to gather in her eyes and erupted down her face, her body rocked back and forth releasing a panicked scream.

"What's wrong Angel? I'm here, I'm here baby...talk to me."

Unable to comfortably speak, only a few words could be uttered.

"You're not." Vince coiled his arms around her and held her tightly.

"I am, you can tell me anything. What's going on here boo."

"I can't."

"You know I love you Daisy, I'd do anything for you." Vince felt a shot of emotion hit him. "Look baby we're strong, me and you, we can do anything."

"Go...just go, I need to be alone!" Daisy screamed at Vince becoming more unpredictable with rocketing emotions.

"I'm not going anywhere. I'm not leaving you like this."

"I just can't right now. I just can't. Please just leave me." Daisy cried falling deeper into her dark hole. Pushing Vince away from her she became unstable.

"STOP IT DAISY!"

"GO!"

"Talk to me." Vince tried to stay calm feeling the stress attach itself to him.

The longer Vince stayed and tried to figure out what the issue was and the reason behind Daisy's bizarre behaviour, the harder it was for him to follow her orders and leave. His heart began to ache with the unknown. Eventually, he forced himself to leave the unsettled environment and kept over analysing trying to figure out what had just happened.

Vince re-connected with the seat of his van feeling distressed. He didn't drive for a couple of minutes deciding to take his frustration out on the steering wheel, punching hard with his fists.

"I just don't fucking understand." Vince's face turned red in the reflection of his mirror. "I've not done anything, all I've done is work, work and fuckin work." Stomping and getting himself in a rut he twisted his keys and started the van.

A covered hand by leather dialled Vince's number.

"Who the fuck is this?" Vince answered the unknown callers number. "I'm not in the mood for bullshit. Who is this?"

"It's Kane. Get down here now. It's going off mate. That fuckin supplier did me over. Can you get your hands on a bat? Get to our place ASAP no fucking about it's a big one."

"Slow down."

"Just get here now. FUCKIN FAST!"

"I've told you I'm not working today."

"Vince. Like I said I need you on this one." Kane firmly stated.

Vince contemplated his decision still feeling hot from his unresolved issue, he pushed down the pedals and drove towards Ardwick. Stopping at a red light he spoke out loud to himself. "A bat? I've got a strap." Vince opened his glove compartment where his newly owned Makarov pistol sat with eight rounds heated inside waiting to be christened. The colour red exposed itself, Vince pushed on to Ardwick Green. Within a matter of fifteen minutes his van arrived outside house 121. Sean waited outside the house for Vince's van to appear.

"Vince come on inside we're all waiting for you." Shouted Sean.

"What's going on?" Vince shouted from his window.

"Get out and come in. Kane's got it all on lock down." Vince left his firearm inside the car and paced firmly inside wearing a grey Adidas tracksuit with a hood up covering his head and an unbound receptive energy consuming. Vince felt the adrenaline scent burning from Kevin and Sean.

"I'm glad you can all make it." Kane humoured feeling passion. "Right boys, I want this to be the first and last time this cunt tries to throw one on us. We've already agreed someone's got to teach this bastard a lesson. Vince you'll take Sean and Kevin with you to the garage. Whatever you feel the need to do, just do it....whatever you think is necessary." Kane spoke with leadership.

"What you and Lucas doing?"

"I've got some more business to attend to. But I'm leaving you with my priority." Kane walked into Vince's personal space. "Because I know you'll get it sorted."

"All I am is a driver, I do what you need when it comes to deliveries."

"That's exactly why you're doing this."

"What?"

"In a way it's your fuck up."

"I didn't even know what was in the parcel."

"What I asked for wasn't a bag of DAZ it was one key of coke. We had a 40K return on street value."

"But."

"No buts Vince. You either do this job for me or you owe me what you lost."

"What the fuck." Vince replied.

"Just fuckin do it you pussy. You get me?" Lucas blurted. Vince stared giving an intimidating look in response. Kevin and Sean listened in as they prepared themselves for the job, Sean stashed a knife in his pants and picked up a wooden bat.

"This will do. You fuckin what lad?"

"Are you ready yet? Burning daylight." Kevin picked up three balaclavas.

"Right! I'll do it! As a favour and when I come back if he's still here I'll spark him straight." Vince spoke with boiling aggression. "Alright you little shithead." Vince directed his comment straight towards Lucas. "What we waiting for then?" Vince walked out of the house following behind Sean and Kevin.

"Remember I want results. It's an opportunity to prove yourself." Vince shook his head and lead the others to his van.

"SHOT GUN!" Sean shouted fully fuelled excitedly running towards Vince's van. Kevin crunched open the door and shuffled inside. Vince strapped himself to his seat and pushed down on the acceleration shifting gears quickly. "I can't wait. This dickhead is getting it." Sean smiled with excitement. Kevin held the balaclava in his hand and stretched open the opening and slotted it on his head.

"Perfect fit. Nice and snug, right Vince get a move on we haven't got all day. Take this left it's a quicker route." Vince responded turning the wheel, he felt his stomach turning inside whirling against his nerves.

"Have you got one of them for me?"

"No. Did you not bring your own?" Kevin replied.

"Fuck sake. I didn't know we was going to be doing this."

"That will teach you to be fucking prepared for anything wont it." Kevin pulled out another balaclava from inside his jacket. "Here, I brought a spare."

"Fuck off Kevin." Vince continued to drive the van down the street.

"HAHA," Sean laughed, "You crack me up Vince."

After some painfully quick ten minutes passed on the road, the street to the garage opened itself to the wheels of Vince's van.

"Slow down." Kevin spoke assured. "Right this is what we're gonna do. I'll bang on and see if he answers, if not, we'll break in."

"Right you two get out and I'll turn this van around."

"I don't think so sugar."

"So we can get a straight home run. A clear exit out of here."

"Stop being a fucking DICKHEAD Kevin." Vince growled.

"What?"

"We've got to be in and out of here in five minutes. We can't afford any fucking about. Just get the money and go."

"Listen to me you little shit. You don't call the shots." Kevin turned stern and clenched his baseball bat that sat in-between his legs. Kevin winked at Vince. "It's show time boys!" Sean and Kevin pulled their balaclavas over their faces and clung to their tools as they jumped out of Vince's van. They made their way towards the garage shutters pacing with adrenaline. Vince watched through the window screen, with eyes slightly swelling with a red tint, he picked up the spare balaclava and turned the van around facing a clean exit. He unstrapped himself from his seat and moved in closer towards his glove compartment. Picking out his leather gloves and his Uncle's gun he slid it in-between his trousers. His eyes glanced in the rear-view mirror revealing his anonymous identity.

Slam! Vince exited the van leaving the keys still in the ignition, yards away from Kevin and Sean he watched them bang on the metal shutters shouting one name.

"DEAN!" Kevin shouted fuelled with aggression. "Come out here now, we've got business."

"Yeah… Dean... Big money business. A great big scam hey." Sean said loud and clear.

After a couple of minutes of hitting the metal shutter and making lots of noise, the shutter started to open slowly, a croaky voice was heard.

"What's all this fuss about?" A familiar voice was heard to the ears of Vince.

"That's him." Kevin and Sean reached under the opening shutter and pushed it open.

"What the fuck is all of this? Who the fuck do you think you are?" In shock, junkie Dean stumbled back, within the matter of seconds chaos broke lose. Kevin charged at Dean waving his baseball bat with fury, he clipped his legs making him crash to the floor.

"Where's the fucking money?"

"I don't know what you're talking about... Fuckin scum." Dean crawled backwards shuffling away from the balaclava figures. The garage was filled with musk and dust, needles were scattered across the floor with a rusty beaten down car standing in the centre that wasn't far from being scrap metal. A small box shaped room stood as an office at the far back of the room. A noise was heard from behind the office door. Dean's face looked towards the door showing fright.

"WHERE'S THE FUCKING MONEY YOU DICKHEAD TWAT?" Kevin hungered. "I'll fucking kill you. You hear me?"

"I don't know what you're talking about. Fucking slimy bastard." Dean croaked muttering and scuffling.

"Don't just stand there, do something!" Kevin ordered as he glanced towards Vince and Sean. Sean leaped with attention and started rummaging, the rusty car caught his eye. Sean held a wooden slab and took a swing at the car. SMASH! What was left of the windows shattered, Kevin gripped Dean from the floor and shook him.

"You're a fucking amateur." Dean spat in Kevin's face and started to throw effortless punches with strain in Kevin's direction. Vince jumped forward from a standing position and pulled the gun from his waist gripping tightly. A bold voice exited his mouth.

"DON'T WASTE MY FUCKING TIME DEAN! YOU DOUBLE CROSSED THE WRONG FUCKING MAN. WHERE IS IT?". Kevin held his hands against his head from the deflection of Dean's scrapes, he quickly kneed with force into Dean's crotch area. Scraping along the metal wall Dean's eyes followed the movements of the gun.

"Ahhh!. You fucking....Ahh!"

Sean searched the car for anything of value but could not find one thing other than rubbish. His ears pierced as he heard the door to the office creek. Turning sharply, he wandered towards it with a burning sensation inside. Kicking open the door to the room revealed one of Dean's workers hiding in the corner of the room. Small build and covered in thick black dirt with tattoos and piercings covering his ears. Thick bushy eyebrows and brown eyes stared at Sean.

"BOY'S, BOY'S LOOK WHAT I FOUND!" Sean bellowed, whilst pulling out his knife simultaneously as he dropped the guy. "I'm going to kill you. Do you hear me? You best tell me where my fucking money is." Sean raised the knife to his lips and licked the blunt side and stared with intention.

Pulling the gun from the embedded skin of Dean's head Vince slightly shook.

"What is it?" Kevin dragged Dean with his nails dug into his scalp. Entering the office, Vince felt the heat on his face, his mind spiralled out of control with danger boiled with power.

"Who the fuck is this?"

"Dead meat." Sean responded staring at the figure in the corner.

"Oscar don't you say a word."

"Oh, Oscars his name." Sean replied.

"LISTEN TO ME WHOEVER THE FUCK YOU ARE." Vince pulled back the slide of the gun pointing it at Dean's head. "Give us the fucking money or he dies. RIGHT HERE, RIGHT NOW!" Dean shuffled side to side, gritting his teeth, with Kevin holding him tightly.

"Don't you dare. Don't you fucking do anything stupid OSCAR." Oscar stood mutely, "Fucking do it you amateurs. I fucking dare you." Sean vaulted at Oscars vulnerability with his knife in hand. Breaking the skin, Oscar screamed.

"Ahhh. Ahhh. My fucking face. I'll get it! STOP STOP!" Sean turned to his feet and started kicking him in the chest. Blood squelched onto the concrete floor, "It's in the boot of the car."

"What?"

"THE BOOT!" Vince pointed the gun square at Oscar's eyes. "Can you see me? Get that boot open, NOW." Sean pulled Oscar by his vest and guided him towards the car. Kevin headbutted Dean in the back of his head viciously like a savage. He fell to the floor unconscious landing on the concrete, head first. Kevin spat back at his body and finished him with multiple kicks to the ribcage.

Shaking like a cowering mongrel Oscar pulled the keys from his back pocket.

"Don't hurt me." Cried Oscar. Whispering softly with the metal barrel of the gun dug into Oscar's neck.

Vince spoke. "Do as we say and you'll live. You're doing great." Oscar opened the boot of the car, inside was black bin liner bags. Vince recognised the bag he dropped off. "Grab them. Grab as many as you can." Vince lead with urgency. "Kevin let's get out of here now! Don't drop them fucking bags." Vince looked at Oscar in the eye with sympathy as blood started to set staining his face. "I'm sorry," Vince whipped the back of his hand allowing the weight of his gun to hit tattooed Oscar in the face. He fell to the floor gripping the car for support with scrawny hands.

Pumping at the top of his lungs Vince called for an exit. "LET'S GO! LETS FUCKING GET OUT OF HERE!" Vince dashed out of the garage, Kevin over took him and was the first to jump in the van. Waving his hands frantically, the gun still held firm. Sean caught up holding a couple of black bags tight. Vince looked to the left of him and shouted to Sean "Come on. Get a step on." BANG! BANG! Sean fell to the floor tumbling to his knees.

"Fucking hell." Sean struggled along the floor as one gunshot exited through his arm. Vince glanced back towards the garage where a vivid figure of Dean fired gun shots towards them. With bullets whizzing past in their direction Vince squeezed a multiple of rounds back in the opposite direction, blind firing. Adrenaline charges hit Vince's body, everything seemed surreal his wrists ached as the recoil rattled him. Vince grabbed Sean by the back of his jacket and rushed him forward with strength towards the van. Sean laughed hysterically, oblivious to his wounds.

"Did you fucking see that? He just fucking shot at us!"

"Get in the van, get in the fuckin van now." Vince pulled open the door and pushed Sean inside.

"Drive, fuckin DRIVE!" Kevin shouted.

The van took off with speed leaving the garage behind, the conversation inside the van started to boil as the reality of the situation started to come back to the present moment amongst the group. Vince pulled off his balaclava and pulled off Sean's. Kevin copied.

"He's been hit. It's his arm." Blood started to pour from Sean's arm, panic awakened him.

"Fuck, FUCK, FUCK, AHHH! JESUS!" Sean repeated and threw up, choking onto the floor of the van.

"Fuckin hell, I can't do this." Kevin howled.

"Wrap your jacket around it, use anything. There's a scarf in the glove compartment." Vince spoke urgently.

Sean looked at his arm and witnessed a fifty pence sized chunk of skin dangling from his arm where blood poured.

"I think it's a graze." Kevin coiled the scarf around his arm and pulled it tightly.

"Fuck! it burns!" Sean cried.

"You will be alright." Kevin responded trying to keep him calm. Breathing heavily and exhaling quickly, Sean bit his lip.

Chapter Twenty-Four

Oden reached for his jacket from the back of his chair and swayed towards the exit of the 'Smoking Barrel.' What was left of his hair was combed back slick with a touch of shining gel. The smell of cologne stained his layer of clothes from top to toe.

"And I will get a young buck. I will, I will. The girl with the pony or curly hair. Were she there, were she in daffodils were she?" Oden sang random words together as his eyes rolled back and forth. He pulled out a hip flask from the inside pocket of his jacket and twisted off the sealed cap. Swallowing the contents clean that sunk into his body, he left a vomiting burp into the atmosphere. The beverage smell lingered but washed away as the wooden doors swung open.

Chris entered the pub and witnessed Oden's stumbling performance, "Alright," Chris pressed lightly on Oden shoulder.

"I, yes I am. I'm indeed I am. Indeed."

"Okay." Chris smirked.

"What's so funny laddie?" Oden held his paws in front of his face. "Put them up, Put them up, Boy, Small boy, I'll fist you boy."

"Nothing's funny. does Mick know your drunk?"

"I said put them up, I'll fight ya," Oden paused taking a breath. "I'm my own man, I'm going out, on the walk, I am."

"Alright, you want me to get you a taxi."

Oden laughed to himself.

"Fuckin taxi, I have legs…legs boy. Do you? Look at my hands." Chris looked down slightly. "Aaaah BANG!" Oden clapped his hands loudly intending to make Chris jump. "Made you jump boy, iron these." Chris looked down with his eyebrows raised.

"Best get busy then. Have a good night." Chris left Oden's presence.

Dave warmed up his Mercedes engine with a couple of strokes of the accelerator, keys in the ignition. Sat outside Scott's flat patiently, he turned off the radio and listened to the sound of the street. Sirens in the distance and other screeching cars, annoying burglar alarms screaming and muffled sounds of young tearaways shouting.

Dave smiled, "I can feel it... coming in the air tonight." He tapped his hands on the steering wheel and beeped on the horn. "Peace will come tonight and it will be all over. No more fuckers fucking with me. I'M THE MAIN FUCKING MAN!" Dave smiled to himself and glanced in the wing mirror to the outline of Scott. Dave winded his window down and bobbed his head out. "Are you coming or what? Hurry your arse up!"

"Did I just catch you talking to yourself again."

"Oh shut up and get in."

Scott jumped inside to the warmth of the air conditioning, "Fuckin hell it's roasting in here. Turn it down a bit." Dave took a cigarette from behind his ear and sparked a lighter then pushed the off button to the heat.

"How you feeling?"

"Good." Dave exhaled a puff of smoke. "You ready?" Scott looked at Dave's face and the answer was clear.

"Always." Dave pushed down on the clutch and raced through his gears gliding with steam like speed. Heading through the overwhelming streets of concrete and council houses he moved onwards towards his acquired destination.

Oden covered a fair amount of ground on the pathway to his pot of gold, he staggered towards a pub in Ardwick. The night was dark with the clock hitting eleven pm; the wind blew in his face but he faced no struggle as he wandered. He entered with a pleasant drunken smile and swayed towards the bar.

"Can I have.... Er? You look really pretty." Oden spoke gibberish to the barmaid holding a smile. "I mean. You know?"

"We've got shots for a pound and we've got some cans of Fosters, Koppenberg's, even that Guinness." Oden smiled at the barmaid, swaying side to side.

"I'LL HAVE A PINT PLEASE." The barmaid pulled Oden a pint of Guinness. "Just one moment. I think.. er..." Oden pulled out a twenty pound note and placed it on the bar. "There it is. You know your nice. You've been good to me. Fuckin hell." Oden started to laugh stumbling in drunken words. "This is for you." Oden glowed. "Keep that for yourself, it's enough isn't it."

"Thanks." The barmaid returned the smile.

Oden found a table to sit at alone, even in his drunken state he wasn't fond of mixing with others especially by himself. He stared into the atmosphere of other lost souls making the same choices. Sinking into his chair wandering his eyes at the most pleasant sight, his ears pricked up on the music what wasn't to his taste. He missed the sound of his genre of music playing, there was nothing but the latest hits on repeat. Entertainment was low as he missed his queue for the karaoke hour.

Dave entered an upper-class estate in the South side of Manchester, he noticed a change of environment in comparison to his own.

"Rooster Avenue, no. 12, it says here."

"It can't be wrong we're on it now." Dave parked outside the house, Scott and himself left the comfort of the car and strolled towards the door. Wearing a leather jacket and familiar gloves, Dave had no concern for concealment; he knocked firmly. No response came from the knocking until he connected his fist with the door the third time. Through the frosted window of the door the pair saw an outline of a person's body coming towards the door, it was large and dark.

Dave could smell the scent of another man behind the door, he watched as his hand touched the knob of the door's handle. His ears peeked as he heard the key crunching through the hole twisting towards the opening. Dave's eyes smiled with overwhelming relief, his intuition connected. The door handle gently crunched open; Dave's eyes watched as his hand reached for his freshly owned blood stained revolver, his hands gripped with his finger at biting point. The figure of the man became apparent to Dave. His unknown danger man had been found. Big C. Carmen held a young child in his arms, his heart beat slower than seconds, time became apparent that his days were numbered. "Noooo!" Scott ejected. "Not like this Dave." Dave spoke clear with the words "Every dog has his day and yours has just ended." Before his finger jaws locked with the violent bite of a pit bull. Unable to break lose, the bullet left the gun into its rightful place of Dave's hunger. Dave's ears became muffled and silent with his thoughts of redemption. The sound of a female child with long blonde hair screamed as Carmen's hands lost their grip as his body collapsed to the floor with a giant thud, splashing blood onto the white marble hallway. Scott pulled Dave as he stood straight with his gun still pointing, his eyes scrolled down towards the girl sat in her father's blood. Smoke vapoured from the barrel of the gun and entered the atmosphere.

Oden left a row of empty glasses on the table that he was sat near, the hands of the clock struck midnight, he knew it was time to go instinctively. He took his last swig of the pint glass and burped.

"Bastard." He made his way to the toilet before leaving and felt the stench of human waste on the tip of his nose. "Eww.. disgusting." He passed the bar on his way out but noticed the barmaid staring at him. "YOU KNOW YOU CAN COME HOME WITH ME?" Oden's volume went louder and louder as he continued his interaction with the barmaid.

"You're charming and straight to the point, aren't you?"

"I'm not married." Oden yarned a smile.

"Maybe another time." The barmaid winked. She had brown hair with extensions and a deep Mancunian accent.

"You like music? I like..I like to DANCE, I'd offer a hand haha." Oden laughed.

The barmaid acknowledged his flirtation.

"I best be off SWEET. I'll see you around I?"

"Yeah! I'll see you around."

Oden left with a warm sensation inside, just like a school boy bewildered by life with love he mellowed and moved with a spark in his step towards the exit of the door. Oden looked back as he got to the door and waved,

"I'm going now, Bye." Oden marched down the Ardwick streets, the lampposts shined bright light onto him but he began to realise he was lost. He sat on a stone bollard and read out a sign that offered the information of the street he was at, he pulled out his mobile phone and called a taxi service.

"Hello, I need a taxi for....." Oden's eyes squinted at the sign. "Hollinwood Close please. Thank you." Oden sat with the cold air touching his cheeks, red with blood pressure risen with the alcohol inside his blood stream. After a ten minute wait a taxi flashed its lights at him.

"It's me fellow, Oden, I ordered the taxi." The taxi pulled up next to him. Oden entered the vehicle. "I've only got this, I think it's five pound. Can you take me as close as you can to Mary Lee Lane please?" The taxi driver was an Asian man with a long beard.

"Of course Sir. Good night, yes?"

"Eye." Every couple of minutes Oden listened to the driver's radio.

"Paddock Lane 2234" The radio streamed.

"Busy night?" Oden offered small talk.

"Quiet today. Yesterday busy."

"Oh right, good." The taxi travelled towards the top of Mary Lee Road and came to a steady stop.

"Sir, five pound has passed my meter. Unless you have more money you will have to get out here Sir." Oden gave the five pound to the taxi driver and left the car seat.

"Bastard," He mumbled under his breath.

Inside Dave's car was a silence like no other. Dave drove down Mersey Lane that lead to Mary Lee Road. Dave spoke breaking the silence.

"It's over now."

Scott stared at the passing houses from his seat and looked at Dave with a slow movement of his neck and held a disapproving face.

"One more thing to do off the list." Dave looked at his phone and opened a photo text message.

"This one lives around here." Dave pushed down on the clutch and changed to first gear, driving smooth at a slower pace with his head lights on.

"What happened back there shouldn't've happened like that Dave." Scott plucked up courage.

"What?" Dave responded bringing the car to a stop.

"That child will be affected for the rest of her life because of you."

"Are you growing soft on me? It's a fucking kid."

"Exactly, a child?" Scott repeated with frown marks glazed across his head. Dave bit his tongue and pushed his foot down on the pedals moving the car forward. Dave shook off Scott's conscience and started scanning his eyes for his second target. In the near distance lights shined on a figure walking, swaying side to side, wearing a tweed jacket. The stench of alcohol reeked from the man.

Moving in closer, behaving like a wild animal hunting down prey Dave beeped his horn at the man mounting the pavement. Bewildered and in another world, the man looked at the car moving towards him, he stared starry eyed. Dave replicated the person's movements swaying the car left to right as he pulled out his gun to take aim.

"NOT LIKE THIS!!" Scott screamed, he jerked forward from his seat and pulled back Dave's arm adding pressure to the steering wheel. Scott pulled Dave back into his seat as the car became uncontrollable, swerving into the unarmed man. Wheels turned right then left with the metal body hitting the legs of the victim sealing his unknown fate with devastation.

"FUCKING HELL! SCOTT WHAT THE FUCK'S WRONG WITH YOU TONIGHT!" Dave shouted pulling back onto the road. Passing the 'Smoking Barrel' Dave's engine hissed pushing his wheels into a full rotation of speed. The body of the man vaulted into the air unconscious and unaware he had rolled over onto the concrete ground with bones broken in multiple places. The nerve endings in his legs became numb to the twitch of muscular spasms exploding inside the victim's body.

Mick lay in his bed of warm covers, the atmosphere of an empty house hit a bone in his body.

"VINCE!" Mick shouted picking his nose slightly.

"Yeah," Vince's voice was heard in the distance. "Have you heard from Chris? Come here." Mick's voice bounced off the walls.

"I'm just getting ready for work."

"Alright," Replied Mick.

Vince pulled of his clothes from the night before and shoved them in a black bin liner, he stepped back from the bin before opening its lid. Standing in boxers in the garden of the pub he shoved the bag to the bottom of the bin and ran back inside. He noticed the stains that Sean's blood had left on his skin. Pacing to the bathroom feeling anxious he slammed the door behind him and pulled the curtain around the bath where he stood in the hot water. Bathing his head under the pressure of the water Vince scrubbed his body with Lynx shower gel. His thoughts began to hit a speed of panic.

"I can't do it, this isn't me." Vince's body crouched down in the bath tub with the hot water pouring over him. Vince felt cold, his arms began to shake as his face changed colour. "I can't, it's too dangerous. Fuck the money, I don't need it." Vince's mind exhaled with stress. "That could off gone worse, I could have been the one. We all could have died. Sean got lucky." Vince fell to the fright of his circumstances, feeling sick inside he tried to rotate his right-hand but it became unmoveable to the shock of the power he held. "Fuck!" Vince cried quietly alone. The sound of the water hitting the floor drew attention to Vince's eye. A red liquid bubbled down the plug hole of the tub which wasn't his shower gel. "I've got to tell him. That's it I'm done. I can't live this life. I can't. What future do I have if I end up dead? What about me and Daisy?" Vulnerability and struggle emerged inside Vince, fear bolted inside as his power levels deflated. "It's got to be this week. Ahhh fuck. What happened to you Vince? You're becoming what you hated. This is not for you." The self-talk spiralled out of control internally and spilt out externally into words and sounds.

Vince's posture changed, it became apparent as he got out of the shower and looked at himself in the mirror; hardly recognisable to himself, his eyes spoke of fear.

Ring ring! Ring ring! The repetitive sounds of the landline in the hallway spread up the stairs of Mick's home. Throwing on black pants and a shirt un-ironed, Mick plodded along his stairs into the hall. The call stopped and started to ring out again. Mick grabbed the phone from the docking station.

"Hello?" Mick spoke with confusion. "Who is this?"

"Hi is this Mick Haze?"

"Yes who's speaking?"

It's Joanne from North Manchester General Hospital, a family member of yours arrived here in the early hours of the morning. Your brother was in a car accident, we're calling to let you know he is here."

"Fuck me. What the hell."

"I understand this is a shock to you, but this is the circumstance." Mick slammed the phone back onto its hook feeling the pain of devastation.

"VINCE! Vince. I've got to go." Feeling anger and upset Mick phoned Chris on his mobile. "Where are you?"

"I'm just coming down the street now. What's wrong?" Chris recognised the sense of urgency and panic within Mick's tone.

"Oden's in the hospital! We need to get there now." Mick walked outside his pub and stood on the street watching Chris's van arrive to his needs.

"Get in!" Mick put the phone into his pocket, his still half-dressed appearance didn't raise any concern to him.

"What's happened?"

"They've just rang, he's at North Manchester General."

"SHIT!"

"They said he was in some kind of car accident. He's not been back long and now this has happened. Fuck me, fuckin bastards."

"Don't worry Mick. They'll be looking after him."

"I know, it's just a shock."

Mick entered the hospital feeling beaten by the world with his head lurking towards the floor. The reception to the hospital housed a waiting room that had a fair amount of people sat patiently.

"Hello?" The receptionist spoke out loud in response to Mick's movements towards her.

"My brother is in here. Oden Haze." The receptionist smiled and began to type away into her computer.

"Room seven. It's straight down the corridor." Mick looked towards the door that he entered and saw Chris stumble inside.

"It was hard to get a parking space."

"Come on, it's this way." Mick pushed his feet forward down the corridor and felt a striking pain of anxiety. "Fuckin hell." Mick stared at the isolated room where a bed accompanied Oden lying there, eyes closed. A nurse was in the room with him checking that his heart monitor was working and all other recovery equipment was in place. The nurse had attractive features that Oden would admire when awoken. The nurse noticed Mick and Chris looking in, she approached them opening the door.

"I'm Oden's brother, can I come in?"

"He's stable and resting."

"Please let me in." Mick's emotions started cracking revealing a tear from his face.

"What's your name." She spoke softly.

"Mick."

"Okay Mick, you can come in but I strongly advise that you do not disturb him as he needs to regain his strength." Mick looked at her blue eyes and blonde hair.

"Thank you." The nurse left the room and Mick entered.

"I'll wait out here." Chris said respectfully.

Walking into the room with held emotions, Mick sat on the chair next to the bed. He looked at Oden's face and realised just how old they had both become. He sat quietly putting one arm on the bed gentle covering Oden's free hand with his. He closed his eyes trying to take himself to a place of peace as a strange calmness crossed his spirit.

Kane was waiting to find out Kevin and Sean's version of events in the usual place. Kane waited anxiously for their return. They arrived with a bang at the door to Kane's beaten down safe house.

"Where the fuck have you all been? You stupid fucks."

"Easy now Kane, let them come in." Lucas interrupted.

"Get fuckin in here." Kevin stepped inside behind Sean. "You didn't get back to my calls. What the fucks with you two?"

"You weren't there Kane. And my phone died."

"Fuck. What happened?"

"Everything went mad."

Sean held is arm firmly. "I got hit! Vince pulled a strap."

Kane's face twirled in confusion. "He was carrying? This doesn't make any sense." Kevin raised his hands as he spoke.

"Everything was going to plan but Dean wasn't having any of it. Playing stupid."

"How did this happen to Sean?" Kane grunted clenching his fists.

"After a big song and dance to finally getting the money, we ran. All of a sudden gun shots rang out. I jumped straight in the van." Kevin explained.

"It's fucking Vince's stupid fault." Sean hissed. "If he didn't pull out a fucking strap Dean wouldn't've shot at us?" Sean angered inside insisting the blame was Vince's.

"I'll fucking sort this coward out." Kane's cigarette burned replicating a poison inside. Moving closer towards Sean, he spoke gently. "Did he shoot you?" Kane wiped sweat from his face. Sean looked at Kane with a teary eye. "Did he do this to you?" Becoming more firm in his tone he became more physical holding Sean by the scruff of his neck, waiting for a response. "DID HE AIM THAT GUN AT YOU AND PULL THE TRIGGER? Breaking what was silent, Sean muttered in upset still shaken.

"Yes."

Mick fell into a sleep sitting on the chair by Oden's bed, still with his hand resting on Oden's. The sound of the beeping machines and ticking of the clock become very noticeable with the silence. A flickering hand started to move ever so slightly, Mick didn't notice still oblivious in a sleep. Oden's fingers moved with more strength. Mick's eyes started to open with the blinking of his eye lids. As they opened he noticed Oden had become conscious with his head snugly glued to the pillow and his face staring at the wall.

"Oden?" Mick gently spoke. Oden's eyes scanned left to right before Mick shuffled up the chair into his brother's eye line.

"Soft bastard." Oden mumbled to himself before he became clear. "How long have I been here?" "You've been here the night. What happened to you?"

"Fucking bastards." Oden shouted. "I don't know what happened. All I remember was being carried away in one of those flashing boxes."

"The doctors said you got hit by a car."

Oden stared at the arms on the clock mounted on the wall in front of him.

"I can't feel anything." Cried Oden in distress.

"It's going to be alright little brother." Mick squeezed a little tighter on his hand. "The Doctor's here are going to fix you up."

"I don't fuckin trust any of them."

"Oden listen to me." Mick held strong. "We're going to get through this."

"We?" Oden's face shrugged. "You're not the one chained to this fuckin bed."

"You need to calm down Oden."

"Oh right, yeah. Calm. Can't be any more at peace." Restlessness and reality hit Oden as it was the first time he had felt paralysed. "Do you have anything to drink?"

"No, it will affect your tests." The door creaked open and the nurse stepped inside.

"Hi Oden." Oden's eyes analysed staring at her. He noticed her blonde hair and subtle make up.

"Yes" he replied.

"How are you feeling?"

"Shit." A short smirk hit her face but she remained professional.

"I'm just here to check up on you. Our test results will arrive back tomorrow. And dinner will be at three tomorrow."

Vince walked outside to his van holding a bottle of bleach and a bucket of water with a floating sponge. Inside the van the passenger seats were stained by Sean's blood, dry and crisp merging with the fabric, Vince scrubbed with force contaminating the sponge. The bleach burnt away at the fabric sending an unpleasant stench into the air. Vince's thoughts revisited as his eyes reflected the horror and panic of the event that took place.

"I've got to do this today." Speaking out loud. Vince heard a car pulling up outside and didn't take any notice.

"Hello, is this place open?" Vince picked up the bucket and jumped in response feeling startled, he slammed the door and replied.

"Why?"

"I'm from HM Customs. I'm here to collect a payment. Do you know where Mick Haze is?"

"So, you're a bailiff?"

"I have a court document that states me the right to enter this building."

"It's closed."

"Is there any windows at the back?"

"No." Feeling an intimidating vibe from the stranger, Vince analysed his clothes with a clipboard and an identification chain hanging from his neck. "I think you best go." Vince stood with his arms open.

"When's he going to be back?"

"I don't know. Come back tomorrow and we'll sort this."

"Right, I've had enough. Who are you?"

"I work here. I've come to pick up my van."

"Who owns this van?"

"It's in my name, owned by me. Alright."

"I'll be back tomorrow with the Police if he doesn't turn up. Good bye."

Driving along the tarmac of Mary Lee Road, Chris advanced towards the 'Smoking Barrel.'

"Vince!" Chris spoke out of breath closing the door to the van.

"What?" replied Vince slamming his own door.

"Come on get inside." Chris felt anxious as he turned the key to the door of the pub.

"What's wrong Chris?"

"Give me a second." Chris caught his breath and walked inside. "Your Dad's in the hospital."

"What the hell!" Vince reacted with an outburst of despair.

"Oden's had an accident, he got hit by a car last night when he was on his night out." Vince's jaw dropped in disbelief.

"Fuck me. That's crazy. Is he going to be okay? What have the doctors said?" Words rushed from Vince's lips feeling a sick sense of panic, he asked multiple questions. "What's my Dad doing?"

"He's okay. He's just in the room watching him. He sent me back to let you know." Vince found himself a seat.

"I can't believe this. Everything is going wrong."

"Calm down Vince. They're doing all they can."

"I know, I know. God this is gonna kill my Dad. Fuckin hell."

"I know." Vince looked down towards the table and his hands began to shake. He clenched his fist holding the pressure tight in his grip. Feeling confused and stressed he spoke, breaking the silence between them.

"Chris, some weird guy came here just before all of this. I don't have a clue what's going on, he was one of them dickheads. I think he was working for the Council or Government or something. He tried taking our stuff."

Chris exhaled a breath of stress into the air. "Jesus Christ, if things couldn't get any worse." Vince read Chris's reaction realising he was hiding more than he expressed.

"You knew about this?"

"Yeah, it was nothing for you to worry about."

"This is my family home." Vince thrusted his arms against the walls. "I have every right to know if something is wrong."

"You're only a kid Vince." Chris pointed losing his temper.

"FUCK OFF you knob-head. Who do you think you are? I've dealt with adult shit, mad shit and bad shit. And you think I'm just a fucking child!" Chris witnessed Vince blow his top for the first time, feeling threatened he stumbled back with nerves.

Vince's lungs howled with breaths shortening. Retaliating back to cease the trauma Chris opened his arms wide.

"Vince." Chris bit his tongue and held himself responsible. "We can stand here shouting at each other all day long but it won't change everything that's happened. And yes, I should have told you, so you wouldn't have found out this way. On top of everything, if I could have sorted this alone I would. You don't need anything to worry about you don't need to carry it." Vince listened feeling his heart rate increase with his face turning red, sweat joined his face running down his cheeks.

"How much does my Dad owe?"

Chris struggled to reveal.

"Around twenty grand."

"Shit! So that twat will definitely be back tomorrow?"

"I'll rustle up some cash, some of it and try to bargain with him. Buy us some time."

Vince's eyes twinkled, "I've got this Chris. I can cover it. Oden stashed a lot of money in the cellar when he came back."

"What? How could he?"

"I know, it looked like a lot. There must be over twenty thousand."

"Fuck, that's a lot to hide." Chris raised a concerned eyebrow.

"It's not your money or your Dad's...it's not ours to use."

"Family is family, it's got to be done." Vince stood with firm feet. "He's in hospital unaware." Chris unzipped his jacket and sat on the table facing Vince, holding his hands against his cheeks with a deep stare aimed at Vince's eye line.

"I know." Vince replied softly holding his stress. He sighed swiping his tongue across his bottom lip. "This has got to stay between us until things come around." Vince took his last stare at Chris for the night and followed the path that led into the back of the pub with the stairway guiding his feet towards his room.

Return to the hospital day 2

The corridor which lead to room seven was buried in silence that was interrupted by the constant beat of Oden's heart monitor. Feeling a whirling pain inside his stomach Oden belched and began to cough hissing with agony. Mick jumped from the chair he had fallen asleep in.

"It's alright."

"I'm not right Mick."

"I'll get the nurse."

"No, it's ok." Mick ignored him and wiped at the sleep in his eyes. As Mick thudded towards the door he heard Oden's tone lower.

"Please stay." Mick turned his head in response and slowly made his way back down. Gentle and slowly mumbling, Oden's lips moved. "Remember when we were boys?" Micks eyes locked and ears pricked. "We used to run by the lake every morning, with sticks for rods and Dad would sit with his toes in the water. Hairy feet." Oden's eyes smiled. "Morgan fell in and we heard him screaming. Dad jumped in and pulled him by his collar. DON'T FEAR THE WATER YOU! You'll scare the fish." Micks face warmed with the memory. "Don't fear the water he said. Before I got here I couldn't leave, not until I knew everything was alright. The way it should be, Morgan happy, same old Mick happy, same old Mick. But I was never the same. I couldn't rest."

Bang! The sound of the door swung open as the nurse who had been attending to Oden walked into the room starting her morning routine checks.

"How are you feeling this morning?"

"Not good at all," Oden choked.

"We're still running our process, how are your legs?"

"I can't feel them. Didn't you cast them?"

"No"

"Well whoever bandaged them, did them too tight," Oden laughed with a hiss.

"Do you need more pillows?"

"No. I just need a drink." The nurse smiled and made her way out.

Chris woke from the corner couch of the pub's interior seating, his face brushed across the patterned fabric. Opening his eyes, he felt the presence of someone approaching.

"Fuck me! What time is it?" Chris shouted at Vince.

"Half seven, get up." Chris wandered his eyes across the floor focussing to a stop on Vince's trainers.

"Are you coming or what?" Vince grunted pulling himself from comfort, Chris joined the surface clenching his toes along the floor.

Vince placed a wooden box on a table in front of Chris.

"Is this the one?"

"Yeah. It's all in here. Even some euros." Vince felt a sentiment of discomfort, he looked at the fabric that covered the bulk and slightly frowned.

"Holy shit! That's a lot, doesn't he have a bank account?"

"Get counting this here." Vince placed a large handful of notes in front of Chris. The table shortly became covered in pound notes scattered everywhere across the table. It became surreal to Chris's eyes, reminding him of his childhood days playing monopoly, it simply didn't feel real seeing such a large amount of cash spread. Bewildered Chris scratched his head.

"Are you sure this is the right thing to do?" Vince's eyes spoke louder than his lips.

"It's the only thing we can do, alright." Vince began separating the notes stacking them into hundreds.

Thirty minutes passed and the two were coming to the end of the count. They had checked it multiple times to be on the safe side. Vince felt passion in his heart as he placed down the last twenty pound note on the table and fell into deep thought.

"I'll pay you back Oden." He smiled trusting himself that he had made the right decision. The money clotted together bonded by elastic bands and was placed into a blue plastic bag. Bang, the doors thudded and banged aggressively back and forth from their hinges.

Vince and Chris ran to the door and opened it quickly. Outside the pub stood three bailiffs hungry to get inside.

"We have the right to get in here! Right this minute." The leader spoke holding authority standing behind the two colleagues he had brought with him.

"It's alright." Vince spoke staring at the leader.

"No! It's not alright, if you haven't got what you owe." Vince stepped outside followed by Chris who swung the door shut. The leader of the bailiffs held a clipboard with the same court document he posed with the previous day. Revealing the blue bag Vince held it firm.

"I've got it all right here." The opposing group laughed.

"What, the full amount? I'm surprised." Holding his tongue Vince passed the bag to the collector.

"Every single penny is there."

Holding a cocky smile the leader opened the bag counting the money. Of each stack he pulled out he fanned it across his face brushing his fingers along the stack.

"I am the law. And the law pays."

"What's your name?" Vince gently squeezed his fists walking into the leader's personal space. "What's your name?"

"Owen."

"I'll remember that name Owen, now you best clear off out of here and take that money." Vince felt anger inside but resisted, he paused and continued to stare. "And leave, right now!"

"Come on lads, let's go." Owen laughed with a smirk on his face.

"We always get them in the end."

Vince turned away and saw the expression of Chris' face gloom in his sight. He approached the door and slammed it behind him.

"FUCKING PRICK!" The pub echoed with Vince's anger.

Oden took a deep breath then slowly released it.

"No. Not me Mick. Restless. Too much pain to handle. I didn't know who I was anymore. A fire Mick, bigger and more ferocious than the flames, my eyes seen burnt inside my heart." Mick listened with his eyes dilating. "I found them all." Oden's voice altered becoming deeper. "I watched them, followed them. Shared drinks in the same bars as them and not one of them recognised me. One night I played cards with some of them and they didn't flutter an eye lid." Mick's ears grew with sensitivity listening with more concentration.

"What are you going on about?"

"Just listen. I don't have long and you know." Oden stressed straining his voice. "I walked into the bar and he was there… Martin Cahill…he sat with his usual crowd with a smoke in his hand. I couldn't take my eyes off him. Laughing and joking without one single slice of guilt across his face. I wanted to break his face. Right there and then, I imagined my fists driving him off his chair. That night I put the whisky down I could smell his sweat, I could smell the Guinness from his lips." Oden coughed repeatedly. "My body is striking me." Oden's eye slowly gathered a tear but he held back. "All night I waited, he didn't move from his seat until the bar closed, he picked up his blazer and swung it on his arms. I could feel my teeth gritting to the point of crumbling. I watched him leave, as he walked past me where I was sat at the bar…not one eye was drawn to me."

Vince felt his phone vibrate inside his pocket as he stormed around the pub in frustration.

Vince. Come to my house tonight. I'm going to cook us something. Xxxx. Vince read the message but failed to reply, frustration and anxiety had made him reach tipping point. He stormed out of the bar area and fired his keys at his van.

"Where are you going?" Chris shouted.

"Leave me alone Chris." Vince shouted from his window as he pushed down on the acceleration. Driving down Mary Lee

Road with force, his wheels followed the tracks towards Kane's safe house. Vince opened his glove compartment that housed the Makarov pistol, it glued to Vince's eyes as he picked it up and released the cartridge. Frozen in a stare of flashes that continued to remind him of the close call, he returned the gun back into the compartment. He pushed open the door and walked out into the street and gazed at the broken-down house and walked in holding his head held high. His thoughts ran quickly without any logical sense until his emotional strength over powered his weakness.

"What a fucking surprise it is to see you!" Lucas shouted with a high-pitched tone.

"FUCK OFF." Vince walked past Lucas without any concern and entered the room where Kane was sat with Sean and Kevin.

"Where have you been? You've not answered any of my calls." Kane spoke with a tone which matched his body language as he sat sprawled along the beaten couch. Vince looked across the room and noticed the silence, Kevin and Sean looked at Vince with dangerous eyes. Sitting up on the couch Kane shouted, "I said where the fuck have you been?" Kane stood to his feet and felt his veins twitch. "I'm talking to you, you fucking dickhead, arn't you going to speak big man?"

"I'm not fucking around with you anymore. Alright! Yeah I fucking said it." Vince's voice busted.

"HAHAHA." Kane laughed. "You want fucking out? Arn't you going to tell me what happened the other day?" Kane approached Vince moving in closer. "Hey, are you? Because someone needs to explain why Sean's been limping around this fucking place. Because the way I fucking see it, you tried killing my fucking brother!" Kane's hand raised quickly and smashed Vince across the face. "Who do you think's going to pay for this fucking fuck up?" Vince stumbled back with his cheek turning red. "You better start fucking talking."

"Kane." Kevin shouted.

"Stay out of this Kevin." Kane ordered as he continued to approach Vince cornering him into a small area of the room. Vince felt his nerves spark inside.

"Everything went crazy. That fucking smackhead started firing at all of us."

"Don't fucking lie to me. You pulled a strap on Sean." Kane's anger grew, burning like wild fire inside. His eyes twitched and blood pulsed as his shadow darkened Vince's face. Vince's eyes scrolled to the black vest top Kane wore, a flush of white cocaine had made its stain on the fabric. "Is this true boys? Is this fucking accountable? Because someone's going to die tonight and it looks like it could be you." Kane smirked in amusement to Vince's facial expressions.

"It's true Kane. All of it. We're wasting time!" Kevin paced towards Kane and pulled him back by the shoulder.

"Well he's lucky it's only a fucking scratch." Kane responded. "But something doesn't seem right here." Kane turned back to Vince brushing Kevin from his shoulder. "You want out?"

"Yeah. I've told you this."

"You work for me, I treat you well, I own you. Do you fucking get that?"

"It's not for me, I don't want this." Vince felt his heart skip a beat of vulnerability.

"This! This is a fucking way of life. The good life, the great life. The fucking only life and you throw it back at me."

"We all need to cool off. Vince just needs to cool down." Kevin responded to the situation.

"A cool off?" Kane shouted with excitement. "Yeah, maybe you do need a cool off." Kane smiled.

"I'm out of here Kane. I'm gone." Vince walked out of the room and looked at Kevin with his cheeks tensed. Muttering to himself with whispers Kane watched Vince leave.

"A cool off yeah. He'll be back. Yeah. I own him. Little fucker thinks he can walk away from all of this. Hahaha." Kane continued to hiss and giggle to himself.

Mick's hand held tightly as he listened to Oden speak.

"I'm telling you Mick. One by one they passed me. Each one that drew a flame to our home, our life, everything we had. I followed behind them and watched them enter their cars. They all went in different directions but I knew which car was his. I put my foot down but not too fast, twenty maybe thirty yards apart behind him, he seen no threat. He owned his own plot just like ours, rich green grass and a stone path led to his house. In the darkness of the night I got out of my car with my overcoat, he didn't hear nor see me. The rain started to fall, I remember the rain." Oden licked his dry lips with his tongue and stared at the walls in silence trapped in a stare.

"Oden?" Mick mumbled squeezing his hand.

"Yeah." Oden replied softly. "It dripped and it dribbled, I wiped it from my face as he stumbled into the house. I stood outside the house and let the water absorb my jacket. Water. Morgen fell into the water." Oden gently moved his lips and spoke very quietly.

"Oden. Are you okay? Oden?" Mick grew with concern.

"I'm fine. I'm okay. I was okay. I felt calm. I felt relaxed. Like the rain started to wash me away. The fire inside started to cool but it didn't go out. I put my hand on the front door to the house. There was no lock. No tension in it. It delicately opened it." Oden paused again for a moment and then returned to himself. "I walked up his stairs and I seen him lay on a chair with a desk in front of it. Unconscious. Vulnerable and drunk. From beneath my overcoat I slid my hands down to my side and pulled out a gun that I treasured for this moment. My hands wrapped around it, my fingers coiled around the trigger. But I couldn't squeeze, not until he knew who I was. I couldn't stand how he didn't recognise me. I felt my lungs gasp as I took a deep breath. Wake the fuck up! I roared." Oden's hand raised from his side and hovered in the air in front of him, shaping his hand in a fist that snugly held the gun he described. "He looked at me, stared straight into my eyes like he knew his day was coming. He reached for a thick leather bag that was by the side of his desk.

Don't fucking move I shouted. I walked forward pointing the gun straight at his head. He smiled but tears streamed down his eyes. Do you fucking know who I am? Do you fucking know what you did to me? You fucked up my whole life. You took everything away from me. I felt my body wretch with pain. He looked at me and waited until I released everything I had inside and nodded. I knew it would of eventually caught up to me. I knew I'd be avenged that they'd somehow get me but I didn't care and by the look on his face when I finished. Neither did he. I squeezed and closed my eyes." Oden shut his eyes and started to experience striking pains in his body. "Help!" Oden began to scream. "Ahhh. Help! I don't want to go. Help!" Mick jumped up feeling shaken.

"Nurse! Nurse!" Mick ran to the door and shouted down the corridor grabbing urgent attention. A group of Nurses ran towards room seven with a male Doctor.

"What's going on ?" Mick shouted in a panic.

"We need you to get outside Sir." The male doctor shouted at Mick and guided him towards the door.

"No. No. I can't go. I can't leave him." Mick looked over the doctor's shoulder and saw Oden flinching in pain moving his arms and shaking in distress. Some male nurses entered the room in response to the commotion and spoke gently to Mick holding his arms firmly.

"He's going to be alright. The doctors here now. Come with me." A tall male nurse repeated himself tugging at Mick's arm.

Vince drove around in circles, he didn't want to go back to the pub or arrive at Daisy's, he felt like the world had beaten him to the floor. Even though he had spoken his mind he felt weak, he pulled down his sun visor and looked at himself in the mirror. He turned his face that showed off his red marked cheek in the reflection and closed the visor in anger. Vince pulled his wheel in at a supermarket carpark and turned off the engine. Sitting in silence with his head tilted down towards the steering wheel, he closed his eyes and rested his arms above the wheel in a leaned position. Vince listened to the thoughts in his head, in the silence they grew loud.

"It's over now. You don't have to be afraid anymore." Vince listened to his inner self. "The hardest part is over. Get up." Vince felt his body groan and drain and gargled a sickly sensation in his mouth. Disbelief ran through him, he couldn't believe it was over, he felt an emotional break inside him explode. Tears fell down his face with a swollen throat that followed. His phone vibrated as he entered his pocket it was a text message from Daisy.

Where are you? Why aren't you talking to me? Feeling ashamed by his face and emotionally weak he ignored the message and closed his eyes.

"Get up!" His inner voice tugged and tore him with the negative emotions and feelings that were beating him. Left to his own mind Vince didn't move.

Mick sat in the waiting room with the male nurse beside him, he felt fear that had been felt long ago. He didn't speak or ask questions, silence was written across his sunken face. He didn't stare at anybody, his body sat still. He focused on one point in the room which was the hand gel dispenser. He started to bite his lip and reached inside his pocket for his hipflask, he dug his hand deep but it wasn't to be found. His eyes then locked towards his nails, a yellow tint glazed over his eyes. His focus then turned towards the clock in the room, all his senses escalated enhancing every small sound within the room. The ticking of the clock, his eyes scanned watching the hands turn. The sounds of paper on the reception door being clipped together, Mick squeezed his hand on the arm of the plastic chair. His breath clung tightly holding his stomach in. Mick's eyes noticed a doctor walk past.

"Is he okay? Is he going to be alright?" Mick gasped.

"Oden Haze, he's in room seven. Is he going to be okay?"

"I'm sorry Sir. I've not been attending to that patient." Mick's breath inhaled and exhaled quickly. The nurse began to notice.

"Don't worry Mick. We have the best doctors here. Would you like a drink of water?"

"No! Where is my brother? Why isn't anyone doing anything?"

"I can assure you that he will be receiving the best medical treatment we have."

Frightened and tense Mick felt his muscles lock.

"I'm going in."

"No Mick. You can't." Mick stood up and broke the mould which set his body in the chair, he heard slow footsteps hit the corridor floor.

"Mick, is it?"

"Yeah. Where is my brother?" Mick replied to the doctor who stood in front of him in a white gown. He had black hair and glasses similar to Clark Kent with a face of stone.

"Mr Haze please come with me." Mick followed behind the doctor into a small office, he turned around and faced Mick. "I'm sorry. There is nothing we could do to save your brother. The damage he had was too much for his body to handle. Oden had internal bleeding that caused him to pass." Mick's face dropped lost for words in shock, his body shook.

Vince's phone repeatedly rang, he glanced with his eyes and watched Daisy's name appear on the phones screen. After four rings of the mobile he answered with the speaker icon indicated on, holding the mobile close he heard Daisy's voice break the silence in the van.

"What's wrong with you? You've not spoke to me all day." Vince listened but didn't respond, he stared straight out of window. "Hello? Are you even listening to me?" Daisy muttered. "Why are you being like this? Vince."

"It's not a good time."

"Time? Are you being serious. I've been ringing you all day trying to talk to you and you're the one ignoring me." Vince felt his mind wander blankly.

You don't understand anything Daisy. You just don't get it."

"See this is what I'm on about. You don't talk to me so how am I supposed to know anything."

"Daisy, leave me alone." Vince's voice changed its tone.

"You're being a dick. Today's one of our special days and your acting like a fucking idiot."

"What are you on about."

"It's our anniversary." Daisy sobbed on the phone. "You don't care about me. It's always about you. There's always something going on that's more important."

"My uncle is in the fucking hospital. There's always something bad happening. Shit that you don't get or understand." The phone line turned quiet sharply but whimpers of Daisy's sobs were still heard.

"You know I'm here for you. You know you can talk to me and you never do. Never!" Vince began to boil becoming more aggressive. "I can't do this. You don't care for one inch about me. You say all this but you really don't understand." Vince hurled the phone against the dash board.

"Leave me alone! I need some fucking space," Vince shouted out with tears streaming. "Ahhh! everything I do, I do it for us and when shit happens I don't know how to fucking deal with it. Ahhh!" Vince screamed at the phone and banged his hands on the steering wheel. He thought his actions that followed that day would have made him feel free, but inside he was trapped by his own inner demons and emotional upheaval. Vince made the lonely journey home back to the 'Smoking barrel.' The darkness of the night sky highlighted the flashing lights of red, amber and green at each traffic light he arrived at. He turned his head towards the right-wing mirror and felt disgusted inside with his reflection.

"I fucked up." Vince whispered to himself and continued his journey.

A week of silence gloomed over Vince and Mick, the 'Smoking Barrel' shut its doors. All fell dark with sadness floating in the atmosphere. Bang! A medium sized man with dark hair and facial hair knocked on the door. Vince opened the door with a creek.

"Come in," Vince spoke with a sombre tone. His eyes were layered with tired line wrinkles with purple heated cheeks. Tear stains masked on the side of his face followed by a weak hand shake.

"Alright Vince." Morgan spoke softly with a quiet tone. Vince didn't respond, a sick sensation merged inside his stomach.

Morgan's eyes witnessed Mick standing in the centre of the room wearing a black suit that his eyes were familiar too. Morgan's fingertips felt the chilled draft in the room; he walked towards Mick and held out his hand. Mick's eyes lowered as a pause of silence between them occurred. Mick took Morgan's hand that was followed by his other which hugged Morgan.

"It's going to be okay little brother." Mick whispered holding himself strong.

"I know Mick." Morgan felt a nervous sensation inside with a tear gathering in the corner of his eye. The door was still left open by Morgan's entrance allowing the wind to blow through. Mick opened the buttons on his blazer jacket and reached inside for his hipflask. He twisted away at the lid and poured it down his throat.

"Vince come here." Mick shouted as he offered the flask to Morgan. "Come here my boy, have some." Vince took the bottle from Morgan's hand and joined both in diving into the burning sensation which was left in their throats. "No matter how hard the wolves howl we shall stand for our Oden."

"We shall stand." Morgan responded feeling his emotions spark.

Chris's van arrived outside the 'Smoking Barrel', he opened his door and stepped out onto the street wearing a black blazer with matching pants. He walked towards the front door gently holding his head towards the floor.

"There you are." Vince spoke. "Come on let's wait outside." Mick's eyes twitched with his jaw muscles held tight. Morgan pulled out a small metal tin which was filled with tobacco and pre-made cigarettes. He pulled one from the tin and offered it to Mick. The rolled cigarette scraped across the dry lips of Mick, he opened his lungs and took a deep breath whilst Morgan struck a match for him. Exhaling the smoke from the back of his throat into the air, Mick felt a cooling sensation.

Chris noticed Vince glance at his phone and snugly hid it inside his pocket.

"Take the notice of her Vince. You don't even need to think about her."

"I'm not."

"If she wanted to be here for you she would."

"I don't even know if I'd want her here. She didn't know him." Vince's ears awaited the sound of the hearse to arrive outside the pub. The hairs on his arms stood on end.

"Will follow up in my van." Chris nodded in response crossing eye lines with Vince.

"I'm glad you're here, Brother." Chris felt a warm sensation conflict inside with his beaten feelings.

A black hearse rolled onto Mary Lee Road with Oden's name printed with white flowers. Mick's heart sunk into the bottom of his belly, taking the last puff of the cigarette he threw it onto the ground.

"It doesn't feel real." Morgen looked at the brown polished coffin through the hearse window.

"I know." Mick replied. A tall man wearing a black top hat jumped out of the hearse and opened the doors to the black limousine behind. Mick maintained his strength with his arms held beside him nodding his head to the driver.

"Are you sure you don't want to get in with your Dad?" Chris asked with care.

"No." Vince replied feeling certain. Vince and Chris stepped into the van and followed behind the limousine. The roads were quiet and the fresh morning air could be tasted by the tongue of all travelling towards the church.

Feeling overwhelmed, Mick released the tired tears that had been holding back as they arrived at the church.

"Fucking hell." Mick shouted.

"We've got to do this Mick. For Oden."

"I know, it's too hard." The limousine driver and the hearse driver exited the vehicles and hovered towards the boot of the hearse. The sounds of scraping wood scratched against the rest which Oden's coffin lay. Mick and Morgen carried Oden from the front followed by Vince and Chris at the back, their heads held high with the sun shining on them. The four marched into the Church and laid him onto a wooden stand at the top of the Church.

The priest started his usual speech prepared for cremation send-offs. All four sat at the front of the Church feeling emptiness as their eyes were glued to Oden's coffin. As the priest spoke his final prayers, members of the Church rolled the coffin behind the rich curtains. Mick cried as his heart crumbled.

"Oden!" Mick shouted. "I love you... Brother." Mick sank into his seat. The speakers from the corners of the Church started to ring the sound of Irish folk music.

Vince felt his phone vibrate numerous times in his pocket, he didn't pay any attention as he said his last good byes to Oden. He sat in silence as the music came to an end, the whole day had felt like a dream. A nightmare which he couldn't escape, he turned his head to Mick and watched as him and Morgen attempted to dry the tears from their eyes. Vince wiped his face with shaken hands and looked to Chris.

"I can't stay here." Vince blubbered.

"I'll come with you." Chris replied.

"I'm just going to get some air. I'll wait outside."

"Oh Okay." Chris responded in respect to Vince's needs.

Vibration after vibration, Vince's mobile rumbled inside his pocket as he opened the Church doors to get some air. The wind blew in his face fluttering the black tie he wore with a white shirt.

He placed his hand into his pockets and noticed the missed calls from Daisy. He looked away in despair and gripped the phone with his hand aiming it towards the floor. Ring! Ring! The phone vibrated again in his hands with Daisy's number on his screen. Vince squeezed the answer button firmly.

"WHAT DO YOU WANT!" Vince shouted upset.

"Naughty, naughty Pikey." A male voice answered in a creepy familiar tone.

"Who is this? How did you get this phone?" Vince felt a bolt of confusion.

"I don't think that's what you should be concerned about."

"Who is this?" Vince heard the screams of Daisy's voice in the back ground. "Who the FUCK is this? I'll FUCKING KILL YOU?" Vince roared down the phone with an immediate panic striking him.

"You know who this is. You think you can walk away from me? You think you can take away what I own? I'm gonna cut her up into little fucking slices." Vince stormed towards his van with Kane still on the line.

"Where the fuck are you? I'm gonna fucking kill you if you touch her!" Vince heard a wet tongue slap Daisy's cheek as she squirmed and screamed.

"You created this Vince, your pretty girlfriend here needs to know that." Kane held a knife in the opposite hand to the phone and rolled the blunt side along her face down to her neck. Tears and sweat drooled down her face with her mouth tied with a scrappy piece of fabric. Black stained tears from her eyeliner formed on her makeup covered in blood from the graze on the left side of her face.

Vince hit down on the acceleration with all his strength and sped down the roads towards Kane's hide out.

"She's a fighter this one. Definitely a keeper. That's if you can keep her." Kane laughed down the phone with a crazy belch.

"Don't worry Daisy, I'm coming." Vince shouted with urgency.

"Haha. Your fucking soft. You're not a man otherwise you'd be able to take care of your woman and it looks like she needs taking care of." Kane put the knife into his pocket and slightly pulled down his pants revealing his pubic hairs. "I'm going to fuck you. Do you hear me, I'm going to break you?" Kane held the phone to Daisy's head as she screamed down the phone, Vince's ears rang with horror.

"I'm going to fucking kill you. You're a dead fucking man!" Vince howled down the phone as the line cut out. Vince heard no sound coming from the phone, he felt his heart shudder as his hands trembled. Looking down in silence he saw the call icon had ended. Vince drove into the estate where Kane's safe house hid amongst the other houses. Slamming down the breaks outside the house Vince reached for his gun from the glove compartment and ran towards the door roaring with insane anger and fiery emotions.

"Where are you? You bastard!"

A wooden plank swung sharply from a door at the side of Vince that knocked him onto the floor. The gun vaulted across the floor amongst the smashed glass and needles. Sean uncovered himself from behind the door.

"He's here!" Sean shouted singing his message to Kane. Vince lay on the floor of the hallway with blood leaking from the side of his head. His ears lost sound and eyes grew blurry. He reached for anything he could connect his hands with. Vince's eyes saw a dark shadow in front of him silhouetting across his eyes. Sean screamed and kicked Vince repeatedly in the chest.

"Do you think you're better than me? Do you think your one of us? You're fucking not!" The sound of Sean's remarks was silence to Vince's ears. Sean stamped on Vince's moving hand. "You've fucked with the wrong family." The screeching sounds of Daisy rang horror to Vince's ears as he listened to her fidget and wriggle trying to escape Kane's hand, which gripped her black hair firmly knotting thick strands around his fingers. Daisy tried to free her hands but the ropes Kane had tied her with were firmly tight holding back her pulse from behind her back with her legs banded together in the same fashion.

Vince heard the loud thudding steps of Kane's shoes treading closer towards him, crunching the scattered glass. The bombardment of horror entered his ears extending all senses with hairs raised from his skin and jittering hands. A blood stained hand reached for the gun that casted Vince's fate.

"Vince! Help me. Vince, Vince." Blood dribbled trickling down Daisy's face smearing her lips. Choking on a contaminated mix of liquids that gathered in the back of her throat Daisy released another helpless cry. "I hate you, I fucking hate you!! Ahhh!! You caused this. You brought this to all of us!" Holding the gun's handle firmly Kane plunged it into Daisy's scalp. A scream of terror screeched from Daisy's lungs as Vince's eyes regained their sight, he focused on Daisy's face of intense fright.

"This is my world Vince. And I own everything within it. You could have been one of us. Just like me. I had high hopes for you, but now you'll pay the price." Unable to breath, forcing himself forward moving slowly, Vince gasped for air with eyes that held pain. Kane increased the pressure of the metal barrel from the gun into Daisy's head adding to her bruises of pain. "Don't you have anything to fucking say? You fucking coward, that's what you are. To think I saw hope for you." Kane grunted fiercely and aimed the gun at Vince as his fingers gained lock jaw to the trigger.

"Don't! Stop! Stop." Daisy thrusted her body left and right. "Please, no.....stop, we're having a baby. Vince get up! Please! Please! I love you."

Bang!

The white from Kane's eyes sparked as Vince made his last stare. His eyelids twitched falling to darkness. The sound of screams were heard from the house as a second gunshot was fired. Blood sprayed from Kane's head as his body joined Vince's along the floor. A tall figure from behind held a black Revolver.

The End

Author Interview

What made you write the book?

I had always wanted to create an exciting story where people could find characters they could connect with. The original idea for 'On The Job' was born back in May 2012 when I created a short visual piece where I creatively investigated the mind of a young criminal by writing the character's thought process through a monologue. From there my imagination erupted and I started to write my first pages. Alongside this project, I was already far into another, which was a theatre production called 'Broken Youth' Written and Directed by Author Karen Woods. Working as an Actor for Karen was an amazing experience as we performed at the Lowry Theatre. I shared my first few pages with Karen and she opened me up to the possibilities that I could make it happen.

What inspired you?

I'm inspired by a lot of things in life, when I was a young child I religiously watched hundreds of films that my Gran bought me. Every weekend I'd sleep at my Grans house as a child and become immersed into all stories that I'd watch on screen. I was fascinated by the stories and once I grew a little older I became inspired by the stories of people who have lived hard dangerous lives and defied all odds to achieve whatever they define as success. The idea of achieving the impossible empowers me to keep striving forward in my journey. I grew an interest in Crime stories that I heard and films that I watched. The stories of the anti-hero Criminals excite me, it all started with watching Robin Hood as a child. Living by my own rules is something I identify myself with when I engage with those characters. Although in this novel I broke the conventional rules.

What plans do you have for the future?

To continue to work hard chasing the impossible and inspire as many people along the way. I've always wanted to work in the Media Industry playing a role in creating visual stories that excite me. To create my own films and media products to become a professional storyteller and express my abilities in the storytelling industries.

What advice would you give to those who share the similar dreams to you?

I'm still young and learning new things every day so I'm humbled to share some of my ideas. Everyone has their own belief system unique to them, but I have a belief that if you've got a dream to create something, an ambition inside that pulls you towards your idea, you've got to fight to make it happen. And the biggest fight you will face is yourself because you are the only person who can bring life to your idea. No one will do it for you but you. On your journey, towards whatever it is you desire, you will come across all types of people who will laugh at you and won't have the same belief as you. That it's possible to climb the mountain you wish to face because a lot of people won't come across the mountain of their dream, never mind experiencing the climb. I learnt how time is limited and if you are burning to tell a story use anything you can. You don't need to wait to get the best equipment, all you need is a pad and paper or even your phone. Smart phones these days have word pads that you can write your idea on and develop it from there. That's how it all started for me.